MW00413119

Bucky and the Lukefahr Ladies

Book 2

Songs of Three

Shirley Gilmore

This is a work of fiction. Names, characters, places, and incidents either are the product of the author's imagination or are used in a fictitious manner. Any resemblance to actual persons, living or dead, or actual events or locales is entirely coincidental.

Copyright © 2018 by Shirley Gilmore

All rights reserved. No part of this book may be reproduced in any form without written permission from the copyright owner.

Except where noted that they are from the King James Version, all but one of the scripture quotations are from the New Revised Standard Version Bible, copyright © 1989 the Division of Christian Education of the National Council of the Churches of Christ in the United States of America. Used by permission. All rights reserved worldwide.

Daniel 10:19 scripture quotation is from the Common English Bible. © Copyright 2011 by the Common English Bible. All rights reserved. Used by permission.

For Klova Helfrecht

who, as my Girl Scout Leader,
taught me many essential life skills—
how to build a fire, how to sharpen a knife,
how to make a bed and set a table.
She impressed upon me the Girl Scout motto,
"Be prepared."
She also told me about Bethesda, Missouri,
a health resort town established by her
husband's family and built around a healing spring.
The spring and a stone foundation are all that remain
today.
Perhaps there was no one there to recognize the magic

TABLE OF CONTENTS

Map of Turn Back, Missouri

INTRODUCTION

After I penned my version of the events that took place that strange summer in Turn Back, Missouri, I naively thought it was over. As the summer drew to a close and school started again and vacations ended, I thought all the hubbub concerning the labyrinth and the dreams and the mastodons and the Singing Spring and the mysterious Park Stone would die down. I imagined the walkers would find the drive to the town on the road to nowhere a little too far and too expensive to keep returning. I thought those who came would soon tire of the mundane walk around the square and the hymns we sang. But the crowds grew. And grew.

The dreams continued and they took a menacing turn for some in the town, most notably Simon Carter and his daughter Bucky. At times it became difficult to separate the dreams from reality. That fall was not a pleasant one for the Carters nor for me. There was a death and a fire, threats and accusations. Secrets came to light that perhaps should have remained hidden. But all was not gloom and doom. Through all of it there was Bucky, resilient Bucky, who had a knack for picking out the positive among the negative things in life, who looked past outward appearances and dove straight for the heart, who could see how things should be and not how they are.

I like stories that have a happy ending. Sometimes the characters have to work hard and travel through difficult trials to achieve that happy ending, but that makes it all worthwhile. So sit back and take the road once more to tiny Turn Back, walk the labyrinth, listen to the Singing Spring, dream the dreams.

Margaret "Maggie" Fletcher
Turn Back, Missouri

PROLOGUE

The vow made to Etakkama from the land of Hatti
was to the thousandth generation
We rejoice and sing that his scion continues
in this sacred place
The sound of sorrow has passed
The song of lamentation is no more
Sing and rejoice
We celebrate the return of the song stone
The songs of three are powerful
We sing the songs to accomplish our will
We sing the song to dry our tears

Inscription on the Park Stone in Turn Back, Missouri

The Mansion

1

Welcome Back to Turn Back

The cave dream that had haunted Simon Carter's sleep for several weeks was shorter and more peaceful than the previous dreams of extinct mastodons and ancient sailing vessels which had invaded the nocturnal slumbers of the thousands of people who walked the Turn Back labyrinth each week. And although it visited Simon and the others every night, it didn't dominate their dreams but allowed time for their brains to sort and sift and weave together *normal* dreams unique to each person. In the cave dream, Simon had never gone beyond the entrance to the cavern which sat partway up a rugged bluff above the river. He usually stood in the opening and looked out at the fields and woods and hills across the way.

Tonight the dream changed. Tonight someone was screaming from the depths of the cave. He turned and scrabbled over the boulders that partially blocked the entrance. Once past the rocks the air felt cooler and had an earthy smell. Simon stumbled across the uneven surface of the cavern floor. The outside light penetrated for a few yards, but the piteous cries were coming from the blackness beyond. He halted at the edge of the total darkness and listened. The piercing shrieks sounded familiar. Bucky!

Simon struggled to climb from deep sleep into consciousness. The screams weren't coming from inside the cave but from his daughter's bedroom. Even before he was fully awake, he threw off his blanket and bounded from his bed. He had flipped the switch inside her door and was beside her in only seconds.

Bucky, thrashing and wailing, was on her hands and knees in the middle of her bed. Blood had already soaked through the back of her pink unicorn nightgown.

Simon sat on the bed and wrapped her in his arms, pulling her close against his chest. "It's all right, Lamb. It will pass. It always passes."

"No!" Bucky screamed. "It was Mom!" Her words were garbled, mixed with sobs and shrieks. "Mom was trying to kill me. She was drowning me."

"No, Lamb." Simon caressed her hair. His hand was covered with her blood. "It was a dream. It was only a dream."

"Make it stop, Dad! Please! It hurts so bad."

"I can't make it stop, Bucky. Just breathe. It won't be long until it's over."

"Sing the song," Bucky sobbed. "Oh, please."

"I can't… I don't know…"

"Please." Bucky drew out the word in a low moan.

Foreign words—syllables really—formed in Simon's mind. Where had they come from and what was the tune? He began to intone the words, chanting as in a Hindu mantra. It wasn't long before the syllables took on a life of their own and began to rise and fall in a pattern.

Ah te o ki u ma
Sa pa ah ku me
Le pa ti ah su me tu
Ki ah as ah ku me
La ya

Simon repeated the stanza and he felt Bucky relax in his arms, her cries quieting and her breaths slowing and deepening. Minutes passed. When he thought the episode was over and she was asleep, he gently laid her head on her pillow and straightened her cover over the prancing unicorn on the front of her nightgown. The unicorn gown, the pillow, sheets and cover were stained in blood.

Bucky opened her eyes. "Ian saved me," she muttered. "He pushed her away. But why would my mom try to kill me?"

Simon wiped his bloody hand on his pajama leg and gently slid his palm down the side of Bucky's face. "Oh, Lamb. Your mother would never do that. It was just a dream. Your mind was just… It was mixing up those things that Reverend Bergmann said tonight at the walk. That's all. Try to sleep now."

"How did you learn the song?" Her voice was weak.

"Shhh. Go to sleep."

Simon moved from her bed to the chair beside it. He closed his eyes. Two months ago, on the night of the Methodist church's talent show, the Reverend Carl Bergmann had suffered a heart attack after hitting Simon with a sledge hammer during a confrontation at the new monolith in the park in Turn Back. This evening's prayer walk had been the first time since that July night Bergmann and his flock were present to harangue the walkers, ranting about how they were participating in a satanic ritual. The walks for the past eight weeks had been peaceful, without incident, despite the large crowds which were now numbering more than five thousand each week. But tonight the non-denominational, evangelical preacher had hauled in a huge white cross and propped it up in the center of the park while he and his followers gathered around it. Between the preacher's bouts of amplified fiery rhetoric, condemning the walkers and calling them back to Jesus, his followers sang hymns.

And then Bergmann's comments took a personal turn as he again accused Simon of being Satan, walking at the head of the procession with his demonic offspring named Bucky. It was when the preacher went on a tirade about the whore who birthed Bucky that Simon cried out, "Enough!"

Simon would have broken rank and crossed the park to attack Bergmann right then except for the restraining hands on his arms. Maggie had released Bucky's hand to lay hold on Simon, as had Bucky herself. Pastor Stephen Bradley and Ron Crosson also moved to block his way. But it was ninety-four-year-old Lillian Thomas, walking behind him, who put a hand against his back and spoke the words, "Don't feed the beast. He ain't worth it," that caused him to stop and take a breath and stand down.

There was no doubt in Simon's mind Bergmann's words had triggered Bucky's nightmare and caused her to cry in her sleep, resulting in one of her traumatic "episodes." She had not suffered one since earlier in the summer and that one, too, had been provoked by Bergmann. For all of her short ten years she had always rebounded from the terrible experiences that were accompanied by so much pain and blood loss until that last one. She had recovered physically from it but psychologically had spiraled down into a depression which had held her captive for several days. Simon could only pray tonight's episode would not result in a similar experience.

But where had tonight's song come from? And had it really stopped her pain or was she already nearing the end of the event when he began chanting? Simon wiped both palms down his face. Ever since his head injury, he had been suffering from disconnected flashes of scenes of which he had no memory and yet they seemed familiar. But when he tried to recall exactly what it was he was seeing in his mind, the memory remained just beyond his grasp. Those experiences, along with a disturbing phone call he had last week from Dr. Chip Crosson, the neurosurgeon who had treated him, were causing his own downward spiral. It was time for answers.

He lightly brushed a hand across Bucky's forehead to make sure she was asleep, and then switched off her lamp and left her room. He walked down the dimly-lit corridor and paused at the top of the stairs. His mission would undoubtedly prove fruitless. Even if the Anarianu, the Guardians, were real, how could he communicate with them? And what would tiny green lightning bugs know or care about the disconcerting emotions they were imposing on an entire community with their dreams or the pain they were inflicting on him and his little girl? He hesitated for a moment and considered washing his hands and changing his pajamas before heading to the Spring Room. No, he thought, growing angrier with each passing second. This is Bucky's blood and they did this to her.

When he reached the Spring Room door, he again hesitated before unlocking it and turning off the motion sensor. After taking a couple of deep breaths, he pulled open the heavy wooden door. He stood on the landing a few moments while his eyes adjusted to the darkness. Moonlight coming through the numerous tall, narrow windows bathed the room in a soft light. The ripples in the two pools shimmered with diamond glints. The stream of water splashing into the upper basin sounded louder in the darkness than when he had visited this room in the daytime.

Standing on the landing, he grasped the railing and closed his eyes. "Anarianu," he whispered, "I know you can hear me." Opening his eyes, he raised his voice. "Anarianu, guardians of this spring." He paused for a moment. "I demand you show yourselves." His voice sounded hollow in the stone room.

Only the sound of the falling water answered him.

"Anarianu!" Simon slipped to his knees. He shifted his grip to a lower rail and rested his head against it. "Why are you torturing my daughter? How much longer must she endure this agony? She's just… She's just a little girl." He squeezed shut his eyes. The railing was cool against his forehead.

He knew it had been hopeless to expect them to respond. They probably didn't even exist. The night Bucky claimed to have seen them, the night he had found her floating face-down in the smaller pool, maybe that never happened. When he questioned her later, she couldn't recall anything from that night. He thought he remembered she had found her nightgown draped over his tub where he had left it to dry, but perhaps he had imagined that, too. What if those events and the story she had told him when he dragged her from the water were all a result of his concussion-addled brain? And the flashes of memory he had been experiencing, scenes from another place, another time, they were more than likely also brought on by the head trauma he had suffered when Reverend Bergmann had swung that sledge hammer at him.

Maybe the blow had done more damage than Dr. Chip Crosson, the neurosurgeon, realized. He probably should contact the doctor, let him know about these recent developments, but after the disquieting phone conversation he had had with Chip last week, Simon really did not want to speak with him again just yet.

Simon reached for the top railing again and pulled himself to his feet. The smooth stones on the floor of the landing were uncomfortably cold on his bare feet. He sighed and shook his head. "So now we have to look for answers elsewhere. I should have known the existence of supernatural beings from another dimension was too neat and tidy an explanation for all this. Besides being ludicrous." He turned to leave.

Etakkama.

Simon pivoted. The air above the pool shimmered in a multitude of colors. Tiny green points of lights filled the room. They had not been there a moment before.

Etakkama. A hundred voices were speaking in his mind—no, aloud—but they were not all in unison, so that the word echoed over and over.

We rejoice that you have returned. The sentence also reverberated.

Simon gripped the railing again for support. The shifting colors and the zipping and blinking of the green glints were disorienting. "I'm not Etakkama."

Of course you are. The phrase resounded over and over.

"Who are you?"

We are Anarianu.

"That… That tells me nothing."

Of course it does.

"No, it doesn't. Why are you doing all this? And why can't you help my little girl?"

She must sing the Laya Song to dry her tears. We all must. It's who we are.

Simon slammed his palms against the railing. "She doesn't know the song!"

Teach her.

"I don't know the words!"

Of course you do.

"Stop saying that!" It was like talking to a four-year-old.

You sang them tonight.

"But I don't know them now. They came to me in that moment, but I can't recall them at will."

Of course you can.

Simon bowed his head. The resonance of their voices and their illogical replies and their dizzying movements were overwhelming.

Etakkama.

"I'm not…"

We taught the Laya Song to you when you were here before. We gave you the song stone for Imala.

"I don't know anyone named Imala."

Of course you do.

"I have the song stone—I have three of them—but I can't read them."

Of course you can. The voices overlapped each other and echoed off the stone walls. *The songs of three are powerful.*

"Why do you think I was here before? Why do you call me Etakkama?"

You saved Tikatara. We sing your name in our songs.

"My name is Simon Carter. I was born in Stony Point, New York."

Etakkama. The voices whispered the name this time.

"I'm not…" Simon sunk to his knees again. "What do you want with me? Why have you brought us here?"

When the People of the Land left, we were alone. The word "alone" reverberated for several seconds. *And then you returned. Seraphina.*

Simon swiveled his head as the name of Dr. Southy MacAdoo's daughter was whispered over and over all around him. Southy MacAdoo had founded Turn Back in the nineteenth century and had built the former Mansion Mineral Springs Resort where Simon and Bucky now lived.

"How is Seraphina my family?"

Etakkama, you have many sons and daughters.

Simon slowly shook his head back and forth.

Meredyth.

Simon jerked at the sound of his wife's name. "What about her? What do you know about Meredyth?"

The others took her. She was caught in the Turning.

"Who— What…what others?

The others. The songs of three are powerful. To protect the three they seek to prevent the three. We leave now. The swirling colors dissipated and the green glints began to flicker and fade.

"No!" Simon leapt to his feet. "Where's Meredyth? What have you done with her?"

Wait.

It was the same thing Meredyth had said when he saw her on the sailing ship in his dreams last summer. "Wait? Wait for what? Where is she?"

Etakkama. Their voices were growing more distant as more and more of the pinpricks of light winked out. Within seconds the last of the echoes died and Simon was left in darkness. The only sound was the stream of water pouring into the upper pool below the landing.

"I'm not…" Simon slid down the railing into a heap on the floor. He leaned his head against one of the upright supports. "I'm not…"

The last thing he remembered hearing was a solitary voice whispering, *Of course you are.*

"Dad! Dad, where are you?"

Simon awoke to the sound of Bucky, calling his name. He raised his head and looked around him, disoriented for a moment before realizing he was in the Spring Room. The soft light of early dawn partially illuminated the space. Using the rails, he pulled himself to his feet. He was stiff from sleeping on the cold stones.

"Dad!" This time Bucky's voice was a drawn-out wail.

"I'm coming, Lamb." The words came out as a croak and he cleared his throat and tried again. "I'm coming." He left the Spring Room and hurried down the hallways and up the short flight of stairs and through another hallway.

Bucky was standing in the entry hall. Her pink nightgown was caked with dried blood. Most of the blood was on the back but when she turned to face him, Simon saw that the unicorn on the front looked like it had been in a battle.

"I'm so sorry, Lamb. I was… I was downstairs." He gently swept her hair, the ends matted with blood, away from her face. "Are you all right?"

"Dad, you're all bloody." Her voice sounded weaker than it had a few moments before when she was calling for him.

Simon held out his hands, covered in dried blood, and looked down at the front of his pajamas. He tried to make light of his appearance. "I hope no one sees the pair of us like this. No telling what rumors that would start."

Bucky closed her eyes tight and Simon knew she was fighting against tears.

"Let's go talk." He took his daughter by the hand and led her to his study to the brown leather sofa where they had shared numerous conversations. She curled up next to him, her face buried in his side.

"I dreamed Mom tried to drown me." Her words were muffled. "Why would she do that?"

Simon stoked her hair. "It was only a dream." He felt her head move back and forth beneath his hand.

"But our other dreams came true."

"Well, this one's not going to come true."

"You sang the song last night. I could feel it. It was like… It was like when you ran your hand down my back just now. It was comforting, except it was with words and sound. Did you translate the song stone?"

"No." He didn't know what to tell her. He didn't know if his conversation last night with the Anarianu was real. He didn't know what was real anymore. When he saw her a few moments ago in the hall, at first it appeared she had long, straight black hair, and she was wearing a short white tunic, although it, too, was blood-stained. And when she spoke, the words were Hittite. The image lasted only for a second or two and then she was Bucky again.

"Dad, are you all right?" Bucky, her face still buried, reached up and laid a hand on his cheek.

He clasped her wrist and pulled her hand away from his face. "I...uh...I didn't sleep well last night." He changed the subject back to her. "You...you seem better than usual after one of your...uh...episodes."

"I don't feel real good, but I don't feel as bad as I usually do. Maybe the song helped. Will you teach it to me?"

Simon closed his eyes. "I'm afraid I can't remember it. But I'll work on it, I promise." With his palms flat against her back, he could feel her breathing as she snuggled against him. They were both quiet for a moment.

"Let me tell you an idea I had," said Simon, breaking the silence. "If you're feeling up to it, what would you say to visiting Ian's school tonight? They're having an open house and I thought—"

"Really?" Bucky sat up. "Ian told me about the open house, but I knew you'd never let me go."

"I'm going with you, of course. They're having a chili supper first and Maggie has invited us to go with them."

The Turn Back school had started the middle of August and this was the third week of September. Simon was aware of how much Bucky missed the daily visits with Ian she had enjoyed all summer. With Ian's homework and chores, several days often passed without the two of them seeing each other.

"I thought it might help you visualize where Ian spends his day if you actually saw his classroom. You could even meet his teacher so when he talks about her you would have a mental image of what she looks like."

"Are you serious? You're really going to let me go tonight?"

"I'm not enrolling you. I just thought it would be helpful for you to see the school. Do you think you'll be feeling up to it?"

"I will make myself feel up to it."

"Maybe if you rest most of the day. How about no school work? Just reading time or quiet play time. I'll call Ms. Woods and tell her we're canceling your French lesson for the day." Sadie Jane Woods was in The Lukefahr Ladies Bible Class Bucky attended at the Methodist Church in Turn Back. Since the first of September, Simon had been allowing the retired French professor to come to the Mansion twice a week to instruct Bucky.

"Deal." Bucky held up her hand for a high-five and Simon obliged her.

"Now, I suggest we both clean up in case someone knocks on our door. And I know that's one of your favorite gowns, so don't put it in your dirty clothes hamper. Leave it in your bathroom. I'll soak it and see if I can get out those stains. I'll bring you some breakfast up to your room after I've showered. Okay?"

Bucky put her arms around him and squeezed. "I love you."

"I love you, too, Imala."

Bucky released him. "Huh?"

"I mean Bucky."

2

OPEN HOUSE

"You don't seem yourself tonight, Simon." Maggie and Simon walked down a hallway decorated with childish artwork and papers scrawled by young hands. Simon kept a close eye on Bucky. She and Ian were a few yards ahead of them, the two stopping here and there for Ian to point out something of interest. Other parents and children milled around, examining the posted classwork and drawings or coming in and out of the open classroom doors.

"In fact," continued Maggie, "I've been concerned about you for the past few weeks. Is anything wrong?"

Simon cleared his throat. It was a nervous habit which accompanied his hesitant speech pattern. "I... uh... I think Bergmann's blow to my head did something." He kept his voice down.

"That was almost two months ago. Have you seen Chip about it?" Dr. Chip Crosson, the neurosurgeon who had attended Simon in the hospital, was the son of Ron and Penny Crosson, relatives and close friends of Maggie's.

Simon shook his head. "I'm not in the habit of running to doctors for every slight twinge. I always hope things will clear up on their own. And they usually do."

"The brain's not something you should slough off. You need to take care of yourself. You're all that little girl has in this world." Maggie nodded toward Bucky further down the hallway.

"You're right, of course, as usual. But... uh... that's something else I'm concerned about." Simon leaned in close so others in the school hallway could not overhear. "Bucky had another one of her episodes last night."

"Oh, no. After the prayer walk? What caused it? Oh, let me guess. Carl Bergmann and what he was ranting about?"

"It was during the night. She had a nightmare her mother was trying to drown her. I've tried to tell her it was only a dream, but...in Turn Back—"

"Nothing's just a dream, is it?" Maggie stopped and watched her great-grandson and Bucky laughing together about something they were looking at on the hallway wall. "She seems all right this evening. The way she inhaled that chili dog at the supper just now, I would never have suspected she was recovering from another one of those...those awful experiences. Don't you ever feed that child?"

Maggie's last remark broke through the dark cloud that had settled over Simon and he smiled. "I'd forgotten how much she likes chili dogs. We haven't had any since we left New York. There was a wonderful deli next to our apartment building. I guess I could try my hand at them, but I know they'd taste nothing like that."

"Pfft," snorted Maggie. She patted Simon on the arm. "I'm glad you're here with me this evening. I'm always a little intimidated by these teachers, especially the out-of-town ones. I always feel like they look down on me because of my age and my lack of education."

It was Simon's turn to snort. "I didn't realize there was anyone who could intimidate you."

Simon and Maggie stopped outside the door to Ian's fifth-grade classroom to allow a man and woman and a young girl to leave the room. The couple nodded in greeting to Maggie and paused to exchange a few pleasantries with her. Ian and Bucky had already ducked inside and had rushed up to the teacher, who was standing beside her desk.

"Mrs. Lannigan," said Ian, "this is my friend, Bucky Carter. She doesn't go to school here but she wanted to see my room."

"Good evening. Bucky, is it?" Mrs. Lannigan's face brightened as she smiled broadly. "Oh, you're the girl who leads the prayer walks, aren't you? Where do you go to school?"

Ian often referred to his teacher as "Old Lady Lannigan," but Bucky didn't think she looked at all like an old lady, at least not like the elderly Lukefahr Ladies in the Sunday school class. "I don't go to school," replied Bucky. "My father teaches me."

"I'm glad you came tonight, Ian," said Mrs. Lannigan. "Is your grandmother with you?" Mrs. Lannigan looked toward the doorway where Simon and Maggie were entering. "Oh, there she is. Ian, why don't you show Bucky your desk and our learning stations while I speak with your grandmother."

"Maggie's his great-grandmother," corrected Bucky.

Mrs. Lannigan smiled in response and turned her attention to Maggie who introduced herself and Simon. Maggie had never met Dana Lannigan personally, but had seen her at various school assemblies and other school functions over the years ever since Ian had started pre-school. Turn Back was a small school where almost everyone knew everyone else. There was a feeling of family there, and, rightly so, since many of the students and some of the teachers were related. Mrs. Lannigan, however, was not from the area, and commuted daily from Green River. She had taught at the rural school in the town on the road to nowhere for eight years.

"So, how's my boy doing so far?" asked Maggie.

"I am impressed with him," replied Mrs. Lannigan. "We took a reading test at the beginning of the year. Most students slip a little from their scores at the end of the previous year because of the long summer holiday. But Ian's scores actually improved over the break. And not just a little. They showed a significant increase. And he is so interested in every subject."

"He had a good teacher this summer."

Mrs. Lannigan looked at Simon. "Your daughter said you homeschooled her. Have you been tutoring Ian also?"

"Bucky has been tutoring him," interjected Maggie. "Not in any strict sense of the word. She's just been a good influence."

"He's really a delight to have in class. I wish I could inspire such enthusiasm in a few of my other students."

"Now for the bad news," said Maggie. "What's he need to work on?"

The young teacher looked at the back of the room where Ian and Bucky were huddled in front of an aquarium. "I was surprised just now when he came into the room with Bucky. He does not seem to have any close friends here at school. There are only fourteen in the class this year, and that's not a large pool to choose from, but you'd think he'd find someone with similar interests to pal around with."

"That's nothing I haven't heard before," said Maggie. "He doesn't have any relatives his age or neighbors. Not until the Carters moved next door, anyway. I think he just never learned to socialize."

"We do a lot of group work. He…" Mrs. Lannigan paused as one of her other students came into the room and headed toward the aquarium. "He participates, but only the bare minimum. And he never takes the lead even though I know he's capable. But working together is an important social skill he'll need out in the world. So, I'd say that's the area we need to work on with him. But academically, I don't see any problems at the moment."

While the adults were talking at the front of the classroom, Ian escorted Bucky around the room, pointing out the different points of interest. When they stopped in front of a display of essays stapled to one of the large bulletin boards, Bucky squinted as she read Ian's. The papers were on the different European explorers and conquerors of the Americas. Ian had written about Pizarro, one of the many historical figures he and Bucky had role-played last summer.

"Your handwriting is atrocious," said Bucky, stepping back. "Almost as bad as mine."

"But I got an A," said Ian defensively. "Besides, people use computers for everything now. Who's going to need to write by hand, anyway? Come on over here and see the aquarium. I think I'd like to have an aquarium."

Bucky followed him and together they peered into the tank.

"I've seen your room, Ian. You wouldn't have anywhere to put it."

"I could set it up in the living room so Gram could watch it, too."

"Hi, Ian."

Ian and Bucky spun around at the sudden sound of the girl's voice behind them.

"Oh, hi, Madyson." Ian ducked his head and wiped his hand across his blond curls, dangling over his forehead.

"I'm Madyson Koeller," said the newcomer, addressing Bucky. "That's Madyson with a *y*. You don't go to school here, do you?" Madyson was taller than Ian or Bucky. She had long red hair that trailed down her back in spiral curls.

"I'm just visiting," answered Bucky. "My name's Bucky Carter."

"From the prayer walks? I've never seen you up close. You're always surrounded by those old women."

"They're the Lukefahr Ladies. We started the walks."

"So, do you know where the cave is we've all been dreaming about?"

Bucky shrugged.

"I'll bet Ian will find it," said Madyson. "He can do anything. He's my boyfriend, you know."

"I am not!" Ian drew himself up.

"Sure you are. Our desks are right over there next to each other." Madyson flung her arm in the general direction of the desks. "He's the least disgusting boy in the whole class. Except for Marty Neale but Sophie is his girlfriend."

Bucky was unsure how to respond. Not once during their many conversations had Ian spoken of girlfriends and boyfriends among his classmates.

"You're lucky, Madyson, that Bucky doesn't go to school here or you wouldn't be the smartest one in our class anymore. I'll bet she knows more than even Mrs. Lannigan."

"I doubt that," said Madyson. She gave her head a shake, causing her long hair to flip over one shoulder. "I've heard that your father thinks he's too good to send you to our school."

"That's not true." Bucky crossed her arms. "He just wants to teach me himself."

"I overheard my mother talking to someone at one of the walks and she said you and your father have an unhealthy relationship."

Bucky scrunched up her face. "What?"

"Ian, Bucky, let's go," called Maggie from the front of the room. She and Simon were walking toward the door.

"Madyson," said Mrs. Lannigan, approaching the children. "Is your mother here tonight?"

"She was in my little brother's class. She'll probably be here in a few minutes."

"Good-bye, Mrs. Lannigan," said Bucky, extending her hand to the teacher. "It was nice meeting you. I'm sorry I can't be in your class." When Mrs. Lannigan took her hand there was no feeling of familiarity Bucky experienced when being in contact with those who were somehow related to her.

"I'm sorry, too. To hear Ian's grandmother—pardon me—great-grandmother talk, you'll make a wonderful teacher someday."

Bucky smiled and threw a parting glance over her shoulder at Madyson who was close enough to hear the teacher's compliment.

When they were out in the hallway, Bucky leaned close to Ian and whispered, "Is she really your girlfriend?"

"Of course not," he replied, wiping his hands down his shirt.

"Am I your girlfriend?"

Ian didn't reply.

"Well?"

"Can't we just be best friends?"

"Sure," said Bucky. "No hand holding, no goo-goo eyes. I like that."

When Simon went in to Bucky's bedroom for their nightly conversation ritual, he found her already asleep. He brushed a strand of hair away from her face, and then sat in the chair beside her bed.

"Dad?" Bucky wiped the back of her hand across her face and sat up. The big eyes of the two kittens on the front of her purple pajama top peeked over the top of the cover.

"I didn't mean to wake you."

"I don't think I was asleep yet. I wanted to talk about some things."

They had already spoken at length about the open house adventure after they arrived home. After leaving Mrs. Lannigan's classroom, they had visited the other classes that made up Ian's weekly schedule. They saw the music room and met that teacher, Kena Lacey. In the gymnasium where Ian had physical education, the coach was busy talking to some other parents so they didn't speak to him. They visited the art room with its walls plastered with students' paintings and several tables full of papier-mâché sculptures, and they walked through the library which Bucky noted was smaller than her father's library at the Mansion. Simon was unsure what else there was left to discuss this evening.

"Since I'm ten and Ian's ten and he's in fifth grade, am I in fifth grade, too, even if I don't go to school?"

"I haven't actually tested you since before we left the city, but I'd say you're all over the map. In some subjects or areas you're above that grade level and in some, such as math, for example, you're at or maybe slightly above fifth-grade level."

"So if I did go to school, I'd be in fifth grade?"

Simon cocked his head. "Maybe. Age-wise that's where you'd be, but they'd probably test you. You might be in sixth or even seventh. But, Bucky, you're not going to school. I told you why we went tonight. It was so you could see where Ian was every day."

"I know. But if you don't know for sure what grade I'm in now, how will I know when I'm ready for college? You are going to let me go to college, aren't you?"

"Oh, maybe, when you're eighty or ninety."

"Dad." Bucky drew out the word.

"There are exams you can take to get the equivalent of a high school diploma and then there are more tests you take to get into college. But it will be a few years yet before we have to think about those. Now, what else is on your mind?"

"When Sissy Casteel found out Sadie Jane Woods was giving me French lessons, Sissy said she would teach me how to play the piano." Sissy was also in the Lukefahr Ladies Bible Class and played the organ at the church. "Since Ian has to take a music class," continued Bucky, "I think I should learn music, too."

"We don't have a piano."

"We could get one. You said that one room downstairs was called the music room back when this was a health resort, and you showed me an old picture of people gathered around the piano that used to be there. We could turn it into a music room again, couldn't we? It's just sitting there empty right now."

"I'm not really happy about Ms. Woods coming here. I'm doing it because you need to learn a foreign language. But now you're suggesting we have yet another person invading our home on a regular basis."

"I think Sissy gives the lessons at her house."

"That's out of the question then."

"Please. *S'il vous plaît.*"

Simon smiled. "Don't try to persuade me with your foreign words. Unless it's Hittite, of course."

"I don't know how to say *please* in Hittite."

"*Māntāssu.*"

"*Māntāssu,*" Bucky repeated. "Did Mom play the piano?"

Simon pressed his lips together. "Yes. But when we moved into our apartment, there wasn't room for one."

"But we have plenty of room here."

"I'll think about it. One more question and then it's lights out."

Bucky chewed on her lower lip before responding. "Do you and I have an unhealthy relationship?"

"What? Why would you ask that?"

"Madyson Koeller, the girl who came into Ian's classroom tonight when we were in there, said that her mother said that you and I have an unhealthy relationship. I'm not sure what that means."

"It means… It means I'm a single father rearing a little girl the best way I know how. That situation is not too unusual these days. Although around here, it's probably not as common as in the city. And we—I, anyway—am a little different than folks in this area and… maybe… overprotective of you. So people are bound to read into that all kinds of things. But I often think about what Maggie told you last summer at Ian's birthday party. Do you remember what she said about if your mother ever came back?"

"She said Mom would see you had done an excellent job in raising me."

"So, the answer is no. We do not have an unhealthy relationship. Okay? Now, good night." He stood and leaned over and kissed her forehead, and then switched off the lamp and started toward the door.

"Wait," called Bucky. "One more. Why did you call me *Imala* this morning?"

"It…uh… It means daughter in Hittite."

"No, it doesn't."

Simon stopped, his back to her. He rested a hand on the doorframe. "How would you know?"

"I just know."

"Good night, Bucky. Go to sleep."

3

WHAT'S REAL AND WHAT'S NOT

Simon sat staring at the computer monitor in his study, trying to tease the words out of his brain and onto the screen. Sometimes when he was writing they flowed freely and he covered pages with them in only a few hours. At other times, today for example, they were dammed somewhere upstream and only a few trickled through. The noise from down the hall, where Bucky was pounding on the grand piano in the music room, was not helping at all. It sounded as if she were banging the lid up and down. Finally he could stand the incessant thumping no longer.

"Bucky!" Simon threw open the double doors to the music room. "Will you please stop that racket. I'm sure that's not how Ms. Casteel taught you."

Bucky, sitting on the bench, looked up in surprise as Simon strode into the room. "That's not me. I thought it was you hammering or something."

Simon stopped and listened. The loud knocking continued. It wasn't coming from this room, but from downstairs. "Stay here."

The pounding grew louder as Simon descended the short flight of stairs to the lower level, the original rooms of the house which later grew into the Mansion Mineral Springs Resort. Someone or something was knocking on the locked door from inside the Spring Room. Simon fished a ring of keys out of his pocket and unlocked a box above the right side of the door. He reached inside and hit the switch to disconnect the motion sensor. His heart was pounding.

"Who's there?" He thought he could hear a low keening sound in response, but the wooden door was several inches thick. Even the sound of the spring pouring into the pool could not be heard from this side.

He scanned the hallway for something he could use as a club, a cudgel for protection. There was nothing. The intervals between the knocks were growing longer, the raps themselves fainter. Perhaps whoever or whatever was making the noise was weakening. He fumbled with the key as he tried to insert it into the lock and the entire ring clattered to the floor. He picked them up, found the correct key and tried again and heard the click. Grasping the ornate metal handle he pulled, opening the door only a couple of inches.

A young woman was slumped against the door frame, her right hand raised to knock once more. Her dark wet hair fell over her shoulders onto a long green dress which clung to her as if she had just stepped from the pool.

"Meredyth. Oh, my God. Meredyth."

The woman collapsed into Simon's arms and he sunk to the floor beneath her weight.

"Oh, my God, Meredyth. What... How..." He stroked her hair and face. There was no doubt the woman he held was his wife who had walked out the door nine years before and had never returned. Except for her clothes, she looked the same as she had then. There were tiny droplets of water—or tears—on her cheeks which were tinged with a slight blush. But her smooth face was that of a thirty-year-old, not the forty-year-old she was. Her lips parted slightly as she tried to speak. Only a quiet moan escaped.

"Dad?"

Simon looked up to see Bucky standing at the turn of the hall. "I told you to stay upstairs."

"Is that Seraphina? From the window?" Bucky had twice seen the image of a young woman in a long green dress with flowing blonde hair in the window of Seraphina's room in the lower level of the Mansion.

"No." Simon's voice broke as he tried to force back tears. "No, it's...it's... Go upstairs and get a blanket from my room and take it to the study. I'll try to carry her in there."

A few minutes later, Simon had pulled up a chair to the couch in his study where the woman from the Spring Room now lay. He leaned forward and adjusted the blanket under her chin.

"Dad," whispered Bucky, resting her hand lightly on Simon's arm. "Who is she? Where'd she come from?"

"Simon?" The woman's lashes fluttered and then her eyes opened.

When Bucky saw the piercing blue eyes she had only seen in photographs, she stepped back away from the couch.

"Simon?" The woman struggled to a half-way sitting position, propping herself up on her elbows. "It is you. It is you," she repeated.

"Meredyth?"

"What's happened? Where are we?" Her eyes darted around the room then came back to focus on Simon. She reached out a hand and touched his face. "What's happened to you, Simon? My darling Simon."

Simon clasped her wrist. "Meredyth, you've been away. You've been gone for…years. For nine years."

"No. That's impossible." For the first time, Meredyth noticed Bucky who was now standing several feet away, behind one of the leather recliners. Meredyth sat up, the blanket falling away. "Bucky? Oh, my God, Bucky? My little baby?"

"Dad?"

Simon released his grasp on Meredyth's arm and reached out to Bucky. "It's all right, Lamb."

Bucky stood frozen in place, her mouth open.

"Bucky, let me see you." Meredyth stretched out both hands. "I'm your mother."

"You're not my mother!" Bucky bolted for the door.

Simon stood. "Come back here!"

But she was gone. He heard her footsteps dashing up the stairs.

Simon shifted position and sat on the couch next to Meredyth who rested against him.

"What's happened, Sie?" she crooned. "I don't understand any of this. And Bucky, my little Bucky. She's just a baby and yet now she's almost grown."

"She's still very much a little girl, but I don't understand any of this either. We need to talk and find out what you remember."

"Can we talk later? I'm exhausted."

"All right," agreed Simon. "But you need to get out of those wet clothes. Do you think you can make it upstairs? I... I'm afraid I got rid of nearly all of your clothes when we moved. After nine years, I...I really didn't expect you to return. But you can wear something of mine."

For the next few days, Simon and Meredyth reacquainted themselves with each other, picking up where they had left off nearly a decade ago. Bucky gradually adjusted to Meredyth's presence in the household, but referred to her only as *her* or *she*, never Mother or Mom.

On the fourth day after Meredyth's arrival, Bucky looked up from her science book to see her mother looming over her.

"Your father is busy writing and I thought you and I could explore this big house together." Meredyth was wearing a pair of Simon's sweat pants and a T-shirt. She was barefoot.

"I can't right now," said Bucky. "I have work to do. I have to finish reading this chapter and answer some questions and then I have to practice my French."

"I can help you with your French. I had French in high school and again in college. I don't see why we have to have an outside tutor for you. I can teach you just as well."

"I like Sadie Jane Woods as a teacher."

"At any rate, I think you've studied enough this morning. You need to take a break. I haven't seen nearly half the rooms here yet."

The next thing Bucky knew she and Meredyth were standing outside the door to the Spring Room. "I'm not allowed to go in there," Bucky said. "Besides, it's locked."

"Locked doors are there for one of two purposes—to keep something in or to keep something out. Since the lock is on this side, it must be to keep something in. Let's see what it is, shall we?"

The ringing of the telephone startled Simon. He must have fallen asleep at his desk. He raised his head and looked around. The room was dark. He wasn't in his study, but in his bedroom. The phone was still ringing. He switched on the lamp and glanced next to him where Meredyth had shared his bed since her reappearance. Her side of the bed was empty. He picked up the receiver.

"Mr. Carter!" The young voice on the other end of the line was frantic.

"Ian? What's wrong? Has something happened to your grandmother?"

"No. Something's wrong with Bucky!"

The numbers on the digital clock next to the lamp glowed green. "Ian, it's two-thirty in the morning."

"Please, Mr. Carter. You have to help her. Something's wrong."

Fully awake now, Simon, the cordless phone still in his hand, rushed next door to Bucky's bedroom. She wasn't there. "Oh, my God. Not again."

Simon clicked the phone off and dropped it on the floor at the top of the stairs before hurtling down them. He reached the Spring Room in only seconds. The door was standing open. He slapped his hand against the light switch to illuminate the room. "Oh, my God!"

Bucky was halfway in the first pool, the coldest one. Her head was submerged but she was flailing her arms and kicking her legs against an invisible entity that was forcing her beneath the water.

"Get away from her!" Simon's cry was feral as he rushed down the steps and grabbed the back of Bucky's pajama top, hauling her onto the stone floor surrounding the pool. "Oh, Bucky, my lamb," he said over and over again, cradling her against his chest.

Bucky gasped for air and spit up water. "She was trying to kill me! She was drowning me! It wasn't a dream. It was real."

"Don't cry, Lamb. Please don't cry. You're safe now. She can't hurt you." Simon felt his daughter stiffen in his arms and he knew she was forcing back tears. He lifted his head from where he had buried it against the top of hers. There were red glints darting over the surface of the water. Higher, toward the ceiling, one or two flashes of green appeared. The red pinpoints of light winked out as the green ones became more numerous.

"Why are you doing this?" Simon cried. "This makes no sense."

Etakkama! The voices echoed around him. *We rejoice in the three. The songs of three are powerful. Sorrow is but for a while.*

Simon struggled to stand with his daughter's still form firmly in his embrace. "Let me know when you're ready to speak plainly," he said to the air. "I don't have time for riddles. My lamb, the most precious thing in the world to me, almost died tonight—again—at your hands."

It was the others. They would not harm her, but they are discordant. Protect the three.

"Whatever." Simon carried Bucky up the steps to the landing and out into the hall. He shifted her, trying to distribute her weight differently.

"I can walk, Dad." Her voice was weak, muffled against his neck.

"It's all right. I've got you."

Simon carried her all the way to his bedroom and set her down at the foot of his bed. "Take off those wet pajamas and I'll get you a T-shirt to wear."

"She was wearing one of your T-shirts."

"Because she didn't have any of her clothes." Simon had started to open one of his dresser drawers but stopped and turned around. "Wait. Those are your Thursday pajamas—the kittens."

Bucky had slipped the pajama top over her head. She held it out in front of her.

"You were wearing those when I said good night. That was Thursday, after the open house at school. What day is this?" He looked at his digital clock next to his bed. "It's Friday, the twenty-second. It was all a dream. Meredyth never came back. All of it... All of it was just another dream."

"But you found her in the Spring Room. She was wearing a green dress and she was all wet."

"And you were practicing on the piano in the music room."

"We don't have a piano."

"My God." Simon pulled a T-shirt from the drawer and slipped it over Bucky's head, then sat down next to her on the edge of the bed. He ran a hand over the sheets. "She was here beside me," he whispered. "But she was never here. It was all a dream. You and I, we were dreaming the same dream, the same...nightmare."

"She made me go with her to the Spring Room and then she tried to drown me. But, Dad, that was real. That wasn't a dream." Bucky wrung her purple pajama top with the wide-eyed kittens. "I'm all wet. That really happened."

"Oh, Bucky this is taking a dangerous turn if we can't tell what's real from what's not. My mind has been so messed up recently. How do I even know I'm sitting here talking to you?"

"You saved me from her just now. But in my first dream—last night or Wednesday night—the night I cried, Ian is the one who saved me."

"Ian saved you this time, too. He called me and… Unless that was part of the dream." Simon glanced at the empty phone cradle on his bedside table and abruptly stood and started for the door.

"No, Dad! Don't leave me here alone."

"I'm only stepping out here in the hall to find the phone."

"No." Bucky sprang up and crossed the bedroom in a flash. She wrapped her arms around Simon's waist.

"You're safe now, Lamb. She's not going to hurt you." Simon tried unsuccessfully to disengage her hold on him.

"That's what you said before."

"Look. There it is." Simon dragged her along with him as he crossed the few steps to the head of the stairs where his phone lay in the shadows against the wall. He retrieved it and with Bucky still tightly clinging to him, walked to her bedroom.

"No, Dad," she wailed, bracing one foot against the granite doorframe. "I'm not sleeping in there tonight. I'm sleeping with you."

"Bucky."

"No! Please let me stay with you. Please. *Māntāssu*."

Simon sighed. "I guess I'd feel better about that, too." He escorted her back into his room and over to the bed. "Madyson Koeller's mother would certainly not approve."

"I didn't like Madyson anyway."

"You only met her for a few minutes." Simon helped his daughter scoot to the other side of the bed. "Remember what we talked about how even if you don't like someone, you're to speak to that person in a civil manner?"

Bucky pulled the sheet and light blanket up over her. "She said Ian was her boyfriend."

Simon shook his head and lay down on his back. Only a few minutes ago, Bucky had suffered a near-death experience at the hands of a dream apparition claiming to be her mother, and now she was talking about fifth-grade love interests. "Ian's too young to have a girlfriend." He reached over to turn off the light.

"That's what I think. When will I be old enough to have a boyfriend? Oh, I know what you're going to say. When I'm eighty or ninety."

"Thereabouts."

"I have an idea."

Bucky's voice coming from the dark next to him was reassuring to Simon. It meant she was still there and it meant she was not having a nightmare about a murderous mother.

"Why don't you tie me to the bed? That way I can't wander off to the Spring Room in my sleep?"

"God, Bucky, I'm not going to tie you in bed. Mrs. Koeller would really have a field day if she got wind of that. The authorities would be here before you could say Jack Robinson."

"Who's Jack Robinson?"

"It's an expression. You need to try to go to sleep."

"My hair's still wet."

"It'll dry."

Bucky sighed. "Dad, would you hold my hand so I know you're still there?"

Simon slid his hand under the cover to take hold of hers. "I'll always be here, Lamb."

An unspoken rule in the Carter household, whether in New York or in Turn Back, was that Bucky was not to disturb her father when he was writing. It was not a hard rule to follow. Simon Carter usually sequestered himself in his study in the hours between breakfast and lunch. It was during those morning hours Bucky attended to her lessons alone in her room. After a shared meal, Simon would quiz her or introduce a new subject or provide instruction where she needed assistance. She was then free to spend the rest of the afternoon playing or reading or, after the move to Missouri, exploring the many rooms of the old Mansion Mineral Springs Resort she and her father now called home. Simon used the remainder of the afternoon to read or write or work on Hittite translations.

The routine had changed slightly this past summer when Simon allowed Bucky to spend time outdoors each morning, usually in the company of Ian Fletcher from next door. The unusual events that had transpired in the past few months had also interrupted the strict schedule of the Carter household on numerous occasions. Simon's writing regimen suffered more than Bucky's studies. He was finding it difficult to concentrate on crafting his latest mystery novel while he and his daughter were caught up in a real-life mystery.

And so he was more than a little annoyed when, for the next two days, Bucky refused to leave his side. The events of Thursday night had shaken her and now she was afraid to be alone. On Saturday Ian was supposed to come for their play time, but Maggie had called and said they needed to go to Green River and it would take most of the day. Simon had asked her if Ian had indeed phoned during the night on Thursday to warn him about the events in the Spring Room, but the boy had no memory of it. Maggie had started to tell Simon the cave dreams had changed, but she had been interrupted by someone at her door before she could elaborate.

Bucky did not seem to be at all upset about Ian's absence. She was sitting with her legs crossed Indian-style on the sofa in Simon's study. On her lap was her math workbook, but every time Simon glanced up from his writing, she was staring at him.

"I think it's time you went outside. You haven't been out since, when? Wednesday morning, except to walk up and get the mail with me yesterday."

"I need to work on my math." She ducked her head and scribbled some numbers on one of the pages.

"But you're not really working on your math, are you?" Simon stood and stretched and then walked over to one of the broad stuffed recliners and slumped into it. "It's daytime. The sun is shining. Nothing's going to harm you."

"I saw Seraphina twice in the window in the daytime."

"You don't know for sure who you saw was Seraphina."

"She was wearing the same dress as…as her. But her hair was different. And her eyes."

"Bucky, for the thousandth time, the woman we both saw in our dreams was not your mother. Your mother would never harm you. Besides you told me last night's dream was about the cave again and Mere—the woman—only made a brief appearance, the same as in mine."

"But she went like this with her hands." Bucky outstretched her right hand and made a beckoning motion with it. "She wanted me to follow her again."

"But you didn't, did you? See? You can control some aspects of your dreams."

The phone ringing interrupted their conversation. Bucky listened to the one-sided conversation, but couldn't identify the caller for the first two minutes. She gathered someone was coming here, but her father protested more than once before finally giving in. It was only when Simon called him "Chip" she knew who it was—Dr. Chip Crosson.

Bucky's face brightened at the mention of the name and she hopped off the couch. "Is Chip really coming here?" she asked after her father had hung up.

"In a few minutes. It seems he's in town for his mother's birthday, but he...uh...has some time and wants to stop by."

"But why didn't you want him to come? I like Chip. Do you think he'll bring Dale with him?"

"He didn't say. But now, Bucky, I want you to go your room while he's here. You can stay and greet him, but then I insist you remain in your room. What he has to say to me is private—it's adult matters."

"That's just like in the old days when you used to hide me away."

"I'm not hiding you away. I want to talk to Chip—to Dr. Crosson—in private, without you listening."

"But it's not safe in my room."

"Of course, it's safe." Simon slammed his hand down on his desk. "And if you don't stop arguing with me, Imala, you can march up there right now and not see him at all."

Bucky jumped, her eyes wide. Her dad rarely reprimanded her or raised his voice. And there was that strange name again! She picked up her math book where it had fallen to the floor and sat down again on the couch. Peering over the top of the book, she watched Simon as he straightened some papers on his desk and then ran his fingers through his dark, wavy hair. It must have been the way the light from the window shone on him that, for the first time, Bucky noticed there were streaks of gray in his curls, especially around his temples. Simon turned his back to her and looked out the bay window.

"I guess we should open the front gate," he said finally.

"I'll do it," she said quietly.

"Thank you."

Bucky slid off the couch and scampered out into the entry hall. She flipped the switch that controlled the gates. The light on the panel by the front door turned from red to green. When she came back into the study, her father was still standing at the window, his hands clasped behind his back.

She tiptoed across the polished wood floor to stand next to him. "I'm sorry I talked back to you."

Simon sighed. "And I'm sorry I yelled at you." He put an arm around her shoulders. "I know you've been upset and frightened the last few days. So have I. And…and I've not been myself for a while. Maybe Chip can help me sort things out."

"Look!" Bucky pointed at the turn of the lane where a late-model SUV was coming toward the Mansion. "He's here."

4

THE PAST IS PRESENT

Bucky hung back a few feet behind Simon as he opened the front door to admit Dr. Chip Crosson and a woman she had never seen. But her face lit up when she saw Dale Crosson also walking up the steps behind his brother. She had only met Chip once when Simon was in the hospital, but she saw Dale every Wednesday at the prayer walks and usually again on Sunday at church. It was the first time she had seen the twin brothers together. It was actually the first time she had ever seen any identical twins in person, and she was fascinated by how much alike they looked. Had Dale's head not been permanently tilted to one side and his sandy brown hair with streaks of gray not been a little longer than Chip's, it would have been difficult to tell them apart. That is, until they spoke. Simon had explained to her a problem at their birth had resulted in Dale's brain being deprived of oxygen which had impaired his mental development and caused his physical abnormality.

Because Dale was so slow in speech and in other ways, the people in Turn Back tended to dismiss him, but it was Dale who, over the past few months, had restored the park in the center of town to its former beauty. It was also Dale who had first told Bucky the ships in their dreams last summer would be found not down by the river where everyone was searching, but in the woods near a spring. And that's exactly where they discovered the Hollow Stone with its engravings of ships and spirals and ancient inscriptions.

Dale smiled broadly when he saw Bucky standing behind Simon. "Chip…said…I… could… come…and…vi…sit…with you…while…he…talked…to your…fa…ther."

"That's an excellent idea," said Simon.

"And this is my wife, Lane," said Chip. "She wasn't feeling well earlier this morning and I probably should have insisted she stay with my parents, but she didn't want to pass up the opportunity to see this old place. I actually brought her here a few years ago when it was vacant and we looked through the windows."

"I hope you're not coming down with something," said Simon.

"Oh, it's nothing. I get a little upset stomach almost every time we come down here and navigate through all these hills. I'm feeling all right now. I thought I could stay with Dale and Bucky while you and Chip talk." Lane was thin with short blond hair. Standing next to her tall, lanky husband, she barely came up to his shoulder.

Chip laid a hand on top of Bucky's head. "You don't mind, do you, Newt, keeping my wife and brother company?"

When Chip touched her, the familiar feeling of kinship spilled from Bucky's head down to her toes. She looked up at him and smiled.

"Bucky, why don't you show Dale and Mrs. Crosson to your room. Chip—Dr. Crosson—and I will be in the study."

"Please call me Chip," Dale's brother said, putting one hand on Dale's shoulder and steering him in Bucky's direction.

"And both of you call me Lane."

Bucky narrowed her eyes and looked at her father for a moment. Until the past few weeks, Simon had always insisted she remain out of sight in her room whenever someone came to the door. And now here he was directing her to take Dale and this person she had just met there. Furthermore, she had refused to be in her room without her father since Thursday night and had hardly stepped foot inside except to change clothes and gather what books she needed. Would Dale be able to protect her if the woman in the dream who claimed to be her mother returned?

"Bucky?" Simon clasped her shoulder.

Bucky blinked and nodded. "Okay." She reached out and took Dale's hand. It was a familiar touch, one of warmth and harmony, a feeling everything was all right. She remembered her dad telling her it had been Dale who had carried her, unconscious, home that night from The Hollow after she had experienced one of her terrible episodes. If he had the strength to do that, she thought, surely he could fend off anyone who sought to do her harm.

Simon showed Chip to the door of the study but paused outside to watch Bucky and Dale walk up the stairs, trailed by Lane.

"Do you like trains?" asked Bucky, still holding Dale's hand. She usually raced up to the second floor, but she matched her steps today to Dale's slower pace. Without waiting for an answer, she continued. "I have a really big train track set up. It has tunnels and bridges and houses and all kinds of other buildings and you can flip a switch to make the train go from one track to another. Or we can play a game. I have lots of them. You could visit my castle, but you're so tall, I don't think you'd be very comfortable. It was made for people my size. My Dad comes in sometimes but he has to bend over."

Both Simon and Chip listened to Bucky's incessant chatter until she and Dale and Chip's wife disappeared down the upstairs hallway.

"I hope she doesn't overwhelm him," said Simon as he showed Chip through the study doorway and invited him to sit in one of the broad leather recliners.

"He'll be fine," said Dr. Crosson, taking a seat. He waited for Simon to sit on the couch before continuing. "So, how have you been?"

Simon sighed and shook his head. "I… I don't know. I…uh… Sometimes… Sometimes, I think I'm going crazy. This is…not at all what I expected when I moved here."

"From a neurological standpoint," said Chip, "these dreams have to be driving everyone crazy. And yet, from everything I've heard, more and more people keep showing up, hoping they'll experience them. I haven't set foot in the park. Quite frankly, I'm afraid to."

"But it's more than the dreams," said Simon. "The dreams I can handle. They're interesting, but...they don't scare me. It's this other thing that's been going on. Oh, God." Simon leaned his head back against the couch and swept his hand through his hair.

"What other thing? Tell me about it."

"I can't."

"What I called about last week?"

Simon huffed. "No. I'm still trying to process that."

"Then what is it?"

Simon leaned forward and put his elbows on his knees, his chin cupped in his hands. "I keep... I keep getting these flashes. Scenes. Memories almost. They're of a different place, a different time. And when I say time, I'm talking about millennia ago." Simon tried to describe for Chip some of what he had been seeing. "But nothing's really clear. Except..."

"Except?"

"Thursday morning, I saw Bucky standing in the hallway, but for a few seconds it wasn't Bucky. It was another little girl and she was speaking..." Simon paused and took a deep breath. "She was speaking Hittite. And I called her Imala, but...I don't know anyone named Imala. And I don't know if I really saw her or if I was imagining it or if it was a dream. But just now, a few minutes before you arrived, I again called Bucky by that name. Did that blow to my head do more damage than what you originally thought?" Simon chose not to tell Chip about the shared dream that was partly real he and Bucky experienced Thursday night.

"In what context did you say that name to Bucky the second time? Were you having another vision?"

Simon shook his head. "No. I lost my temper. And it was over nothing. But I yelled at her. All of her life I've tried never to raise my voice to her, but I've shouted at her more in the past few months than I ever have."

"Why do you think that is?"

Simon shifted positions and leaned back again. He recognized Chip was playing psychologist with him, but he really needed to talk to someone about all this. "I… I'm afraid of losing her."

"She's how old?" said Chip. "Ten? She's entering that in-between stage. No longer a child but not an adult. I don't have kids myself, but it's a universal truth children grow up. They become more and more independent. Parents have to continually balance between allowing them that freedom while still maintaining control."

Simon drummed his fingers on his leg. "I keep telling myself that, but…" He sighed. "Bucky's different."

"I know. In just the brief time I spent with her that day in the hospital, I'm aware she's not like other children. And I know you do what you do to keep her safe. But, Simon, she might be different in some ways, but she has the same needs as all children." Chip leaned back, propping his left ankle onto his right knee. "But let's return to these visions of yours, these flashes, as you call them. Have they increased since our phone conversation?"

"No. Yes. Maybe. I don't know." Simon swept his hand along the leather cushion. He picked at the piped seam along the front edge.

"That had to be a shock."

"It was more a confirmation than a revelation. I don't think these are related to that. I think… I think… God, I don't know what I think." Simon leaned forward and buried his face in his hands.

Chip was quiet for a moment before continuing. "Do you believe you really are this Etakkama guy from the stone in the park?"

"What?" Simon raised his head.

"Hey, I'm not here in Turn Back often, but my mother keeps me well-informed of all that's going on *and* all that's being said."

"Then Maggie has told your mother about the Anarianu."

"The what?"

"The Anarianu. The Guardians of the spring. The little green lightning bugs we think are causing all this."

Chip put both feet on the floor and leaned forward. "I have no idea what you're talking about. My mother has never mentioned Anari… whatever or green bugs."

Simon sighed.

"Well?" pressed Chip. "Are you going to tell me?"

Simon ran his open palms down his face. "I think I've talked to them…or communicated with them. And I think Bucky has, also."

"Who? The little green bugs?"

Simon barked a short laugh. "Maybe I am crazy."

"What'd they say?"

Simon stood and walked over to the bay window, his back to Chip. "That I am Etakkama. That I was a Hittite who came here with some Minoan sailors thirty-five hundred years ago. That I took a wife—a Native American—who died in childbirth. And that I sailed back—to Crete, I guess—with my infant daughter."

"Imala?"

Simon made no response.

"And you think these flashes, these visions, are scenes or memories from that life?"

Simon turned around. "But not just from then. I sometimes see battle scenes from what appear to be, maybe, the Crusades. Or sometimes I'm riding in an oxcart down a dirt road and there's a village ahead of round huts with thatched roofs. Or even this—" Simon swept one arm around him. "This Mansion. I've seen it under construction." He leaned against his desk, his hands flat against the surface, his head down. "I don't know. Maybe I've spent too many hours on this blasted computer, writing stories in my own little made-up worlds. Now my mind can no longer sort out what's real from what's not."

Chip leaned back in his chair without comment.

Simon raised his head. "Well, Mr. Neurosurgeon?"

Chip smiled. "That's Dr. Neurosurgeon. Are you on any medication?"

It was Simon's turn to smile. "Nothing. Legal or illegal. An occasional aspirin. And I don't drink, either."

"And you say Bucky has been in communication with these bugs, too? They seem very articulate."

"No, actually they are not. It's difficult to make sense of much of what they say."

"Do they speak English?"

"Not sure. I understand them, but I think it's telepathy."

Chip raised his eyebrows and brushed a hand through his salt and pepper hair. "I believe I'll definitely schedule you for an MRI. We have the scans from July to use as a reference to see if there have been any changes. Have you had any others from back in New York? I could get a copy of them."

Simon shook his head.

"But…" started Chip and then hesitated.

"What?"

"I know what I'd like to try. You'd be an excellent candidate."

"What?" Simon repeated.

"Hypnotherapy."

"No. No way."

"I'm a licensed hypnotherapist."

"And a neurosurgeon? Well, aren't you multi-talented."

"What's the difference from you being a best-selling author and a Hittite scholar? I learned a long time ago not everything wrong with a brain can be fixed with a scalpel. So I chose to delve into another path to wholeness and well-being. And I'm not the only one."

Neither man spoke for a few seconds and then Simon broke the silence. "You're serious? Perform some type of regression hypnosis on me? Take me back to my Hittite roots? Make me cluck like a chicken whenever I hear a certain word?"

"Yes, yes, maybe, and no. I'm not a stage hypnotist. But in a relaxed state and guided by the right questions, maybe we can come up with some answers."

"When?"

"Right now. We could do a thirty- to sixty-minute session. See what happens."

"Now?"

"Why not? I have to head back to the city later today. I'd just need to get my laptop from my car. I want to record the session."

Simon pressed his lips together. "We'd better check on Bucky and Dale and your wife first. Tell them we'll be a while yet."

"Good." Chip clapped his hands together and jumped up from the chair. "Let's go."

Simon followed behind Chip who bounded up the stairs, stopping at the top to wait for Simon to catch up. Although they were close to the same age, Simon was amazed at how much more energy the doctor had.

"Her room's down the hall here on the left." Simon led the way into Bucky's bedroom and on into her study room. They could hear voices coming from her playroom.

Chip paused at the short table in the center of the study room. Several books and papers were spread across it, sharing space with a laptop. He picked up a science workbook and thumbed through it. "Do you use one of the many home-school programs for your daughter?"

"It's a...curriculum of my own design."

"Do you intend to take her through high school?" Chip laid the book back on the table.

"Haven't thought that far ahead."

"Don't shoot!" shouted Bucky from the next room.

Simon and Chip rushed over to the doorway. Bucky, wearing a turban and a long, striped robe, was kneeling on the floor. Dale, with a cowboy hat fastened tightly under his chin, was sitting on the life-sized carousel horse. He was waving a plastic, pearl-handled pistol with one hand while holding a small bag and the reins with the other.

"But...you...will...steal...my...gold."

"No, I promise. Please don't kill me," pleaded Bucky dramatically, her hands clasped over her heart. "If you let me live, I will grant you three wishes." She looked up and noticed the two men standing in the doorway. "Oh, hi."

Lane was seated on one of the small red chairs at the low table. She turned over the book she had been reading and smiled at her husband.

Dale also turned to see his brother and Simon. "Buck...y...and...I...were...playing." He slid off of the horse.

"That's all right," said Simon. "We didn't mean to interrupt. Who are you supposed to be?"

"We couldn't decide between playing cowboys or one of the stories from *Arabian Nights*," explained Bucky, "so we sort of combined the two."

"We...didn't...have...this...many...toys...when... we...were...little,...did we,...Chip?"

Chip looked around the playroom at the castle, the carousel horse, the elaborate train set, the miniature kitchen, the doll houses, the costumes hanging on pegs, and bins and shelves full of games and puzzles and playthings. The scene would have rivaled the toy department of any major store. He shook his head. "Nobody had this many toys." He raised his eyebrows and looked sideways at Simon who turned away.

"I call it my pleasure palace." Bucky clasped one of Simon's hands. "But it didn't work out quite like you planned, did it?"

Simon laid his other hand on the top of Bucky's head. "We came up to tell you we're going to be maybe an hour longer. Can the three of you occupy yourselves for that time?"

"Can—may—we go outside?"

"I would rather you stay up here," answered Simon.

"If I had a room like this as a boy, I'm not sure I'd have ever gone outside," said Chip.

"That was the idea," said Simon. He disengaged his hand from Bucky's. He and Chip went back downstairs to his study while Dale and Bucky resumed their characters and Lane continued reading.

It was almost two hours later when Simon and Bucky stood at the front door and watched Chip and Dale and Lane Crosson drive up the tree-shrouded lane toward the road.

"I'm sorry you had to spend so much time with Dale. My…uh…conversation with Chip took much longer than I intended."

"I didn't mind. We had fun. And Lane's nice. We talked a little but she read most of the time."

"You must be starved. Let's go find something to eat."

Bucky hung her head. "I did get a snack earlier."

"You came downstairs? I told you to stay in your room."

"I used the back stairs. We were hungry. I didn't think you'd mind."

The two of them started toward the kitchen. "So what did you serve them?"

"I got us each a slice of bread and a glass of water."

Simon snorted. "Oh, great. So now Dale's going to tell his mother I gave you bread and water for lunch and she'll tell Maggie and Maggie will scold me for not feeding you right."

"It was whole wheat bread. That ought to count for something." Bucky sat down at the small square table while Simon disappeared into the pantry and reemerged with a can of chicken noodle soup. "And, Dad, I think I can sleep in my own bed tonight."

"Oh?" Simon opened the can and looked in the cabinet for a large bowl.

"Dale said he would protect me from Mom."

Simon set the opened can on the counter and turned to face Bucky. "First of all, that is not your mother in the dreams. And secondly, how can Dale help you?"

Bucky shrugged. "I don't know. But Dale's not like other people, is he? He said I just have to think about him and he would come into my dream and keep her from hurting me."

"So if you told Dale about your dream that means that Lane heard it, too. And she, no doubt, will tell Chip." Simon turned back and poured the soup into a bowl. He added a can of water and stirred.

"Did I do something wrong?"

"No, of course not."

"I'm glad Dale will be in my dreams to protect me from now on. And, Dad, you remember this morning I told you I didn't want to go to church tomorrow because I didn't want to be in class without you?"

"And I told you the ladies in your class would not let anything happen to you and I would be right next door."

"Dale said I should go, so I guess I will."

"I'm glad Dale convinced you." Simon put the bowl of soup in the microwave and punched in the time. "Maggie told me Thursday night at the open house your ladies are going to discuss the future of the prayer walks tomorrow."

"What does that mean? Are they going to stop them?"

"I don't think so, but the days are getting shorter and cooler. It won't be long until winter. Older people often don't like to get out at night and the park is not well lit. Maybe they'll move it to an earlier time and they might even start having them less frequently."

"How will that affect the dreams?"

"I have no idea. I guess we'll have to wait and see. And speaking of winter, we're going to have to get you some warm clothes. I think you've probably outgrown most of last year's."

Bucky's face brightened. "Are we going shopping again?"

"Probably not. I'll look online. Did you wash your hands?"

Bucky held up her hands and squinted at them. "No."

"Then come over here to the sink and do so. I think after lunch you should spend a couple of hours on your studies. I know you didn't accomplish much this morning before the Crossons came. And I… I need to spend some time alone in my study without interruption. All right?"

Chip had discussed with Simon a few things after their hypnosis session but he had left a USB flash drive of the recording with him and Simon was anxious to hear what had transpired in the nearly ninety-minute session.

Bucky washed her hands and dried them on one of the kitchen towels. "Dad, do you want to know a secret?" she whispered.

"Did you promise someone you wouldn't tell?"

"No, but he did say it was a secret."

"Who? Dale?"

Bucky nodded. "When Lane was in the bathroom and couldn't hear us, Dale told me she's going to have a baby, but she doesn't know it yet and neither does Chip."

Simon was pouring a glass of milk for Bucky and stopped halfway. "Then how does Dale know?"

Bucky shrugged. "Dale says it's a boy."

"Well, don't go telling anybody else, because it might not be true. And even if it's true, it would be very early in the pregnancy. Maggie told me they've lost two babies, so she might not carry this one to term."

"How do you lose a baby?" Bucky sat back down at the table.

Simon considered for a moment the best way to explain the phrase to her. "It means something happens during the pregnancy and the baby dies before it is born."

When she did not respond Simon said, "Understand?"

Bucky drew on the tabletop with her finger. "That's sad. Do you think it will be all right if I include their baby in my prayers? It's probably not a secret from God since he knows everything."

"I think that will be fine."

5

THAT'S A WHOPPER

The next morning Simon held Bucky's hand until they reached the end of the hallway outside the Lukefahr Ladies Bible Class room in the Turn Back Methodist Church.

"Remember, I'm just down the hallway here," said Simon. The night had passed without incident, with Bucky in her own room. Simon, however, had not slept much. His recorded responses to Chip's questions during the hypnotherapy session kept replaying in his mind. Unable to sleep, he had sat by Bucky's bed for several hours, trying to reconcile what he had said under hypnosis with what his conscious mind could recall. He didn't want Bucky to wake and find him hovering there so toward dawn he had returned to his own room.

In the church hallway Bucky looked up at him and smiled. "I'll be all right."

"Are you joining us old women today, Simon Carter?" Lillian Thomas, her white, short tightly curled hair neatly framing the brown, lined face, shuffled down the hall with her walker. At ninety-four she was the oldest member of the class, but her sister Leona, who followed close behind her, was only four years younger.

Simon smiled broadly at the sisters. "Good morning, ladies. I was saying good-bye to Bucky."

Lillian shook her head. "Lordy, man, she's just going to Sunday school. She's not headed off to college."

"Not yet, anyway," replied Simon. He dropped Bucky's hand but laid his own hand on her head. "See you after while, Lamb."

Simon moved aside to let the sisters and some other class members through the doorway. He started for his own classroom, but not before he heard Lillian say to Bucky, "Child, it's a wonder you ever learned to walk. I'll bet he didn't let you down on the floor by yourself until you were six or seven."

Bucky's reply, if any, was lost in the babble of the several women congregating in the hallway outside the door.

Once inside the Lukefahr Ladies classroom, Bucky found her usual place in one of the upholstered seats which were once part of the theater in the Mansion Mineral Springs Resort which was now her home. Maggie's chair next to her was vacant. Bucky looked around as the women filtered into the room, some of them standing talking in groups of two or three. They all began to take their seats and still Maggie was absent. Although in the past four months, Bucky had become acquainted with all thirteen of the class members, she was closest to Maggie. Ian's great-grandmother had not missed one Sunday.

Tall, thin Sadie Jane Woods rapped her knuckles on the small table that served as her teacher's desk. "Ladies, we should get started. We have some things to discuss this morning besides the lesson." She waited while the women took their seats before continuing. "We've been talking among ourselves, but I think as a group we should make some sort of decision about the prayer walks."

Just then Maggie came hurrying through the door. The manner in which the seats were set up in a horseshoe shape meant she had to go around to the opening before she could sit in her usual spot next to Bucky. "Sorry, I'm running late this morning," she said to the class. "I declare, sometimes that boy is sprinting fifty yards ahead of me and other times he's as slow as molasses."

The other women smiled and nodded, most of them having been mothers. None envied her position of rearing a child at her age.

As Maggie settled into her seat and set her purse on the floor, Bucky leaned over and whispered. "I was afraid you weren't coming."

Maggie patted Bucky's knee. Bucky soaked in the serene, calming feeling of familiarity that always accompanied Maggie's touch.

Sadie Jane cleared her throat and continued. "As I was saying, we need to decide so we can announce any changes at this week's walk."

"The Baptists were surprisingly accommodating enough to change their Wednesday night services to Thursday when they started up again this month," said Ruby Lower, toying with one of her earrings, "but I think it grates on their nerves to have done so. I'm sure they'd like us to pick a different day."

"But are we the ones to make that decision?" asked Clara Keller. Bucky had noted Clara was one of the women who rarely spoke up in class although she had been the one who suggested the soap bubbles for the talent show last July.

"Who better?" said Betty Fischer, whose husband taught the Men's Class. "We started it."

"And although it's grown far beyond what we ever imagined," said Penny Crosson, Dale and Chip's mother, "I think we still have proprietary rights."

Ruth Mercer and Maxine Ross both started to speak at the same time. "You go ahead," said Ruth.

"What I suggest," said Maxine, "is we pick a day and time that we can agree on. If the other thousands want to join us, then let them. But if not, maybe we can return to the first couple of weeks when the walks were small and truly prayerful."

"People are coming here and walking the labyrinth every day at all times of the day, anyway," said Ruth. "I can't see it really matters if our little group wants to walk on, say, the first Saturday morning of every month."

Lillian spoke up. "I think we should hear what Miss Bucky has to say. After all, she's what started the whole thing."

Bucky found herself the center of attention as all heads turned toward her. She swallowed. "I didn't know you were even thinking about changing anything until my dad told me yesterday." She tried to recall Simon's words. "I realize it won't be long before it's dark at seven o'clock and the lighting's not real good in the park. Someone could trip and get hurt. And some of you who don't live in town don't really like to drive after dark. We could change it to a morning during the week, but then people who work or go to school wouldn't be able to walk then. Saturdays, like Ruth said, would probably be best. But why only once a month?"

"I think once a month might be best during the winter," said Maggie, "because of the weather mainly." She looked at Bucky next to her. "But then next spring, we could go back to a weekly schedule."

"I might be gone by next spring," said Ruby.

"Where are you going?" asked Bucky.

"To be with Jesus, of course," said Ruby. "He might call me home."

"I think Jesus can wait for you a few more years," said Bucky.

The women all laughed good-naturedly at her innocent remark.

Birdie Weber, one of the newer members of the class, having joined during the summer, spoke up, echoing the question Bucky had asked Simon the day before. "But do you think only walking once a month will have an effect on the dreams?"

"I hope it stops them," said Sissy Casteel, the church organist. "I don't like that woman that's been looking at me from the mouth of the cave for the last few nights."

Bucky's head jerked up. "What woman?"

"Haven't you seen her?" asked Sadie Jane.

Several of the women began speaking at once, describing a woman in a long green dress, with long brown hair and vivid blue eyes. Bucky's breaths came in short gasps and she clenched her hands.

Maggie, noticing the sudden change in her, put an arm around her and spoke quietly. "Have you seen her?"

Bucky nodded and stared at her balled fists in her lap. "She's my mother," she whispered.

"What?" said three or four of the others almost in unison.

"I thought your mother had passed on," said Maxine.

Bucky's head twitched back and forth. "No. She's missing."

"It's all right, Bucky," said Maggie, smoothing her hair. "Girls, we need to move on. We're upsetting her."

Bucky raised her head. "I'm all right, Maggie." She looked around the room. "She's dangerous. She tried to kill me. In the dream, anyway."

The ladies looked at one another, not knowing how to respond.

Sadie Jane at the teacher's desk broke the silence. "All right. Let's vote. All in favor of moving our walks to the first Saturday morning of every month at nine o'clock, raise your hand."

"Wait," said Ruby. "Why don't we make it ten o'clock. That way it will be about time to stop in at the café for lunch afterwards."

"Okay," conceded Sadie Jane. "The first Saturday of every month at ten o'clock, beginning in October."

Nine of the fourteen people in the class raised their hands. Bucky was one who did not.

"Those of you who don't agree, do you have a better suggestion?" asked Sadie Jane.

Once again, everyone's eyes turned to Bucky. She lowered her gaze again and shook her head.

"All right, then," said Sadie Jane. "I'll contact the Garton paper and the other news outlets and we'll make an announcement at the walk this week. Now, let's move on to our lesson."

Bucky usually enjoyed the class. She especially liked to listen to Sadie Jane expound on the background of the lesson, citing material that wasn't in the student book. The former university professor taught French the same way whenever she came to the Mansion to tutor Bucky. She didn't just have Bucky memorize words and phrases. She would go into lengthy explanations of the etymology of the French words. Bucky found the lessons fascinating and would try to remember as much as she could so she could later relay the information to her father. But on this day, she found it difficult to concentrate on the passage from Second Corinthians about Paul's suffering. She had enough troubles of her own. She was upset about the coming change in the prayer walk schedule, but she was even more disturbed by the discovery the women in the class, and probably everyone who had walked recently, also had dreamed of her mother. Despite Simon's insistence it was not her mother in the dreams, she knew it could be no one else.

When class was over and the women were beginning to collect their purses and Bibles and quarterlies and visit for a few minutes before heading to the sanctuary, Bucky remained seated. Maggie patted the back of her hand. "I heard you had company yesterday."

Bucky smiled in spite of her brooding thoughts. "It was fun playing with Dale. I miss Ian, though."

"I had an idea this morning. It's such a pretty day and I thought—"

"Excuse me for interrupting," said Sissy Casteel, who had walked over to stand in front of Bucky. "I have to get in and start playing, but I wondered if you had asked your father about the piano lessons. Or do you want me to ask him?"

Bucky shrugged. "I asked. He said no."

"No? Why?"

"He gave me a bunch of reasons. He doesn't want me taking lessons at your house, and he doesn't want you coming to our house because too many people have been coming to our house, and he can't concentrate on his writing. We don't have a piano, anyway."

Sissy glanced at Maggie and rolled her eyes. "Well, there's not much I can do about his first two objections, but I know where the perfect piano is. I have some friends in Cape Girardeau who own the same grand piano that used to be in the music room at your Mansion. I played it there when I was just a little thing, not much older than you. They bought it at the auction years ago and now they're downsizing and need to find it a good home. It's been well-cared for and it's in perfect condition. It would be wonderful to have it back where it belongs." Sissy looked at the tiny watch on a small gold band that was stretched to its limit around her plump wrist. "Oh, look at the time. I need to get to the organ. You tell your dad about that piano."

Bucky remain seated with her head down. Maggie had stood to leave but took her seat again. "Your father will be in here looking for you if we're not in the sanctuary."

"Maggie, is a grand piano one of those big flat pianos with a lid that lifts up?"

"Yes."

"I had a dream a few nights ago I was playing one in the music room. When Sissy told me last week she'd give me piano lessons, I thought she was talking about a regular piano, like the one in the sanctuary. I never thought about a grand piano. But there it was in my dream, and now Sissy says she knows where it is and that it should be back in the Mansion." Bucky tuned her face up toward Maggie's and squinted. "Don't you think that's strange?"

Maggie sighed. "After everything that's happened here this summer, I'd say it's right there in line with the rest. Coincidence? Yes, but I'm not sure there are any coincidences anymore. Not in Turn Back, anyway." She patted Bucky's hand and stood. "Are you going to tell your dad about the piano?"

Bucky shrugged. "I don't know. It wasn't a very nice dream. If we get the piano, it might come true. But, maybe..." She stood and clasped her Bible and lesson book to her chest.

"Maybe what?"

"Maybe it's supposed to be back in the Mansion."

Maggie used the armrests on the old theater seat to push herself up. "We'd better go on."

Bucky slipped her free hand into Maggie's and the pair walked down the hallway and into the sanctuary. Simon was sitting in his usual place about halfway down the aisle with an empty space in the pew between him and Ian who had a large map unrolled and was studying it. The sides of the map kept rolling up.

"What's that?" Bucky asked as she squeezed in front of Ian to sit between her friend and her father.

"It's a map of this part of the county I found at a flea market yesterday. It's a…" He flattened the upper right-hand corner so he could read the word. "It's a topographic map. See all these little brown squiggly lines. They show all of the hills and valleys. Look here." He pointed at a spot along the St. Francis River. "Here's Turn Back and you see right here where all the lines get real close together. You can't hardly tell them apart. That's the bluff on the other side of the river from us."

Bucky bent over the map to see where he was indicating. "Are our houses on there?"

"Sure. Let's see." Ian traced his finger a short distance on the map. "Right here is mine. See that little black square. And here's yours next door. See, this little blue symbol is a spring and it says *Resort* because this is a really old map. It says right here, *1933*, and your place was still a resort then."

"Let me see." Bucky pulled the map closer to her and turned it slightly. "Look, Dad." She pointed out the spot to Simon. "And here are some more resorts. I've wondered where they all were. Oh! Look here, Ian." She moved her finger along the lines. "Here's The Hollow. It even says it. But it's not spelled right. It says *The Hallow*. And there's the spring in The Hollow. Look." She swept her hand along the map. There are some other hollows on here but they all have names, like Brushy Hollow or Turkey Pen Hollow. Ours is just *The* Hollow, or, rather, *The Hallow*."

Ian pulled the map back toward him.

"Put that away," said Maggie. "Church is about ready to start."

"I'm going to use this map to help me find the cave," whispered Ian to Bucky.

"How?"

"Don't know. But I think it will be useful."

While Ian rolled the map, Maggie leaned around the back of the children's heads toward Simon. She had to dodge the rolled map as Ian looked for a place to keep it until after the worship service. "Simon, it's so pretty out today, Ian and I are taking a picnic lunch down to the river after church and going fishing. Now, I've asked you several times to go fishing with us and—"

Simon held up a hand to stop her. "I don't think so. Not today."

Bucky twisted toward Simon. "Please. I've never been fishing."

"Not today," Simon repeated.

Bucky pressed her palms together. "*Māntāssu.*"

Simon shook his head and sighed. "Maggie, I don't even have any fishing equipment or gear or whatever you call it."

"Tackle. And I have enough for all of us. And I have enough fried chicken and potato salad, too."

"I don't have a fishing license."

"As soon as you get home, get on your computer and go to the Missouri Department of Conservation website and get one. It will only take a couple of minutes. And if you don't want one, then you can just watch us have all the fun."

"Does Bucky need one?"

"No, you have to be sixteen before you need a permit. Now, the two of you go home after church and change clothes and meet us down on that big gravel bar just north of the mastodon site. We'll eat while we catch some minnows for bait."

Bucky whispered in Ian's ear. "Minnows are awfully small to catch on a hook, aren't they?"

"Silly," said Ian, pushing her away. "We use a minnow trap. It's a big jar with a funnel. The minnows swim in but they can't swim out."

Sissy had been playing the organ softly for several minutes, but now turned up the volume, signaling it was time for the service to begin. They were late starting this morning. Pastor Stephen Bradley also served the Methodist church in Garton. Their worship service was earlier and he must have been delayed this morning.

Bucky clasped one of Simon's hands and squeezed it. "Thanks you," she whispered. "It will be fun."

Simon put his arm around her and leaned close and whispered in her ear. "If you like ticks and chiggers and mosquitos and sunburns and smelly hands and fish guts and getting hooks stuck in your fingers."

"Oooh," whispered Bucky. "It sounds like fun already." She giggled and Simon playfully clapped his hand over her mouth.

A disapproving look from Maggie hushed them both.

A little over two and a half hours later, Simon, Bucky, Maggie, and Ian were sitting on a gravel bar on the St. Francis River. They had eaten Maggie's picnic lunch and now the two children were at the edge of the water near where Ian had earlier set the minnow trap. The river was shallow there and clear enough so the two could watch as the minnows, attracted by the cracker crumbs in the jar, swam near the opening of the funnel.

The day was warm and Bucky wiggled her feet in the water. She and Ian both were wearing old sneakers. She remembered last summer when her father had yelled at her for dipping her feet in the spring at The Hollow, but today a glance from Maggie overcame his objection to her getting her feet wet. Bucky adjusted the baseball cap she wore. "Don't you think there's enough already? I want to start fishing."

"We need to wait a few more minutes," said Ian. "There's four of us so we need a bunch."

"I don't understand why the minnows swim in through the funnel and can't get out. The hole's still open. You'd think they'd see that."

"A minnow's brain is only about that big." Ian held up his thumb and index finger barely a hair's width apart.

"If I were a minnow," said Bucky, "I think I could figure it out. Maybe I should write a story about a smart one. *Mary the Magnificent Minnow.* No, I know. I'd name her after your gram. *Maggie the Magnificent Minnow.* That way you'd not only get the main words all starting with an M, but you'd also get MAG in Maggie and Magnificent. There's a word for when the same letter starts all the words." Bucky twisted around to look where Simon and Maggie were sitting about twenty feet behind them. "Dad, what's it called when all the words in a sentence start with the same letter, like the big brown bear bounced the ball?"

"Alliteration," answered Simon.

Bucky turned back to Ian. "Alliteration. *Maggie the Magnificent Minnow.*"

"You could add some more," suggested Ian. "*Maggie the Magnificent Merry Minnow.*"

"Or…" Bucky held up an index finger. "*Maggie the Magnificent Merry Minnow from Missouri.* Maybe change it around. *Merry Maggie, the Magnificent Minnow from Missouri.*"

"If you'd write the story, I could draw the pictures for you."

"We could publish it and be famous authors like my dad."

"And get rich and have all the money we need to fix up the museum in town. We could buy all the buildings so it could be really big."

"You can't buy all the buildings," said Bucky. "There would still have to be a café and a grocery store and the bank and the hardware store."

"We wouldn't even have to buy all the buildings. We'd have enough money, we could build our own."

"I love to hear them chattering," said Maggie, keeping her voice low. She was sitting on the gravel with her knees drawn up to her chin. "The night Bucky stayed with us while you were in the hospital, I didn't think they would ever shut up. I put them to bed in separate rooms and they talked through the wall for half the night. If he can be that way with her, why can't he make friends at school?"

Simon sifted a handful of gravel through his fingers. "I've been thinking about that. I can't recall having any close friends until I was in college. When I entered my degree field, I found myself surrounded by people with the same interests and aspirations and became good friends with several of them. Maybe there's no one in his class who has the same interests as he does. As his teacher pointed out, the pool is not large."

"So you don't think I should worry about it?"

Simon shook his head.

"What about Mrs. Lannigan's comments concerning him not working well with others?"

"I wouldn't worry about that, either. I have...occasionally watched them playing in the garden when they're working on some project, constructing something like their sail boat. They get along fine. There's plenty of back and forth as to who takes the lead. They cooperate with each other without being bossy. It astonishes me Bucky learned those skills, having been reared in isolation, but I certainly don't see anything wrong with Ian's behavior in that regard."

"So, I should just make sure he keeps his grades up and you think the rest will work itself out?"

"I'm no expert on child-rearing, but I'd say whatever you're doing, don't stop. Perhaps the most important thing is to keep open the lines of communication. As long as he feels free to talk to you about his problems, about…about anything, that's half the battle."

Maggie reached over and laid a hand on Simon's forearm. "Thank you." She directed her attention to the children. "Ian! If you don't start fishing soon, it'll be time to go home and you won't even have got your lines wet. Get those minnows in the bucket and show Bucky how to bait her hook."

Ian had instructed Bucky earlier how to cast and now he showed her how to slip her hook through one of the wriggling minnows. Simon had been concerned how his daughter would react to that, but she seemed unperturbed. Maggie and Simon, still seated on the gravel bar, watched for a few minutes while the children fished.

"Now, Simon, what's troubling you?"

Simon turned and looked at Maggie and then looked away. "I suppose you won't take 'nothing' for an answer."

"Not likely."

"What did Penny report to you on the meeting I had with her son yesterday?"

"Not too much except Lane especially enjoyed spending time with Bucky. And Dale, too. Did you really feed them bread and water for lunch?"

Simon barked a short laugh. "I knew that would get back to you. I didn't find out about it until afterwards. I think maybe Bucky was having a tea party. Or more likely they were camped out in the Arabian Desert or being held prisoner in the Tower of London." He fell silent and sorted through some rocks in his hand before speaking again, his head down. "Maggie what would you do if you were working in your garden and suddenly you weren't in your garden but in the middle of a battle from the Crusades and then just as suddenly back in your garden only to pull up a weed and discover it's not a weed at all but a dagger? And then a few minutes later you're in an oxcart, traveling toward a village of round huts with thatched roofs and then you're transported to a sailing ship like those in our ship dreams last summer? But it isn't a dream because you're still in your garden or, at least, you think you are."

Maggie studied him for a moment, frown lines creasing her brow. "Is that what you're experiencing?"

"It's as if someone in my head is switching channels through different time periods and different places.

Sometimes… Sometimes when I'm in my study, I hear music and I go down the hall to the music room and I can see people in there. It's only for a moment, but they're there. Or I hear dishes clattering and snatches of conversation and laughter from the dining room. The empty dining room." Simon raised his head and looked at the older woman next to him. "What would you do?"

"I think I'd go mad."

"I think I'm already there. On the way down here, Bucky and I walked past the mastodon site. Dr. Smallin wasn't able to come this weekend and I told him I'd check on it. And there…" Simon caught his breath and shook his head. "There right in front of me was a knight in full armor on a black horse. It was a living, breathing horse. It reared and I jumped backwards and about knocked Bucky down. And then it was gone."

"Did you tell Chip all this?"

"Yes."

"What did he say?"

"He's going to schedule an MRI. But, Maggie. I don't need an MRI. We had a… We had a hypnotherapy session yesterday. He hypnotized me. I listened to the recording afterwards. Those… Those aren't hallucinations. They're memories. I'm…remembering. Past lives. So many lives."

Simon stuck both of his hands in the gravel and scooped up rocks. "I've been here before. Right here. Here, next to this river. I was here thirty-five hundred years ago on a ship from Crete. And I think I was here just over a hundred and fifty years ago. Maggie, I think

I'm that crazy ancestor of yours, Southy MacAdoo, who laid out this stupid town and built that ridiculous Mansion and duped all those people for all those years into thinking the springs here have some sort of magical..." Simon let the stones slide out of his hands and he buried his face in his palms.

Maggie laid a hand on Simon's shoulder. "Maybe that's why he was crazy. Maybe he had all those past lives to remember, too."

"Do you think I'm crazy, too?"

"Rich people aren't crazy. They're eccentric."

Simon sat up and flashed Maggie a wry smile. "But what do I do?"

"Have you tried prayer?"

"Pfft," Simon scoffed. "I need something practical. Something to either make them go away or something to help me remember them completely so I don't get all of these disconnected and...disorienting bits and pieces."

"You asked me what I would do. And that's what I'd do. Pray."

Simon looked away. "God doesn't seem very close to me right now."

"Oh, Lamb." Maggie patted his shoulder. "Don't you know that's when he's closest? *Be strong and bold; have no fear or dread of them, because it is the Lord your God who goes with you; he will not fail you or forsake you.* That's from Deuteronomy 31:6. And Proverbs 18:10 says, *The name of the Lord is a strong tower; the righteous run into it and are safe.*"

"Just words."

"But they're good words. True words. Words we can cling to when our world is collapsing around us. I know, Simon. I've been there. Not what you're going through, but I lost three generations all far too young. My husband, my son, my grandson. It's my faith that carried me through those dark times. God will get you through this if you let him. I believe that."

A squeal from Bucky brought both adults to their feet

"I've got one! I've got one!" Bucky's rod bowed against the pull of the fish.

"Don't reel it in too fast," ordered Ian. "You'll break the line. Here, maybe I should do it." Ian laid down his own rod and reel and tried to grab Bucky's but she turned away from him.

"Ian, you let Bucky bring it in," scolded Maggie as she and Simon hurried to the edge of the gravel bar.

"But she's going to lose it," Ian protested.

"Give it some slack," said Maggie. "Let it play out a little. But keep a tight grip on your pole. You don't want the fish to yank it out of your hands."

"Oh my gosh! Oh my gosh!" Bucky squealed again as she reeled in the fish.

"You sound like a girl," said Ian.

"I am a girl," replied Bucky, gritting her teeth as she clutched the pole with all her might.

"Here," said Simon. "You just about have it." He reached out for the line to help her hoist the large smallmouth bass away from the edge of the water and onto the gravel where it flopped a few times.

"That's a whopper!" shouted Ian. His own pole went skidding across the gravel as a fish took his bait. He lunged for it and kept it from being dragged into the river. Maggie attended to him while Simon helped Bucky with her catch.

"Take a picture, Dad."

Simon used his cellphone to snap a few shots of Bucky kneeling beside the fish she held up.

"Can we keep it?"

"Smallmouths have to be at least twelve inches," said Maggie, "and that one looks like it's a good fourteen. Let's put it on the stringer. I think Ian's pulling in a nice one, too. If we get enough, I'll fry them up for supper tomorrow night and you and your Dad can come over."

Bucky watched as Maggie took the hook out of the fish's lower lip and then slipped one of the clips of the stringer through its gills. She hooked the stringer to a large branch she stuck in the gravel and put the other end with the bass in the water.

Simon took a picture of Ian and his fish, also a good-sized one, and then Ian added it to the stringer.

Bucky knelt down and reached into the water and stroked her fish. "You think it hurts them?"

"They're fish," answered Ian.

"They probably still have feelings."

"So did that chicken whose leg you ate for lunch. Maybe you should be a vegetarian, but you'd probably still worry about the potatoes in the potato salad and whether or not they felt it when Gram boiled them." Ian pulled her hand away from the fish. "Stop playing with it."

Simon intervened. "I think I'll try my luck. Ian, would you show me how to put a minnow on the hook?"

"But, Dad, you go over there." Bucky pointed further down the gravel bar. "This is my spot."

It was over two hours later they decided to call it a day. Among the four of them they had caught quite a mess of smallmouths, bluegill, sunfish and one goggle-eye. Maggie demonstrated how to clean and filet them, and then let Bucky try. They packed the entrails and other refuse into the now-empty minnow bucket to take back to bury in Maggie's garden compost pile. After wrapping the fish filets in foil, Maggie put them in the picnic basket.

"I can carry some of this back to your house," offered Simon.

"Oh, no," Maggie replied, putting the last of their belongings into the picnic basket. "Ian's got the poles and the bucket and I can carry the basket. There's room for the minnow jar in it. I can get the tackle box in my other hand. That's no more than we came down with."

Simon picked up the basket and the tackle box. "I'll carry these for you until we veer off toward our place."

"I won't say no," said Maggie. She stood with some effort and brushed off her capri pants.

After they parted ways as they neared the back of Maggie's barn, Bucky took Simon's hand. "It was a good day, wasn't it, Dad?"

Simon watched as Maggie and Ian struggled with their burdens past the barn.

"Wasn't it?" Bucky repeated.

Simon looked down at her and smiled. He pulled the bill of her cap down over her eyes. "Sure it was."

6

SECRETS AREN'T FOREVER

"**M**y hands smell like fish." Bucky sniffed her palms. Still wearing her sparkling pink princess Sunday nightgown, she was sitting at the small table in the kitchen waiting for the pancakes Simon was cooking.

"After breakfast, I'll put some lemon juice on them," said Simon, his back to her. "That might help."

"I had fun yesterday, but you were right about the fish guts. They were disgusting."

"Did you find your fish picture in your room this morning?" Bucky was already asleep when Simon had gone into her room for their nightly chat. He had left the photo he had printed of her and her first fish on her bedside table.

"Do you have a frame for it?"

"We can get one the next time we have to go to Garton or Green River." Simon lifted the edge of one of the pancakes.

"It was the biggest of all the ones we caught yesterday. But what I really liked was after I caught it. For a little while, for the first time in a long time, you weren't so glumpy."

"I'm not sure *glumpy* is a word. I'll have to look it up."

"If it's not, it should be. It's a cross between gloomy and grumpy."

Simon, holding a spatula in his hand, turned around. "You think I've been glumpy?"

"For weeks. You're always pretty serious, but I think the last time you looked really happy was at the talent show at church and that was over two months ago."

Simon turned his attention back to the pancakes on the griddle. "You were glumpy, too, for a few days recently. It was only after Dale Crosson came over Saturday your mood brightened."

"Maybe that's what you need, Dad. Maybe you should have a friend over, like the Moyers who were here last summer and are helping you translate the Hollow Stone."

"They live in Chicago and they have classes this semester, so I doubt they can get away. But, you're right. I haven't talked to them for a while. I need to send Nick what I've translated so far of the Hittite portion and see if he's made any progress."

"I thought his wife said you only had two months. It's been longer than that, hasn't it?"

"I think she was teasing us." Simon carried a plate with two pancakes on it over to Bucky. "We'll eat these for breakfast and, since we're going to Maggie's tonight for our fish dinner, we'll just have a light lunch. Maybe bread and water."

Bucky looked up at him and grinned. "Now you're teasing me."

Simon returned her smile. "Is that better?"

Bucky buttered her pancakes and poured syrup over them. "You and Maggie talked an awful lot yesterday."

"We had a lot to talk about." Simon set his plate on the table and took his seat across from Bucky.

"Did she tell you everyone's been dreaming about my mom—about the woman in our dreams?"

"What? What do you mean by everyone?"

"Everyone in my Sunday school class."

"What does she do in their dreams?"

"From what they said, it sounded like mostly what she's been doing in mine the last couple of nights. Standing at the mouth of the cave. She's not acting like she's my mom like she did in my dream and in the dream we shared the other night. They didn't even know it was Mom."

"You told them?"

"I know you told me she's not, but..."

Simon exhaled loudly.

"I'm sorry, Dad. You can punish me, if you want."

Simon shook his head. "I'm not going to punish you. I just wish you hadn't mentioned that to them."

"Can I clean the—may I clean the library today?"

"What?" Bucky's quick change of subjects always caught Simon off-guard.

"The last time I got a book out of there, I noticed they were all really dusty. There's even some cobwebs. You have so much to do and you're always working so hard, I thought I could help you a little more around the house."

Simon tilted his head and narrowed his eyes. "Why?"

"I'm just offering to help."

Simon considered her proposal. "I suppose. But it's right next to my study. Do you think you can do it quietly?"

"Sure. Can I—may I climb on the ladder?"

"Absolutely not." The shelves in the library reached to the twelve foot ceiling and a sliding ladder allowed for access to the books on the higher shelves. From the first day they had moved into the Mansion, Simon had told Bucky the ladder was off-limits. It was not only for her safety he was concerned. One of the upper shelves held the books he had written, and he did not feel she was yet old enough to be exposed to them.

"Please," she begged. "I'll be careful. I can't reach very high and all of the books on the higher shelves are dusty, too. I'm not a little kid. I'm old enough to catch and gut my own fish."

"No. And it's *clean* your fish."

"Ian said it was gut."

"It may be, but that sounds gross."

"It was gross."

"I agree, but you're still not climbing the ladder."

"*Māntāssu*." Bucky repeated the Hittite word for please.

"I wish I'd never taught you that word."

The two held a staring contest for about thirty seconds before Simon blinked. "All right. But if you fall and break your arm—"

"I'll be careful."

Even though Bucky had asked her father if she could dust off the library books, she considered it to be a punishment, albeit a self-imposed one. She could not name a particular infraction she had incurred recently, but she felt there was a growing chasm between her and her father. For weeks he had acted more aloof, more distant from her. She was beginning to see how her troubles affected him, caused him stress, added to his worries. It was her fault they moved here. She was the one who started the prayer walks that resulted in the dreams and the crowds that poured into the little town. She was the one who lashed out at Reverend Bergmann that night in the park, a confrontation which ended with her father's concussion. That injury seemed to begin his slide into his current depression and dark mood. Sometimes she tried to cajole him and tease him to help bring back the man she had always known, but at other times she just stayed out of his way.

In the library, she had reasoned she should start at the top since the dust she was brushing off would fall down, some of it landing on the lower books. It was easy to imagine herself scaling the stone wall of a castle as she climbed the antique decorative metal ladder to reach the upper shelves. If she could find the secret doorway in the wall, she could slip inside and rescue the princess who was being held there by an ogre. She had promised her dad she would be careful and she was. The ladder slid sideways easily, but she pulled it along slowly while hanging on with one hand. She was also careful not to overreach when taking a book off the shelf to dust it.

She had started on the east wall where the bay window was that matched the one in her father's study. The ladder was designed to slide over the window but there was nothing to grasp to pull it, so she had to climb back down, position it next to the bay and then climb back up. Since that wall was interrupted by the large window, there were fewer books there and she finished the upper reaches in a little over forty minutes. But she was beginning to realize this was a job she was going to have to spread over several days. She probably could have done it faster, but the books up high were ones she had never been able to examine before. It had even been difficult to read most of the titles on the spines from down below. Some of them were really old, judging from their covers and the types of yellowed paper inside. From the amount of dust on them and the fact it would be inconvenient to reach them on a regular basis, she reasoned her father had probably not taken them down since they were put there last April. Most were history books, many of them about Turkey, Egypt, Greece and other countries in that part of the world.

The track to which the old metal ladder was attached had been designed so the ladder could even turn the corner when she was ready to start on the south wall. It was on that south wall, on the topmost shelf that butted against the ceiling, that her father's books rested. She counted sixteen books, each with a colorful dust jacket which did nothing to protect the top of the book from getting dusty. Even in their apartment in New York, Simon had kept the books he had written on the top shelf and she had been forbidden to touch them. And here in the Mansion, they had been out of reach until today.

Bucky's heart beat a little faster as she reached for the first book. He had told her often that she could read them when she was older. Since he had not specifically told her this morning to leave them alone, maybe she was old enough now. The front of the dust jacket was mostly red and black with overlapping scenes of a woman in a strapless gown, a gun, a taxi and some skyscrapers. The title of the book, in bold white letters, sprinkled with blood was *At Destiny's Door* and there was her father's name, Simon Carter, in big letters across the bottom. She opened the book to the inside cover and read the synopsis where she discovered the Destiny referred to on the cover was the name of a woman. Opening the book to a random page, she began reading. After only three sentences, she slammed the book shut. Maybe she wasn't old enough yet.

She dusted that book and replaced it. Perhaps, she thought, she should just swipe the tops of the remaining Simon Carter books with her dust rag and not risk the temptation of peeking inside them. When she came to the fourth book, though, she saw the title on the spine, *The Lion of Lyon*. That was the book she remembered overhearing Sadie Jane Woods mention to her dad last summer. The former French professor, and now Bucky's tutor, had told him it was her favorite.

Bucky reached out with her right hand. The hardback book was heavy and the dust jacket was slick. She braced it against the side of the ladder and opened it to a page containing an envelope addressed to her dad in care of Healey Publishing Company in New York. Matt Healey was her dad's friend from college who later became Simon's publisher. Bucky learned a few weeks ago it was also Matt Healey whom Simon had chosen to be her guardian if something happened to him. There was no return address on the envelope but it was postmarked Chicago on June 21 the year after she was born. The top of the envelope had been slit open and Bucky took out the folded letter. It was awkward unfolding it because she was still pushing hard against the book to keep it from slipping and hanging onto the ladder with her left hand. Inside there was a photograph of a baby wearing a Cubs baseball shirt. Bucky's hand trembled as she held the picture and the letter and read the hand-written words.

Simon, next door in his study, heard a loud *thunk!* followed by the rattling of metal and another loud *kerplunk!* He threw open the door that separated the library from his study, expecting to find Bucky flat on the floor. Instead she was standing next to the ladder, holding a piece of paper.

"What happened?" Simon crossed the room and saw the book where it had crashed to the floor. Its dust jacket had come partially off and was bent. He picked it up and smoothed the jacket. *The Lion of Lyon.* Simon swallowed and twice tried to speak before the words would come. "What… What… What's that in your hands?"

"Dad, it's Ian."

Simon snatched the photograph and letter from her. "Of course it's not Ian."

Bucky balled her fists and squeezed shut her eyes. She could feel the tears starting and she knew she had to stop them.

"Bucky, there's no reason to be upset. It's not Ian. Why would you even think that? It's not… It's not anybody."

Bucky opened her eyes but kept her fists clenched. "That's not what it says in the letter. It says 'your son.' 'Your!' And she's writing to you. It says right there, 'My Dear Simon.'" Her lower lip quivered.

"Bucky, listen to me! You need to calm down. This is not your concern. This is… This is something from a long time ago."

"But it's a baby picture of Ian!"

"It's not Ian!"

"You're lying! Liar!" Bucky lunged at Simon and pummeled him with her fists.

Simon dropped the book and grabbed her wrists. The letter and picture he still held in one hand crumpled in his grip. "Stop that. What do you think you're doing?"

"What do you think *you're* doing? Let me go!" she shrieked.

"Bucky, I can't deal with this right now. You need to go to your room and calm down. We… We can talk about it later."

"No!" She tried to wrench away from his hold on her.

"What did you say?"

"I said 'No!'"

Simon released her and stepped back. "Go to your room."

"No."

"I'm not going to argue with you, Imala. Go!"

"My name's Bucky!" Bucky ripped the letter and photograph from his hand and threw them to the floor. She turned and fled, flinging open the double doors that led to the hallway and then tearing up the stairs to her suite of rooms. When she reached the inner sanctum of her castle in the playroom, she threw herself on the pillows and then drew her knees up to her chin, hugging her legs tightly and squeezing shut her eyes. She must not cry. Not now. She didn't want him to hold her. She didn't want to hear his voice telling her it would pass.

After Bucky left, Simon stood there for a minute before picking up *The Lion of Lyon* where he had dropped it and again trying to smooth out the crease in the cover. He set it on the library table in the middle of the room. He stared at the letter and picture on the floor for a moment before bending over and retrieving them. "Oh, God," he said aloud, "what am I going to do now?"

He collapsed into the chair at the table and spread the letter with its neat, precise handwriting next to the photograph of the smiling baby wearing a blue Chicago Cubs T-shirt. The plump toddler was sitting up and was practically bald with only a few wisps of blond hair. He turned the picture over but the back was blank. He read the letter he had not read in nine years, but there was no mention of the baby's name, and it was simply signed Kara. No last name. He traced the outline of the little boy. How could Bucky possibly have known it was Ian Fletcher in the photograph? He didn't recall seeing a similar photo when he was in Maggie's house last June. But Bucky had stayed all night there. Maybe there had been one upstairs or maybe she had looked through a photo album. It didn't really matter how she knew. His secret was out and he now had to deal with it.

Chip's phone call almost two weeks ago about the results of the DNA tests he had ordered for Simon and Bucky was good news. Whatever the Anarianu had changed when they had healed the newborn Bucky had not altered the X-DNA she had inherited from Simon. She was definitely his biological daughter. Simon audibly gasped when he heard Chip say that.

But what the neurosurgeon said next confirmed what Simon had suspected all summer. Chip had uploaded Simon's Y-DNA and autosomal DNA to an online testing site, the same one Maggie had used for her own genetic studies which also included DNA tests for Ian. Simon had researched the subject enough to know the Y chromosome DNA test, or Y-DNA, is a genealogical DNA test which is used to explore a man's patrilineal or direct father's-line ancestry. The autosomal DNA test can be used to identify relatives. Simon's autosomal, and even more importantly, his Y-DNA matched Ian's to such a close degree it could only be a father-son relationship. Chip had immediately changed the results to "private" so Maggie would never see the match. But knowing there was now irrefutable proof Ian was his biological son had contributed to Simon's dark mood.

After the DNA confirmation from Chip, Simon had decided to withhold that information from Ian until he was older, more emotionally mature, and better able to understand. At that time he would also tell Bucky. He never dreamed Bucky would discover it this soon and in this manner. She was only ten and, although she was intelligent, he was not sure how detailed his explanation to her should be, but he knew she deserved an explanation.

Simon waited about thirty minutes while he sorted through different ways of approaching the subject. He finally pushed himself off of the library chair and stood for a moment staring down at the wrinkled picture and letter which had exposed his secret. He swept them up in one hand and headed upstairs.

Bucky was not in her bedroom or study room. He stopped just inside of her playroom. She was not visible, but he knew where she was. "Bucky, are you all right?"

"No." The answer came from within the wooden castle with the painted stone walls he had had the workmen build for her during the remodel of the Mansion.

"Can we talk?"

"No."

"I… I would really like to talk. I think we need to."

"You'd just tell me more lies."

"No. No, I won't. It's time for some truths to be told."

There was no reply from within the castle.

"Please."

He heard some shuffling and then Bucky emerged through the rounded doorway. She was on her hands and knees although the doorway was tall enough she could have stood upright. Once outside the castle and on the drawbridge that was painted on the floor, she stood.

"Let's…uh… Let's go in here and sit in the window." Simon gestured toward her study room. He led the way to the cushioned built-in seat in the small bay window that looked out over the walled garden below. He knew this spot was her second favorite place to curl up and read.

Bucky stopped in front of the window. "The sky's getting dark." She spoke with no inflection.

"They're calling for some pop-up showers. I hope we get under one of them. We could certainly use the rain." Simon sat on one end of the burgundy cushion and Bucky sat at the opposite end. She drew her knees up to her chin and wrapped her arms around her legs. It was a distinctly defensive position.

"First of all," began Simon, speaking calmly, "I apologize for losing my temper and yelling at you a while ago. I shouldn't have acted that way. Do you accept my apology?"

Bucky closed her eyes and nodded her head against her knees.

"Good. Now for the subject at hand." He held out the picture of the baby. "May I ask how you knew this was Ian in the photograph?"

Bucky shrugged.

"Have you seen a similar picture over at Maggie's?"

Bucky shook her head.

"Then how did you know? He's only a year old here. It doesn't look anything like him. He's practically bald for one thing." Simon smiled, hoping to get a smile in return but Bucky sat stony-faced. "How did you know?"

"I just knew, but…" She buried her face in her knees.

Simon continued to speak slowly and calmly. "Please don't be upset. But what?"

"But why did you say it wasn't Ian when you knew it was? Why did you lie to me?"

Simon cleared his throat. "I think I was really lying to me. You just happened to—"

"But I don't understand how he could be your son." Her head was still down and her voice was muffled. "Who's Kara? I mean, I know she must be his mother, and he talks about his father sometimes, but he's not talking about you."

"I'm going to tell you all that. I'm going to try to explain it to you. That's why I came up here now. To tell you."

"The truth?"

"The truth. No more lies." Simon cleared his throat again. "It…uh… It all began the year before… The year before you were born." Simon turned away from her. "Bucky, it's going to be hard for me to tell this story. It's been inside of me for so long and I've buried it so deeply. Please bear with me."

Bucky raised her head. Part of her wanted to crawl into his lap and lay her head again his chest like she had done so many times in the past but the other part felt so betrayed by him. So she stayed where she was at her end of the window seat, her chin braced against her knees.

Simon turned and faced her once again. "In the few years before you were born I was just beginning to make a name for myself as an author. My few books I had out were starting to sell well, but I had to do a lot of promotional work. Book signings, personal appearances, speaking at conferences, that sort of thing. About eleven years ago there was this large writers conference in Chicago. Three days. There were established authors and new authors and wannabe authors along with agents and publishers and book buyers. I was one of the guest speakers and so was Matt Healey, who had been publishing my books from the beginning, and we flew there together.

"Matt loved all that, hobnobbing with all those people and making connections and going to all the different receptions and parties. I hated it. I would much rather have spent the whole conference holed up in my room reading a book. But Matt insisted I attend the different gatherings.

"And Matt introduced me to this girl named Kara who was part of the group which organized the conference. And she was all over me."

Bucky raised her head at his last remark.

"I mean… She was… Gosh, I was around thirty at the time and she was…much younger. Several years younger." Simon avoided looking at Bucky at the other end of the couch. "And…uh…this was during a difficult time for your mother and me. We…uh…" Simon cleared his throat, "We were arguing a lot. She didn't like it I was away so much and we…uh…were trying to have a baby and that didn't seem to be happening and…oh, there were lots of little things. And it was nice having someone like Kara make over me. And, well, I guess I got a little drunk, and when people are drunk they sometimes say and do things they would never do when they're sober and—"

"But, Dad," interrupted Bucky. "I've never seen you drunk. I didn't even know you drank."

"I used to have a beer occasionally or a glass of wine, but I never drank to excess, even in college. I just never did. Until that Saturday night at that writers conference. We were at a table, Kara and I, Matt and some girl he had hooked up with. Of course, he wasn't married. It was all right for him. And there was another couple—some friend of Matt's. And Matt kept pushing one drink after another at me and it wasn't long before I was… I was drunk. And the next thing I know I'm in Kara's hotel room and the next thing I know it's morning. And that's all I'm going to tell you about that. Except to say I was so ashamed of what happened that I avoided her completely the next day, never spoke another word to her, and was so glad to leave Chicago." Simon paused. "You do know what happened that night, don't you?"

"I think so. It's how you became Ian's father."

Simon nodded. "On the flight back from the conference on Sunday night, I made up my mind to tell your mother what had happened, to confess what I'd done. But when I arrived home, your mother had the most wonderful news for me and it knocked all thoughts of Kara and my shameful behavior out of my head, and so I never told her."

"What was the wonderful news?"

"After several years of trying to have a baby it was finally going to happen. She was pregnant."

"With me?"

"Yes." Simon paused again, taking a big breath and exhaling slowly. "However, the following summer, I received a letter from Kara and a picture of a baby—a boy—and she claimed I was the father."

"That picture?" Bucky pointed at the photograph Simon still held in his hand.

"No. It was a photo of a newborn. I don't have that picture because I destroyed it along with the letter so your mother wouldn't see it. Sometimes women will claim that sort of thing, especially if the man is well-known or wealthy, in order to get money. But she said in the letter she didn't want anything from me. She just wanted me to know, and she would send me a photo every year so I could see him. And she said her husband did not know—nor would he ever know—that the baby was not his. But she never told me the baby's name. I never knew her married name. When I met her at that convention, she said she wasn't married."

"So this picture here is from the next year when he's a year old? Why didn't you tear it up, too, or was Mom already gone by that time?"

Simon leaned over and buried his face in his hands.

"Dad?"

Thunder rumbled outside and the first few raindrops splattered against the window.

"Dad?"

Simon sat up. His eyes were red and full of tears. "Oh, Bucky." He swallowed hard. "You know how periodically we'll get a large mailbag or two of letters that have been sent to me at the publishing house? Your mom used to help me go through them and answer them. The first letter from Kara came that way, but I was the one who opened it. But the next letter, this one—" He waved the wrinkled letter. "Your mother opened this one and read it." Simon stared at the letter. "She had the same reaction as you did in the library when you read it. Oh, God." Simon put his head in his hands again.

Bucky had not changed position during Simon's narrative, but now she stood up on her knees and reached over to her father and touched his hair. "It's all right, Dad."

"No, it's not. It will never be all right." He raised his head and looked at Bucky. "Don't you understand? This is why your mother left. This is why she walked out the door that day and never came back." He bunched up the letter and photograph in both hands. "This is what I did that made her leave."

Another growl of thunder shook the window and the rain hit it harder and harder.

Bucky sat back down, her legs tucked under her. "But, Dad, if you hadn't done…what you did, then Ian wouldn't be here, and I… I wouldn't have a best friend. We probably never would have gone to church, and I wouldn't have met the Lukefahr Ladies, and the prayer walks would never have happened, and—"

"No!" Simon spoke so loud he startled her. "Stop it! You can't put a positive spin on this. What I did cost you your mother and it cost me my wife, my companion, the person who completed me, the woman I loved."

Neither spoke for a moment. The rain pelting on the window was the only sound except for Simon's ragged breathing.

"Is what you did that night in Chicago a sin?"

Simon exhaled sharply. "Oh, yeah. It's one of the big ones. Right up there in the top ten."

"Every Sunday in church, we say the Lord's prayer. And that one part says, 'forgive us our trespasses as we forgive those who trespass against us.' And you told me trespasses are sins or things people do wrong. And at the end of that other prayer, Pastor Bradley says, 'God forgives our sins' and all the people say, 'Thanks be to God. We are forgiven.' So doesn't that mean God has forgiven you?"

"Lamb, God might forgive our sins, but sometimes people can't forgive themselves. And I will never forgive myself. No matter how many good things you say came out of it, it destroyed the very best thing in my life."

Bucky was quiet for a moment, her brow creased in concentration. "I think you should have told me the truth a long time ago, but I forgive all your trespasses, Dad."

Simon looked at Bucky for a moment, and then opened his arms. She crawled over the space separating them and climbed into his lap and settled into a comfortable position. They sat there for a few minutes, neither speaking while the rain continued.

"I've got some questions," she said, putting a hand along his cheek.

"I'm sure you do. How about three questions now and we'll save the rest for later."

7

QUESTIONS AND ANSWERS

"First question," said Bucky. "Did you know Ian was your son all along? Is that why we moved here?"

"I had no idea. When no more letters came, I assumed Kara had decided not to continue, although now it makes sense. She and her husband died in the wreck when Ian was only a year old. The first time I met Ian, if you remember, I was so busy yelling at him to get out of the garden and never return, I certainly wasn't aware of anything then. But the next day when he returned your crown, I watched the two of you from the kitchen door for a few seconds. Something... Something seemed familiar about him. And at church the next day and on the following Wednesday at Ruby's birthday party at the café when he and I sat at the booth and had lunch together, there was just...something about him. And each time I was around him or when we would walk the labyrinth together, I couldn't help feeling there was a connection of some sort. But to be honest, like you, I do get a feeling of connection or familiarity with certain people in town, especially when I shake hands with them."

Simon paused and Bucky tapped on his cheek with her index finger, indicating for him to continue.

"The night he and I worked on his telescope, the night of his birthday, there were a couple of times when we were in contact with each other. And I don't know if he was aware of it, but, oh man, I was aware of something. And the more I learned from him and from Maggie about his background, I really began to suspect. But the thing that clenched it was the night he led me through the woods to find you at The Hollow. He asked me to hold his hand. It was... It was like this revelation flooding over me. I was so worried about you that night, but I almost stopped dead in my tracks when I took his hand in mine. After that, every time I was around him, it was as if I were looking at a younger me. Our hair color is different, but the curls are the same. I've wrestled with those curls all my life. And he's built like me and...just so many things."

Simon paused again and Bucky shifted and tapped again on his cheek.

"But remember two weeks ago when Chip called with the results of our DNA test? We were both excited because they proved you were my biological daughter and not a...not a changeling or something. And we celebrated down at the café with ice cream? Well, Chip had other news for me in that phone call. I didn't share that news with you. He had DNA proof I was Ian's father."

Simon knew his answer to her question was longer than it probably needed to be and she didn't respond immediately. He couldn't see her face from the angle she was sitting in his lap, but she kept her palm on the side of his face. He suspected it was there so she could detect any falsehood on his part, so he was trying to be as open as possible.

"So," Bucky began, but paused. "So if Ian is your son, then he's my brother?"

"Yes. Technically he's your half-brother since you have different mothers."

"But that doesn't count as a question. Because what I want to know is this. If his father—not you, I mean his other father—was Maggie's grandson, but he's not Ian's real father, then Ian's not really related to Maggie, is he?"

Simon cleared his throat. "No, and that's why we have to keep this to ourselves. You are not to tell anyone what I've told you today—not Ian, nor Maggie, nor any of your old ladies, nor Dale. Not anyone, do you understand me?"

"Why not? Shouldn't Ian know?"

"I will tell him someday, when he's older, when he can understand it better."

"He's the same age as me, and I understand it."

"But it's not about you, Bucky. I've heard him talk about his parents. He can't remember them, but Maggie's told him things. He idolizes his father. And for him to find out the man he has built up into something bigger than life is not really his father would be devastating."

"I think I'd want to know now instead of later. I think I'd be more upset other people knew and didn't tell me."

"You have to trust me on this. I want you to promise me, promise me with all your heart you won't tell. And no crossing your fingers or eyes or legs or toes or anything else. Crosses don't count. Promise me, Bucky."

"I don't think I can keep that promise."

"You have to. Now promise me."

Bucky exhaled long and loudly. "Okay. I promise. But, Dad? Wouldn't Maggie know if Ian wasn't related by blood to her? She wouldn't have that...feeling those of us who are related have."

"I've wondered about that, too. I get that feeling whenever I've been in contact with her, as do you. Maybe he gets it from me somehow. So now I think you have used all your questions and more."

"No." She drew out the word into two syllables. "One more. I know it takes nine months to have a baby, human babies, anyway. And I know I'm not good at math but I think I've got this one figured out. If Ian was born nine months after your Chicago conference, and Kara said her husband thought the baby was his, was she already married at the conference or even if she wasn't, wasn't she committing a sin, too?"

Simon placed his hand over Bucky's on his cheek and pulled her hand down to her lap. With his other hand he smoothed her hair. "The Bible says we aren't to judge other people. We're to leave that to God. We're each responsible for our own actions...and the consequences of those actions."

Bucky twisted off of his lap and scooted back to the other side of the cushioned seat. "I think I want to be alone for a while to think about all this."

"I understand." Simon got to his feet. "I'll be in my study. I'll fix us some lunch after a while." He walked across the room to her bedroom door. "Oh, and I guess I'll call Maggie and cancel our dinner tonight."

Bucky's mouth dropped open. "Why?"

"Because we've both had an upsetting morning. I don't think we'd be good company."

"But I want to eat my fish I caught."

"I really don't think it would be a good idea to see them tonight."

"Please," she whined. "*Māntāssu.*"

Simon sighed and studied the floor for a moment and then raised his head. "Say *māntāssu, Atta.*"

"*Māntāssu, Atta,*" repeated Bucky, mimicking him perfectly. "What does that mean?"

"Please, Father." Simon smiled at her and winked.

"*Māntāssu, Atta,* may we go to Maggie's tonight for supper so I can eat my fish? What's the Hittite word for fish?"

"That one is always written as a logogram, so scholars are unsure how it was pronounced. I think it might be *parhus.*"

"*Māntāssu, Atta,* I'd like to go have supper at Maggie's tonight so I can eat my *parhus.*"

Simon laughed. "I can't say no to that. We'll go if— and only if—you remember your promise. You are not to mention any of this conversation we've had to anyone."

"I won't tell." Bucky drew her thumb and index finger across her tight-closed lips.

"And I think you need to take a bath before lunch and wash your hair because you are covered in dust from the library." Simon nodded toward the window. "It looks like the rain is over."

Bucky turned and looked out the window. The dark clouds were gone and the gray and white ones that remained were breaking apart and allowing through streaks of sunshine. When she turned back around to say something to her dad, he was gone.

Late that afternoon Bucky held Simon's hand as they walked up their tree-shrouded lane toward the road. "I've been thinking hard all afternoon about what you told me this morning."

Simon stopped and picked up a small leafy branch that had blown down in the morning's brief rainstorm. He tossed it off the lane. "And?"

"Since Maggie is poor and she's raising Ian, but he's really your son, shouldn't you give her some money?"

"I've given that matter some thought also in the last couple of weeks. I'm establishing a trust fund for Ian, similar to yours, which will be his when he's twenty-one."

"That's a long time from now. I think the two of them could use some of your money now."

"That would be difficult to do without telling our secret. And even when I eventually find a way to tell Maggie, if not Ian, well, Maggie's a proud woman,

Lamb, and I'm not sure she would take any money from me."

"But Ian's always having to buy stuff at flea markets and yard sales."

"Do you think Ian is any less happy with his second-hand items than you are with your playroom full of toys?"

Bucky frowned.

"Well?"

"I'm thinking." She hesitated a few seconds. "He acts like he made a good bargain when he's paid fifty cents for something that might have cost ten dollars when it was new."

"And so he has. He's learning the value of a dollar which, unfortunately, is something you have yet to learn."

"I've never been to a flea market. Maybe we should visit one so I could learn the value of a dollar."

"We'll see."

When they came to the ornate black iron gates at the road, Simon released Bucky's hand to punch in the code which unlocked them. He swung open one side enough for Bucky and him to slip through and then slammed it shut.

"It's going to be different seeing Ian tonight, knowing he's my brother." Bucky again took her father's hand in hers as they started down the road.

"But you can't let yourself think about that. You have to act the same around him as you always do."

Bucky exhaled a long, drawn-out sigh. She looked down at the brown river-gravel on the road bed and scuffed the toes of her sneakers.

Simon halted their walk. "What's wrong?"

"Do you have any other children I should know about?"

Simon barked a short laugh. "Definitely not."

"Who's Imala? Why do you sometimes call me that?"

Now it was Simon's turn to sigh. "That's…uh…a little difficult to explain. I think… I think she was Etakkama's daughter from a long time ago. She was the one who was born here and healed by the Anarianu just like you were."

"What did she look like?"

Simon fixed his gaze on a crook in a tree across the road from them. "She had jet-black hair like her mother's and beautiful brown skin, also like her mother's. I'm not sure what she got from her father. Maybe the way her eyes crinkled when she smiled. Or maybe her desire to explore and experience more than a scribe's life at court."

Bucky looked at the tree, wondering what was there that held her father's attention. She looked back at Simon's face. His eyes were full of tears. "What was she like?"

"She was intelligent and clever and charming and…" Simon looked down at Bucky whose face was upturned toward his. "And every bit as headstrong as you. That's probably why I say her name when I'm angry with you."

Bucky reached around and took her dad's other hand. "Are you—were you—Etakkama?"

Simon nodded. "It's beginning to look that way."

Bucky released both of his hands and stepped back. She tucked her chin. "I thought you were his great-great-something-grandson."

"I think I'm both." Simon dropped down on one knee and took Bucky's left hand in both of his. "Have you ever read a story or seen a movie where a person gets hit on the head and they develop amnesia and can't remember anything, not even who they are? I think that's what's happened to me except in reverse. Instead of forgetting everything, I'm remembering. I'm remembering everything. But it's not coming back all at once. Just little bits here and there." He lowered his gaze. "Your old man's a mess right now, Bucky. This… This thing that's going on inside my head and this matter with Ian and…and the shared dream you and I had and…and just everything that's been happening. It's as if my world is closing in on me and I… I'm trying to keep it together—I have to keep it together—for you. But it's difficult."

Bucky laid her free hand on top of her father's head. "This is why you've been so glumpy, isn't it?"

"Gloomy and grumpy and short-tempered and…and just not myself. I'm trying to sort it out and some things are becoming clearer, but it's going to take some time."

"Maybe I can help?"

Simon smiled and Bucky noticed for the first time his eyes did crinkle at the outside edges as he had described Imala's. Her right hand slipped from the top of his head to lie against his cheek.

Simon covered her hand with his palm. "You can help by just being you. I love how you always see the good in people, how you always find the sunshine amongst the clouds, how you can't stay angry for very long because it isn't in your nature. Hang in there with me on this and I'll get through it."

"I love you, Dad."

Simon kissed her forehead. "I love you, too." He let go of her hands and pushed himself off the ground. He brushed the bits of gravel from the knee of his khaki pants. "Now, if we don't get a move-on, we're going to be late for supper and Maggie will chew us both out."

After Maggie's wonderful meal of fried fish, hush puppies, baked beans, slaw, and banana pudding for dessert, Bucky helped her clean up in the kitchen while Simon stayed with Ian in the living room. When Bucky glanced at them as she carried the last of the supper dishes from the dining room table, both Simon and Ian were kneeling by the coffee table, looking at the topographic map Ian had showed Bucky at church.

"I was worried when you were a little late getting here this evening," said Maggie as she put some aluminum foil over the leftover bowl of baked beans. "It's not like your father to be late."

"Oh, we had to stop and talk about some things on the road." Bucky had her hands in the suds at the sink.

"What kinds of things?"

Bucky bit her lower lip. She didn't want to lie. "Oh, just things. You know my dad. He likes to go into long explanations. If I ask him about one king of England, he'll have to tell me about every single one of them."

The phone on the kitchen wall rang and Maggie answered it after wiping one hand across her apron. Bucky noticed the long cord on the receiver that enabled Maggie to carry on with whatever she was doing in the kitchen and still talk.

"Oh, no," Maggie said. She had picked up the bowl of baked beans to put in the refrigerator but set it back down on the counter. "What happened?" She held the phone between her shoulder and ear while she sorted through a stack of papers at the edge of the counter. She found a pad of paper and an ink pen. "Was she alone?" The person on the other end of the line must have said something and then Maggie said, "Oh, that's awful." She scribbled something on the note pad. "How'd you find out?" There was another pause. "Listen, Penny, I have company. Would you please call my person on the prayer chain—it's Betty—and pass it on? I just feel terrible about this." Another pause. "All right. Let me know as soon as you hear something." Maggie replaced the receiver in its cradle and stood there for a moment staring at the phone.

Simon came to the doorway. "What's wrong?"

"That was Penny. Clara Keller died this afternoon." Maggie turned toward Bucky who was still standing in front of the sink. "You know, Clara from our Sunday School class."

Bucky's eyes widened. "But she was in class yesterday. She didn't look sick."

Simon, not sure how Bucky would react, crossed the kitchen to her and put an arm around her shoulders. Death was an abstract for her. It was something she had only experienced in books and movies. She had never had a relative or close friend or even a pet that had died.

"They think it was a heart attack," said Maggie. "Her daughter had come down from St. Louis for a couple of days. She said Clara had laid down for a nap and when she went to check on her, she was gone."

"Where'd she—?"

"She means she died," explained Simon before Bucky could finish the question.

"Did it hurt?" asked Bucky.

Maggie picked up the bowl of baked beans and opened the refrigerator door. "I don't think so. I think she just went to sleep."

"Are you sad?"

"Bucky," said Simon, "why don't you go in and visit with Ian. I'll help Maggie finish up in here."

Bucky dried her hands on a kitchen towel and went into the living room and joined Ian who was still sitting on the floor in front of the coffee table. "Did you hear Clara Keller died?"

"Yeah," said Ian. "I was listening. She was old."

"Do you ever think about dying?"

Ian shrugged. "Sometimes I think about Gram dying. She's pretty old, too. And I don't know where I'll live if that happens. I'm related to lots of people around here, but they're all like third cousins or something. I don't have any aunts or uncles or grandparents."

"You can come live with us. You already picked out your room, remember?" One day last summer Bucky and Ian had explored the many rooms in the Mansion and Ian had chosen an upstairs corner room as his own.

"Your dad's pretty strict. I don't think he'd want me living there."

"Sure he would." Bucky thought she had better change the subject before she blurted out the secret she had promised to keep. "Do you still think this old map will help you find the cave?"

"I've read a lot about caves in the past few weeks. Most caves in the Ozarks are found in sinkholes and along stream banks. The dream looks like the cave is on a bluff. The bluff across the river has some caves in it, but people have been all over them ever since the cave dreams started. But there are other streams around here and other bluffs that just aren't that big. Look here." Ian pointed to some brown lines on the map that were so close together it appeared to be a brown smudge. "This is not too far from here. See? This is the stream that comes down from The Hollow. And here is where it enters the St. Francis River. Your dad said that would be a good place to look. I'm going to explore there this Saturday."

Bucky had been leaning over the low table, studying the map, but she sat back and crossed her arms. "I wish I could go with you."

Ian glanced toward the kitchen door but no one was in sight. He lowered his voice. "Maybe you could sneak out like that one time."

Bucky snorted. "Not likely. What's that?" She pointed to a cloth bag leaning up against the couch.

"That's just my backpack from school."

"Can I look in it?"

"I don't care. It just has a couple of books in it and some papers. Gram cleans it out every once in a while or else it'd be stuffed full."

Bucky dragged it over to her and opened it and took out his math book.

"I already did today's assignment as soon as I came home this afternoon so I wouldn't have to do it while you were here. See, it's that paper folded up in there."

Bucky took the paper from the book and looked at the problems. "You go through an awful lot of steps to get the answer."

"That's the way we have to do it and we have to show our work. Gram checks over it for me and she hates it. She says it was a lot easier the way she learned it in school."

"Maybe if I learned to do it your way, I'd be better at math. She replaced the paper in the book and pulled out a single sheet of folded paper from his bag. "What's this?"

"Don't look at that!" Ian tried to snatch the paper from her hand but she pulled it away.

She twisted away from him so he couldn't reach it and read aloud. "'Dear Ian. I like you very much. Do you like me? I don't think you should be friends with that girl Bucky. She's as weird as her name. My mother said I'm not to talk to her if I see her again. Madyson.'"

"I told you not to read it."

Bucky folded the note. "She must like you a lot. She even put glitter heart stickers all over the page."

"I told you the other night I don't like her. I have to sit next to her, though, because the teacher makes me. And she's always putting things like that in my backpack when I'm not looking."

Bucky, not too carefully, stuffed the paper back in the bag between his math book and a workbook. "I agree I do have a weird name."

"I like your name. And I don't think you're weird." Ian pulled the backpack away from her in case there were any other notes in there. "Madyson is just jealous because I was with you at open house."

"Wonder why her mother doesn't like me. Oh! You think she's part of Reverend Bergmann's group?"

Ian shook his head. "I don't think so. I've seen her walking with the big crowd on Wednesday nights."

"Point her out to me at the walk this Wednesday."

Simon strode through the dining room from the kitchen and stopped at the door to the living room.

"Bucky, we need to be leaving. Maggie has some phone calls to make about Clara. Go thank her for the meal and then we'll be off."

Bucky stood. "So soon? It's still light out."

Simon replied with one of his looks Bucky knew meant, *Do as I say.*

Later that evening, Simon sat down by Bucky's bed as part of their nighttime ritual. He listened to her say her "Now I lay me down to sleep" prayer and tonight her "God blesses" included Clara and her family, which he could understand, but also Madyson Koeller's mother. He did not inquire further as to why she chose the mother of Ian's classmate to receive a special blessing.

"Dad, when I told Maggie goodbye tonight, she said she would let me know about Clara's visitation and funeral. I know what a funeral is, of course, but I'm not sure what she meant by *visitation.*"

"It's…uh…sometimes called a viewing. Family and friends gather to pay their respects and offer condolences to the family. They often share stories about the deceased. It's their way of saying goodbye."

"So I should tell her daughter—and I think she had a son and another daughter and they had kids—that I liked being in Sunday school with her and I will miss walking the labyrinth with her."

"Yes, you would say something like that, except we won't be attending the visitation or the funeral."

Bucky had been lying down, but she bolted upright. "Why not?"

"Because those events are sad occasions. There will be people crying and, Lamb, crying is contagious."

"I'm pretty sure she would come to my funeral if I had died."

"Probably, but you're not going to hers."

Bucky crossed her arms and pouted. "But I need to tell her goodbye. That's not fair."

"Maybe not, but, as in all things, I have to do what I believe is best for you. Now, I think you should go to sleep. You have your French lesson with Sadie Jane tomorrow morning and you want to be in top form for that."

8

A WALK TO REMEMBER

When Bucky met Sadie Jane Woods in the library the next morning for her French lesson, she noticed the dust rags still draped over the top of the bookshelf ladder where she had left them the day before. She was unsure whether her dad would let her continue cleaning after her discovery of her father's secret. For a brief moment she wondered if he had any other secrets hidden among the books.

Bucky took her seat on the opposite side of the library table from the tall, thin, woman who had been a university French professor for many years. The elderly Sadie Jane seemed preoccupied this morning and distant as she shuffled through some papers.

"I went fishing with Maggie and Ian Sunday afternoon," said Bucky. "My dad taught me the Hittite word for fish. *Parhus*. What's the French word for fish?"

"What?" Sadie Jane laid a paper with some French phrases on it in front of Bucky. "Oh, it's *poisson*."

Bucky giggled. "That sounds like poison. But both the French and the Hittite words start with a *p*. My dad says Hittite is the oldest Indo-European language. Do you think that's why?"

Sadie Jane was rummaging in her purse for a pen. "Do I think what's why?"

"Why they both start with a *p*. Because they're related."

"Poisson comes from the Latin *piscis*. Before that, I'm not sure."

"Of course that doesn't explain why fish starts with an *f* if it's related to them also. I'll have to look it up. I could ask my dad, but he'd tell me to look it up myself. Can—may I write myself a note on this paper so I won't forget?" Bucky giggled again. "Wait till I tell Ian we ate poison last night for dinner."

"But you need to pronounce it correctly. *Poisson.* We should begin our lesson."

"May I ask you something first? Are you sad Clara died?"

"It was such a shock. I've known Clara most all my life. We went to school together right here in Turn Back. I was a year ahead of her, but, you know, it's such a small school, even back then. We were all like family." Sadie Jane reached into the pocket of her skirt and pulled out an embroidered handkerchief. She dabbed one eye and then the other. "She was one of my closest friends. I'm going to miss her."

"If my best friend died, I don't think I could stand it. I would be so sad, I'd think I'd die, too."

Sadie Jane half smiled. "I know Ian is your best friend so you aren't going to have to worry about that for a long time. But when you get to be my age, you learn to accept it. Funerals become a regular occurrence."

Bucky glanced at the closed doors that connected the library to Simon's study. She knew her father was on the other side and could probably hear them. She lowered her voice to almost a whisper. "My dad won't let me go to Clara's funeral."

"Maybe he thinks you're too young. Although a ten-year-old who's interested in the etymology of the word *fish* seems old enough to me. But, then, I'm not a parent."

"I think I should be there to tell her goodbye."

"I received a call from Maxine just before I came. She said that it's Thursday morning at the funeral home in Garton. We'll have a dinner afterwards at the church. One of us could take you if your father doesn't want to go."

Bucky doodled on the margins of the paper Sadie Jane had given her. "He wouldn't let me go without him."

"Maybe some of us could say something to him at the prayer walk tomorrow night. Now we had better begin today's lesson."

"That sweater is too small on you. Look how short the sleeves are." Simon raised Bucky's arm as they walked from their car to the park. "You must have grown this year when I wasn't looking."

"You said you were going to order me some warm clothes."

"I did. Some of them are supposed to be here by Friday."

"This is too hot right now." Bucky tried shrugging her free arm out of the pale pink sweater but Simon stopped her.

"Leave it on. The sun is already down behind the bluff and the temperature will be dropping. You'll be glad I made you wear it after a while."

The two of them came around the corner where they could see the crowd that had already gathered all around the square. The smells from the food vendors filled the air along with the cacophonous sound of several thousand voices.

"I'm going to miss this," said Bucky.

"It will probably be the same on a Saturday." Simon had to raise his voice to be heard above the din.

"But it won't be every week."

Simon gripped Bucky's hand tighter as they wound their way through the mass of people and headed toward the spot in front of the café where the Lukefahr Ladies assembled every Wednesday. When they reached the safety of the knot of women, Simon released his hold on his daughter and surrendered her to the elderly ladies who greeted her with handshakes and hugs and pats on her head and shoulders.

"I see the good reverend is at it again." Maggie stepped away from the other women and drew Simon's attention to the cluster of people in the center of the park and the large white cross they had planted there.

"Yeah, well, maybe…"

"Simon?" Maggie laid a hand on Simon's wrist.

"Maybe he's right. Maybe I am an…abomination."

"You wouldn't be out here walking with us if you thought that."

"He has said all summer I'm leading you astray. Maybe I should give in to him. Tell him he's right, that he's been right all along. Maybe he can exorcise my demons."

"Simon, now you hush. That's crazy talk and you know it. It's coming from all that mixed up jumbled mess in your mind. Once you get it all sorted, you'll be okay." Maggie pulled out a slip of paper from her pocket. "Tonight's verse is for you, I think. It's Daniel 10:19. *Don't be afraid. You are greatly treasured. All will be well with you. Be strong!*

Simon smiled ruefully, shaking his head. "*Be strong.* I think a more apt verse for me would be Mark 5:9: *My name is Legion, for we are many.* I know how that possessed man in Mark felt. Every day there are times when…I'm fine, when I'm me. And then it's like these others who are also me begin fighting their way to the surface and I'm in another time, another place. Sometimes the scenes switch so rapidly, I literally feel sick to my stomach."

"I'm here if you need me, Simon. We all are. You and Bucky are part of this town now, part of our family. You pulled out the last sentence of that verse from Daniel, but the other three are equally important. *Don't be afraid. You are greatly treasured. All will be well with you.*"

While Simon and Maggie were conversing, Bucky slipped away from the women and found Ian nearby. "Have you seen Madyson Koeller's mother yet?"

Ian had his head down, staring at the small compass he held. "I haven't been looking for her. It's hard to see anybody in this crowd."

"I told you I wanted to find her."

Ian pulled his attention away from his compass and looked at Bucky. "That was two days ago. You expect me to remember since then?"

Bucky put her hands on her hips and huffed.

He shoved the compass into a pocket of his jeans and swung his head around first one direction and then another. It was difficult to see past the adults who surrounded them. Just then a break in the crowd occurred and he had a clear view for about forty feet. "There she is, right over there with the Baptists. That makes sense. Madyson told me she went to the Baptist church."

"Which one is she?" Bucky craned her neck to see where Ian was pointing.

"The woman with the tan jacket. Move this way a little. See? There's Madyson right next her."

"Come on." Bucky grabbed Ian by the arm and hurried toward the group from the Turn Back Baptist church. Since the early days of the walk last June, it had been traditional for the Baptists to walk directly behind the Methodists in the procession around the park.

Before Bucky could reach Mrs. Koeller, a hand clamped her wrist. "Good evening, Miss Bucky. Where are you hurrying off to? The walk is about ready to begin and you need to be on the front line." The woman who spoke to her was Lydia Schell, a second cousin to

Maggie, and one of the Baptist women Bucky had met at Ruby's birthday party the day they had first walked the labyrinth.

Bucky knew who it was as soon as Lydia touched her. There was a feeling of familiarity which flooded over her through the contact. "We still have a couple of minutes, I think," said Bucky. "I need to talk to someone."

Lydia smiled. "I thought maybe you had decided to walk with us Baptists tonight since I hear it's to be our last evening parade." She released Bucky's wrist. "You'd better get a move on, then."

The crowd had closed ranks so there was no longer a clear path to Madyson and her mother, but Bucky, with Ian in tow, squirmed through the milling bodies until she drew herself upright in front of Mrs. Koeller. "Good evening, Mrs. Koeller. I haven't ever met you before. My name's Bucky Carter." Bucky had dropped her hold on Ian, who stood beside her, staring at his feet, and she extended her hand to the heavyset woman.

Mrs. Koeller, surprised by Bucky's forwardness, took the girl's hand in a limp handshake, but didn't speak.

"I met your daughter at the open house at school last week." Bucky nodded toward Madyson who was standing beside her mother, but kept her eyes focused on Mrs. Koeller. "I don't think you've met my father, either. He's a single parent, trying to raise his child the best way he knows how. As Madyson's mother, you must realize the difficulty in raising a headstrong daughter. Yes, he's overprotective of me, but we don't have an unhealthy relationship. I just thought you ought to know that."

Bucky twisted and looked back toward where the Methodists were gathered. "Oh, look, here he comes now. He's probably going to yell at me."

Simon broke through the crowd and grabbed Bucky's upper arm. "What were you thinking? You know better than to wander off like that."

"Dad, this is Mrs. Koeller and her daughter Madyson. I met Madyson at the open house. She and Ian are in the same class."

Simon, remembering the conversation he had with Bucky the week before about Ian and Madyson and her mother, put his hands at his side and quickly composed himself. "Good evening, Mrs. Koeller." He tilted his head toward Madyson. "Madyson." Neither of the Koellers returned his greeting. "Bucky, the walk is about ready to start. We need to go." He took Bucky's hand and put his other hand on Ian's shoulder. "Ian."

"Bye, Ian," said Madyson.

As they headed off, even above the noise of the crowd, Bucky distinctly heard Mrs. Koeller say, "What a strange little girl." Bucky turned back and flashed a smile at Mrs. Koeller and gave her a thumbs-up sign.

When the three of them took their place alongside Maggie and some of the other Lukefahr Ladies who would walk at the head of the procession, Ian whispered in Bucky's ear, "What was that all about?"

"Dad said I should learn to be civil to people I don't like. I was practicing."

"You might have been all smiles on the outside, but I think you got a couple of digs in."

Jim Runnel from the Methodist church was running the projection system this evening. Some of the paleontology students had continued to drive down every week to provide the music and run the projector even after their mastodon field class had ended, but tonight the projectionist was unable to be there. Methodist Pastor Stephen Bradley, at the microphone in the gazebo, introduced the prayer walk and the Bible verse for the evening from Daniel 10:19. Runnel had been showing the words from that verse on the large screen for the past hour and would continue to do so throughout the walk. They had decided to wait until the end of tonight's walk to announce the change in schedule for the winter months.

A hush fell over the crowd when Pastor Bradley began speaking and when he was done, the mass of people began to slowly move along the road which encircled the park. Reverend Carl Bergmann's followers had increased after his eight-week absence. There were over sixty of them clustered around the cross at one end of the park. His amplifier was in good working order tonight and the radical preacher continued to spew his attacks against the walk, claiming its participants were being led by Satan. Since he had noted the rise he had gotten from Simon the week before after bringing up the famous author's absent wife and mother of his demon spawn, Bergmann hit on those topics tonight with a stream of taunts and verbal attacks.

Maggie did not usually hold Simon's hand when she walked next to him, but on this night she did. Whenever

SHIRLEY GILMORE

Reverend Bergmann would utter a particularly vile comment, she would squeeze Simon's left hand. Bucky usually held hands with Maggie, but Simon had kept a tight grip on her after bringing her back from her encounter with Mrs. Koeller, and tonight she walked on Simon's right. Whenever Maggie squeezed his hand, Simon would pass it on to Bucky.

"Is he talking about us again?" whispered Bucky to her father as they rounded the curve and were now walking away from Bergmann's group.

Simon leaned down slightly so he could whisper in her ear. "Try to ignore him."

"He's hard to ignore. It's pretty loud."

"Concentrate on praying."

It was obvious from the whispers and audible comments from hundreds of others that many of the walkers were upset by the continual diatribe coming from the preacher and his group of protesters.

It was at that moment when an "Oh!" sound of surprise rippled through the crowd. The sound grew in intensity as more and more people turned to see what had caused the response. The air in the center of the park, about twenty feet above the ground, shimmered in a multitude of colors before coalescing into a spinning flat disc. Twilight had settled over the town but the colors that swirled and wavered shone brightly. Everyone stopped and stared at the shifting, swirling colors and then the mass of people began to move back as the display expanded to the edges of the park.

"Listen," said Bucky to those around her.

A low hum emanated from the shimmering colors and then other sounds, in harmony with the first one, began.

Simon scanned the area for some kind of beam that could be projecting the holographic-looking scene. The LED projector in the park was aimed at the screen. Jim Runnel had made a hasty exit from his post as the rotating disk of colored air grew closer to him. Reverend Bergmann's group, who had been within the park, also retreated to the roadway as the phenomenon grew.

Bucky looked around at the hundreds of upturned faces. Almost everyone's mouth was open as they stared at the mesmerizing dance of colors.

"You are looking at Hell!" Reverend Carl Bergmann, one hand upraised, holding his Bible, stood apart from the crowd at the far end of the park. He advanced toward the sidewalk encircling the square. "Of course, it's beautiful! Satan wants you to think that. He wants to draw you into his lair. I'm not afraid of you, Satan or Simon Carter or Etakkama or whatever name you go by. God is on my side and he will protect me. He will shield me from all unrighteousness."

With her free hand Bucky tugged on the sleeve of Simon's sweatshirt and whispered, "Are you doing that?"

"What? No, of course not."

"What do you think it is?"

"I don't know for sure, but it's... It's like what you described the night I found you in the pool and you said you had been there...to the Anarianu. And I've seen it, too, in the Spring Room, last week. I think… I think we're glimpsing their world. A doorway."

"And to prove that Hell has no power over me," Bergmann continued, "I walk, unafraid, into its heart because God walks beside me. He will not forsake me." Bergmann stepped off the sidewalk into the grass. The disc of swirling colors tilted and then wobbled.

Everyone at the same time took another step back, but there was nowhere to go because the crowd in many places was already pressed against the storefronts which surrounded the main street around the park. The people squeezed together.

"The demons scatter before the power of Almighty Jehovah God!" Bergmann kept moving forward, closer to the spinning disc.

The rotating saucer flipped so its broadside was directly in front of Bergmann. Those looking at it from the side could see it had no real depth to it.

"I walk boldly into the mouth of Hell. Are you listening, Satan?" Carl Bergmann turned and stared directly at Simon and then turned back to face the swirling colors.

"What's he doing, Dad?"

Simon answered by squeezing Bucky's hand even more tightly. He had lost his grip on Maggie's hand when the crowd moved back, but he could feel her presence and that of some of the other Lukefahr Ladies. He wanted to look down and see where Ian was, but his eyes were locked on the scene playing out in the park.

The mass of onlookers uttered a unison gasp as Bergmann stepped through the disk. Except he didn't step through. He walked into the whirling colors, but did not walk out. He disappeared.

"Carl!" A solitary voice cried out from the end of the park where Bergmann's followers were gathered on the roadway. A woman ran toward the center of the square where the circle of colors wobbled again and flipped over as its circumference began to shrink.

"Oh, my Lord," said Maggie breathlessly. "That's Jewel, Carl's wife."

The crowd watched in stunned silence as the woman stumbled toward the still-spinning disc which, as it grew smaller, moved toward the Singing Spring near the gazebo. Jewel Bergmann had not even reached the center of the park when the disc erupted into a fountain of colors, sending multi-hued streamers in all directions. And then it winked out and was gone. And there on the ground lay Reverend Bergmann.

Dr. Bukhari, who operated a health clinic in Garton and had been participating in the walks for many weeks, rushed from his place near the end of the procession toward the motionless body of the preacher. The two emergency medical technicians stationed in the town that night also sprinted across the park to him, reaching the reverend at the same time as his wife. The rest of the crowd remained frozen in place.

As the sky darkened it was increasingly difficult to see what was happening. The colored lights shining on the spring and the white lights outlining the bandstand provided limited illumination. A long two minutes passed and then the shadowy figures near the gazebo moved aside and Bergmann sat up.

A sigh of relief went up from the crowd. His presence at the walks was annoying, but no one wished him dead. After another minute, the EMTs helped him to his feet and the people clapped and cheered. The paramedics shone their flashlights on the couple as Bergmann's wife clung to him. The tears streaming down her cheeks were visible even in the growing darkness.

Bucky tugged on her father's sleeve again. "Dad, look at his face."

Bergmann had been clean-shaven when he entered the mass of swirling colors. He stood before them now with at least a three or four-day growth of beard. The preacher staggered a little and appeared to be disoriented, but physically uninjured. The fiery rhetoric was absent as he and his wife, assisted by the EMTs, walked slowly down the length of the park toward his group of followers

"Well," blurted Lillian Thomas, standing behind Simon and Bucky, "are we going to finish this walk?"

Bucky twisted around to look at the elderly woman leaning on her walker. Her dark brown face was almost hidden in the shadows. "I think we should since it's our last one," said Bucky.

Simon looked at Maggie who nodded. "Let's go, then," he said and started walking.

Many in the crowd were hesitant at first to resume their slow walk around the square that would lead eventually along the spiral path which ended at the bandstand. With the numbers here this evening only a few would get anywhere near the bandstand, but most were unsure they wanted to be in the park where the phenomenon they had just witnessed had spun and gyrated and swallowed a man then spit him back out. Their nervousness was understandable. The Lukefahr Ladies began to spread out across the road, followed by the rest of the Methodist congregation who were followed closely by the Baptists. A hush settled over the crowd as others fell into place, and soon the mass of walkers were circling the park once again. By this time, many were using flashlights or the lights on their cellphones. The moving beams of white lights, like candles in a cathedral, made the walk seem even more sacred.

As the front line moved onto the spiral path, Bucky glanced back to where Reverend Bergmann and his followers stood motionless and silent at the far end of the park. She was still puzzled about his changed appearance when he had reappeared. When she and the other walkers in the lead reached the gazebo, she scanned the ground where Bergmann had lain but there was no evidence of the colorful spinning orb.

As the other walkers were moving into place in the park, the university students on stage began singing "Just a Closer Walk with Thee." Jim Runnel had resumed his position at the projector and the words filled the screen. After the frightening experience they had just been through, those in the crowd lifted up their voices and sang loudly. There were many non-Christians present, but even they sang the Christian lyrics with enthusiasm. They didn't have to believe in the same thing to be part of this shared experience that something otherworldly was definitely happening in Turn Back. The students led the crowd in two more songs, "Bringing in the Sheaves" and "It is Well with My Soul." Pastor Stephen Bradley from the Methodist church then took the microphone to announce this evening's walk would be the last one on Wednesday.

The crowd responded to the announcement with shouts of dismay and it was a few seconds before it was quiet enough for him to continue with the explanation of the new arrangement. He explained that for the next few months the walks would be held on the first Saturday of each month at ten o'clock, but folks were welcome to walk the labyrinth, whether in the park or the streets of the town itself, at any time. He tried to tell them the strange events that had transpired this evening had no bearing on the change in schedule, that the decision had been made days ago, but many expressed disbelief about that. The fact the park was now almost in total darkness had it not been for the many individual lights people held should have been enough to convince them continuing the walks as they had done since June was not practical. It wouldn't be long before it would be dark by five o'clock. There was so much disagreement being expressed by the crowd Pastor Bradley finally threw up his hands and asked the students to lead one more hymn to conclude the walk. The students obliged with

"Amazing Grace," as the Lukefahr Ladies and the others at the head of the procession began to wind their way past the Singing Spring and the mysterious Park Stone and on out of the square.

When Simon went up to Bucky's room later that evening he found her lying on her back in the middle of her bedroom floor surrounded by a circle of books.

"What on earth are you doing?"

"You can't see me. I'm invisible." The sparkles on the front of her pink unicorn nightgown glittered in the dim light of her bedside lamp.

Simon shook his head. "I can see that it's past your bedtime."

"I'm not done thinking."

"You can finish your thinking in bed."

"But I think better here in my Circle of Power."

Simon bent down and picked up one of the books, *White Fang*.

"Oh, Dad," whined Bucky, sitting up, "now you've broken the Circle."

Simon extended his hand to pull her to her feet. "Get to bed. Did you brush your teeth?"

"Of course." Bucky crossed over to her bed and crawled in it. "I couldn't very well think with dirty teeth, could I?"

Simon settled into the chair next to her bed. "You didn't have much to say after the walk. Is that what you were thinking about?"

Bucky nodded.

"Sounded as if quite a few people were unhappy about the change."

"I know we can't walk in the dark," said Bucky, "and I know a lot of those people drive a long way to come here and I know the roads are not that good, but still…"

"Let's try it this way and see how it goes. But that's not what's really troubling you, is it?"

Bucky pressed her lips together and shook her head. She twisted the edge of her top sheet. "Why did that thing appear tonight?"

"I don't know, Lamb."

"Did it come for Reverend Bergmann? Did the Anarianu know he would walk into it?"

"It certainly looked that way, didn't it?"

"But where did he go and why did it look like he hadn't shaved for a while when he came back?"

"That night I found you in the spring pool, you told me the Anarianu can manipulate time, that they can stretch it and squeeze it and turn it inside out. I don't know exactly what you meant by that, but what if what happened to him was the same thing that happened to you when you were a baby? They took you and kept you for a few months but then returned you the same night. What if they kept Reverend Bergmann for three or four days or maybe even a week or longer and then returned him here after only a minute or two had passed?"

"I think you should talk to him and find out what he remembers about it."

Simon scoffed. "I don't think he'd want to talk with me. Maybe word will get back to us."

"He was missing his Bible when he came back."

"What? How do you know?"

"Don't you remember? He was holding it when he walked into the colors but he didn't have it when he was lying on the ground."

"Maybe it was there beside him."

"It was too big to fit in his pocket and he didn't have it in his hand when he was walking back across the park. I looked for it when we reached the gazebo. We were the first ones there afterwards. I didn't see it."

"The paramedics or Dr. Bukhari might have picked it up."

"No, the Anarianu have it."

"Maybe. But let's change the subject. Tomorrow morning when you get up, I want you to wash and put on something nice like you'd wear to church because we're going to Clara's funeral."

"What?"

"Some of your ladies convinced me tonight I should take you, if you still want to go. It is against my better judgment, and tomorrow morning before we go we'll discuss about what to expect, but—"

Bucky sat up on her knees and reached over and hugged Simon. "Thank you! Are we going to the visitation, too?"

"Yes, it's right before the funeral."

"And the dinner afterwards?"

"No, that's only for family. Now, it's time you went to sleep." He helped her lie back down and smoothed the covers over her.

"Aren't you going to punish me for running off tonight to see Mrs. Koeller?"

"Do you want me to?"

"No, but I kind of expected it."

Simon sighed. "Bucky, I don't think you realize how dangerous it is for you to go off on your own like that, especially with thousands of people there."

"Ian was with me."

"That's not the point. Both of you are still children."

"I heard you tell Maggie once we were special children."

Simon couldn't help smiling. "But that doesn't mean you can do whatever you want. That's all the more reason for you to mind me."

"I think we're special children because we are your children and you are special."

"I think you need to go to sleep. Goodnight, Lamb." He leaned over and kissed her forehead. "Love you."

"I love you, too, *Atta* Etakkama."

9

WHEN WE ALL GET TO HEAVEN

"It doesn't look like her." Bucky and Simon stood beside Clara Keller's open casket in the chapel at Holman's Funeral Home in the county seat of Garton. For several seconds Bucky had stared without speaking at the woman lying before her. Clara, her hands crossed over her stomach, was wearing a rose-colored dress and was clutching a white, delicately-embroidered handkerchief.

"That's because it's just her body. Her spirit is gone." Simon kept a firm clasp on Bucky's left hand.

"Is she with Jesus?"

"Yes," Simon replied automatically although he wasn't sure anymore what he believed about the afterlife.

"She looks like she's breathing. How do we know she's really dead?"

"That's just your mind playing tricks. She's been embalmed."

"Like the Egyptians?"

"Not exactly, but similar."

"Can I touch her?"

"No, of course not."

Bucky twisted slightly and pointed at someone nearby. "That woman over there touched her. I saw her while we were waiting in line."

"She's probably a relative. We need to move along. Other people are coming."

"Is this the last time I'll see her?"

"Maybe. They might close the casket before the funeral starts. If they leave it open during the service, we might file by afterwards. It just depends."

Bucky touched the side of the white and gold casket with her index finger. "Good-by, Clara. I'll miss you."

Simon led his daughter to the back row and took seats on the aisle so they could make a quick exit if they needed to. "Are you all right?" He put his left arm around her narrow shoulders.

Bucky nodded. "It looks a little like a church in here."

"It's designed to provide a comforting setting."

Several of the women from the Lukefahr Ladies class stopped by and spoke a few words to Simon and Bucky. Sadie Jane Woods greeted Bucky with, "*Bonjour*," and told her she was sorry they had to cancel their French lesson for the day. Maggie had been standing and talking with some younger women toward the front of the chapel, but she came down the aisle to say hello to the pair.

"Is Ian here?" asked Bucky. "I haven't seen him."

"I didn't think there was any reason to take him out of school today," explained Maggie. "Most of us from the class are sitting together over there. Do you want to come sit with us?"

Bucky looked up at Simon who gave an almost imperceptible shake of his head. "No, I think I'll stay back here. Maggie, are those people standing up there at the front Clara's children?"

Maggie turned to look at the cluster of people who stood near the bier and casket. "The two women on the left—the one in the navy-blue dress and the other one wearing the black pantsuit—are her daughters, Donna and Nancy. The man on the right is her son, Steve. I haven't seen him in years. Some of the rest of the others up there and those who are seated near the front are their spouses and children and grandchildren."

Sissy Casteel began playing the small organ which was a signal for those present to take their seats. Pastor Bradley from the Methodist church stood behind a wooden lectern and welcomed everyone on behalf of Clara's family. He then read some Bible verses and said a prayer. A woman Bucky had never seen before sang "In the Garden." It was a hymn they sometimes sang at the prayer walks. The pastor read another passage from the Bible and then read the story of Clara's life, when and where she was born, who her parents were, which members of her family had died before her and the names of her relatives she left behind. To Bucky it seemed like only a bare outline of Clara's life. A woman who had lived so long must have had many interesting experiences and to have her life condensed in a few sentences didn't seem right.

After he read the obituary, Pastor Bradley asked if anyone wanted to say a few words about Clara before he began his message. Simon had told Bucky funerals often included this, and Bucky waited for someone to go up front to speak. During the visitation, while she and Simon had stood in line to see Clara for the last time and later when they were seated, Bucky had listened in on the conversations around her. She heard people speak fondly of Clara and tell stories about her, some of them funny. And yet, now when the preacher asked if anyone wanted to share anything with all of those in attendance, not one person responded. Everyone just sat there.

When Simon had talked to Bucky over breakfast about what to expect during the visitation and funeral, Bucky had thought immediately of what she would like to tell people about Clara. She had come prepared but she didn't want to go first. But it appeared as if no one was going to talk. The preacher shuffled some papers on the lectern and started to move on with the service.

Bucky jumped to her feet and waved one hand. "Pastor Bradley, I'd like to say something."

Simon cringed and pulled down her hand. "No," he whispered.

"Well, come on up here," said Pastor Bradley.

Simon sighed in resignation and Bucky squirmed between him and the back of the pew in front of her to get to the aisle.

As she was walking toward the front, Pastor Bradley introduced her. "Folks, this is Bucky Carter. She's one of the younger ones in our church in Turn Back where Clara was a member."

Bucky was short for her age and when she stood behind the lectern she could barely see over it. The pastor had her stand off to one side so people could see her. He adjusted the microphone stand the singer had used so Bucky could speak into the mic.

Bucky licked her lips before she began. There were more people here than in the Turn Back Methodist Church congregation on Sunday mornings. For a moment she felt the same way she did when she had stood up front at the talent show. That night nothing had come out her mouth but a squeak at first. She recalled Sissy's instructions before the talent show to speak slowly and distinctly and to talk into the microphone. She looked at her dad, still seated in the back. He nodded his head to her. That was all she needed to calm her.

"I was surprised," she began, "when Pastor Bradley said Clara was 83 years old. That's a long time and some of you have known Clara her whole life so you must be very sad today. Because I've only known her for a few months and I'm sad. I'm in the same Sunday school class as Clara—the Lukefahr Ladies Bible Class—and I think we're all here. We've come, like the rest of you, to say goodbye to Clara for one last time." Bucky lowered her gaze for a moment and bit her bottom lip as she thought of what her next words would be.

"Most of the women in our class don't say a whole lot during the lesson, and Clara was like that. But that's all right, because when you're with friends, sometimes you don't have to say anything. It's like when Pastor Bradley asked if anyone wanted to speak just now. I know all of you have some wonderful things to say about Clara, or else you wouldn't be here today. I heard some of you talking about her before the service started about what a good cook she was and how she grew such beautiful roses and made quilts, and someone told a funny story of how she got her car stuck in a ditch one night and she had to walk home, but a cow was on the road and it startled her and she was so scared she ran all the way." Soft laughter rippled through the listeners.

"I didn't know any of that about Clara. I wish I would have known her longer so I could have known her better. But I'll remember Clara this way. As I said, she didn't speak up in class usually, but she was the one who gave us the idea of blowing bubbles at the church talent show last summer. If it hadn't been for her, we might never have entered that talent show. We had a good act. It was funny and we made people laugh, and that's a good thing." Bucky paused and looked at the group of Lukefahr Ladies sitting on the left. They were all smiling, even if some of them were dabbing their nose or eyes with a tissue or handkerchief.

"So whenever I see a soap bubble I will think of Clara and remember that Sunday night when we sang and acted silly and made people laugh." Bucky reached into the pocket of her dress and pulled out a little bottle of soap solution. She fumbled with the lid but finally got it unscrewed. "So, Clara, this is for you. Thank you for your wonderful idea." Bucky turned toward the open casket, tilted her head back and blew gently. A stream of iridescent bubbles filled the air above Clara. Some of them popped in the air, some floated to the carpet before dissipating, but three came to rest on the spray of pink roses on top of the casket and lingered there for a few seconds.

Bucky replaced the lid and walked back to her seat next to Simon who moved over so she could slide into the end of the pew. Her heart was racing.

Her father put an arm around her and leaned over and whispered in her ear, "That was beautiful."

Stephen Bradley took his place at the lectern and asked again if anyone else wished to speak. No one stepped forward. "Thank you, Bucky," Pastor Bradley said, "for reminding us that people will often remember us for the little things we do and say. Whether it's a friendly smile or a helping hand, a kind word of encouragement or comfort, maybe a pot roast cooked to perfection or a rose in all its glory picked from our flower garden or a maybe a simple suggestion to blow bubbles for a talent show. We never know which of our words or actions will define us to others, which ones will be what someone remembers about us after we're gone. The Apostle Paul said in…"

Bucky knew the pastor was continuing to talk but she could no longer focus on his words. The tears which she had been successful in repressing ever since she entered the funeral home were threatening to surface. She squeezed shut her eyes and clenched her fists. Not here, she screamed to herself. Not now.

She bolted for the door before Simon realized what was happening. The double doors to the chapel were closed but she crashed through them. More than one person turned to see what had caused the jarring sound. Wide-eyed, her heart pounding, she pivoted one way and then the other in the open reception area outside the chapel doors. She had to find somewhere to hide where she could try and stop the tears. She tore off to the left toward a hallway. Another hallway entered that one and she turned left again and then right. There was a niche behind a fake potted fern on a stand and she crawled into it and hugged her knees to her chin, rocking back and forth.

"Bucky!" Simon whispered loudly as he chased after her. Reaching her hiding place, he shoved the stand with the potted fern out of the way and knelt beside her. "It's all right, Lamb,"

A man in a suit, an employee at the funeral home, stopped beside them. Simon looked up. "She'll be all right in a minute," he said. "She's just upset."

The man nodded and walked away.

"Dad, I don't think I can stop it."

"Yes, you can. Yes, you can," he repeated. "Just breathe." Simon wrapped her in his arms.

Bucky's breath was ragged and she was shaking. "Sing the song. Dad, please."

"I can't, Lamb. I don't know the words. They're nonsense sounds. You can do this. You've done it lots of times. Go inside yourself. Find a calm place."

Bucky buried her face in her knees. Within a minute her breathing became smoother and Simon could feel her relax.

"I'm sorry, Dad," she said, her voice muffled. "You were right. I shouldn't have come today. I thought I could control it."

"But you did control it."

"Barely."

Simon continued talking quietly, hoping the sound of his voice would continue to calm her. "You did such a beautiful job when you were up there speaking. I was so proud of you."

"Was it all right what I said? I didn't make anyone mad by blowing the bubbles, did I?"

"Of course it was all right. It was wonderful. I wish I could talk like that in front of people. All I do is stammer and hem and haw. You have the makings of a true orator."

"What's that?" Bucky, breathing normally now, raised her head. The crisis had passed.

"What's an orator? A public speaker like Patrick Henry or Winston Churchill or Nelson Mandela, Martin Luther King."

"Aren't there any women orators?"

"Hmmm. Sojourner Truth, Susan B. Anthony, Maya Angelou. But I'll bet none of them were half as good as you when they were ten. You showed presence and poise. It was as if you gave speeches every day."

"I guess I do, in a way. When I pretend to be people like George Washington or Julius Caesar or Queen Elizabeth I, I recite the speeches they gave or sometimes I make up my own."

"Your imagination has served you well, then." Simon smoothed her hair. "Are you ready to leave?"

"I'd like to go to the cemetery with everybody and see where they bury her."

"I think we'd better go by there another day."

"How about our flowers?" Simon had showed her earlier the arrangement he had sent from him and Bucky.

"We don't get to take them home. They're for the family. Since they were fresh flowers, they'll probably be left at the cemetery. Or some family member might take them home." Simon stood and extended his hand. "Let's go."

Bucky took his hand and stood. "Is the funeral over?" They wound their way back through the maze of corridors.

"I don't think so. There would be people out here." The reception area outside the chapel was empty except for two funeral home employees behind a counter.

Simon led Bucky out to the parking lot. He opened the back passenger-side door for her and she climbed in and fastened her seatbelt while he walked around to the driver's door.

"Are you hungry?" Simon asked after he had started the car. "There are several places here in Garton where we've never eaten or we could go back to Joe's in Turn Back or we could go on home if you'd rather."

"We passed a Chinese place on the highway just as we were coming into town."

"I've seen that the few times we've driven this way. We haven't had Chinese since we left New York."

"Dad, remember how we used to have it delivered from that place down the street and it came in those little boxes with the wire handles? And I always wanted to save the boxes but you wouldn't let me because they were cardboard and we couldn't wash them. So one day you ordered our meal but you also ordered a whole bunch of empty cartons for me."

Simon looked back at his daughter before pulling out of the funeral home parking lot. It was good to see her smiling again after narrowly averting one of her episodes. "I had forgotten that."

"I still have a couple of the boxes. One has fake money in it and the other one is full of broken crayons."

Bucky continued to prattle on about various subjects for the short drive to Wu Lan's Chinese Restaurant. Once inside they had to stop so she could watch the large goldfish in a small rock-lined pool. Simon asked for a side table away from the main dining area. He hoped they would not be recognized in the dimly-lit establishment and so be able to eat undisturbed.

While waiting for their food, Bucky's mood turned somber. Simon tried to keep her talking about other subjects to divert her thoughts from the funeral but she kept returning to what she had seen and heard at the funeral home.

"I saw Clara's daughters cry. They're adults so I didn't think they'd cry like that. Do you think they miss her even though they're grown?"

"I was already an adult when my parents died. I still miss them."

"You don't talk about them hardly at all."

"I think about them sometimes, though. Especially when I'm writing. I'm sorry my father didn't get to read any of my books except the first one. He would have loved the action and the adventure and especially the mystery. Mystery books were his favorite."

"How about your mom?"

Simon smiled. "Oh, I can hear her clicking her tongue at me in disapproval whenever I'm writing a particularly steamy scene."

"What does *steamy* mean?"

"Sexy."

Bucky giggled. She remembered the little bit she had peeked at while dusting his books earlier in the week. "Is that why you won't let me read them until I'm older?"

"That and there's other content I think you will appreciate and understand better when you're more mature."

When their food came, Bucky struggled for a few moments with the chopsticks. Simon had taught her how to use them when she was not much more than a toddler, but it had been several months since she had eaten with them. It didn't take long, though, for them to fit comfortably in her fingers once more.

Once she had the chopsticks moving again, she continued the conversation by stating matter-of-factly, "I don't miss Mom."

"That's understandable. You were only a baby when she left."

"But even if she came back, I don't think I could love her." A piece of chicken kept rolling out of the way of her chopsticks, so Bucky stabbed it with one of them.

"It's been nine years," said Simon. "I don't think you need to be concerned about her returning."

"She could be dead."

"I hope she's alive somewhere and…and happy. Let's talk about something else, shall we?"

Bucky switched to a spoon to eat some rice. "When we were looking at Clara, I asked you if she was with Jesus and you said, 'Yes.'" Bucky lifted her head to look at her father who raised his eyebrows but said nothing. "But that's not what you were thinking."

"What was I thinking?"

Bucky shrugged and took a sip of her hot tea.

"There is some disagreement among Christians on the matter," explained Simon, "and they are both based on Biblical passages. One is we go to Heaven immediately after we die and the other is we have to wait for the Second Coming of Christ."

"My Sunday school class likes the one where we go see Jesus right after we die."

"That's a comforting thought to many people. And perhaps it's not an either-or dilemma. Immediately upon death our souls might be in the presence of God, but later, at the Second Coming, we will receive new bodies. People have tried to puzzle this out for two thousand years. Many, many, many books have been written on the subject. I think it's one of those things we will have to wait and find out the truth when it happens."

As Simon reached for the pot of tea, Bucky laid her hand on his. "But that's not what you were thinking when I asked you about Clara. I was holding your hand, remember?"

Simon gently pried Bucky's hand away. "You need to finish your meal."

Bucky took up her chopsticks again and attacked her garlic chicken. "You want to know what almost made me cry at the funeral?"

"Not if there's a chance it will make you cry when you tell me."

"I got to thinking about this whole life after death thing and you. If you really have been different people, like Etakkama and the others, then when you die you don't get to go to Heaven. You're born all over again as someone else. I know reincarnation is a belief in Hinduism and Buddhism, but we never talk about it in Sunday school and I've never heard Pastor Bradley preach about it."

"That's because it's not a Christian belief," explained Simon.

"But if you're a Christian, then how have you been those other people?'

Simon shook his head.

"That's what you were thinking when we looked at Clara lying there, wasn't it?"

"And that's what you were thinking about that made you cry?"

"It's not fair you don't ever get to see Jesus."

Simon opened his mouth twice to speak but nothing came out. Finally, on the third time he had formulated an answer he could verbalize. "Some of the memories running around inside my head seem to be separated by many years—decades or even centuries. Maybe in between times, I get to go to Heaven."

Bucky nodded thoughtfully. "That would be good. Do you think I have been other people, too?"

"Don't know."

"Do you think you've ever been an animal?"

Simon smiled. "I don't remember being one. But in those Eastern religions, the whole idea of reincarnation is you're supposed to be bettering yourself, moving up each time so eventually you don't have to be reborn. I think I've really messed up this lifetime. I'll probably have to start all over."

"I don't think so."

Simon glanced at his watch. "Oh, look at the time. We need to get home. I'm expecting a delivery this afternoon."

"My new clothes? You said they weren't coming until tomorrow."

"No, this is something else. I think you might like it even better than new outfits. Finish eating so we can go."

After returning home from the funeral and lunch in Garton, Bucky had gone upstairs to work on her studies.

Simon had promised to call her when he heard the delivery truck. He had left the front gate open when they drove in so the truck could come on up the lane without having to stop and push the buzzer at the gate and wait for a response from the house.

Earlier in the week, Bucky had downloaded information about the fishes of Missouri, and she was deep into reading about the habitats and life cycles of bass and crappie and catfish and bluegill and the many others found in the state's rivers and lakes when Simon called to her from the bottom of the stairs. She hopped down the stairs like a rabbit even though Simon stood frowning at the bottom. Ever since they had moved here last April, she had longed to slide down the curved polished wood banister but was afraid of getting caught. One day she would, though, she told herself.

When she landed with a thump at the bottom of the stairs, Simon, out of habit, took her by the hand and walked across the entryway to the double doors. He opened one door as a panel truck was backing up to the front steps.

"Is it furniture?" asked Bucky.

"You'll see."

Simon and Bucky watched as two men got out of the truck and went around to the back. One of the men called out, "Are you Simon Carter?"

Simon answered, "Yes."

"Wouldn't want to unload this beauty at the wrong place and have to load it back up again. It's a little bit on the heavy side."

One of the men pushed a button which opened the lift gate that served as the back door of the truck. He then raised the upper part of the back so it was fully opened. The hydraulic lift gate lowered to the ground and the men stepped on it and it rose again to be level with the truck floor. Simon opened the other front door so they would be able to easily bring their cargo into the house.

It was dark in the interior of the truck, and Bucky, watching from the doorway, could only see a large, bulky object which was heavily padded. The delivery men fiddled with some straps which had secured it during the move and then skidded the object onto the lift gate.

At that moment, Bucky realized what was being delivered. She jerked her hand out of her father's grasp and backed away.

"What's wrong?" asked Simon.

"No, Dad! How could you?" Bucky spun around and fled up the stairs.

Simon called after her but he had to turn his attention back to the men who were ready to carry the grand piano up the steps and into the music room.

10

PIANOS AND DREAMS

"I really thought you'd be excited about the piano." Simon stood in front of the castle in Bucky's playroom. He knew she was inside. Through the doorway he could see one foot covered by a white sock. "Sissy Casteel caught me after church Sunday while you and Ian were still looking at the topographic map and told me about it. And Maggie mentioned it to me that afternoon at the river. I thought you wanted to take lessons. I even talked to Ms. Casteel Tuesday morning on the phone while you were having your French lesson, about her possibly coming here to teach you."

There was no response from within the castle.

"Bucky, come out here and let's talk about this."

"It's too late," came a voice from inside the structure. The foot that had been visible disappeared.

"What's too late?"

"The dream's going to come true now and we can't stop it."

"Bucky, come out here. That's an order." Simon waited an anxious ten seconds to see how she would respond. He let out his breath in relief when he heard her rustling. When she walked out, he noted her head almost touched the top of the doorway now.

Bucky crossed over to the small table and plopped down in one of the little red chairs. She folded her arms across her chest. Simon lowered himself into the chair opposite her.

"Last Thursday night," he began, "we experienced a shared dream in which you were in the music room, practicing on a grand piano, a piano which you—which we—had seen before only in a photograph. Right?"

Bucky nodded, her eyes focused on a blemish in the wood on the table.

"And now I've gone and brought that same piano back into that same room where it stood until fifty years ago. But, Lamb, we had talked about you taking lessons only a few hours before you—before we—had that dream. It was just an image, an idea that wove its way into that nightmare. There's nothing evil about the piano. Having it here in the house does not mean the dream will come true. It's an inanimate object. But…it's a beautiful object. It needs to sit and rest for a couple of weeks, and then a tuner will come in and make sure it's on pitch, but even now the sound it makes is so mellow and deep and rich. You need to come down and look at it."

"Do I have to?"

"No. But I bought it for you. Ms. Casteel's coming over tomorrow morning to see it. Maybe she'll even give you your first lesson—show you middle C."

"I already know where middle C is."

"How do you know that?"

Bucky shrugged. "Internet." She uncrossed her arms. "Do you really think it was your idea to buy that piano?"

Simon tilted his head. "What do you mean?"

"Do you think you did it because you wanted to or do you think you were being made to buy it, maybe by the Anarianu, and that it was all…a…set-up by them?"

Simon reached across the table and took one of her hands in his. "I bought it at Sissy Casteel's suggestion. I thought it was fitting that it originally came from this place. And I thought my daughter should be exposed to music lessons, something which I do not feel I know enough about to teach her."

Bucky was silent for a moment. She knew from his touch he believed what he was saying. "Dad," she said finally, "you look silly sitting in that little chair."

Simon grinned and pulled back his hand. "Well, I'll wager you yourself will be too big to sit in them by this time next year."

"That's something I've wondered about. Madyson Koeller is probably my age since she's in Ian's class, and she's lots taller than me. But I'm still taller than Ian. Shouldn't we all be the same height since we're the same age?"

"People are all different sizes. You know that. Look at all the people at the prayer walks."

"I thought people started out the same when they were kids and then grew up to be different sizes."

"The differences begin even before they're born. Some babies come out weighing more than others and some are longer or shorter by a few inches."

"How big was I when I was born?"

"Let me think." Simon closed his eyes for a moment and then opened them. "You were nineteen inches long and weighed seven and a half pounds. That's about average, which is the one and only thing about you that has ever been average in your whole life." He smiled.

"And women get fat where they're going to have a baby?"

"Not fat exactly. They get big because…well…after all, they're carrying a baby inside them. But then after the baby is born, the mother loses a lot of that extra weight and most women will lose the rest in a few months."

"Will Chip's wife, Lane, get big since she's going to have a baby?"

"Yes, but, remember, you aren't to mention that to anyone until they announce it."

"Did Mom get big when I was inside her?"

"Yes, but then after you were born, she was anxious to shed those baby pounds."

Bucky was quiet for a moment as she rolled her tongue inside her cheek.

Simon had always tried to be forthright in answering her questions, but he dreaded where this particular conversation seemed to be headed. He was pleasantly surprised by her next question since she seemed to have skipped the track and reversed direction.

"So do you think I will always be taller than Ian, especially since I'm two months older than him?"

"Your age doesn't have anything to do with it, except for the fact that yes, for the next year or two or three, you will probably be taller than Ian. You might even grow to be a whole lot taller than him. Boys usually have a growth spurt around ages 13 or 14. It varies. But then he will shoot up and probably be taller than you."

Bucky put her elbows on the table and cupped her chin in her hands. "This growing up business seems awfully complicated. Things were a lot simpler when I was little."

"You'll get no argument from me about that." Simon looked at his watch. "It's almost four o'clock and you have done little school work today. While you are in this contemplative mood, I want you to work on your writing skills. I want you to write me your thoughts on… I'll give you a choice. I want you to describe what happened at the prayer walk last night or at the funeral this morning." He paused. "Or about what all this was about with the piano this afternoon. Or you can talk about two of them or all three. And it needs to be in cursive and at least two pages long."

"Two pages!"

"And what are the three parts of a paper?"

"A beginning and a middle and an end."

"And I want you to have it finished by supper, which will be about six o'clock."

"Dad," Bucky whined. "*Atta.*" She repeated her whine in Hittite.

"Hop to it." Simon put his hands on the table and pushed himself up. He *was* too big for these little chairs.

Bucky sat on the bench at the grand piano in the music room of the Mansion Mineral Springs Resort. Her bare feet did not sit flat on the floor. She stretched her right foot to touch one of the pedals, but she would have to grow a couple of more inches to do that gracefully while she played. She placed her right thumb on middle C and positioned the rest of her fingers of her right hand on the next four white keys. She played the notes one at a time.

"No!" The woman next to her on the mahogany bench spoke sharply. "How many times do I have to tell you? You strike each key thusly with your fingers. Keep your hand and wrist still. We're playing *legato*, not *staccato*." The woman's fingers moved effortlessly over the keys.

Bucky tried again.

"This is hopeless! You will never learn." The woman slammed the fallboard down across the keys. Bucky snatched her hand out of the way just in time to keep her fingers from being smashed.

Bucky turned to look at the woman beside her. It was the woman from her dream with the flowing brown hair and she was wearing the same long, green dress. Her piercing blue eyes were opened wide. Bucky tried to slide away from her and off the bench but the woman grasped her by the wrist.

"You should never have been allowed to live." The woman stood and yanked Bucky off the bench and to her feet.

Bucky screamed for her dad, but the woman clamped her other hand over Bucky's mouth.

"Shut up, you unholy child."

Bucky kicked and flailed her free arm as the woman dragged her across the room and through the doorway, turning left and heading down the hall in the direction of the Spring Room. Bucky tried to grab a door knob as they passed one of the rooms but her strength was no match for her abductor's. She tried punching her but the woman seemed unaffected by the blows. Bucky managed twice to slip the woman's hand from her mouth and cry out, but her screams were swallowed in the vastness of the Mansion.

When they reached the Spring Room, the woman shifted Bucky and wrapped one arm around her waist and held her off the ground while she touched the door with her open palm and hummed some notes. Bucky screamed for her dad once more, but the woman slapped her across the face. She dropped Bucky to her feet and pulled her aside as the door swung outward. Down the steps to the first pool the woman dragged her captive. With both hands clutching Bucky, she forced the child to her knees at the edge of the pool. Bucky continued to fight and scream. She pulled the woman's hair and tried to gouge out her eyes, those blue eyes which were the same as Bucky's mother's in all the pictures.

"Stop!" The male voice came from the landing at the top of the stairs. "Don't...hurt...Bucky."

The woman turned in surprise at the sudden intrusion. Bucky chose that moment to pull away from her and run toward the stairs, but she slipped on the stone walkway. The woman grabbed one of her ankles.

"Dale!" shouted Bucky. "Help me! Please!"

Dale Crosson slowly descended the steps.

The woman dragged Bucky by the ankle back into her grasp.

"Let...her...go," ordered Dale, reaching the walkway.

"I'm her mother and she has to die." The woman hissed at the lanky young man with the tilted head.

"No!" Dale grabbed the woman's arm. There was a *pop!* and the woman was gone.

Dale knelt beside Bucky. She wrapped her arms around him and buried her face in his neck.

"You're...shaking," Dale said.

"You came," said Bucky, her voice muffled. "You said you'd come."

"Bucky. Bucky, wake up. You're having a nightmare." Simon laid a hand on one of Bucky's arms and gently shook his daughter. She was thrashing about so wildly her covers were twisted. One foot was uncovered and the sheet was wrapped around the other one. Her screams were so loud they had awakened him next door. Afraid she was experiencing one of her episodes, he had rushed to her bedside. She was deep in the throes of a bad dream, but there were no tears. "Lamb, wake up."

Bucky's eyes opened wide and she sat up, tugging at the sheet that had her left foot ensnared. "Dad! Where's Dale?"

"Dale's not here, Lamb. You're in your bedroom. You're safe."

"No! She tried to kill me again. She was going to drown me, but Dale saved me."

Simon sat on the edge of the bed and laid his hands on Bucky's shoulders to try and calm her. "It was just a bad dream. It's all over."

"No, Dad. It was Mom again. I know you said it wasn't, but it was. She said I— Oh, Dad. She said I—"

Simon tightened his grip on her shoulders. "Bucky, you need to calm down. Try taking some big breaths. In through your nose and out through your mouth. That's good. Breathe some more."

Bucky put her own hands on top of Simon's and gradually her breathing slowed and Simon could feel her relax.

"Are you sure Dale's not here? He carried me here from the Spring Room."

"Look around." Simon indicated the room lit only by the small bedside lamp. "There's no one here except you and me. It wasn't real. It was only a dream."

"Did you dream it, too?"

Simon thought for a moment. What was he dreaming when her cries interrupted? "No, I was dreaming about the cave, I think." He stood and began to straighten her covers. "You have your bed in a terrible fix." He put his hand on her jaw and turned her head to the right so he could see it better. "You have a red mark on your cheek. It looks like you hit yourself in the face with all your thrashing about." He untwisted the sheet from around her foot. "Okay, you need to lie back down." He sat in the chair next to her bed. "I'm probably to blame for your nightmare. I shouldn't have made you write that paper this afternoon. I thought writing it down might help you process some of the experiences you've had the past couple of days."

"But tonight after you read it, you said it was good."

"It was. I'm not sure, though, it accomplished what I hoped it would."

"Maybe you should try it."

"Try what?"

"You said you have all those people and things running around inside your head. Maybe you should write about them instead of your old mystery books."

"Hey." He ran a finger down her nose. "My old mystery books have been pretty darn successful."

"But writing about what's happening to you might help you…process it."

"Out of the mouths of babes."

Bucky crossed her arms under the covers. "I'm not a baby."

"That's an expression, Lamb. It means when a child says something surprising because it seems wise beyond her years. It actually comes from the Bible. Now, I think you should try to go back to sleep. I'll stay here until you do, if you want me to."

"I'm afraid she'll come for me again."

"She'll have to get through me…and Dale Crosson, apparently."

"Will you teach me another Hittite word?"

Not tonight"

"Please. *Māntāssu.*"

"Mmmm." Simon rubbed his chin. "How about *it sēs?*"

"*It sēs,*" Bucky repeated. "What does it mean?"

"Go to sleep."

"Oh, Dad…"

"Close your eyes and *it sēs.*"

⁓

The next morning, Bucky was in her room when she heard the doorbell ring. She crept to the top of the stairs and listened. Simon had told her Sissy Casteel was coming this morning to check out the piano. Bucky had refused to enter the music room yesterday and again this morning, despite her father's insistence there was nothing to fear.

"Good morning, Ms. Casteel. Welcome to the Mansion, although I hear you've been here before when it was decked out in all its glory."

"Good morning, Simon, and, although I'm old enough to be your mother, maybe even your grandmother, you need to call me Sissy." The plump woman spun around slowly in the foyer. "This is beautiful. Even if it is a bit smaller than I remember. I used to come through these front doors and imagine I was a princess in a palace. Speaking of princesses, where's Bucky?"

Simon cleared his throat. "I'm afraid Bucky won't be joining us this morning. There's been a...a development with the piano. I don't know if she'll be taking lessons." Simon led the way to the music room on the opposite side of the entryway from the library and his study.

"Oh, no. What's wrong?"

"I'm not sure." Simon had hoped all morning Bucky would change her mind, but all his persuasive logical arguments couldn't convince her there was no danger in having the piano back at the Mansion.

Sissy put both of her hands over her heart when she entered the music room and glimpsed the grand piano. It sat at an angle near the bay window, but not so close the morning sun would fade the finish, nor would the heat or cold from the window affect the sound. The movers had reassembled the instrument and had left the lid propped open. Sissy sat down on the bench and ran one hand over the smooth wood of the music shelf above the keyboard.

Simon smiled and imagined her as a young girl sitting there.

Sissy's fingers danced lightly up the keys as she played a simple scale and then went down them toward the deeper bass tones. "It's remarkable that it's not too badly out of tune after the move and for as old as it is. But I'd still call that piano tuner from Green River I told you about after you let it settle for a few weeks." The church organist followed her comments with a rousing rendition of "My Hope Is Built on Nothing Less."

"You need some more furniture in here to soften the sound," Sissy said when she had finished the hymn. "Some couches, maybe an area rug. Some paintings on the walls. Drapes, for sure." She played a few random notes and then looked up and cleared her throat as she nodded toward the door.

Simon, who had his back to the door, turned and looked. Bucky was standing at the edge of the doorway.

"Don't you want to join us?" Simon asked.

Bucky shook her head. She traced one finger along the swirled lines of the granite doorframe.

Sissy patted the bench next to her. "Come sit next to me and we'll have our first lesson."

Bucky shook her head again.

"A lot of people would give their eye teeth to own a magnificent piano like this," Sissy said.

"They can have it."

"Bucky," admonished Simon, "if you're going to talk like that you can go back up to your room."

Bucky fled back up the stairs.

"I'm sorry, Ms.—Sissy. That's not like her. She's just…upset over some things."

Sissy had to lay her hand on the piano to help herself stand. "Well, there's lots been going on, what with whatever that thing that happened at the walk Wednesday night and then poor Clara's funeral. Bucky did such a good job speaking at Clara's service. You should be very proud of her, Simon." She patted Simon's arm. "We can overlook it if she's a little out of sorts occasionally."

"Thank you for understanding. I'm sure she'll come around. I believe she really does want to take lessons."

"Say, I don't want to be presumptuous, and I know you're busy and don't like people around, but while I'm here, could I have a peek at the spring and the pools? My grandmother had arthritis real bad even as a young woman, and I remember coming here with her sometimes when I was little. She would always say she was going to 'take the waters,' and ask if I wanted to come along."

"After all you did to help me procure this piano, it's the least I can do." Simon ushered her out into the hallway.

They walked down the hall and down the stairs to the lower level. When they passed the rooms with the nameplates on the doors, Sissy stopped at Seraphina's. "You know, I can remember Seraphina, but just barely. She was already ancient when I was born. At church, she sat off to the side away from everyone, even her own family. My mother used to comment that she thought she was too good to associate with anyone." Sissy had a faraway look on her face. "I recall seeing her once here at the Mansion Resort, and even though I was a young child, I noticed that although she was smiling, her eyes didn't match her smile. Her eyes were sad. She was strange. I'm surprised she ever got married, although the truth be told, the story is her father arranged the marriage."

"If he hadn't," said Simon, "the population of Turn Back and the rest of the county would be somewhat diminished, wouldn't it?"

Sissy laughed good-naturedly. "It does seem that most of the town and half the county's descended from her. My mother always prided herself on the fact we weren't related to any of them. I don't know why. Most of them are good people."

Simon and Sissy continued down the hall and turned the corner but Simon stopped suddenly.

"What's the matter?" Sissy stopped, too. "You look like you've seen a ghost."

"The door to the Spring Room is open."

"I take it that it's not supposed to be."

"Not only that, it should be locked and…and…and there's a security monitor—a motion sensor—on it. An alarm should ring upstairs if it's opened." Simon could feel his heart racing. He had not been down here since the week before, but he thought of the nightmare Bucky had suffered last night. What if it had been another waking dream? What if she had really been here in the night? He remembered going in to her room last night. But what if that was part of the dream?

"Are you all right?" Sissy lightly touched Simon's arm.

Simon's head jerked back and forth. "Yes, I'm… I'm… I'm fine. I was…uh…thinking how it could have possibly been opened. Perhaps I left it open by accident the last time I was down here. Well,…uh…let's step inside and see if it's smaller than you remember."

That night when Simon went in to Bucky's room to tell her goodnight, he did not know for sure if he should broach the subject about the open Spring Room door. After her reluctance about going in to the music room that morning, Bucky had been her usual, cheerful self the rest of the day. Just after noon, Frog Bryland, the mailman, drove up the lane and delivered several packages containing the new clothes Simon had ordered. Bucky insisted she put on a fashion show on the stage in the old theater. She had made Simon drag in a chair so he could watch while she paraded back and forth on the stage in the various outfits, describing each one in detail to her captive audience of one. And during supper, they had held a lively discussion on fish since that seemed to be her new interest. She seemed especially preoccupied with their mating habits and procreation, regaling Simon with such facts as the female smallmouth bass, like the one she had caught, can lay over twenty-one thousand eggs at a time which are guarded by the male in his nest.

"Bucky, do you remember learning a new Hittite word last night?"

Bucky sat up in the bed. She was wearing her Friday-night, short-sleeved, navy-blue gown with silver stars.

"With the weather getting cooler, I thought you'd wear one of the new pajamas I bought you."

"You didn't buy seven of them."

"You don't need a different one each night."

Bucky rolled her eyes in response.

"So? Do you remember last night's Hittite word?"

"*It sēs*. You said it means *go to sleep*."

He recalled when he had gone into her room the night before when he had heard her cry out, she was indeed having a nightmare. Since she could remember the Hittite word for "go to sleep," then that must have really happened. But then why was the door to Spring Room open this morning? He feared if he discussed it now with her, it would only trigger another frightful dream.

"But, Dad, I'm not really sleepy. I guess I'm still excited over those new clothes. I don't feel like *it sēsing* yet."

Simon laughed. "That's not how the Hittites formed tenses."

"Can I tell you something?"

"You may tell me anything, Lamb, you know that."

"I'm sorry I couldn't go into the music room this morning to see Sissy. I wanted to, but I just couldn't."

"I think you owe Sissy an apology for speaking so rudely. And I expect you to tell her so Sunday morning."

"Do I have to?"

"Yes."

Bucky huffed and lay back down. "Do you think Sissy is her real name?"

"I suspect it's a nickname."

"Why do parents name their children one name and then call them something else? Why don't they name them whatever they're going to call them?"

"I don't know, Bucilla Rose." He paused to see if his response elicited even a hint of a smile, but none was forthcoming. "Now, I really think you should *it sēs*. Tomorrow's Saturday. Won't Ian be coming over in the morning?"

"No." Bucky stuck out her lower lip. "He told me he's going to look for the cave, using his old map. And I know you won't let me go with him."

"No, I won't. Maybe he can come over later in the day."

"And maybe it'll rain pink ice cream cones."

Simon sighed in exasperation. "I really don't like this new attitude of yours. What happened to always looking on the bright side?"

"What's the bright side of him getting to go off on his own exploring?"

"He might find it. After all he found the mastodon bones and the Hollow Stone."

"But I want to help him."

"The answer is still *no*." Simon leaned over and kissed her forehead. "I love you."

She did not say the words back to him tonight.

11

SEARCH AND RESCUE

"And who are you today?" Simon was standing at the kitchen counter, cleaning up the remains of their breakfast waffles when Bucky came down the back stairs wearing a bandana wrapped around her head.

"Harriet Tubman. I'm headed back into Maryland to rescue some slaves and help them escape to Canada."

"So, what's this?" Simon pulled out the plastic pearl-handled pistol she had stuffed into the waistband of her jeans. "I didn't realize Harriet was armed."

"The book I read said she carried a revolver. She was in danger of the slave catchers and their dogs. Plus she threatened to use it on any slaves who wanted to turn back because she thought that would threaten the safety of the others." Bucky took the toy gun from her father and slipped it back into her jeans.

"Well, Ms. Harriet, it's cool out this morning." Simon grabbed a zippered sweatshirt off a hook by the back door. "Wear this."

Bucky sighed. "I'm not cold."

Simon gave her a stern look and held out the sweatshirt.

Bucky snatched it out of his hand and put it on, frowning the whole time. "I think she probably wore a shawl."

"I don't have a shawl for you. You'll just have to imagine it. Off you go. I'll be in my study. And remember…"

"I know. Don't leave the garden. You tell me that every day."

Simon finished straightening the kitchen and stopped at the French doors that looked out onto the walled garden. Bucky was in the small rowboat Ian had pulled from the shed last summer. The two of them had converted it to a sail boat after everyone started dreaming the ship dreams. The sail, one of Bucky's old bedsheets on which she had painted a red bull, hung limply from the center pole, one corner having come undone from the upper crossbar. Bucky, however, was using an oar this morning. Simon smiled, wondering what imaginary body of water she was crossing and who was in the boat with her.

The next second, Simon staggered and grabbed the doorframe for support as a wave poured over the sides of the ship. "Imala!" He reached for the toddler who was sliding across the drenched deck. Falling to his knees, he crawled toward the child and wrapped his arms around her as another wave hit. The vessel lurched to the side, almost tossing them both into the sea. Simon clung to a post with one arm, the other one securely around his daughter.

And then it was over and Simon was on the stone floor of the kitchen, clutching only air. He sat back on his heels and wiped his hands down his face, fully expecting his hair and skin to be soaked, but they were dry. The vision had been so real. He could feel the sting of the spray and taste the salt on his lips. He could hear his baby's cries for help.

"Process," he said aloud. Process. Maybe this morning he could forego working on his book and instead write down everything he could remember about Etakkama. Perhaps that would be one less of his incarnations cavorting in his mind amidst a jumble of memories.

"Dad! Dad!"

Simon looked at his watch. It had been two hours since he had sent Bucky out into the garden. He jumped up from his desk and rushed over to the door of his study as she came bounding through the doorway and into his arms.

"Dad! It's Ian! Something's wrong!"

"What? Where is he? Is he outside?"

Bucky was wild-eyed and breathless. "I don't— I don't know where he is. I think he's hurt. We have to find him."

Simon grasped her by her upper arms. "Calm down, Lamb. Tell me slowly. How do you know?"

"I just know." She pulled at the bandana that was now tied around her throat. "I was… I was… I was…"

"Take a deep breath and tell me."

"I was standing by one of the doorways in the garden wall and I felt… I can't describe it, Dad. I just know we need to get to him. Oh, Ian." She turned away from Simon and looked back out into the hallway.

"But he could be anywhere."

"No. He's by… I think he's by a river, but not the big river by the mastodons. And there's a bluff, but not the big bluff across the river."

Simon straightened. "Oh, my God. I showed him on the map when we were at his house Monday night. Let's go."

Simon pushed Bucky ahead of him through the entryway and down the hall to the kitchen. Pausing only long enough to grab his own jacket from the hook by the back door, he ushered her out the door. Once outside, Bucky took off running and was across the garden almost before Simon had cleared the steps. He had to yell at her to wait at the doorway in the wall for him.

He was already breathing heavily when he caught up with her. "I don't think it's far. It's in that direction." He waved his arm toward the southwest. "There's the stream over there that comes from our Spring Room and runs on down to the river. And then on the map there was a much larger stream past that one that had some bluffs along it. But there are some hills and deep ravines between here and there. I think our easiest path would be to go to the river and head south."

"Come on!" Bucky grabbed his hand and began running.

It was open land until they neared the river. The mastodon site lay off to their right but they veered left through the trees. The flood plain along the river was uneven, and they had to contend with roots and fallen trees. Where the Spring Room stream entered the river, they splashed through the shallow water as they crossed over the rocky bottom.

Not far past that stream, Simon pulled Bucky to a halt. "We're going to have to stop a minute." He doubled over.

"We can't stop, Dad." Bucky pulled at him. "We're getting closer. I can feel it."

"Let me catch my breath." He put his hands on either side of his waist and straightened. "I've seen you and Ian chase each other around the garden. You're in better shape than I am." He wiped the sleeve of his jacket across his red, sweat-drenched face. "All right, but let's take it a little slower. We have a ways to go yet."

It wasn't long before the tangled growth along the river grew thicker.

"Maybe this route was not such a good idea," said Simon holding some bramble runners up so Bucky could get through. "Let's move away from the river up along that rise over there. It looks a little clearer. We just don't want to lose our direction. I know that stream runs into the river at some point."

Twenty more minutes of scrambling through the undergrowth brought them to a clearing.

"Look!" Bucky pointed to the center of the clearing. There stood the remains of a stone chimney, partially obscured by vines and brush. Most of its rocks lay scattered at its base, but enough of the upright portion was still intact to tell what it was.

"Oh, my God." Simon was panting, but smiling at the same time.

"What is it?"

"I saw that on Jennifer's LIDAR scans." Dr. Jennifer Brockman, a lithics specialist, had been one of the archaeologists Simon had called in last summer to verify the age of the Hollow Stone. During the investigation, she had surveyed the area by air, searching for evidence of early occupation. "She had discounted it as the remains of a nineteenth- or early twentieth-century cabin. A chimney. It's not." Simon laughed, but it was a strange laugh.

"Dad? What's wrong?"

"We found... There are mines near here. I remember. Some holes in the ground. We found copper and...and zinc...and silver. Just trace amounts, but near the surface. And iron. And lots of lead. We built a smelter. We weren't going to return home empty-handed." Simon laughed again. "That's why this clearing is here. The fumes from the lead and the sulfur dioxide poisoned the vegetation and the soil. Even after three thousand years."

Bucky was staring at her father, her mouth open, sweat rolling down her cheeks. "What are you talking about?"

"When I was here before. With the Minoans. When I was Etakkama."

Bucky clamped her mouth shut and closed her eyes, listening. She turned away from Simon and then back toward him. "I can hear water running. Come on, Dad. We have to find Ian."

Simon blinked several times, forcing himself back to the present. "I know. It's not far. We're actually on top of the bluff. It's just past those trees there."

Simon led the way until they came to the edge of a precipice. Through the trees that grew from narrow ledges and breaks in the cliff face they could see the stream below. Simon surveyed the area for a moment. "It looks like there's a way down over here."

Bucky trailed behind him, still holding his hand as they walked along an animal track at the edge of the bluff. Simon stopped between two large boulders.

"It's not going to be easy going down. Grab hold of any branches or saplings as you pick your way, but make sure they're alive. If you pull at a dead one it could break off and you'd tumble on down. If you start to fall, sit down on your bottom and slide."

The cliff was as not smooth as the high one on the western side of the St. Francis River across from Turn Back. This bluff consisted of huge stones jumbled together and perched precariously on a steep slope. There was no guarantee the boulders were secure in their positions. Simon worried he would put his hand on one and start it cascading down.

When they reached the base of the cliff, there were more large rocks along the stream. But there was less vegetation here and a clearer path along this creek than along the river.

Bucky let go of her father's hand and took off her bandana. She knelt by the edge of the stream. Surprised Simon didn't stop her, she dipped the bandana in the water and wiped it across her face and neck. She had tied her sweatshirt around her waist not long after they began their trek.

"Good idea," said Simon, kneeling beside her, and using his own handkerchief in a similar fashion. He cupped his hands and drank from the stream. "Are you picking up anything?" He did not have a clue as to what connection existed between Ian and her that she could sense something had happened to her friend. But he didn't doubt that it was real.

Bucky shook her head. "I don't know which way to go. Is the cave near here? Can you remember?"

"Nothing looks familiar about all this." Simon indicated the boulder-strewn bluff. "Maybe there was an earthquake or something."

They both stood and looked around.

"Let's try upstream first," said Simon, taking Bucky's hand once again.

They had gone less than thirty yards when Bucky cried out, "There he is!"

Ahead of them, just off the path, Ian lay crumpled on his side on the ground, one arm draped over a large rock.

"Stay here," ordered Simon as he rushed to Ian and knelt beside him. He felt his neck for a pulse and put his ear against his chest.

"Dad?"

"Hush." Simon sat up. "He's alive. Come on." He beckoned to Bucky to join him, and she dropped to her knees next to Ian's unmoving body."

"Are you sure?" Bucky reached out and lightly touched one of Ian's legs. His jeans were streaked with dirt. Even through the material she could feel the spark that connected them.

"Course I'm sure." The side of Simon's face and hair were bloody where he had put his head against the boy. "But he's badly hurt. Give me your bandana." Simon wadded up his own handkerchief and pressed it against a wound on Ian's stomach. He used Bucky's bandana to wipe Ian's forehead which had a gash in it. Neither wound was bleeding profusely. A flashlight protruded from under Ian's torso.

"Can you carry him back home?"

"I don't think we should move him. It looks like he fell from up there." Simon jerked his head up toward the bluff with its sprawling huge stones. "He could have some broken bones and maybe internal injuries."

"So what are we going to do?

Simon dug in his pocket for his cellphone, but he already knew what it would indicate. No service. He slammed it against his thigh. "We should never have come to this God-forsaken wilderness."

Bucky laid a hand on his arm. "You stay here with Ian. I'll go get help."

"Bucky, we've walked... We've walked an hour and half to get here. There's no way..." Simon slumped.

Bucky untied the arms of her sweatshirt from around her waist and spread the garment over Ian who had on a long-sleeve T-shirt, but no jacket. As she sat back down on the ground, the sunlight on the water in the creek sparkled and she saw a reflection. She twisted and glanced up at the rocks on the bluff and then looked again at the stream and then back at the bluff. "Dad! Look!"

Simon raised his head. "What? Where?"

"She was there!" Bucky scooted as close to her father as she could. "She was up there, Dad. I saw her. I saw her reflection in the water, but she's gone now."

"Who?"

"The woman from the dream. And she was going like this." Bucky held out her hand and curled her fingers in a beckoning motion.

"Bucky, there's no one there. You're hot and you're tired and you're scared for Ian. It's just your mind playing tricks."

"*Your* mind plays tricks. Mine doesn't. Maybe she pushed him. Maybe that's why he fell."

Simon put an arm around his daughter. "We need to think about Ian now. I honestly don't know what to do."

Bucky nervously eyed the cliff above them as she offered a suggestion. "Maybe we could build a travois.

There are lots of limbs around here. We could put him on it and drag him out."

"I told you we can't move him. We couldn't make one, anyway and even if we did, how could we possibly drag it through all this?" He swept his arm around, indicating the trees and boulders and rough terrain. "I can't leave him here alone while we go back. I can't leave you here by yourself with him while I go for help."

"I'm not staying here, anyway. Not with her up there. I don't care whether or not you believe me." Bucky jumped to her feet. "I'm going back. I'll get Maggie. She'll call 911."

Simon grabbed her by one wrist. "You're not going anywhere. Sit down."

Bucky pulled away from him, and Simon scrambled to his feet. "No! Dad, Ian's going to die if we don't get him some help. When you were hurt they sent an ambulance, but Maggie said they might send a helicopter. An ambulance could never get back in here— there's no road. But a helicopter could land in that field up there where your chimney is."

"There's no way I will let you go off by yourself. How would you ever find your way home?"

"I led us here, didn't I?"

"I led us here," said Simon.

"Dad," Bucky spoke calmly, "while we're arguing, Ian might be dying. You have to let me go."

"Bucky, I can't. If anything happened to you, I… I'd go mad with grief."

"Dad." Bucky took one of Simon's hands in both of hers. "Pretend that I'm eighty years old. It's finally time to let me go."

Simon drew Bucky to him and wrapped his arms around her. "I can't."

"Yes, you can. You need to stay here with…with your son."

Tears ran down Simon's face as he caressed Bucky's hair. He couldn't speak for almost a minute. "You need… You need to drink some more water from the stream before you leave. And… And it's afternoon now. You'll want to go north so make sure the sun is always on your left. And… Oh, Lamb, I can't do this. I can't let you go alone."

"It's the only way to get help. No one's going to find us here."

"Oh, God, help me."

"Dad, I can do this. Please, Dad. *Māntāssu, A*tta"

Simon buried his face in the top of Bucky's head for a few seconds and then straightened.

"Oh, God. Four months ago, I wouldn't even allow you to go out in the garden by yourself. How can I possibly let you go off through these woods?"

"A lot's changed in four months."

Simon tightened his grip on his daughter. The first time he tried to speak, no words would come out. Taking a deep breath, he tried again. "Please be safe, Bucky. I can't lose you, too." He released her and she went and knelt beside Ian.

"Dad, how do you say *be strong* in Hittite?"

"*Dassus ēs.*"

Bucky put a hand on Ian's arm. "*Dassus ēs*, Ian. It's going to be okay." She walked over to the edge of the creek and went down on her knees and leaned over the water. After she drank several handfuls, she sat up and wiped her mouth. "You told me once the springs in the Ozarks were polluted. Should we be drinking this?"

Simon shook his head. Here he was panicking over allowing his precious child to head out on her own through the woods and she was concerned about what's in the water. "At this point, it's more important you are hydrated. We can deal later with whatever illness you might get from it. One more thing. Here." Simon handed her the topographic map that had been sticking out of Ian's back pocket. "You'll have to direct the helicopter pilot back here to the clearing. You've never flown. Things look different when you're up there." He pointed on the map where they were. "Show this to the pilot. Remember, on the way back here, you'll cross this stream here that comes from our house and then this one will be the second stream. But with all the trees they might be hard to see from the air. Hopefully, the pilot will know what to look for. This spot here is the clearing on top of this bluff."

Bucky rolled up the map and stuffed it into the waistband of her jeans. Somewhere on their trek, Harriet Tubman's pearl-handled revolver had fallen out.

Simon embraced her again. "I love you so much, Lamb."

"I love you, too, Dad." She leaned her head back and looked up at his face. "I'll be back in no time. I can run pretty fast for an eighty-year old."

It was two hours later when Simon heard the distinct thrumming of a helicopter rotor. He jumped up from the spot beside Ian where he had kept vigil and listened as the helicopter landed. With his heart pounding, Simon sprinted down the path to the spot where he and Bucky had descended earlier from the top of the bluff.

It wasn't long before a male voice called out to him and Simon responded, "Over here! We're over here! There's a way down!"

Two paramedics, a male and female, finally came into view through the trees above him and there with them was a little girl.

Simon threw back his head and let out an uncharacteristic whoop when he saw her.

When Bucky caught sight of her dad at the bottom of the cliff, she jumped in front of the emergency responders and half-ran, half-slid down the bluff, bouncing from one boulder to another. If Simon had not been at the base to catch her, she would have tumbled on into the creek. But she flew into his out-stretched arms and he swept her up in an embrace, holding her off the ground.

"I told you I could do it," she said, laughing as she covered his face with kisses.

"Oh, my beautiful, brave, bodacious Bucky."

Bucky squealed with laughter but then stopped. She was still in Simon's arms, but she pushed herself away a little. "What does *bodacious* mean?"

"Bold and courageous and awesome and wonderful and...just a little bit sassy." He pressed her head against his neck. "Oh, Lamb, you will never know how scared I was."

The medical team had reached the bottom of the bluff and Simon pointed down the path where Ian was. With Bucky still in his arms, Simon trailed after them.

"How's Ian? Did he wake up?"

Simon let Bucky slip down so her feet were on the ground. "Not yet. He moaned a couple of times and I thought he might wake, but he's still unconscious." Simon pulled her close. "Oh, Bucky, how on earth did you ever— What's this?"

Bucky let the backpack she was wearing slide off and she held it out to Simon. "It's some sandwiches for you. I made them myself. And Maggie put in a thermos of coffee and some water. But she said you'd probably like the coffee better."

"Where is Maggie?"

"She stayed by the helicopter. She didn't think she could climb down the cliff. What are they doing, Dad?"

The man and woman were kneeling beside Ian.

"They're assessing his injuries. Let's stay back here out of the way." Simon leaned against one of the big boulders and rummaged through the backpack. He pulled out a turtle shell. "I hope you don't expect me to eat this."

Bucky chuckled. "Of course not. Look, it still has the bottom part on it. I had to stop sometimes to catch my breath, and there it was, right in front of me. I thought Ian would like to see it if he was awake."

"I'm sure he would. It will make a nice addition to his collections."

"Oh, no." Bucky took the bleached turtle shell from her father. "This is for my new collection. He already has a couple of these. One of his even still has some bones inside."

Simon reached into the backpack again and drew out a little clear plastic bag containing a ham sandwich. It didn't take him long to devour it. It had been a long time since breakfast. "Did you say there was coffee in there?"

Bucky reached in the bag for the thermos. She unscrewed the top before handing it to Simon, but she almost dropped it as something behind her dad caught her eye. "Dad, look!"

Simon turned around. Three green fireflies flitted near him and then darted toward where Ian lay.

"They've been here since you left. There are a couple of red ones, too."

"The Guardians," whispered Bucky. "Anarianu. Two of them were with me the whole time I was headed toward Maggie's. And they weren't making any noise but it was like I could hear them talking inside my head. They kept saying *Protect the three*. What do you think that means? Protect the three. The three what?"

Simon lowered the thermos from his mouth. "We three? You and Ian and I?"

Bucky shrugged. "They didn't do a very good job of protecting Ian."

"I don't know. Look right there next to him. See that pointed stump?" A slender tree stump, no more than three inches in diameter, projected from the ground next to where Ian lay. "That's a beaver tree. That point is where the beaver chewed it. If Ian had fallen on that, it would have gone right through him."

The two of them watched the paramedics for a few more minutes.

"You need to start back up to the helicopter," said Simon. "They're going to take Ian up on a stretcher and I don't know if they're going to need any help with that."

"They said we can't go back in that helicopter because it'll be too crowded when they get Ian in there."

"We have to walk out?" said Simon. "That will take a couple of hours. I really think we should be at the hospital with Maggie."

"No, Dad, there were all kinds of emergency people at Maggie's. There was a fire truck from the Garton Fire Department. I don't know why they were there. When Maggie called 911, she didn't say there was a fire. And the two deputies who are at the walks most of the time came. But right before we took off, another helicopter landed from the Highway Patrol. And when this helicopter that's in the clearing right now leaves, that helicopter is going to pick us up. Have you ever flown before, Dad?"

"Sure, but never in a helicopter."
"You're going to love it."

12

A REVELATION

The last time Simon had been at the hospital in Green River was as a patient. He had no memory of being admitted, but did recall leaving through the front doors in a wheelchair and Maggie's truck had been under an overhang just outside the doors. He was unsure today where he should go to locate Maggie and Ian, but decided to head toward the main entrance.

It had been almost three hours since the helicopter had lifted off from the clearing with Ian and Maggie. As Bucky had said, the Missouri Highway Patrol helicopter arrived then, but before allowing Bucky and Simon to board, the officer insisted on viewing the scene of Ian's accident. So Simon and Bucky again had to descend the bluff and show him where Ian had fallen and answer a slew of questions. Simon hedged on a few of the questions and outright lied on a couple of them. How could he possibly explain the reason they were even out here was because Bucky had a "feeling" something was wrong? At each half-truth and lie Bucky squeezed his hand, but, fortunately, made no comment.

The officer finally allowed them to hike back up the bluff and to the helicopter which flew them to the field adjacent to the back wall of the garden behind the

Mansion and left them there. Simon and Bucky took a few minutes to clean up and change clothes before traveling by car to the hospital in Green River, an hour's drive away. Bucky had fallen asleep in the back seat of the car and Simon wished he could have joined her. He was exhausted from the exertion of the search for Ian and the stress over the boy's condition and his worry over Bucky's solo trek back to Maggie's. They stopped for a hamburger when they arrived in Green River and ate in the car on the way to hospital. Simon feared it would be a long night and vending machines might be their only food source. It was almost six o'clock by the time he parked the car and they crossed the parking lot to the front doors. Simon held Bucky's hand. He wasn't ready to let her go again.

Once inside, they hurried across the lobby to the information desk.

The woman behind the counter checked her computer in response to Simon's inquiry about Ian. "He's in PICU. That's the pediatric intensive care unit," she explained. "Bed four. But I can't tell you anything else about his condition."

Simon scanned a laminated map of the hospital on the counter. "How do I get there?"

"The elevators are around that corner over there and PICU's on the lower level. But I'm sorry, you won't be able to go down there."

"Why not?"

"Hospital policy is to not allow children under twelve in the patient rooms," explained the woman, nodding at

Bucky. "And we also do not allow unattended children to remain in the lobby."

"Well that's quite a catch-22, isn't it?" answered Simon. "I can't take her with me and I can't leave her here." He looked down at Bucky who looked up at him. "Not that I would." He turned his attention back to the woman behind the counter. "I— *We* really need to see that little boy and find out his condition."

"I'm sorry, sir. There's nothing I can do."

Bucky spoke up. "When my dad was here a couple of months ago, Dr. Crosson let me in the room to see him."

The woman hit some keys on her keyboard and peered at the monitor. "Dr. Crosson's not here."

Simon tried to remain calm but he had little patience for bureaucracies. "Then find someone who can make the decision to allow my daughter to accompany me."

"There's no one here who can do that. You'll have to wait in the lobby and, perhaps, someone will inform you about the patient."

"And if we should just head on down to PICU?"

"I'd have to call security, sir."

Simon stared at the woman for a few seconds and then backed up and turned toward the seats in the lobby. With Bucky in tow he chose some chairs far enough away from the Information desk that the woman would not overhear them. There were two other people in the lobby, but they were seated on the other side.

"What are we going to do, Dad. I really need to see Ian."

"I know. First off," said Simon, digging in his back pants pocket for his handkerchief, "maybe the sergeant-major over there would have been more accommodating if you didn't have ketchup smeared on your face." He held out the white handkerchief to her. "Here. Spit on that and wipe the corner of your mouth."

"Ew, Dad, that's gross."

"You want me to spit on it?"

Bucky spit and swiped the handkerchief across her mouth. "Better?"

"No, you missed a spot. Right there." Simon touched her left cheek.

Bucky rubbed the spot and handed the handkerchief back to Simon. "I wish Chip Crosson was here. He'd let us in there."

"We'll see Ian," Simon whispered. "I have a plan." He looked around the lobby and the adjacent wide hallway leading to the elevators. "We'll need a diversion."

"Like in the movies?"

"You see that mural over there on the wall? I want you to casually stroll over there and pretend to look at it. But keep an eye on me and when you see me do this—" Simon touched his eyebrow and then flicked his index finger, pointing forward, "you scurry around the corner. I saw on the map where there's a staircase just beyond the elevators. We'll take the stairs down."

"What are you going to do?"

"Do you remember at one of the early prayer walks that man from the TV station was there and he interviewed Maggie, but you got all worried because you couldn't see me and you didn't know where I was?"

Bucky nodded.

"I was right there all along. Hiding in plain sight, so to speak. It's a matter of getting people to focus their attention elsewhere." As Simon was speaking, the glass front doors slid open and he turned to look. "Ah, the cavalry has arrived."

"Dad!" exclaimed Bucky, swiveling to look. "It's the Lukefahr Ladies. Some of them, anyway."

Penny Crosson and Maxine Ross, followed by Ruby Lower, pushing her walker, and Ruth Mercier with a cane, entered the lobby. Simon was not quick enough to stop Bucky from leaping out of her seat and rushing over to greet them. The women surrounded Bucky and escorted her back to her father. He quickly filled them in on what little he knew and his predicament.

"The last update I had from Maggie was about an hour and a half ago," said Penny. "Evidently Ian needs surgery but they're delaying it because he has a rare blood type and they're trying to locate some. I've called Chip and he said he'd head on down here, but it'll be a while."

"Poor Ian and poor Maggie," said Ruth. "I can only imagine what she's going through."

"It's going to be a long night, I'm afraid," said Maxine. "That's why we've come. We're going to take turns sitting with her so she won't be alone."

Simon had caught his breath at Penny's words of "rare blood type." "Ladies, it is imperative I get in there to see him. Bucky, too. We don't have time to wait for Chip. Will you help?"

"Of course," said Ruby. "You just tell us what to do."

Simon gathered them all in closer and explained his simple plan. He then sent Bucky over to the mural across the wide hallway from the information counter. He sat back down in his seat and, keeping one eye on Bucky, watched the elderly women go into action.

The four ladies approached the counter from the side. Penny took the lead and asked the woman for the room number of a fictitious person. Simon waited until the woman looked at her computer monitor and then she turned back to the women who all insisted the person they were looking for was a patient. He stood up and tried to be nonchalant as he moved part of the way across the lobby to where Bucky was standing by the mural. Suddenly Ruby yelped and pretended she had caught her little finger in the brake handle of her walker. She cried out in pain as the other three women sought to extract her finger. The woman stepped from behind the counter and bent over her just as Ruby pulled it free and sobbed about it hurting.

That, of course, was the diversion Simon was hoping would capture the woman's attention and give him a chance to slip away. He gave the sign to Bucky and she disappeared around the corner in a flash and he followed. They opened the door to the stairs and hurriedly made their way to the lower level.

When they reached the bottom of the stairs there was another closed door. Bucky turned and gave Simon a high-five but he cautioned her they weren't out of danger yet.

"There will be people on this floor as officious and rule-abiding as the sergeant-major back there. We have to act as if we belong, as if we have permission to be here. Okay?"

Bucky nodded and Simon reached around her and started to open the door, but stopped. "Listen, Bucky." He kept his voice low. "Remember when you came here to see me and you were a little upset about me being in bed and having my head wrapped up and all? Well, this is going to be upsetting, too, I'm afraid. Ian might still be unconscious and he might have all kinds of tubes and wires attached to him. You need to steel yourself."

"Dad, ever since we got out of the car, I've had to steel myself. It's like… I don't know how to describe it. It's like I can feel the sadness and pain of everyone in here. I felt that way at Clara's funeral, but I wanted to be there so I fought past it. And it was like that when I was here before, too, but I needed to be here then because of you. And I need to be here now because of Ian. So I can put up with it for a while."

Simon wrapped his arms around her and drew her close. "Oh, my darling lamb."

Bucky let him hug her but then pulled away. "That's one reason why I like the prayer walks. When we first get there and there's all those people, I can feel all kinds of things—some of them not so good. But after we start walking—I don't know—there's a kind of peace that surrounds me. It's like that at church, too."

"I'm so sorry. I never realized that just being around other people could cause you so much pain."

"It's not really pain. It's more like an unsettling in my soul."

Simon shook his head. "Words no ten-year-old should ever need to speak. Let's find Ian."

Simon opened the door and they entered another lobby area, although this one was much smaller than the main one upstairs. Simon scanned the informational direction sign on the wall opposite the nearby elevators. "This way."

He led Bucky down a hallway that opened into the pediatric intensive care unit. There was a circular nurses station and a complex of individual patient rooms with glass doors in a concentric circle surrounding it.

"She said bed four, Dad," whispered Bucky.

"There," said Simon. The rooms had large numbers on the glass.

They made it to the room without being accosted. Maggie, seated in a chair inside, stood when she saw them at the open door. The bed was empty.

"Where's Ian?" asked Simon.

Maggie hugged Bucky and kept her in her arms. "They took him to surgery about forty-five minutes ago."

"Penny said they were having difficulty locating blood for him because he has a rare blood type," said Simon.

"Oh, that Penny. She only hears half of what I tell her. It's not that rare of a blood, but the nearest blood bank had none in reserve, so they had to call around to others. The surgeon wanted as much as four units. There was internal bleeding, I guess." Maggie had to release Bucky from her grip to dab at her eyes with a tissue. "They couldn't find that much, but they felt they couldn't postpone the surgery any longer. Oh, Simon..."

Simon, usually reserved in showing affection with anyone besides Bucky, put his arms around Maggie and let her sob into his shoulder. It took her a few seconds to recover. She stepped back. "I'm sorry, Simon."

"There's nothing to be sorry for, Maggie." He glanced back toward the nurses station. "I need to find someone here who knows something. I was a patient here not that long ago. Surely they have my blood type on file. It might be a match."

"I said it's not rare, but it's rare enough that would be a pretty big coincidence."

"We both know there are no coincidences in Turn Back."

"Maggie," said Bucky, pulling on the sleeve of the older woman's sweater. "Some of the Sunday school ladies are here. They said they would take turns sitting with you tonight."

"Oh, bless them. The last I heard from Penny before she left to drive up here was that Pastor Bradley would be here, too, later. He was in Cape Girardeau when she got ahold of him."

"I'll sit here with you, too, Maggie," said Bucky, "unless they throw me out for being under twelve."

Maggie drew Bucky against her again. "Oh, Lamb, you've done so much today. You saved my little boy's life." Maggie looked at Simon. "I can't lose him. I've lost everyone else." The tears she had stopped earlier started running down her cheeks again.

"Bucky," said Simon, "stay here. I'm going to step over there to the nurses station." A temple bell chimed softly. "What the—"

"It's your phone, Dad."

"I know it's my phone. It's just been several months since I've heard it ring."

"I saw some signs on the wall outside telling people to turn off their cellphones."

Simon pulled the phone from his pocket and peered at the screen. "This is strange. It's a call from Behring Memorial Hospital."

"That's where we are," said Bucky.

He swiped the screen. "Hello?"

A voice on the other end asked, "Is this Simon Carter?"

Simon hesitated before answering. "Yes."

"My name is Susan LaPlant at Behring Memorial Hospital. We've had a request from Dr. Darrin Crosson to ask if you would come to the hospital immediately. There's an urgent need for your blood type. I'm sorry that because of privacy regulations we can't tell you any more than that except to say Dr. Crosson said to tell you he's been trying to reach you at your home with no answer and that's the only number he had for you. But, fortunately, we had your cellphone information on file. When you arrive, you need to come directly to the—"

"B-but wait," stammered Simon. "Wait a minute. I'm already at the hospital. I'm in the pediatric intensive care unit, room four."

"Oh,…oh, in that case…uh…" Ms. LaPlant's voice became muffled as she spoke to someone else and then said to Simon, "If you are willing to donate, I'll send someone down there right now."

"Of course, I'll donate." Simon ended the call and put his phone back in his pocket. He stood there a moment without speaking.

"Simon?" Maggie pressed. She and Bucky had only heard his side of the conversation.

Simon flicked his head back and forth. "Oh…uh…Chip Crosson's been trying to get hold of me. I think my blood might be compatible with Ian's—that is unless there's someone else here tonight with an urgent need of a transfusion. They wouldn't tell me who it's for. They're sending someone now."

"Will it hurt?" asked Bucky.

"You remember when Chip drew some blood out of your arm? It's like that except they take more than just a little vial. I'll be all right."

A technician holding a clipboard arrived at the glass door to the room. "Simon Carter? Will you come with me?"

Simon looked at Bucky. "I promised myself today I would never let you out of my sight again, at least not this soon. But will you stay here with Maggie? I'll only be gone a half hour or so, maybe not that long."

Maggie put a protective arm around Bucky's shoulders. "She'll be all right. Oh, look, here comes Penny to keep us company."

It was almost an hour before Simon returned to the room in PICU. Maggie and Penny Crosson were sitting in the two chairs and Bucky was asleep on Maggie's lap. Ian's bed was still empty.

"Maggie," whispered Simon, "she's too heavy for you to hold her like that." He started to take his daughter in his arms.

"I need to talk to you, anyway." Maggie stood and together they slid the sleeping Bucky back into the chair. "Penny, we're going to go down to the lounge for a few minutes. I need to stretch my legs."

There was a family area not far down one of the hallways. Simon felt as if he were being escorted by his teacher to the principal's office. He did not know for sure what Maggie had to say, but he was afraid he was going to have to come up with more lies.

The family lounge was empty. Maggie closed the door then turned on Simon. "How did you know you were a match for my Ian?"

Simon looked away and closed his eyes. He took a big breath and let it out slowly. "Chip must have remembered from when I was here in July."

"No, you knew before the call from Chip came through. I want the truth, Simon Carter."

Simon opened his eyes but could not look at her. Any story he might have fabricated seemed hollow, so he tried to stall. "This isn't the time. Let's wait until Ian is out of danger."

Maggie took Simon's jaw in her hands. She turned his head from side to side, and he stood there and allowed her to do it. "The older he gets," she said, "the less I see of my husband and son and grandson in him. As much…" She dropped her hands to her side as tears welled up in her eyes. "As much as I look for it."

"Maggie, please."

"Tell me."

Simon swallowed twice before the words would come. "Chip did a DNA test on me. It… The father-son Y-DNA test… It's a perfect match for Ian's that you had done."

"How?"

Simon scoffed. "How? How did it happen? The way it always happens. What? Do you want me to tell you the little green lightning bugs had something to do with it? They didn't. I… I'm to blame. I'm totally to blame. I'm sorry, Maggie. I was going to tell you. But not like this."

Maggie clenched her fists. For a moment Simon feared she was going to pummel him. Instead she turned away.

"I know I'm just a simple country woman, but I grew up on a farm. I know it takes two. But Kara was married to Seth over two years before she became pregnant with Ian. How long did your affair with her last?"

Simon grunted. "There was no affair. It was one night, a night which I have regretted every single day of my life since then."

Maggie shook her head and turned back to face him. "I just… I mean I've only known you for a few months, but I never would have thought that of you. You always seem so…so reserved. Kara, on the other hand, I could believe it of her. My son, Robert, did not have a high opinion of his daughter-in-law. She had a… Well, back when I was in school, we would have said she had a reputation."

Simon sniffed. Tears blurred his eyes. "I'm so sorry, Maggie. I didn't know… When I moved here, I didn't know… I had no idea Ian lived here. His mother, Kara, sent me a picture of him when he was born and…and another one after his first birthday, but that was the only contact I ever had with her and I didn't respond to either of those because she didn't want me to. She didn't even give me an address. She said as far as Ian's father knew…" Simon paused. "As far as he knew, the baby was his. And then I didn't hear from her anymore."

"Because she and Seth died in the accident."

"I have money, Maggie. You know I have money. Ian will never want for anything and neither will you."

"I don't want your money, Simon Carter. You save it all for that little girl of yours. Ian and me will make out all right on our own."

Neither spoke for a few moments. Muffled noises from the hall filtered in through the closed door, but other than that there was silence in the room.

"I don't want to lose your friendship, Maggie. You mean the world to Bucky and…and to me."

"But I can *feel* him," said Maggie. "He has that family touch. If he's not really my great-grandson, through blood anyway, why can I feel him? Is it through you?" She laid her hand on Simon's wrist.

Simon shook his head. The familiar warmth of Maggie's touch coursed through him. "I don't know."

"At least I know now where he gets those curls. I've always wondered. Bucky doesn't know any of this, does she?"

"She found out by accident just this past week."

Maggie sighed. "And her reaction?"

Simon shrugged. "She seems fine. She doesn't like keeping it a secret from him."

"He needs to be told. We'll wait until he's past all this, though. Oh, Simon…" Maggie hugged him and Simon put his arms around her. He could feel her shoulders shaking.

"I'm so sorry, Maggie. I've only added to all your worries and made things worse for you."

"I'd like to hate you for this, for what you did. I think I need to hate you, but I can't. He probably would have died out there today if you hadn't found him, and you might have saved his life again this evening with your blood. And you gave me this beautiful child to raise. Maybe tomorrow, when he's out of danger, maybe I can hate you then. Tonight I'm still going to think of you as my boy's savior."

"We'd better…" Simon cleared his throat. "We'd better get back. There might be news."

Simon and Maggie had barely entered Ian's room when Dr. Chip Crosson swooped in behind them. "Good news!" he announced. "Ian's out of surgery. He's in recovery. Doing fine. All his vitals are good. He should be back here in an hour or so."

Maggie gripped Simon's arm and closed her eyes in relief.

"Hi, Mom." Chip crossed over to his mother and kissed her on the cheek. "Where are all your cronies?"

Penny stood up and embraced her son. "They're waiting upstairs in the lobby. I'd better go and give them the news." She walked toward the doorway and slipped behind Simon and Maggie, but didn't leave.

"And who's this?" Chip tousled Bucky's hair.

Bucky yawned and stretched. "Is Ian back?"

"No, but he will be soon." Chip turned to Maggie. "Are you doing okay?"

"Better now that you've brought us good news. Did you have to operate also?"

Chip laughed good-naturedly. "Oh, no. There was no call for a neurosurgeon. I've looked at his scans, though, and they're all good. He did suffer a concussion, but there's no bleeding on the brain. Everything looks fine. Dr. Keogh's an excellent abdominal surgeon. And that's where his worst injuries were. I can't believe there were no broken bones, but he evidently fell on his flashlight and that's what ruptured his spleen and caused the internal bleeding."

Bucky stood and stretched again. "If you didn't have to operate, why did you come all the way here from St. Louis?"

Chip lowered his lanky frame into the chair Bucky had vacated. He took one of her hands in both of his. "Well, Newt, I will impart to you one of the great lessons in life. Now, listen carefully because this will serve you well and avoid countless trials and tribulations. No matter how old you are, when your mama tells you to do something, you'd better do it. Isn't that right, Mama?"

Penny was still standing in the doorway. She didn't answer but her face was beaming.

"Or, in your case, your dad," continued Chip.

"Like in the Ten Commandments?" asked Bucky. "Honor your father and mother?"

Chip counted on his fingers. "Number five. You see? God thought it was such an important lesson for people to learn he made it a commandment. Listen to your father."

"Even when I'm eighty years old?"

"Age doesn't matter. He'll always be your dad."

"I think you'll be a great dad," said Bucky.

Chip's brow furrowed and he stared intently into Bucky's gray eyes. The golden specks in them sparkled in the reflected light of an overhead fixture. He brushed away the hair covering one of her ears and leaned in close to whisper, "I hope so, too." He sat up and looked gravely at her.

Bucky, whose back was to the others in the room, winked and grinned at him.

Chip returned her wink and then looked up at Penny who was still in the open doorway. "Oh, Mom, Dale called after you left and while I was driving down here. He was so excited Dad was taking him to milk Maggie's cow."

Penny put a hand on Maggie's shoulder. "Oh, Maggie, I'm so sorry. I hope your old milk cow survives that experience."

"And gather the eggs," added Chip. "The words were tumbling out of him so much faster than normal, it took me a while to figure out what he was talking about. Oh, hi, Simon. Didn't even notice you standing there. I only heard a brief summary of today's events. I hope you will give me the whole story later."

"Of course," replied Simon. He noticed how the anxiety level in the room had decreased significantly since Chip's arrival. The easy-going, relaxed demeanor of the neurosurgeon had not only calmed their fears but also lifted their spirits.

Chip stood, but still held onto one of Bucky's hands. "I'm going back to recovery to check on Ian. Now, the major-domos here in PICU are pretty adamant about only two visitors at a time in the room. So, Simon, stay here with Maggie, if you will, until Mom's replacement gets down here and then you and Bucky should hide out in the family lounge until Ian gets back. After you see him and convince yourself he's all right, I suggest you go home and come back tomorrow when he'll be more alert." He looked down at Bucky. "I can't believe they haven't run you out already."

"I'm hiding in plain sight," Bucky said, grinning.

Chip smiled and squeezed her hand. "You must be doing a good job of it. Mom, wait up and I'll walk with you to the elevator."

13

MORE CAUSE FOR CONCERN

Early the next morning, Bucky leaned against the doorframe of the main doors to the music room and peeked inside. She was barefoot and still wearing her teal-and-gray-striped pajamas she always wore to bed on Saturday night. Her hair had not seen a brush since she awoke. The sound of someone playing the piano had drawn her downstairs and she was curious to discover the identity of the musician. Her mouth dropped open in surprise when she saw her dad sitting on the bench. There was no music in front of him. He was playing with both hands, and from where she was standing, she could see he even had a foot on one of the pedals.

Simon stopped playing when he saw her. "I'm sorry, Lamb. I didn't mean to wake you."

Bucky stepped into the open doorway. "You never told me you played the piano."

"You didn't ask. You only asked if your mother played." He smiled at her.

"How do you know what notes to play if you don't have any music?"

"The music is in your head, and, for those who are exceptional, it's in your heart. And your fingers translate what is in here," he said, pointing to his head, "and what is in here." He pointed to his heart. "Come over here and I'll show you."

Bucky, still in the doorway, took two tentative steps forward and then stopped, remembering her dream. "No. I can hear you from here."

"But you can't see my hands on the keys. Come here." Simon held out his right hand and cupped his fingers. It was the same gesture the woman in front of the cave made.

"No!" yelled Bucky. She spun around and the woman in the green dress with the long dark hair was standing behind her. Bucky screamed and the woman grabbed her and held her fast.

"Let her go," yelled Simon, propelling himself off the bench.

The woman pointed a finger at Simon and he went flying backwards against the piano, knocking awry the support for the lid which came crashing down.

"Bucky, call Dale for help!" wheezed Simon, grabbing his chest.

Bucky kicked and twisted and bit one of the woman's arms, but the woman only tightened her grip and began to pull her out into the hall. "I can't, Dad! He has to look for the blue eggs."

Simon crawled on his stomach toward the doorway. "What?"

"Willow lays blue eggs!"

A temple bell sounded as Bucky and the woman disappeared from Simon's view.

"Dad!" Bucky called from down the hallway. "Your phone's ringing!"

Simon opened his eyes and struggled to slow his breathing. He was on his stomach. The alarm clock was buzzing next to his bed. He reached out and slapped it off. Turning on his side, he propped himself up on his elbow so he could see the clock. "Sunday," he said aloud. They hadn't arrived home from the hospital until after midnight and he had no intention of going to church this morning, but he had forgotten to turn off the alarm that was automatically set for six-thirty on Sundays. He didn't even bother with an alarm for the other days. He flipped onto his back and stared at the ceiling, trying to recall the dream interrupted by the alarm. And then he remembered. "Oh, my God. Bucky!"

He leapt out of the bed and rushed next door to Bucky's room. Her bed was empty. "Oh, God! How many times do I have to go through this?" He hesitated in the middle of her bedroom, his mind still groggy from being suddenly awakened. Her castle! He hurried through her study room and into her playroom. Bending down at the castle doorway he could see her inside, curled up on the stack of pillows. He went down on his knees and pressed his palms against his thighs.

A temple bell sounded again.

"Dad, your phone's ringing."

The voice came from behind him and he spun around on his knees, almost losing his balance. He put a hand on the floor to catch himself. "Bucky, what are…"

Bucky was standing in the middle of the playroom in her teal and gray pajamas, the same ones she had worn in the dream.

The temple bell continued to ring.

"Aren't you going to answer it?"

"I don't carry my phone in my pajamas. This is... This is still a dream. I... Who's in there?" Simon turned back toward the castle door where now stood the little brown-skinned girl with jet-black hair he had mistaken for Bucky. "Imala?"

"Answer it, Dad."

Simon fumbled in the pocket of his pajama bottoms. He swiped the front of the phone. "Hello?"

But the phone continued to ring even as the voice on the other end of the line spoke.

Simon opened his eyes. The alarm clock next to his bed was going off again. He leaned over and silenced it. He must have hit the snooze button the first time. He sat up abruptly. "Bucky!"

Jumping out of bed, he ran to his daughter's room. Bucky was asleep in her bed but her disheveled covers said she had not slept peacefully during the night. Simon dropped into the chair beside her bed. The first dream had seemed so real and then the second dream had seemed even more real. But was he still dreaming? He considered looking inside the castle, but fear of what he might find kept him by Bucky's bed. After a time, when no other events unfolded, he decided this was real and he was awake. Returning to his room, he discovered he had neglected to fix his coffee before collapsing in bed, so there was no fresh brew to revive him this morning. Maybe just a hot shower would clear his mind.

A half hour later Simon was standing at the back door of the kitchen, eating a piece of toast, and staring out at nothing. Popping the last bite in his mouth he picked up his coffee mug off the counter and headed toward his study. However, when he reached the broad entryway, instead of turning left, he turned in the opposite direction toward the music room. It had been years since he'd played, and when he bought the piano he had no intention of taking it up again, but the dream had tickled something in his brain. He wondered if he retained any of his schoolboy lessons.

He set the cup of coffee next to the music rack. Probably not the best place for it, he chided himself. With his right hand he played the C major scale, remembering the fingering. He added his left hand. He then played a lullaby he recalled from one of his earliest lesson books. He sat back and smiled and took a sip of his coffee. Sissy was right. There needed to be some carpeting and other furniture in the room. In this empty space the sound bounced off the walls. He started to get up from the bench but decided to play another tune, a haunting melody from… He tried to remember for a moment when he had learned it. Setting his cup down, he hesitantly stroked a few keys in succession, then started playing. That led to another song and another.

"Dad?"

Simon had been concentrating on the keyboard and did not notice Bucky standing at the door until she spoke.

He stopped playing and reached for his coffee again. "I'm so sorry, Lamb. I didn't mean to wake you."

"You never told me you played the piano." She was still wearing her pajamas, the teal-and-gray-striped ones.

"You didn't ask. You only asked if your mother played."

Both Simon and Bucky jerked their heads at the same moment.

"That was what you said in my dream," said Bucky.

"*Your* dream?" Simon's hand that was holding the mug trembled and he replaced the cup on the piano. "Was I playing this piano in your dream last night?"

Bucky, looking left and right, started backing up into the hallway,

"It's all right. There's no one here." Simon stood and walked toward her. "Let's go in the kitchen. I'll fix you some breakfast."

Bucky stopped, and when Simon reached her, she wrapped her arms around him. Simon stroked her hair, smoothing some of the tangles. "It's all right. It was just… It was a just a dream."

"But you had the same dream, didn't you, Dad? Are we still dreaming?"

"No, I think we're both awake now. Come on." He took her hands from around his waist and steered her toward the kitchen.

"But, Dad," said Bucky, sitting at the kitchen table while waiting for Simon to finish frying some eggs, "how could I dream about you playing the piano when I didn't know you even knew how?"

Simon put some bacon in the microwave and punched in the time. "I don't know. And you said something about Willow laying blue eggs? What was that all about, I wonder. Isn't Willow Maggie's cow?"

"Yeah, but maybe it was because last night at the hospital Chip said that Dale was excited because he was going to get to gather the eggs for Maggie and help do the milking. You know how sometimes you dream about real things but they're all jumbled? If these dreams are from the Anarianu, maybe they get things mixed up, too."

Simon set a glass on the table in front of Bucky and poured some milk into it. "But why blue eggs?"

"Didn't you know Maggie has a chicken that lays blue eggs?"

"No, I didn't."

"She does. Her other chickens lay white or brown eggs, but she has one brown chicken that always lays a little blue egg. I saw it when I stayed all night there when you were in the hospital."

Simon flipped over the eggs and retrieved the bacon from the microwave. He soaked up the excess grease with a paper towel. "But I didn't know that so how could I have dreamed it?"

"The same way I didn't know you played the piano, I guess. Did you take lessons?"

"For three years. When I was in elementary school, somewhere around your age I guess."

"Why did you stop? Did you get too good?"

"Hardly. I suppose I got interested in other things."

"Like what?"

"Oh, sports. And girls. Mainly girls."

Bucky giggled, ducking her head.

Simon squeezed the back of her neck playfully and made her squirm. "Are you laughing at your old man?"

"Girls," squealed Bucky, drawing the word out into two syllables.

Simon went back to the stove and dished up the eggs and bacon on two plates and took them over to the table and then went back for the two pieces of toast he had set on a smaller plate. He poured some fresh coffee in his cup and joined Bucky at the table and then waited while she said a prayer.

"Dad, shouldn't we be getting ready for church?"

"I thought we'd skip today. Half of your Sunday school ladies are up at the hospital, anyway."

"Skip church? Won't we go to Hell?"

"Where did you get an idea like that? People don't go to Hell for skipping church. I thought we'd leave here about ten and go see Ian."

The phone rang and Simon walked over to where it hung on the wall and answered it. After about fifteen seconds, he said, "Oh, that's good news. We're coming up later this morning, if that's all right." After a few more exchanges with the person on the other end, he replaced the receiver. "That was Maggie." He sat down at his breakfast again. "She said Ian ate breakfast this morning and is in good spirits, but sore. And that he's anxious to see you."

Bucky audibly sighed. "I was so worried about him. He looked awful when they brought him back into the room last night. Will he go home today?"

"Oh, no, I imagine they'll want to keep him for a few days. But they're moving him to a regular room sometime this morning, which means we'll probably have to stop at the information desk and find out where he is. I was hoping to sneak by that spot again."

"Meaning they might not let me in?"

"Don't worry. You'll get to see him."

Father and daughter ate in silence for nearly two minutes before Bucky asked, "Who was that on the phone?"

Simon, startled by her question, said, "I told you. Maggie."

"No, not just now. Your cellphone in our dream."

Simon cleared his throat and took a sip of coffee. "It was... It was only a dream."

"You answered it. Who was there?"

Simon set the cup down. "No one."

"Was it Mom?"

Simon looked away. "Yes." He turned back toward Bucky. "But not the evil woman in your dreams that's trying to kill you. It was your real mom. Well, not your real mom, because it was a dream. But it was the woman I remember."

"What did she say?"

"*Wait.*"

"Wait? That's what she said in your ship dream last summer."

"That's what she always says."

"You've dreamed about her before?"

"Lots of times, especially since we moved here. She always says, *Wait*."

Bucky laid her fork down on her plate. "If Mom comes back, I don't think I could ever love her. I'm sorry, but every time I think about her now, I think about her trying to drown me. I know you say it's not her, but—"

"Bucky, listen to me. First of all, it's been nine years. She's... She's not coming back. And secondly, for the thousandth time, the person you see in your dreams is not her. And... And she wouldn't even look like that today. When I see her in my dreams, I see her as I remember her, and, since you can't remember her, the woman in your dreams is how she looks in all the photos you've seen. Maybe... Maybe it's time I put away all those pictures."

Bucky slid off her chair and went around to Simon and put her arms around his neck. "I'm sorry I upset you. But what do you mean she wouldn't look like that if she came back. Why would she look different?"

"Because she'd be older. Do you look the same as you did nine years ago?"

"No, but I'm a kid. You look the same."

"That's because you see me every day and don't notice the changes. I have some lines in my face that weren't there before and my hair's getting a little gray. And, unfortunately, I'm about ten pounds heavier than I was nine years ago."

Bucky kissed him on the cheek then took her seat again. "I wonder what she wants you to wait for."

Simon shook his head.

"Can we take some water from the spring to Ian? Maybe it will help him get better faster. You said you thought it helped you."

"I believe I said it was probably psychological, but sure, we can take some. I'll find something to put it in. But I'll get it. I don't want you going down there. Now, if you're finished with your breakfast, why don't you go upstairs and get cleaned up."

"May I wear one of my new outfits?"

"Of course. Pick a top with long sleeves you can wear with tights or leggings. We won't be there as long today, but it was rather chilly in that hospital last night."

"The Lukefahr Ladies gave me a get-well card last summer when I was upset and stayed in my castle for several days. Should I make a card for Ian?"

"I think he'd like that. It will be a while yet before we leave so you have time."

Later that morning, at the hospital in Green River, Simon and Bucky stopped at the information counter in the lobby area to find out if Ian had been moved. It was a different woman at the desk on this Sunday morning. She had on large, black-rimmed glasses with thick lenses which made her eyes look bigger than they were. She peered down her nose at Bucky but didn't say anything and then checked her computer screen. "He's in room 212. Oh, there's a note here." She squinted at the monitor then looked back up. "May I ask your names?"

"I'm Simon Carter and this is my daughter Bucky."

"Okay, then. It seems Dr. Crosson has authorized your under-aged daughter to visit this patient. The elevator's around the corner there. Second floor."

Bucky grinned. "Thank you!"

"Thank you," muttered Simon and led Bucky away. When they turned the corner and were out of earshot, he said, "You see, when you have a clean face that's not covered in ketchup, people are much more agreeable."

"Oh, that's not why she didn't argue with you like the other one did. Chip set it up so I could see Ian."

Simon let Bucky push the elevator button.

"That Chip's pretty special, isn't he?" said Simon. "Just like his brother Dale."

"But, you know, it's twice now I've heard him call you *Newt*. I'm not sure I like that."

"Newts are amphibians."

"So?"

"Most amphibians have gills when they're babies."

"And?"

"You said I told you the Anarianu told me that the scars on my back were from gills. So that kind of makes me an amphibian, doesn't it?"

"No. You're not an amphibian."

"Maybe not, because when you were in the hospital, Chip told me he thinks if my scars were from gills they'd be on my neck. And he's a doctor, so he should know. I think he calls me Newt to tease me. It's just his nickname for me."

"You already have a nickname. It's Bucky. I'm going to tell him to stop."

"No, don't do that. I don't mind."

The elevator arrived, and Simon and Bucky waited for two people to exit before stepping inside. When the doors closed and they were alone, Simon squeezed Bucky's hand. "How are you holding up this morning with all the emotional pressure of this place?"

"I'm all right. I'm a tough old bird. That's how Maggie always describes herself."

"But I'm afraid Maggie's got a lot on her plate, right now. So we have to be extra supportive."

They found Ian's room with no trouble and his door was open. The first bed was empty and there was a curtain hiding the second bed, but Maggie was sitting in one of the two chairs by the window and she saw them come in.

"Ian," Maggie said, "you have visitors."

Simon and Bucky peeked around the curtain. Ian was propped up in bed and he smiled broadly when he saw who it was. Simon let go of Bucky's hand and she immediately went to Ian's side while Simon walked around to the other side of the bed. "You look a whole lot better than the last time I saw you," Simon said.

"But I hurt in lots of places. I have a bruise that covers my whole right side and stomach." Ian turned to Bucky. "You wanna see?" He started to reach under the hospital sheet and cotton cover and raise his gown.

Simon laughed and put a hand on Ian's. "I don't think you need to show everyone."

"And they made me get up a while ago and walk, but it really hurt. But the worst was when this mean old nurse made me cough. That hurt really bad and she kept trying to get me to cough deeper and deeper. She said it was to keep my lungs clear."

"They don't want you to lie here and waste away," said Simon. "They want you to get better as quickly as possible so you can go home." Simon turned to Maggie. "Where are your other women?"

"They left about a half hour ago. You probably passed them on the road. Penny's taking them home and then she's going to stop by my place and get me a few things. She's going to rest a while and come back up here this evening."

"Maggie, you're welcome to take my car and go home for a few hours. We can stay here with Ian."

Maggie narrowed her eyes. "I think not." She stood up. "But I will let you walk down the hall with me to the lounge. I can get me something to eat from the vending machines there. They'll probably be bringing him lunch soon. But that way the young'uns can visit without us."

Simon hesitated at the door, but Maggie put a hand on his shoulder. "She'll be all right. Remember what she did yesterday all alone."

After Maggie and Simon left, Bucky reached through the safety rails on the side of the bed and put her hand around Ian's wrist. "I was so scared yesterday when I saw you lying on the ground. I thought for sure you were dead."

"Gram told me you ran all the way back to our house so she could call an ambulance."

"I didn't run *all* the way, but it was a long ways. And I got to ride in a helicopter. So did you, but you were unconscious."

"I wish I could remember that part of it. And your dad let you do all that by yourself?"

"We didn't have much choice. We had to get you help."

"Gram said you and your dad saved my life. But, Bucky, listen to this. I found it. I found the cave."

"Where?"

"Right where I fell. I was backing down the bluff and one of the rocks I stepped on gave way, I guess."

"Ian, there was no cave there."

"There is. It's not a big opening like in the dreams. It might have been at one time, but now the entrance isn't any bigger than the spring opening in The Hollow. Remember last summer when it was dry and you got down on your stomach and looked in it. Something must have happened to this one—a land slide or an earthquake—and covered up the entrance."

"Did you go in it?"

"The opening was too tight for me to squeeze through, but I shone my flashlight in."

"What did you see?"

"Last summer when we played Howard Carter and Lord Carnarvon and the discovery of King Tut's Tomb,

Lord Carnarvon asked that same question almost. And what did Howard Carter say?"

"*Wonderful things*," whispered Bucky. "Did you really?"

"I didn't see any gold. But there's something in there. There was a chest, like a pirate's chest. Maybe there's gold in it."

"Oh, my gosh. You've got to get better real fast so we can go back there."

A shadow crossed Ian's face. "Bucky, I had a dream yesterday or last night. It was a strange dream."

"Was it about the woman in front of the cave?"

Ian shook his head. "I dreamed you told me that your dad was my dad, too."

Bucky released her hold on Ian's wrist and stepped back. "Why would I say something like that?" She thought back to the previous evening. After Ian was brought back to the PICU room and the adults had smothered him with their attention and he had groggily acknowledged them, he fell asleep. Bucky had stepped up to his bedside and touched his hand to reassure herself he was okay. She wanted to feel the tiny spark that always passed between them when they made contact. But she had never revealed the secret Simon had made her promise to keep. Could Ian somehow read her much like she could read her dad or others when she touched them?

"Here," said Bucky, wanting to change the subject. "I brought you something." She had a book bag she had dropped on the floor, but she bent down and pulled out the plastic cup of spring water and took off the lid. "It's from the spring at my house. If it's really a healing spring, maybe it will help you get better."

"Am I supposed to drink it?"

"My dad told me the springs in the Ozarks are polluted but it looks clean. And he drank some of it when he got hurt. But you could just put some on your bruises. There's a bandage on the cut on your head and I suppose there's one on your stomach where they did the surgery, but you could maybe dip your fingers in it and kind of pat around the bandages."

Ian took a few sips from the cup and then did as Bucky had suggested. "How long does it take to work?"

Bucky had turned around and faced the other way when he pulled up his gown to apply a few drops to his abdomen. She turned back to him. "I don't know. It probably takes a while to get into your system." She bent down to the bag again. "Here. I made you a card. I didn't have any glitter heart stickers like Madyson. That's supposed to be a mastodon on the front."

Ian opened the card.

"And that's the museum inside."

"You're a really good artist." Ian closed the card and stood it up on his bedside table next to the cup of spring water. "Are you going to tell your dad about the cave?"

Bucky considered the question. "I think I have to. You shouldn't go back there by yourself and, despite what he let me do yesterday, he's not going to let me go back there with you without him. And I don't know that I'd want to anyway. I saw her up on that bluff, Ian. In real life. The woman from my dreams. The one who's trying to kill me. The one who looks like my mom. I don't think you slipped. I think she pushed you."

"But why would she try to kill me?"

Bucky shrugged. "I don't know. Why's she trying to kill me?"

"Don't you know?" A man's voice spoke from the doorway. "Isn't it obvious?"

Bucky yanked back the curtain at the sound of the familiar voice and then froze in place when she saw who stood there. Reverend Bergmann.

"They explained it all to me when they brought me into their realm," said the preacher. "I was caught up to the Third Heaven and they showed me I was right all along. My only mistake was thinking it was just the man and the girl-child who are an abomination." His eyes narrowed as he focused on Ian. "I now know it's you, too." He stepped toward them.

Ian grabbed the remote control lying on his pillow and frantically pushed the call button over and over.

Bucky recovered her initial fright and screamed, "Leave us alone!"

An orderly responded faster to Bucky's screams than the call button and appeared in the doorway as Bergmann reached the foot of Ian's bed. Bucky took up a defensive position in front of Ian. "Help! He's trying to kill us."

"Sir, please step away," said the orderly.

The preacher immediately assumed a humble stance and turned toward the orderly who was now backed up by two nurses in the doorway. "I'm Reverend Carl Bergmann. You've probably seen me here visiting my church members. I didn't mean to frighten these children. We're all from down around Turn Back and I heard the lad was injured and came to see how he was."

"He's a liar!" yelled Bucky.

Reverend Bergmann continued in a syrupy voice. "I think I caught them behaving in an inappropriate manner and now they're trying to cover it up." He turned to look at Bucky. "You children had better be careful."

Simon and Maggie had been walking back from the lounge when they saw the rush of people head toward Ian's room. Simon left Maggie and sprinted for the door, shoving his way through the two nurses. "You!" He spat out the word. "Get out of my son's— Get out of this room! How dare you show your face here."

Reverend Bergmann held out his hands, palms up. "Obviously, everyone's a little upset by the tragedy suffered by this young boy. Of course, I'll leave." He turned and put a hand on the end of Ian's bed. "You just get better and mind my words."

Everyone moved aside and let the preacher pass through the doorway where he brushed up against Maggie who had just arrived.

"Carl Bergmann. What are you doing here? What have you done?"

"Nothing. Yet." He smiled and ambled down the hallway.

The nurses moved in beside Ian and checked to make sure he was all right. Bucky backed out of the way and Simon put his arms around her. "He didn't hurt us, Dad, but he meant to. Both of us."

"I never dreamed we'd have to worry about him here," said Maggie, watching Ian closely as the nurses hovered over him.

One of the nurses moved the bedside tray aside, knocking over the cup of spring water onto Bucky's card. The orderly grabbed some paper towels from the bathroom and mopped up the water and then left. After the nurses were sure Ian was okay, they also left the room. Maggie took their place and squeezed Ian's hand.

"It's Sunday morning," said Simon. "Why isn't Bergmann in church?"

"I think their services start pretty early," Maggie said, ruffling Ian's blond curls. "You can bet I'm not leaving you alone again while we're here."

"I can't do anything today because it's Sunday," Simon said, "but I think it's time I check on taking out a protection order against him or filing a harassment suit or...or something. I should have done that a couple of months ago."

"Oh, he'll fight that and he's got people behind him."

"And I... And since I have some notoriety, I'm afraid something like that will make the news, and I really... I really don't want that."

Simon still clasped Bucky in his arms but her back was to him. Sensing his agitation, she tilted her head back and looked up at him. "Aare you all right?"

He smiled down at her and nodded. He looked back at Maggie. "When my wife left nine years ago and no one could find her, there were all sorts of rumors and stories in the news that I had something to do with her disappearance. I'm afraid that will all come up again when word gets out I'm taking him to court. I thought after his experience last week at the walk he would have changed his attitude. I don't know what happened to him in the colored cloud, but I was hoping they'd set him straight."

Bucky twisted around in his grasp. "He said something about being caught up in the Third Heaven and they explained everything to him and that he was right all along. I thought it was the Anarianu who did that to him."

Simon blew out a long puff of air. "So did I. Maybe the Guardians are not as benevolent as we thought. Or... I don't know. Something's not right."

14

STORIES FROM THE PAST

Ian was released to go home on Wednesday afternoon. Maggie had stayed with him the whole time, sleeping in the recliner in the room. Several friends and people from church visited, some staying for only a few minutes and some camping in for several hours to keep her company. As Ian's condition improved he became increasingly restless and lost some of the good-natured disposition he had always possessed. Simon and Bucky made the ninety-mile round-trip drive to visit him every day but they stayed for only an hour each time.

Simon couldn't help noting Maggie's attitude toward him had changed after his revelation to her on Saturday evening about his relationship with Ian. She was congenial but there was now a wall between them. When Simon took Bucky to see Ian on Wednesday morning and found out the boy was probably going home that afternoon, Simon offered to take them back to Turn Back since Maggie's truck was still at her house. Maggie refused, replying curtly that Penny would drive them.

"When will you be able to go back to school?" asked Bucky.

Ian frowned and shrugged. "The doctor said I have to stay home all next week."

"And restrict his activity," added Maggie. "That means lots of lying around on the couch. You have to give those tears inside your stomach time to heal."

"It wasn't my stomach, Gram. It was my pancreas and liver and spleen. Don't you know anything?"

"Ian!" said Simon. "Don't talk to your grandmother like that."

"Thank you, Simon," said Maggie, "but I can do my own scolding."

Simon bit his lower lip and looked away.

"What will you do about school?" asked Bucky. She was standing beside his bed, but it was raised so high this morning her chin barely topped the side safety rails.

"Somebody will probably bring me all the stuff I miss so I don't get too far behind."

"Maybe I could come over and help you with it." Bucky raised her eyebrows and looked over at her dad who was sitting in the chair next to Maggie.

"I don't need your help," replied Ian, turning away from her. "I just want to go home."

"I only meant it'd be more fun working together."

When Ian didn't respond, Maggie said, "I think he needs to rest for a while."

"I'm tired of resting," said Ian.

Simon stood. "We'd better be going."

"But we just got here," protested Bucky.

"Why don't you call tomorrow morning," suggested Maggie to Bucky. "He'll probably be in a better mood after he gets home today."

"No I won't be, if all I get to do is lay on the couch."

"It's *lie* on the couch," corrected Bucky. "I have my French lesson with Sadie Jane Woods tomorrow morning. Can I call in the afternoon?"

Simon put a hand on the top of her head. "It's *may* I, since you're doing the correcting now."

"Why's everyone concerned with the way everyone else talks?" demanded Ian. "I can talk any way I want."

"Maggie," said Simon, taking Bucky's hand to leave, "please let me know if there's anything you need or anything I can do. Well, except the milking. I've never milked a cow and I don't think your Willow would appreciate my efforts."

"I thought you could do anything," muttered Ian.

"He'd probably be the best milker in the whole world once he learned how," said Bucky.

Simon squeezed Bucky's hand. "Come on. Let's go. Goodbye, Maggie."

Someone wheeled in a food service cart, loaded with covered lunch trays, through the door.

"Bye, Ian," said Bucky but he didn't reply to her.

"Goodbye, Ian," said Simon. "This should be the last hospital meal you'll have. I'll bet you'll be glad to get back to your gram's cooking."

Once they were out in the hall, Bucky didn't say anything until they were several doors away from Ian's room. "Why was he all glumpy?"

"Glumpy? Oh, gloomy and grumpy." Simon said, remembering Bucky's made-up word he had discovered was an actual word, although little used, meaning sullen. "He's confined to a small room, most of the time stuck in bed and he's probably still in some pain. If you were in a similar situation, I guarantee you also would be out of sorts."

The elevator doors opened as soon as Bucky pushed the button. "But Maggie didn't have an operation and she's not been very friendly, either, this whole time."

They were the only two in the elevator as they rode down to the first floor. "She's tired of being cooped up here, too. She's not been home since Saturday. And she's under a lot of stress right now."

Bucky waited until they were in the parking lot to continue the conversation. "But sometimes Maggie acts like she's mad at you."

Simon cleared his throat but didn't answer until they were standing by their car. "Maggie's known since Saturday night I'm Ian's biological father."

"And she's upset about that?"

"Of course she's upset. For many reasons. It means… It means a lot of things, but basically it means she has no descendants. Ian was her only one. He was the only child of an only child of her only child."

"But he's not dead. He's still her great-grandson, isn't he?"

"But not by blood. You know how much she loves genealogy and figuring out how everyone around here is related. It was a shock to learn it the way she did. That's what I told you might happen and why I wanted to wait and find a way to…to soften the blow."

He opened the back door for Bucky to get in but she stayed where she was. "But, Dad, for almost all my life, you didn't think I was related by blood to you, but you told me that didn't matter, that you loved me anyway. You told me even if I was your real daughter it would be impossible for you to love me any more than you already did." Simon had released his hold on her when he opened the door, but she took his left hand in both of hers. "Were you lying when you said that?"

"I… No, I wasn't lying. Of course, Maggie still loves Ian, but it's… It's going to take some time for her to accept this new relationship and to accept that her next-door neighbor is responsible. And I imagine she's wondering how she's going to break the news to Ian."

Bucky released her Dad's hand and dropped her gaze to the pavement. "Ian already knows."

"What? I told you not to—"

"I don't think I told him."

"What do you mean you don't *think* you told him?" Simon put his hand under her chin. "Look at me!"

"When we went to see him on Sunday morning, he said he'd had a dream where I told him. But I don't remember having a dream like that. And when he told me, I acted like I didn't know anything about it, because I promised you I wouldn't tell. But—" She waggled her index finger at Simon. "You came busting through the door when you saw Reverend Bergmann in the room and you yelled, 'get out of my *son's* room.' Ian would have had to have been deaf not to have heard you."

Simon stepped back and shook his head. "So for the past three days, we've all four been in that room, and we all knew, but we haven't spoken of it. No wonder the tension's been so thick. Come on. Get in the car. We need to find something to eat and then I have a stop to make before we head home."

From the backseat, Bucky expressed surprise when, after lunch, Simon pulled into the parking lot of the Green River Powersports Center. "What are we doing here?"

"I ordered a new toy and it's supposed to be ready today. Oh, I think that might be it." Simon drove up near the front of the building and parked near a trailer on which sat a recreational vehicle Bucky would learn was called a utility task vehicle, commonly referred to as a UTV or a side-by-side. Simon got out and went around and opened Bucky's door and then walked with her over to the trailer. A man came out of the showroom and joined them there.

Bucky remained quiet while the man and her dad discussed the vehicle and trailer and then she went with them inside to his office and they talked some more. Simon filled out some paperwork and wrote a check for the man. When they all went back outside, someone had already pulled the trailer with the UTV around and had hitched it to the back of Simon's car. The man and Simon shook hands and then Simon opened the back door of the car for Bucky.

Once they were back out on the highway, Bucky finally broke her silence. "Is this new toy for me?"

Simon laughed. "This is my toy, but you can ride in it."

"Dads don't have toys."

"Of course they do. Ours are usually just more expensive."

"Dad, do you have more money than you know what to do with?"

Simon glanced at his daughter in the back seat. "Where did you hear that?"

"At one of the prayer walks."

"You seem to overhear a lot of things at those walks."

"Probably because I'm a kid, people forget I'm there or maybe they think I don't understand what they're talking about. So, do you?"

"I wish. The reason I bought this utility vehicle is because I thought it would come in handy when we want to visit the mastodon site or The Hollow. We wouldn't have to walk. And I am anxious to further investigate that area where Ian had his accident and I certainly don't want to go all that way again on foot. I looked on some satellite images and there might be an old logging road or trail that comes off the gravel road that goes in front of our place and then goes on back through the woods. If that pile of stones is the remains of our furnace from back then, the cave we stayed in must be near there."

"Ian said he found the cave."

Simon glanced back at her again. "Where? When?"

"Right where he fell. I didn't want to tell you until he was better and could go there with us."

"But there was nothing there."

"He said it wasn't big like in our dreams. In fact he couldn't even get through the opening."

"So why does he think it's the cave from the dreams?"

Bucky didn't answer his question, but instead asked, "Who owns that land?"

"From the maps, it appears the land on the south side of the creek is National Forest. We own the property on the north side. God, I had no idea how much land I was getting when I bought this place. I think we rival Central Park. Maybe more." Simon was quiet for a minute before asking again, "So, if the opening was too small for Ian to get in, why does he think it's the right cave?"

"He looked in with his flashlight."

"And?"

"He saw a pirate's chest."

"A pirate's chest," repeated Simon. "Do you think Ian was being just a little imaginative about what he saw?"

"There could have been pirates around here, couldn't there?"

"Highly unlikely."

"But you said there couldn't be Minoans or Hittites around here, either, and yet—" Bucky shrugged and held out her hands, "here you are."

"Oh, my God! *Nāhhus!*" Simon swerved to the right and onto the broad shoulder of the four-lane highway. The person in the car behind them laid on his horn as he passed. Simon's car with the trailer behind it traveled almost a hundred yards before he could bring it to a full stop. He slammed it into park and slumped over the steering wheel.

"Dad!" screamed Bucky.

Simon sat up but his hands were trembling and still gripping the steering wheel. "Are... Are... Are you all right, L-Lamb," he stammered.

Bucky unlocked her seat belt and leaned forward over the seat. "What's wrong?"

"I... I... I'm sorry, Imala."

"I'm Bucky."

"Of course you are. I... I'm sorry, Bucky."

"What happened?"

"Oh, my God. I could have killed you."

"You almost killed both of us. What does *nāhhus* mean?"

"What?"

"*Nāhhus*. It's what you said when you ran off the road."

"It's...uh... It's what I saw. It means *ship*. It was right in front of us. And you were swept overboard. No, not you. Imala."

"You told me this morning at breakfast you were better the last few days. That the visions had stopped. Did I cause it when I said *Hittite*?"

Simon took his hands off the wheel. His breathing had returned to normal. "No, of course not. I'm sorry I scared you. I'm all right now."

Bucky laid her hand on Simon's shoulder. "Dad, did Imala die when she fell off the ship?"

"There was a terrible storm. The ship rolled almost all the way over. And she was on the deck and I couldn't reach her and she went overboard. She was only a

toddler. She couldn't swim. But the mast broke and…
And I guess the rigging got tangled around something
because the mast fell but it was still attached to the ship.
And after the storm cleared, there was little Imala in the
sea, clinging to the end of the mast just above the water
line."

"She was alive?"

"Oh, yes! I don't know how. It was a miracle."

"So the story has a happy ending?"

"A very happy ending." Simon nodded his head a
couple of times. "I think we'd better go. I'm all right. Sit
back down and buckle up."

Bucky, still leaning over the seat, put her arms
around Simon's neck. "Maybe I should drive."

"Not likely. Sit down. I'll try to keep it on the road
this time."

From where she was sitting, Bucky could see the right
side of her dad's face and she watched it the whole way
home for any sign he might be shifting into another
vision, but there were no further incidents. She didn't
speak again until they turned off just past Garton and
were on the final leg of their journey back to Turn Back.
"Dad, even though they decided to only have the prayer
walks on the first Saturday of the month, since it's
Wednesday can't we go into town this evening and walk
anyway?"

"No," Simon answered quickly. "I imagine there will
be people there—well, there seems to be people there
every day—but maybe more tonight because some might
not have received word the walks had been changed. But

people know you are one of the leaders, and if you're there, that would somehow make it official. We don't want them thinking that. As Pastor Bradley said last week, they are welcome to walk anytime, but the only officially sanctioned walks, so to speak, are going to be on the first Saturday until spring."

Bucky sighed audibly. "I could wear a disguise so no one would recognize me."

"Saturday is only a couple of days away. You can wait until then."

"But then it will be a whole month until the next one."

"You'll survive."

It was early afternoon when they arrived in Turn Back and there were at least a hundred people walking in and around the square. Simon slowed as he approached the Singing Spring. He lowered the two windows on the driver's side, but the car's engine as well as the noise from a few other vehicles drowned out the ethereal sound emanating from the fountain. He pulled off to the left of the roadway next to the sidewalk that circled the park and turned off the motor. Bucky unfastened her seat belt and scooted across the seat to put her face up to the opened window. The glass wouldn't roll completely down or she would have stuck out her whole head and half her body.

Simon twisted around so he could see her. The spring and the sound it made were mesmerizing, but they always seemed to have a special effect on her. After two minutes, Simon started the engine.

Bucky sat back down and fastened her seatbelt. "I wish the spring was close enough to our house that we could look out and see it and hear it anytime we wanted to."

"Perhaps, then, we'd grow too accustomed to it and not even notice it."

They drove the short distance up the gravel road to the Mansion.

"What's that?" Bucky pointed to something tucked between the ornate black iron gates that blocked the entrance to their driveway.

A newspaper fluttered to the ground as the gates opened when Simon pushed the remote control. He parked the car and stepped out to retrieve the paper. "There's a note on here from Penny," he said as he got back into the car and read it aloud, "'Thought you'd want to see this article.'" He took off the sticky note and looked at the headline. *Local Pastor Caught up in Heavenly Cloud.* The subhead read *Thousands Witness the Prayer Walk Miracle.* "That's a little different slant than the major news agencies put on it," Simon said aloud.

"Can I read it?"

"May I," corrected Simon. "Not until I've looked at it. It might not be appropriate for you."

Bucky huffed and crossed her arms. "When am I ever going to be old enough to read anything I want and look at any movie or TV show I want and do anything I want."

"You'll be there in a few years," replied Simon, as he started driving down the lane toward the Mansion.

He parked the car and trailer by the front steps and got out and opened the back car door for Bucky and escorted her up the steps. As he unlocked the front door and ushered her inside, he said, "With all that's been going on the past few days, I know you are woefully behind in your lessons. So I want you to get down to work this afternoon. I'm going to be outside, playing with my new toy."

"That's not fair." Bucky pouted.

"Later, when I'm comfortable with it, we'll take it for a ride."

"Aren't you woefully behind in your work, too?"

Simon smiled. "Yes, but I can write after the sun goes down. I need to check out the UTV while it's light out. Now, upstairs with you."

Simon watched while she dragged herself up the broad staircase, and then went into his study to deposit the newspaper. He opened the packet which contained the papers and informational material for his UTV, took out the operating manual and went back outside.

That night when Simon went into Bucky's room to tell her goodnight, he found her sitting cross-legged in the middle of her bed. Her pink unicorn gown survived the soakings and the numerous blood-stain-removal efforts Simon had put it through after her episode two weeks earlier. It had emerged almost stain-free and still sparkled when the light hit it just right. Simon sat down in the chair beside her bed and casually propped his left ankle on his right knee. He waited for her to initiate the conversation but she just sat there and stared at him. He finally spoke first. "You were quiet at supper and earlier when we rode down to the mastodon site. I guess you don't share my enthusiasm for my new glorified golf cart or have you run out of things to say?"

Bucky tucked her chin. "I did something wrong."

"You did tell Ian I am his father."

She jerked her head up. "No. I told you he said he dreamed it. I didn't lie." She put her head back down.

"So? Look at me and tell me what you did."

She raised her head. "I read the newspaper article about Reverend Bergmann."

Simon broke eye contact and turned his head. "I wish you hadn't done that."

"He said the angels told him to stop us, although he didn't actually use our names. I'm just a kid, but it was pretty clear to me who he was talking about. He still thinks we're doing Satan's work, but you told me what I said when I visited them and it didn't sound at all like the same place. And is that why the Anarianu are called Guardians? Are they guardian angels? I'm all confused, Dad."

Simon bowed his head. He studied one of his fingernails for a moment, trying to sort through his own theories to find a satisfactory explanation for her. "I don't know for sure, of course, but here's what I think." He raised his head and looked at her. "Is everyone on earth one big, happy family?"

Bucky narrowed her eyes. "No. That's why we have wars."

"But we've been referring to the Anarianu as one set of beings, as a single group. They might be more advanced than we are and able to manipulate people's dreams and make massive engraved stones appear overnight, but what if they, too, are divided into factions who don't always get along, who disagree with each other about the course of events? Remember what I told you I saw when I was with Ian by the stream? Even though it was daylight, there were green flickers of light, but there were also red ones."

Do you think they are both Anarianu, but like different races? Like white people and black people?"

"This is only speculation," continued Simon, "but I don't think we're looking at racial differences. In their own dimension, maybe they look the same, but maybe they manifest in different colors in our dimension because they have different needs or goals or ideologies. Two weeks ago when they spoke to me in the Spring Room, it was filled with mostly green ones and they spoke of the *Discordants.* As I told you it was hard to make much sense of what they were saying, but what if the green Anarianu get their energy from us, especially during the prayer walks when everyone is in harmony and feeling uplifted and singing the hymns. You know how the Park Stone mentions singing and songs?"

Bucky nodded.

"The Hollow Stone does, too, and you told me there was music when you visited them. So music is an important part of their realm. But the fact they referred to the others as Discordants…" Simon paused. "Do you know what a dissonant chord is?"

Bucky shook her head.

"That's why you need to take piano lessons. In music there are consonant and dissonant intervals. To the western ear, consonance refers to intervals that are pleasant and harmonious. Dissonance is chords that are inharmonious and jarring and harsh and unpleasant. Dissonant chords are also called *discordants*. So what if the Discordant Anarianu draw their energy from disharmony, from antagonism, from chaos. When Reverend Bergmann stirs up trouble and incites anger, maybe that energy is feeding the Discordants."

Bucky chewed on her bottom lip, thinking, before she responded. "So last week when that colored cloud took him, he wasn't in Heaven like he said he was? He was with the Discordants, the red Anarianu?"

"That's my theory."

"So why did he call them angels?"

"Maybe they looked like angels to him. We interpret experiences against our frame of reference. The Anarianu—the green ones—told me it was the Discordants who make us dream those nightmares in which you think your mother is trying to harm you."

"But why are they doing that? Why pick on me?"

Simon shook his head. "Maybe they get energy from the terror those dreams generate in you, but why they are targeting you, I don't know."

Bucky put her elbows on her knees and cupped her chin in her hands. "Are you going to punish me?"

"Why? Oh, for reading the paper? I should but I'm not."

"Thank you. I think you were probably right. It wasn't appropriate. But, Dad, he called you Etakkama and you say you are or were Etakkama. So what I don't understand is when you talk about the Hittite writing on the Hollow Stone, you say the guy who wrote it was not very good and that made it hard to translate. But if Etakkama was the Hittite who came here and he was the one who wrote on the stone, aren't you saying that you were not very good?"

Simon laughed. "I'm sure old Etakkama could speak Hittite better than I can today, but I think I know more about written Hittite than he did. And I know why. My father—Etakkama's father—forced me to go to scribal school because, well, he was a scribe, and it could be a good occupation if you landed a position in the royal court or with some rich merchant. But it was not what I wanted to do. I wanted to travel. I wanted to see the world. A few years of schooling was all I could take, so I… I ran away from home."

"Did you ever go back to see your parents again?"

Simon shook his head slowly. "No," he said quietly.

"They must have missed you."

"They had other sons…and daughters. And now, I think it's time you went to sleep."

"One more. When you told me the story today of Imala falling off the ship, you didn't tell me the whole story, did you?"

"What?"

"She didn't fall off the ship in the storm, did she?"

Simon closed his eyes and looked away. "The…uh… When I was here before and we finally got the ship repaired and headed home, the others didn't want me bringing Imala back home with me."

"Why?"

"She was different. Her mother was a Native American for one thing and remember she, like you, changed overnight. Sailors are a superstitious lot, and so when that first terrible storm broke, they blamed her for it. They… They ripped her from my arms and they… They threw her into the raging sea. I… I thought she…"

Bucky sat up on her knees and leaned over to put a hand on Simon's arm. "It's all right, Dad. The part about the happy ending was true, wasn't it?"

"Yes." Simon's eyes were filled with tears. "Yes it was. And it's a good thing, too, because I—because Etakkama—had no other children. And so if you and I are really descended from him, it's through Imala."

Bucky sat back and then crawled under her covers.

Simon tucked her in. "I'm actually enjoying writing what I can remember about him and his adventures. I think it will make a good book. It will certainly be a radical departure from what I've written in the past. But, unfortunately, I have to first finish the mystery I'm currently writing."

"But Matt Healey probably won't like your Etakkama book, will he?"

"If he doesn't, I'll just find another publisher. Good night, Lamb." Simon kissed her forehead. "I love you."

"I love you, too, Dad. I hope Maggie lets me see Ian tomorrow afternoon."

"I hope so, too. Good night."

15

COMING TO AN UNDERSTANDING

Bucky knocked on the front door of Maggie Fletcher's house. When she and Simon had visited last summer, there was only the screen door. The sun was shining this afternoon, but the weather had turned cold here in the first week of October, and the solid wood door was shut. From within the house came Ian's voice, "Gram, someone's at the door."

"Now, remember," said Simon, holding open the screen door, "we don't want to stay too long. Ian's recuperating and needs his rest."

"And he might still be out of sorts and really not want me here at all."

Simon ran his fingers through her hair, pulling it back on one side behind her ear. "I'm sure that now he's home, he's in a better mood."

There was the click of a lock and then the door opened to reveal Maggie. "Come in. I didn't hear your car. Oh, what's that?" Maggie looked beyond them at the utility vehicle parked in her driveway.

"It's my dad's new toy," answered Bucky. "It's a UTV and it's electric, so it doesn't make much noise."

"I want to see," called Ian from the couch.

"You stay where you are," said Maggie. "You can see later." She stood aside to allow Simon and Bucky into the living room and then locked the door behind them. "I've lived here all my life and never locked my doors until this summer when all those yahoos started nosing around looking for those mastodons and ships. And after that incident with Carl Bergmann in the hospital, I'm going to be even more cautious."

Bucky crossed over to Ian while Maggie was talking. "I brought you a couple of my books. One's on dinosaurs and one's about King Arthur. Oh, my gosh!" She gawked at the stack of books on the floor next to Ian. "Are those from your school?"

"Yeah." Ian was propped up on several pillows with a light blanket over him. "Mrs. Lannigan brought them over this morning while the class was at music. It's all the stuff I've missed so far this week plus what I'll miss next week."

"Wow, that's a lot." Bucky plopped down on the floor and looked through the workbooks and textbooks. There were also some library books. She turned around to the coffee table which was littered with cards Ian's classmates had made. One with glitter and hearts on the front caught her attention. "I bet I know who this is from without even looking." She held it up in front of Ian.

Ian tried to grab it from her but she pulled it away and brought it up to her face and inhaled. "Oooh, she even used a strawberry-scented marker for the hearts."

"I told you she's not my girlfriend," growled Ian.

Bucky laughed. "I'm just teasing you." She opened the card and read it to herself. "She even signed it Madyson Koeller Fletcher. You might not like her, but she loves you." She exaggerated the word *loves*.

Maggie and Simon watched their exchange and then Maggie said, "You kids visit for a while. Simon and I are going to be in the garden."

"What?" asked Simon.

"You said if I needed anything to let you know. Well, it's going to freeze tonight and I still have some things I need to bring in. How are you at picking green beans?"

"I…uh…I guess we'll find out." He didn't follow Maggie when she headed into the dining room.

Maggie came back and grabbed his arm. "Come on. They'll be all right."

After Maggie and her dad were out the back door, Bucky cleared a spot on the sturdy coffee table for her to sit. "Does it still hurt?"

"Yeah, especially when I move too quickly or when I stand up. I have to go back next week to get the stitches out. Why did your dad get a UTV? I would have got a four-wheeler ATV."

"I don't know what the difference is, but he bought this so we don't have to walk to The Hollow or the mastodon site. And tomorrow he wants to go back to where you had your accident. He thinks he can get there with it on an old logging road."

"You didn't tell him about the cave, did you? Cause I want to go there with you when you explore it."

"I told him, but if the opening is as small as you said, we won't be able to get inside without doing a lot of digging or moving those rocks. He said it's probably not a pirate's chest that you saw."

"How would he know?"

Bucky shrugged. "He knows an awful lot."

Neither spoke for a moment and then Bucky asked, "Do you want to do some school work?"

"I don't want to do anything."

"You just can't lie there and do nothing. You'll turn into a toad. I had a French lesson this morning with Sadie Jane Woods. Do you want me to teach you some French?"

"No, I'm never going to France."

"My dad's teaching me a few Hittite words. Yesterday I learned *nāhhus* means ship."

Ian frowned and toyed with the edge of the blanket. "About your dad."

"What about him?"

"You know. What I said you told me in my dream. That your dad was my dad."

Bucky bit her lower lip before replying. "I think that was just a dream."

"No, it wasn't. I heard Gram and Mrs. Crosson talking when they thought I was asleep. It's true, isn't it?"

Bucky clenched her fists and looked away and then turned back to him. "Don't be silly. How could we have the same father? We're almost the same age and you were born in Chicago and I was born in New York."

"I can tell when you're lying, Bucky. Those little gold flecks in your eyes sort of dance around."

Bucky pressed her fists against her eyelids. "Stop it, Ian. Just stop talking about it."

"Oh, my God! You're not going to cry, are you? Please don't cry, Bucky." Ian leaned toward her, reaching out with his left hand, and winced at the pain in his abdomen.

Bucky, her eyes still covered, fought to keep the tears at bay by taking some deep breaths, and then said, "I promised. I promised my Dad I wouldn't tell."

"It's all right. Please, Bucky, don't cry. I don't think I could stand to watch you suffer like that again. Here." Grimacing, he twisted and picked up a book from the top of the stack on the floor next to him. "Let's do some math."

A long minute crept by before Bucky took her hands away from her eyes and onto her lap. "I'm sorry, Ian. I want to tell you. I want to tell you so bad, but I promised I wouldn't."

"Promises are important. And I don't want to get you in any trouble. But I don't think it would count as telling if you just answered yes or no. But I already know the answer is yes."

"Can you really tell I'm lying by looking at my eyes, or did you just say that?"

"I noticed it way back last summer."

Bucky grabbed his wrist with one hand. The tiny electrical pulse was there. It was that little spark she had desperately felt for when he was lying injured on the ground. "I can tell when you're lying, too."

He pried her fingers from around his wrist. "Then that kind of makes it hard for either of us to keep secrets, doesn't it?"

"Let's make a pact," said Bucky. "From this day forth, we'll always be truthful with each other. Pinky swear?"

"Sure." Ian and Bucky locked the little fingers of their right hands together. "I, Ian Michael Fletcher, do solemnly swear I will always speak the truth to you, and the only secrets I keep from you will be only those good kinds like about Christmas presents and stuff. Cross my heart and hope to die, stick a needle in my eye."

"I, Bucilla Rose Carter—" Ian giggled and Bucky swatted his head with her other hand. "Don't laugh at my name." She finished the oath, repeating Ian's words.

"We should shake on it, too." Ian pulled his hand away and spit on his palm and held it out to Bucky. She did the same and they clasped hands.

Bucky wiped her hand on her leggings.

"Now will you tell me what you know about how we came to have the same father?"

Bucky shared with him the story Simon had told her. When she finished, she added, "And he was going to tell you when you were older because he thought it would upset you too much now. He knew how much you loved your father and he didn't want to take that away from you."

Ian was quiet and turned his head toward the back of the couch. "I never even knew my real father—or mother—since I was still a baby when they died. I only know them from the stories Gram has told me. But wait." He turned back toward Bucky. "That means I'm not really a Fletcher, am I? I'm a Carter. But Gram's a Fletcher. So I'm not really her great-grandson."

"Of course you are. I spent my whole life believing my dad was not my real dad, by blood, anyway. It was only after we got the DNA results back a few weeks ago that we found out we really are related. But for all those years, he was still my dad. I think family is who takes care of us and loves us."

Ian nodded but didn't say anything.

"And," continued Bucky, "I think it's pretty cool we're not just best friends, but now we're brother and sister."

"How come you inherited all the smarts?"

"Oh, Ian, you're smart, too."

"Do I have to come live with you?"

"I don't think your gram would let you do that."

"Good. Because, well, you know, your dad is kind of strict."

"He probably wouldn't be as strict with you because you're a boy."

"Do you think I look like him?"

Bucky bobbed her head up and down. "I've seen pictures of him when he was your age."

"What am I supposed to call him? You call Gram by her first name but I've always called him Mr. Carter."

Bucky's face brightened. "I just thought of something. Since you're my brother that makes your gram my gram, too."

"No, it doesn't."

"But I never had a grandmother of any kind."

"Well, you can't have mine."

"I'm sharing my dad with you."

"That's not the same."

"I think it is. I'm going to ask Maggie."

"Ask me what?" Maggie called from the kitchen. Neither child had heard Maggie and Simon come in through the back door. Maggie appeared at the dining room doorway. "What do you need to know?"

"Uh…" Bucky hesitated.

Ian spoke up. "She thinks chocolate milk comes from brown cows. I told her she was crazy."

"How about you not use the word *crazy*, and just say she's misinformed," said Maggie.

Simon came in behind Maggie and shot Bucky a quizzical look.

Ian looked at Bucky and winked. The way the couch was positioned, the adults could not see the gesture. "You're misinformed," he said, "and crazy."

"I need to wash my hands," said Simon.

"You can use the sink in the kitchen. There's a hand towel next to it."

"Did you get all the things in from the garden?" asked Bucky.

"Your father dug the last of the sweet potatoes and I picked what remained of the beans and peppers and tomatoes. Let's see, today's Thursday. I think tomorrow I'll can some green tomato relish. Maybe your dad will let you come down and help." Maggie sat down in the easy chair and fanned herself with a magazine. "It's cold out there today, but I worked up a sweat."

"Don't count on me eating any of that old relish," said Ian, scowling. "That stuff's nasty and it'll stink up the house when you're cooking it."

"The ladies at church who don't have their own gardens think it's a treat when I give them a jar for Christmas," replied Maggie.

"They probably dump it out as soon as you leave."

Simon joined them in the living room but remained standing. "Did you two make any progress on Ian's assignments?"

Neither Ian nor Bucky answered.

"Hmm?" questioned Simon.

"No," said Bucky. "We just talked."

"Yeah," said Ian, still petulant. "We talked about how people have lied to me my whole life about who my father was." He looked at Maggie. "And you're the biggest, fattest liar of all."

"Ian!" hissed Bucky, abruptly standing.

"Bucky!" scolded Simon, accusingly.

"I didn't tell him, Dad. Honest. He already knew."

Maggie pushed herself up out of the chair. "Simon, I think you and Bucky should leave."

"No!" shouted Ian. "I don't want Bucky to leave." He sat up and winced and lay back again against pillows. "She's the only one I can trust anymore."

Maggie went to the couch and, bending down, laid her open hand on Ian's head. "Lamb, you need to rest."

Ian swatted her hand away. "Leave me alone! I'm not your lamb. I'm not anybody."

Maggie straightened and looked at Simon. Tears glistened in her eyes. Bucky had crossed over to her dad and was holding his hand.

"Maggie…uh…" Simon hesitated, unsure of his next move. "Why don't… Uh…Bucky tells me you have a chicken that lays blue eggs. Do you suppose there is one in the hen house this afternoon that you and Bucky can look for? I'd like to talk with Ian."

"No!" screamed Ian, struggling to sit up again. "Don't leave me alone with him."

"Ian," scolded Maggie. "Calm down or you're going to pull out your stitches. Bucky, let's you and me go collect eggs." She took Bucky's free hand.

"Dad?" Bucky looked up at Simon who nodded and released his hold on her.

When he heard the back door slam, Simon went over to the coffee table where Bucky had been sitting and lowered himself onto it.

Ian pulled one of his pillows over his face. "I don't have to talk to you."

"No, but you have to listen to me and I like to look at the person to whom I'm speaking." He took the pillow from Ian's face and placed it on the boy's stomach. Ian crossed his arms over his chest. "Ian, I don't know how much you know or what Bucky has told you, but I want you to hear the truth from me." Simon told him the story of what happened in Chicago that night eleven years ago and the two different times Ian's mother, Kara, had contacted him.

"But, Ian, no one has lied to you your whole life. Your grandmother had no idea. She was not aware of any of this. And when I moved here last spring, I didn't know who you were. I didn't find out until less than a month ago when Chip Crosson got the DNA results back. And your grandmother only found out on Saturday and the only reason she learned the truth then was because you needed more blood during your surgery."

"But why didn't you tell me when you found out or why didn't Gram tell me?" It was the first time Ian had spoken since Simon began.

"I guess we both knew your reaction would be what it has been. You'd feel hurt and confused and betrayed and you'd probably lash out at everyone and everything. I was hoping to wait until you were older and maybe you'd be able to understand better how and why these things happen. And your grandmother certainly didn't want to tell you while you were recuperating from your injuries. I wish… I wish Bucky hadn't told you."

"She didn't. Well, she kind of did, but it was in a dream, so it really wasn't her. So don't be mad at her. Bucky said you don't think the chest in the cave is a pirate's chest."

Simon shook his head. Here he was focusing on this life-altering revelation and Ian completely changed the subject, as Bucky did so often. "I think it is unlikely."

"Why? You haven't even seen it."

"Pirates made their living by attacking and pillaging other ships and coastal settlements. They would not find much to plunder along the St. Francis River, would they? And I can't imagine it being too old if it is wooden. Most of the caves in Missouri are damp and the wood most likely would rot and disintegrate in a matter of years."

"So you think I lied about what I saw?"

"Of course not. I'm anxious to see it for myself."

"But Bucky said you're going without me."

"Only to try and find the opening you described. It sounds as if it might take some excavation to gain entry and that can certainly wait until you're able to participate."

"It might not even be the right cave since it doesn't look like the one in the dreams and I'm still dreaming about it."

"So am I, but remember, the mastodon dreams and the ship dreams continued for a while after we discovered the bone bed and the Hollow Stone." Simon smiled. "Or, rather, after you discovered them."

For the first time since Simon sat down to talk to him, the corners of Ian's mouth turned up, but the expression was short-lived and he became somber again. "So what's all this mean?"

Simon raised his eyebrows.

"I mean about you being my dad. Is everything going to change?"

Simon hesitated before answering. "I... I'm going to take my cues from you. Nothing has to change. I can still be your next-door neighbor, the father of your best friend and—"

Ian interrupted, "But she's not just my best friend now. She's my sister."

"There is that."

"So will you explain to her we can't get married?"

"Married?"

"Bucky told me last summer she was planning to marry me some day. You need to tell her that since she's my sister, that's never going to happen. It was never going to happen anyway."

Simon suppressed a smile. "I think she's figured that out for herself."

"Do I have to change my last name to Carter?"

"Of course not. I think the Fletchers would be proud to have a young man such as you continue their family name."

"So where does my dad—my real dad—come into all this? Well, I guess you're my real dad, but what about my dad that I thought was my dad?"

"Your father is still your father and always will be. I'm not taking anything away from him. He loved you. And because he was Maggie's grandson, I can only imagine he would have been a wonderful father to you had he lived. So you must never consider him anything other than your father."

"But what about you?"

"As I said a minute ago, that's up to you. I will always take an interest in your life, your education, your career choice." He leaned forward. "And who you marry. But I will only intervene or interfere if and when you want me to. And our relationship might change over time. Right now this is overwhelming for you, and you wish I'd back off and leave you alone, and that's all right. But later on, you might need my advice or expertise on something, and that's the important thing I want you to take away from this conversation. I will always be here for you, Ian. Always. Okay?"

Ian frowned.

"Okay?"

Ian nodded.

"Good." Simon stood up from the coffee table and turned away and then pivoted back. "I need to amend my last statement." He resumed his seat. "I am going to interfere on something I think is important. I was…appalled a few minutes ago at the way you spoke to your grandmother and I also witnessed that same behavior a few times while you were in the hospital. I don't allow Bucky to speak to me in that manner and I will not allow you to do so, either. For all these years, Maggie has been both mother and father to you. She loves you more than life itself and she would do anything in her power for you. You know that, don't you?"

There was no response from Ian except he tucked his chin.

"Don't you?" Simon repeated.

"Yes, sir," Ian muttered.

"You owe her respect. I know you are in pain right now, but she is hurting, too. So, you don't have to do it while we're here—you can wait until we're gone—but I want you to apologize to her for the way you've been acting and the hurtful things you've said to her. And that's for starters. For the time you're confined here at home, until you go back to school, I want you to tell her 'thank you' at least once a day for something. It can be something as simple as bringing you a glass of water or maybe changing the dressing on your incision. But every day I want you to remember to say 'thank you' to her. Capisce?"

"What does *capisce* mean?"

"Got it?"

"But you won't be here. How will you know?"

"I'll know."

"Because Gram will tell you."

"No, your grandmother need never know we've had this conversation. I'll just know. Will you do that?"

Ian nodded. "Are you really Etakkama?"

"Yes."

"That makes you really old."

"I've been around the block a few times. Or, maybe, here in Turn Back, I should say I've gone to the creek and back a few times."

"Or," suggested Ian, "you've circled around the square more than once."

"Oh, good analogy," said Simon. "You're pretty sharp."

"I am?"

Simon squeezed Ian's leg which was under the cover and stood. "Of course you are."

The back door opened and Bucky pranced into the living room. She held the blue egg up for Simon. "See, I told you it was blue. And Maggie said I could have this one."

Maggie came into the room, holding an open egg carton. "I said you can have that one plus eleven more brown ones. Here, put it in here with the others so you don't break it on the way home."

"Which is where we need to be headed," said Simon. "Thank you, Maggie, for the eggs and for showing me how to dig sweet potatoes."

"Are you sure you don't want some of the green beans?"

"I…uh…wouldn't know what to do with them," replied Simon.

Maggie shook her head. "Bucky, I think you'd better come back tomorrow and start your cooking lessons. You need to know how to make something that doesn't come in a box or a can."

A few minutes later Simon and Bucky were riding in Simon's new vehicle up the gravel road toward their private lane. "You know, Dad, if Sadie Jane Woods teaches me French, and Maggie teaches me to cook, and Sissy teaches me to play the piano, pretty soon all of the Lukefahr Ladies will be my teachers. Maybe one of them can teach me to sew and another one to dance and one of the others to paint and—"

"Wait a minute. I thought you weren't going to take piano lessons."

"I've been thinking about it. Maybe it *was* just a bad dream. And you can play and I want to learn to do everything you can do."

"That's nice," said Simon, putting his arm around her and steering with one hand. She was sitting in the seat next to him which she was never allowed to do in the car.

"Besides," continued Bucky, "Ian has a music class at school and I don't want him learning anything without me." She was quiet for a minute while Simon got out and opened the front gate, drove a few feet in and then climbed out to close it. When he came back, Bucky said, "You know, Dad, when you and Maggie were outside and it was just Ian and me—should that be 'Ian and I'?"

"Yes."

"When Ian and I were talking, he was mostly like his old self. He didn't act like he did in the hospital or when he talked awful to Maggie."

"I told you he would be upset if he found out…" Simon cleared his throat. "If he found out I was his biological father. And I think that is exactly what happened."

"What did you talk about when you sent me outside with Maggie to get the eggs?"

"I believe that conversation should stay private between Ian and me."

"Shouldn't that be 'Ian and I'?"

"No."

Bucky crossed her arms and frown. "I'll never get that straight."

Simon laughed. "Yes, you will."

They continued toward the Mansion. Although the peak of fall color was still a week away, the leaves on the trees shrouding the lane overhead were rapidly changing from green to yellow and red and orange and brown. Bucky caught a falling leaf as it drifted in through the open side of the UTV. She traced a finger over the veins of the yellow leaf with red splotches.

"Lamb, I don't think I've expressed my appreciation of how well you have handled this whole new relationship between you and Ian and Ian and me. After that first day, you've seemed to have accepted it. I keep expecting behavior from you somewhat like Ian's."

She continued to look at the leaf as she answered. "I don't like sharing you, but if Mom hadn't left, I would probably have a whole bunch of brothers and sisters by now."

"Probably not a whole bunch," said Simon. "Maybe one or two."

"And this way, getting a brother who's already grown, I don't have to put up with dirty diapers or crying all the time. And Ian's not going to take my things or break all my stuff like a bratty brother would do. In fact, if he's not even going to live with us, it's not going to be hardly any different than it was before." She looked up at Simon next to her. "He asked me what he should call you."

"Oh? We didn't talk about that. What did you tell him?"

"I told him I think I'll start calling Maggie *Gram*. She is kind of like my grandmother now, isn't she?"

Simon shook his head. "Technically, no."

Bucky's face fell. "Oh. That's what he said. That's what we were talking about when you came in. Dad, I know chocolate milk doesn't come from brown cows. He made that up so you wouldn't know what we were really talking about."

"Oh, good. I was afraid my little city girl was *misinformed*."

"He thinks you're strict."

"He probably really thinks I'm strict after our little talk."

"Dad, since it's going to freeze tonight, shouldn't we bring in our geraniums we got from church at Pentecost?" Simon and Bucky had brought home two little pots of red geraniums in May and had planted them in a concrete planter on the back porch outside the kitchen. It had been Bucky's job to care for them all summer.

"Lots of time people don't overwinter geraniums. They let them die and buy new ones the next summer."

"But I read about them. They're perennials, but they can't stand the cold. We could bring them inside."

"If you want to. I think there's a pot in one of the sheds you can transfer them to. I'll get it for you. There's that small room with the bank of windows off of the dining room. You could put them in there so they'll get light. They probably don't need too much water over the winter, but don't forget about them."

"Thank you. I'd hate to see them die."

16

CAVES, COOKIES, TEARS, AND GREEN TOMATO RELISH

Bucky looked up at her dad's face. He was smiling and his eyes were half-closed. "Dad," she whispered, "are you remembering?" Simon and Bucky were sitting in the grass about twenty feet from the tumbled stones Simon claimed were the thirty-five-hundred-year-old remains of a smelting furnace.

"Yes."

Early on this Friday morning, Simon had set out with Bucky in the utility vehicle to see if they could get close to the clearing and the site of Ian's accident. Simon had downloaded some satellite images of the area and had compared those with the LIDAR scans Dr. Jennifer Brockman had made in July. What he had identified as an old logging road through the woods was in much worse condition than the one which led to The Hollow. Father and daughter had to get out numerous times and clear the trail of limbs. Fallen trees twice forced them to make a new path. They did finally get within a hundred yards of the clearing before they had to abandon the UTV and continue on foot.

"I'm remembering, too," said Bucky.

Simon glanced down at his daughter. "What are you remembering?"

"When we discovered this place last Saturday when we were looking for Ian, you told me it was what was left of the furnace the Minoans used to melt—"

"Smelt," corrected Simon.

"That the Minoans used to smelt the minerals you found. But you said one of them was iron. I think you were wrong."

"About?"

"The iron. I remember reading the Iron Age began with the collapse of the Bronze Age, but that was 1200 BC. And I've heard you say lots of times you were here, or rather Etakkama was here, with the Minoans thirty-five hundred years ago. That would be more like 1500 BC. That's three hundred years before iron was invented."

Simon squeezed Bucky's knee. "Oh, how did I get such a smart daughter? You're right, except the events as presented in your textbooks are…simplistic. Real life is much more complicated. First of all, let me correct your last sentence. Iron wasn't *invented*. The technique for iron *smelting* was invented."

Simon continued. "When your books or Internet articles state the Iron Age began in 1200 BC, well, everyone didn't wake up one morning and suddenly start using iron for weapons and armor and plowshares. It was a gradual process, spanning centuries. And the Hittites were one of the first of the ancient civilizations to discover the process. There was iron smelting on a small scale for many years before they learned to produce it in large quantities."

"So Etakkama knew how?"

"Not exactly. He was training as a scribe, remember? But you know what you told me recently about sometimes you overhear things because people think you're a child and they overlook you?"

Bucky nodded.

"Etakkama's father was a scribe in the royal courts during the reign of Hantili I. That's one reason why I can approximately date when I was here before. Hantili I was king of the Hittites from around 1526-1496 BC. Etakkama's father would often take me with him to various sites where he worked as a scribe, including the smelters."

"Dad," interrupted Bucky, "you mix up a lot whether you're talking about you or Etakkama or when you were Etakkama."

Simon chuckled. "I'm sorry. I will try to speak of him in third person. Since iron was already known to be superior to bronze, it was a closely-guarded state secret. But no one thought twice of allowing a child to view the smelting process. Etakkama's father would never have been allowed to leave the country because of the things he had seen and had written about in the state documents. But when teen-aged Etakkama slipped out of the kingdom, no one suspected he was carrying in his head state secrets he had seen as a child.

"And you never saw your father again?"

"Now you're doing it."

"Etakkama never saw his father again?"

Simon shook his head. "No. But I don't think he missed him. His father had been rather cruel. However, he did miss his mother. And, as I told you earlier, he left behind brothers and sisters. He was especially close to one of his brothers whom he had unsuccessfully tried to persuade to leave with him."

"That's sad."

"To continue the story, when Etakkama reached Crete, he eventually joined an expedition that was sailing to a faraway place today called the British Isles in search of tin, which had become a scarce commodity and was needed to make bronze. Those are the ships that were blown off course and ended up at the mouth of the Mississippi and eventually here."

"It's a wonder Etakkama survived all of that."

"Many of those he sailed with did not. There were enough miners and smiths in the expedition who survived that wherever the ships stopped, they would search for evidence of any mineral resources. When we became stranded here for months because of the damage to our one remaining ship, we had plenty of time for the miners to search for minerals and ores they could smelt. But it was Etakkama who introduced to them how to build a furnace and instructed them in the process that was capable of smelting iron."

"Did it work?"

Simon laughed. "You would ask that. No, it didn't work well. For the iron anyway. It did work for the lead, though. It was much more efficient than the process they knew. But those miners and smiths who survived long enough to reach home took Etakkama's idea with them."

Bucky's face brightened when she realized the implication. "Dad! You—I mean Etakkama—was responsible for spreading the state secrets of the Hittites to the Minoans."

Simon turned to her and winked. "Maybe. Or maybe they figured it out on their own."

"Ian would love to hear this story. But he should hear it from you because you would tell it better."

Simon grunted as he got to his feet.

Bucky sprang up and said, "But if this furnace was used for smelting, shouldn't there be some evidence which would have shown up on Dr. Brockman's scans?"

"If she had used the GPR, the ground-penetrating radar, here, I believe something would have shown up. There must be copious amounts of slag around here just beneath the surface. Even a metal detector would help."

"Remember? I asked you for a metal detector last summer and you told me I was too young."

"And my answer remains the same," said Simon.

Bucky crossed her arms. "What does *copious* mean?"

"Abundant, numerous, many. Whatever lay on the surface all those millennia ago, probably lies a few feet under today. Thirty-five hundred years is a long time. I suspect there has been a lot of runoff from the hills there and there." Simon pointed to the trees to the north and east of the clearing.

"There's been copious amounts of runoff," said Bucky.

Simon pulled the baseball cap she was wearing down over her eyes.

"Do you think Etakkama ever brought Imala here to see the furnace when she was a baby?"

"Oh, I know he did. I—I mean he—shaped a hollow log into something rather like a modern car seat or baby carrier. And he would prop it up on the ground, oh…" Simon turned in a circle and then pointed to one corner of the clearing. "Over there in the morning and on the opposite side in the afternoon so the sun wouldn't be in her eyes. That way he could keep an eye on her while he worked. Of course, we—I mean they—were here over the winter so some days the weather was brutal. Remember, the Minoans were from an island in the Mediterranean and most of them weren't at all used to that sort of weather. Some of the miners were from the mountainous areas of Crete where it gets colder and snows so they coped well. Etakkama was from what is today central Turkey so he was accustomed to harsh winters."

"So what did he do with Imala when the weather was bad?"

"If it was really bad, we didn't work outside. We stayed in the cave. But if it was just cold, he would bundle her up in furs." For a moment, Simon stood still, staring at the spot he had pointed to.

"You're remembering a lot."

Bucky's words broke his reverie and he replied. "Yes, I am." He put an arm around her shoulders. "It's going to make a good book, don't you think? Come on, let's see if we can find Ian's cave."

When they reached the stream below the clearing, Simon made Bucky remain on the path while he scrambled over the rocks on the bluff above the spot where they had found Ian. His foot slipped once and Bucky put her fist in her mouth to avoid screaming. Her mind flashed images of him meeting the same fate as Ian and she thought of different scenarios of how she would respond and summon help again. She had studied the way he operated the UTV and thought she would be able to handle it. That would certainly be the fastest way to get back to the Mansion and to a phone.

"I found it!" Simon finally called down to her. "I think it is, anyway. Ian was right. There's no way in at the moment."

"Can you see the pirate's chest that's not a pirate's chest?"

"Give me a minute."

Bucky could see her father's shoes sticking out from where he was sprawled on his stomach on a small ledge, but the boulders obscured her view of the rest of him and the opening he had discovered. "Be careful, Dad." She chewed on her lower lip and looked around for signs of the woman in the green dress or for any appearance of the Anarianu. It seemed she and her father were here alone today.

Two long minutes crept by before Bucky heard scrabbling sounds above her.

Simon's head popped out from behind one of the large rocks. "There's something in there." Most of his body came into view as he turned toward the bluff face. "But I don't know how we're going to enlarge the opening. We might have to call in some experts. Let me get some pictures."

That afternoon Simon did something which astonished Bucky. He dropped her off at Maggie's house and left her there by herself, telling her he would return for her in two hours. Just the week before, after she had to run alone through the woods to get help for Ian, Simon had exclaimed he was never again letting her out of his sight. Bucky stood on the front porch with her eyes wide and her mouth open and watched as he backed his toy vehicle out of Maggie's driveway and headed up the gravel road toward the Mansion. The front door opening behind her startled her, and she turned to see Maggie.

"Where's your father going?" Maggie stepped out onto the porch.

"He said he'd be back to pick me up in a couple of hours."

"I suppose he has things to do," said Maggie. "Come on in." Maggie ushered her into the living room and closed and locked the door.

"Can— May I talk to Ian for a while before you teach me how to cook?" The house had a sharp, metallic aroma to it today.

A smile broke across Maggie's face. "Of course."

After Maggie had disappeared through the dining room, Bucky cleared a spot on the coffee table so she could tell Ian, still lying on the couch, about their trip to the cave. When she was finished, she added, "And he said he was going to talk to Dr. Smallin who might have an idea or know someone who has had experience with that sort of thing, so we can make the entrance bigger. Of course, like the other discoveries, he wants to keep this a secret as long as possible until we can explore the cave."

Ian had been following her re-telling of the morning's adventures with great interest. "But why doesn't it look like the cave in the dreams?"

"Dad thinks there must have been an earthquake or something that caused the collapse of the front part of the cave to make it look like it does now and not like he remembers from…well, you know."

"From when he was here as Etakkama," said Ian.

Bucky nodded. "But the cave wasn't all we looked at this morning. There's a clearing near there—it's where the helicopters landed last Saturday to rescue you—and there are some big rocks piled up. He says they're left over from that other time, too, when the Minoans and Etakkama were here. Listen, I'll tell you the story." Bucky recounted her father's tale of how Etakkama left his homeland and ended up in present-day southeast Missouri and how he taught the Minoans how to build a better furnace to smelt the minerals they found nearby. "I wish you could have heard him tell it. I guess that's why he's a writer. He's a good storyteller."

"Why didn't he stay here with you today?"

Bucky shrugged.

"Maybe he doesn't want to see me," Ian said, tucking his chin. "I wasn't very nice to him yesterday."

Bucky scoffed. "Oh, he understands. He probably thinks you don't want to see him."

Ian shook his head. "I don't know. It's kind of confusing."

"Do you still hurt?"

"Yeah," said Ian, "especially when I sit up or stand up and walk. It's getting better, but I'm going to miss tomorrow's prayer walk. I asked Gram if she'd get me a wheelchair and then you could push me around the square, but she didn't go for that idea."

"She's going to miss it, too, isn't she?"

"She's sure not going to let me stay here by myself. She's treating me more like your dad treats you."

"Like *our* dad treats me. You mean overprotective? She's just worried about you." Bucky glanced at the dining room doorway. "I need to go in the kitchen. She's going to teach me how to cook."

Ian clasped Bucky's forearm when she tried to stand. "No, don't go. I have loads of school work to do."

"Yesterday you acted like you didn't want my help."

"Today's different. Please stay."

"But I told your gram that I would help her make the green tomato relish."

"Don't you smell it? She already made it this morning."

"Oh." Bucky frowned. "Maybe she's going to teach me how to make something else." She pried Ian's fingers from around her wrist and stood and started toward the kitchen.

"Please, Bucky."

"What's all the noise in here?" Maggie appeared in the dining room doorway.

"Ian said you already made the green tomato relish. May I see it?"

"Of course." Maggie put an arm around her shoulder and escorted her to the kitchen.

"Gram!" called Ian from the living room. "Tell her I need help with my homework."

Bucky stopped in the middle of the kitchen while Maggie opened a drawer and took out some utensils. From a cupboard she pulled down a mixing bowl. The jars of green tomato relish stood on one of the counters.

"We can start your cooking lesson with something simple," said Maggie.

"Bucky!" yelled Ian.

"Maybe I should stay with Ian. But I do want to learn to cook." Bucky turned in the direction of the living room and then swiveled back to face Maggie. "I don't know what to do." Without warning, tears welled up in Bucky's eyes. She squeezed shut her eyes as tightly as she could and balled her hands into fists, her arms stiff at her sides.

"Bucky, what's wrong? Oh, my Lord," said Maggie. "You're not having one of those fits here in my kitchen, are you?"

"What's the matter, Gram?" Ian shouted.

Bucky continued in her trance, trying to keep the tears at bay. She was aware of the others talking but couldn't afford to listen to them. She had to concentrate.

"Lamb, I think she's having one of her spells." Maggie started to put a hand on Bucky's shoulder but recoiled, unsure whether or not she should touch the young girl when she was in this state.

Ian threw off the quilt that was over his legs. He winced as he sat up and again as he stood. Gritting his teeth he made it to the dining room and used the back of the chairs for support as he passed through to the kitchen. He had been walking, per doctor's orders, several times a day, but at a much slower pace than his current one. He reached Bucky and threw one of his arms around her shoulders and the other across her chest and drew her to him.

"Lamb, be careful," cautioned Maggie. "Don't pull your stitches out."

"You have to hold her, Gram," whispered Ian. "It's the only thing you can do to help her." Ian flashed back to that dreadful night in the woods when he had sat beside a screaming, wailing Bucky and held her until she blacked out. Tears pooled in his own eyes now as he remembered how he had thought she was dead as she lay there on the ground amidst those ancient oaks. She wasn't crying now but he could feel her breathing rapidly, and then gradually the breaths grew slower.

Bucky's eyes popped open. She turned her head so quickly toward Ian's face, their noses touched before they both jerked back their heads. "What are you doing?"

"I'm holding you. It's what you told me to do that night when you... When you..."

"I'm all right now." Bucky ducked out of Ian's grasp, careful not to bump against him. "I almost cried but I didn't."

Maggie put her hands on both of Bucky's shoulders. "Are you sure you're all right? Should I call your father?"

"No! Please don't tell him. It was... It was nothing."

"It didn't look like nothing," said Maggie. "You scared the living daylights out of me. What brought that on?"

Bucky shrugged. "I don't know. I guess I wanted to do two things at the same time, but I could only do one, and I didn't know which to choose."

"Lamb, you don't need to make that decision. There'll be plenty of time for cooking lessons when Ian goes back to school. These days while he's home you should spend with him. Besides, folks have brought over enough food to feed an army. I really don't need to cook anything for a while."

"But I didn't want to hurt your feelings like I hurt Sissy's."

"Sissy Casteel? You mean about the piano lessons?"

Bucky nodded. "I was rude to her. Dad told me to apologize last Sunday, but we didn't go to church, so I guess I'll have to tell her I'm sorry tomorrow at the prayer walk."

Maggie scoffed. "You mind your dad, but I don't think Sissy was offended. Confused maybe. I think she really does want to give you piano lessons, and she thought you wanted to learn."

"It's…complicated," said Bucky.

"Ian," said Maggie, "since you're already up, do you think you could sit here with Bucky at the kitchen table and have some cookies and milk? Ruby brought over two different kinds, but she tends to bake them on the long side, so they need some good dunking."

Bucky pulled out a chair for Ian and then she sat opposite him at the white wooden kitchen table with spindly legs. "That tomato relish in those jars looks pretty, Maggie. What does it taste like?"

Maggie set the plastic container of cookies on the table and brought over two empty glasses. She retrieved a gallon jar of milk from the refrigerator. "I'd let you try some but I really don't think it goes with cookies. Maxine brought over enough roast beef and potatoes and carrots to last Ian and me for a week. I'll make up two plates to send home for you and your dad for supper tonight and put in a little half pint of the relish so you can try it."

Ian had already nibbled on one of the crisp chocolate chip cookies before Maggie poured his glass of milk. "Thank you," he said, plunging the rest of the cookie into his glass. He let it soak in the milk for a few seconds before popping the whole thing in his mouth. Milk dribbled down from one corner of his mouth but he wiped it on the sleeve of his T-shirt. "You're right, Gram. These cookies do need a good dunking."

"But they taste good," said Bucky, narrowing her eyes as she studied Ian. His attitude toward her when she almost cried and now his words to Maggie were like the old Ian. "Tell Ruby thank you for them," she said to Maggie. "I'll also try to remember to tell her tomorrow at the walk. I'm sorry you won't be there, Maggie. I've always walked beside you. It won't be the same."

At that moment, one of the canning jars of relish made a popping noise and Bucky sat up straight.

Maggie laughed. "That sound means the lid sealed. After they've cooled I'll show you one so you can see the dimple in the lid." Maggie picked up one of the cookies. "You be sure and say a prayer for the two of us at the walk."

Bucky and Ian spent the next hour and a half working together on the various assignments Ian's teacher had brought for him. The time flew by quickly until a beeping sound from the front yard startled both of them.

"Oh, I think that's Dad," said Bucky, standing up. Her right leg had gone to sleep from where she had been sitting on it next to Ian's couch. She shook it, trying to rid it of the pins-and-needles feeling. "That thing he bought has a really funny-sounding horn." She hopped on her left foot over to the picture window. "Yep, that's him."

Maggie came from the kitchen to the living room doorway. "Is he not going to come inside this time either?"

Bucky looked back out the window as the horn beeped again. "Doesn't look like it. He's just sitting there."

"Let me get the food I fixed for you," said Maggie, heading back through the dining room toward the kitchen. She returned with a plastic bag with the logo on it of Turn Back's small grocery store. "In the big container in here there's plenty of meat and potatoes and carrots for the two of you and there are two cottage cheese containers. One has a gelatin fruit salad in it and the other one has gravy. It's heavy but I double-bagged it. Can you carry that?"

"Sure." Bucky slipped on her jacket she had thrown across the arm of the couch when she arrived. She took the bag from Maggie.

"And here." Maggie pulled a small jar of the green tomato relish from the pocket of her apron. "Put this in your pocket." She slipped the jar into one of the pockets of Bucky's jacket. "Now don't forget it's there. Let me get the door for you."

The horn beeped again when Maggie was opening the door.

"Thank you, Maggie, for the food. And please don't tell Dad I almost cried."

"You come back tomorrow afternoon with news of how the prayer walk went."

Bucky was using both hands to clutch the bag, but she turned and nodded at Ian. "Bye, Ian."

"Bye," he replied. "See you tomorrow. Thanks for your help on my work."

"I hope she made you look up the answers for yourself." Maggie held the door open for Bucky. "Be careful going down the steps."

Bucky turned to see Maggie wave at Simon, but when she turned back she saw Simon's head was down and he did not return the gesture. The door closed behind her. She shifted the bag to one hand and held onto the railing as she picked her way down the steps. Approaching the UTV, she sensed something was wrong. The closer she got the more intense the feeling became. Her breathing quickened. She started to set the bulging plastic bag with its containers of food on the seat so she could climb in, but as she did so, a surge of emotions struck her with such force she fell backwards.

Bucky had never been on a real boat, but the pounding of the waves in the ship dreams last summer gave her a frame of reference to later describe what she was feeling now. Wave after wave of emotions, emanating from her father, slammed against her.

"Bucky!" she heard Simon yell as he jumped from the vehicle and came around to her. The direction of the invisible emotional assault changed as his position changed. When he grabbed her wrist and yanked her to her feet, his touch was almost too overwhelming. She recoiled and pulled away.

"Dad! What's wrong?"

"Get in! Nothing's wrong." Simon bent to pick up the bag. Two of the containers had rolled free, but their lids had stayed on so none of the contents had spilled. "Get in," he repeated and returned to the driver's seat.

The waves subsided enough for Bucky to crawl into her seat, but she could still feel them rolling off of her father. For all of her life she had been aware that being in contact with Simon allowed her also to be in touch with his emotions. As the years passed she had learned to sort them, to categorize them so she could interpret what he was feeling. It's how she could always tell when he was lying. Touching him intensified her reception of his state of being, but by just being near him she could usually feel his emotions. It was what she had tried to describe to him about being at the hospital or at the prayer walks or at the open house at school or every Sunday at church. Whenever she was around lots of people she was unconsciously picking up all of their emotions at once and she had learned to build a mental wall to prevent herself from being overwhelmed by them. But never in all of her ten years had she experienced what she was now feeling coming from her father.

Simon started the motor and backed out of the driveway. Bucky was almost scared to look at him, afraid the raging wave would strike her again. She stole a glance. His eyes were red and the skin around them was dark and puffy. The rest of his face was splotchy. A slight tremor shook both of his hands on the steering wheel.

"What's wrong, Dad?"

"I told you *nothing*. "I'm just… I… I'll be all right."

"I've never seen you like this."

"I… I had a phone call. I… I'll tell you later. Just… Just let me be for a while."

"Did someone die?"

"No. No one's dead. Just let it go for a few minutes. Please, Bucky." Simon straightened and appeared to regain some of his usual controlled demeanor. He looked down at the plastic sack on the seat between them. "What's this?"

Bucky took her cue from him and tried to act normal. "Maggie sent home supper for us. It's roast beef and potatoes and carrots. And look." She pulled out the jar of tomato relish from her pocket. "Isn't this pretty? But I don't know how it tastes. Maybe like green ketchup. What do you think?"

"I guess... I guess we'll find out. Did you thank her?"

"Yes. I told her we'll miss her and Ian at the walk tomorrow."

"Oh, the walk."

Bucky was afraid from his tone he was going to say they weren't going to the walk but he didn't.

Simon had left the front gate open and after he drove through, he stopped and started to get out.

"I'll close it for you." Bucky hopped out. Only one side was opened and she pulled it shut and lowered the latch that locked it. She climbed back in the UTV and neither she nor Simon spoke again until he pulled up in front of the steps leading to the front door of the Mansion.

"While you were gone," Simon said after he had stopped, "Ron Crosson brought out that little portable tent shed to shelter this thing. See it over there at the side of the garage? We ran an extension cord so I could plug it in to charge the batteries." He twisted in the seat to face Bucky. "Now, I want you to go to your room and stay there until I call you for supper."

"But—"

"No *buts*. I'm having a hard time dealing with this, and I need you to give me space. Please, Lamb." He set the plastic bag upright on the seat. "Does all this need to go into the refrigerator?"

Bucky nodded. "Except this." She handed him the half pint of the green tomato relish. "It's sealed. See the little depression in the lid. It can stay out until we've opened it."

Simon's eyes had filled with tears but he smiled. "All right. So study, read, do whatever you want until supper." His voice quivered. "Just stay in your room please. I... I have to work this out."

Bucky could still sense the emotions coming from him but she leaned over and kissed him on the cheek. There was a slight twinge of electrical energy, similar to when she and Ian touched. "I love you."

"I love you, too, Lamb. More than you'll ever know."

17

THIS CHANGES EVERYTHING

Bucky waited the rest of the afternoon to hear her father say supper was ready but the call never came. She imagined different scenarios of what might have happened to cause Simon's strange behavior. He said no one had died but what else could have transpired to trigger the overwhelming tide of emotions? Her father was usually so calm and reserved, that is, until the past few weeks when he began experiencing the visions of past lives.

Maybe, Bucky thought, he had seen another vison, this one with terrible horrors. Perhaps he had committed an awful crime, even murdered someone when he had lived as someone else. But he had said it was a phone call. Who could have called?

Maybe Chip Crosson had given him awful news. Maybe Simon was dying. Or maybe Chip had made some new DNA discoveries. Maybe Bucky was not really his daughter, after all. Or maybe Chip had discovered yet another child belonging to her dad. On the day Simon had first confessed to her that Ian was his son, he had denied having any other children. But he had laughed when he said *no*. He had once explained to her people often laughed when they were uncomfortable or unsure about a situation, that it released the tension. She herself had been upset that day and now she couldn't remember if she had felt at the time that Simon was lying.

Maybe the Moyers had called concerning the translation of the Hollow Stone. There might have been something dire in the Minoan inscription Jan Moyer was trying to translate, or maybe Nick Moyer and Simon had a big argument about something in the Hittite message that they were translating.

Bucky tried to think of all the people who her father usually communicated with by phone. Simon had said he was going to contact Dr. Smallin this afternoon about the cave. Bucky tried to imagine what the mastodon paleontologist might have told him that would be upsetting. Simon was often on the phone with his long-time friend and publisher, Matt Healey. She had overheard her father arguing with Matt sometimes, but never anything that would upset him like this.

Bucky had retreated to her playroom castle after Simon had ordered her to stay in her room. After she had exhausted all the different reasons to explain his state of mind, she had begun reading. There were no electric lights inside the fortress, but there was a battery-powered fixture on the wall above where she liked to sit on the pillows and read. It had been light outside when she had first settled into the cushiony pillows, so she had not needed it. Now she touched it with her hand to turn it on. She could tell through the narrow castle windows the playroom was growing darker. It was past time for supper.

She finally heard a knock on her bedroom door, but by the time she had marked her book and unwound herself from the contorted position in which she had been reading and exited the castle and crossed through the study room and through her bedroom to the door to the hallway, there was no one there. A tray of food sat on the floor. "Dad?" She stepped over the tray into the hallway and walked over to the stairs, but there was no sign of him. She reviewed some of the possible explanations she had come up with earlier, but she was no closer to understanding why he was acting so strangely.

Plopping down on the floor, she decided to sit right there in the doorway and eat, scooting back a little so that technically she was in her room and wouldn't get in trouble for disobeying him. She didn't want to miss him if he returned.

Simon had warmed the roast beef and potatoes and carrots Maggie had sent home with her and they partially filled a plate. Off to the side was a small bowl of gravy which she poured over the chunks of potatoes after breaking them up with her fork. Two tiny bowls held ketchup and the green tomato relish. She was glad he had included the ketchup because her first bite of the relish on the roast beef was not to her liking. It looked prettier than it tasted. Another small bowl held a serving of the cold, jiggly gelatin salad. There must have been some of Ruby's cookies in the bag, also, because Simon had put two of them on her tray.

Bucky was upset over Simon, but she was also hungry, so she ate everything he had brought on the tray, except for the relish, and drank the tall glass of milk. She sat cross-legged in the doorway long after she finished, listening in vain for her father's footsteps on the stairs. The dim lights on the wall along the hallway came on and she brightened for a moment, thinking he was coming, until she remembered the lights were on a timer.

She caught herself falling asleep and decided she had waited long enough. It had been a long day with their trip to the cave and her afternoon visit with Ian and then several hours of worrying. She left the tray on the floor, retrieved her Friday nightgown, navy blue with silver stars, from her dresser, and trudged to the bathroom to prepare for bed.

Lying on her back in her bed, she stared at the soft circle of light the lamp beside her cast on the high ceiling. Surely her father would not miss saying goodnight to her. Their bedtime talks were a long-established ritual. It was a time for the two of them to sort the events of the day, to discuss the highs and the lows. It was a time for her to ask questions, to present observations and for him to soothe her fears, clear up misunderstandings, and elaborate on items of interest. In the dim glow of the bedside lamp he would sometimes let down his guard, become less reserved, smile more, and even laugh. Surely tonight of all nights, he would come and tell her what was troubling him. But he didn't come.

Bucky's imagination took a dark turn. Maybe her father was in such despair he took his own life. Maybe, like the character in a book she had read, he had wandered off into the moors never to be found. Bucky didn't think there were any moors around Turn Back, but there were plenty of woods where it was possible to get lost. And the river. What if he had drowned himself in the river. Or the spring? He might have gone down to the Spring Room. What if the woman in the shared dream had held him under the water? Bucky briefly entertained the thought of searching for him, but she was afraid of what she might find. Was he even now lying dead on the floor in his study? Is that the sight which would greet her when she went down in the morning? And what would become of her? Shipped off to Matt Healey, Simon's publisher, a man she didn't know, the man Simon had named as her guardian? Torn away from Ian and Maggie and the Lukefahr Ladies and Turn Back and the labyrinth?

As the ideas tumbled and twisted and swirled in her mind, she felt the sting of tears in her eyes. She squeezed them shut and balled her fists. Her body stiffened as she shut out the room around her and attempted to force back the tears.

"Oh, my God! What's wrong?"

Bucky's eyes flew open at the sound of the familiar voice and the touch of his hands on her arms. "Dad! You're alive!" She bolted upright and wrapped her arms around Simon's neck.

"Of course, I'm alive. Why wouldn't I be?" Simon sat on the edge of the bed and untwined her arms but kept hold of her hands. "Did you have another nightmare?"

"No, I was just so worried about you."

"I'm sorry, Lamb. I never meant … I'm sorry I upset you. I needed some time to think about some things. And I needed to tell you something but I wanted to wait until I was sure I could do it without breaking down, but the tears…" Simon swallowed past the lump in his throat. "The tears refused to stop all afternoon and on into the night."

"And tears are catching."

"Yeah, they are." Simon managed a wry smile.

Only a few minutes before, Bucky had imagined never to see that smile again. She hugged Simon again. "And now you're ready to tell me?" She could still feel his heightened emotions, but they weren't rolling off of him as they had done earlier.

"Maybe not just yet. Let's talk about your day first. How was your visit with Ian? And Maggie? Did you make the tomato relish and that delicious pot roast I ate tonight?"

Bucky laughed. "No. Maggie said she would start teaching me after Ian goes back to school. She said people have been bringing food over for her and Ian. Maxine made the roast, but I don't know who made the salad. Ruby made the cookies. We didn't take any food over there. Shouldn't we?"

"I don't think Maggie would appreciate one of our frozen dinners. But we're helping out in other ways. You're keeping Ian company for a while each day and I helped Maggie bring in her garden produce yesterday. Was Ian feeling better today?"

"I think so. He acted better. And we sat at the kitchen table for a few minutes and had cookies and milk. Ruby's cookies are better if you dunk them in milk."

"I found that out except I softened mine in coffee."

Bucky flashed a fleeting smile. Simon sounded like his old self, but she could still feel his tension, even without touching him. "What did you do while I was gone?"

"I told you about Ron coming over and setting up that little shed for the UTV. That took about an hour. I gathered from some comments he made that he and Penny still don't know Chip and his wife are expecting, so you be sure you keep that a secret for a while yet. And then after that I called Michael Smallin and told him about the cave. He's coming down anyway tomorrow, so I thought he and I could go see it maybe in the afternoon after the walk."

Bucky sighed. "Another decision."

"What do you mean?"

"I told Ian I'd come over tomorrow afternoon to tell him and Maggie about how the walk went, but I probably won't have time to do that and go with you and Dr. Smallin to see the cave. But I want to do both."

"How about if I make that decision for you? Dr. Smallin and I will go see the cave and you go see Ian."

Bucky stuck out her lower lip. "Just a week ago, you told me you were never going to let me out of your sight again and now you act as if you don't care."

Simon squeezed her knee. "Of course I care. And if it were anyone but Maggie I wouldn't let you go without me, but when you're with her at her house, I feel you're safe."

Bucky lowered her head and picked at one of the shiny stars on the front of her gown. "So Ron Crosson came and then you called Dr. Smallin. But what happened after that?"

Simon glanced away for a moment and took a breath. "I… I got a phone call from Matt Healey."

"Your publisher?"

"You always say that after I say his name. Yes, Matt Healey, my publisher and my friend. He's the only Matt Healey I know. In fact, I think he's the only Matt I know personally."

"What'd he want? Oh, no! He doesn't like your new book. He's not going to publish it. We're going to go broke, aren't we? We aren't going to be able to live here anymore. That's why you're upset."

The words tumbled out so fast from Bucky that Simon had a hard time jumping in. "No, none of that. Stop racing ahead and just listen." Simon swallowed and took a couple of breaths. "The reason Matt called was to tell me… He told me… Bucky, your mother's back."

Bucky had slouched down after being reprimanded but she sprang upright again. "What? Where is she? When did she come back?"

"Slow down. I'll tell you what I know."

Bucky could feel the tide of emotions pulsating again from her father but now they were colliding with her own.

"Evidently, according to Matt, she showed up last summer, but she couldn't remember anything. She didn't know who she was or where she lived or where she'd been for the past nine years." Simon managed to get that much out without hesitating but he paused before continuing. "She was in a hospital for a while until—"

"Was she hurt? Is she all right?"

"They wanted to try to figure out what was wrong with her and discover her identity. But they eventually transferred her to another facility—a group home of some type where she could be cared for. She had no memory, no money, no ID."

"Was it where they send crazy people?"

"She wasn't insane. She just couldn't remember."

"Amnesia," said Bucky matter-of-factly.

"Yes, amnesia. But I don't understand why the police couldn't identify her. Yes, it's been nine years—yes, it's a cold case—but they had all the information on her."

"But you said she would look different, older. Maybe she didn't look like her old pictures at all."

"They have artists who are skilled at aging people in photographs or drawings to give some idea of how they would look as older adults. Anyway, let me continue. A couple of weeks ago, the residents of the home went on an outing, a field trip, I guess, and one of the places they went to was a bookstore. Your mother saw one of my books and it must have jogged something in her mind. Matt said she didn't remember right off, but it must have seemed familiar to her and—"

"Which book was it?"

"I don't know."

"If it seemed familiar, it must have been one of your early ones."

"I suppose it must have been. Well, she didn't have any money but someone in the group bought it for her. And over the next couple of days, bits and pieces of her life started coming back to her—not the whole story but enough that she remembered where we had lived. I still don't understand. At that point it looks like whoever was in charge of that group home would have contacted the authorities. Maybe it was because when she did convince someone to take her to the address of our old apartment, the couple who live there now had no idea what she was talking about. Remember? Our lease was up the first of May and there were new tenants. Perhaps the leaders of the group home were convinced she was crazy, after all. But her next course of action was to go to Healey Publishing Company. Matt said she just showed up there one day. I don't know how she got there if she had no money for a cab or other transportation. She...uh... She caused quite a commotion in the lobby, I guess, and Matt came out of his office and recognized her right off." Simon paused and Bucky could see that his eyes glistened with tears. "She's been... She's been staying with Matt for the past two weeks." He wiped a hand across his eyes. "I'm sorry, Bucky. I thought I was all cried out."

"So, Dad," Bucky whispered, "if your friend Matt knew who she was two weeks ago, why did he wait until today to call you?"

"I don't…" Simon closed his eyes and covered them with his palms. "I don't know. When she pieced together her story for him, what she was able to remember, anyway, at that point, and she learned she had been gone for all these years, Matt said she didn't want him to tell me. She wanted to wait until she could come in person, to try to explain to me herself what had happened. She…uh… Matt said she was afraid we wouldn't want her in our lives."

"We don't."

"God, Bucky!" Simon pulled his hands away from his face. "Of course we do. She's my wife. She's your mother."

"Not if she's coming here to kill me."

"She's not… She's not going to kill you. How many times do I have to tell you? Those were dreams."

"I still don't understand why Matt called you today."

"Matt… Matt leased her a car, set her up with a credit card, phone, ID—he's got a lot of connections. Even a driver's license. All without the authorities even knowing she'd been found. I don't understand that at all. New York's a big city, but still… She left this morning and is on her way here."

Bucky had been sitting up on her knees for most of the story but now sat down with her legs under her. "When will she get here?"

Simon shook his head. "It took us three days, but we didn't travel very fast and made numerous stops. I don't know. The earliest she could get here would be tomorrow night, but that would be really pushing it, and if she's not used to driving… It could be Sunday, Monday maybe."

"She's just going to show up at our front gate?"

"I guess so."

"So if she didn't want Matt to tell you, why did he call you today?"

"Maybe he thought I should know. He told me he was afraid if she suddenly appeared I would have a heart attack. But there was… There was something he wasn't telling me."

"What?"

"I don't know. He didn't tell me. But I could feel there was more to the story than what he was saying."

Bucky put her head down again and scratched one fingernail across the largest star on her nightgown.

"So, Lamb, I'm sorry again, for the way I acted this afternoon and for avoiding you all evening. I just… It was a lot for me to take in. After all this time… For so many years it was what I hoped for, but as time passed, I really, really never thought it would happen." He paused when Bucky didn't respond. "Maybe I should talk to Maggie and have you stay with her for a few days until your mother comes and I can find out—"

"No! I should be here. She might be coming to kill you, too, and I can help protect you."

Simon shook his head.

"Dad, can I sleep with you tonight? *May* I sleep with you tonight?"

"I don't think that would be a good idea. I'm afraid I'm not going to sleep well."

"Please. *Māntāssu*. I don't think I'm going to sleep well either."

Simon sighed.

"*Māntāssu, Père.*"

"Now you're mixing Hittite and French. Don't do that."

Bucky chewed on her bottom lip. "I can't remember the Hittite word for father, Oh, wait. *Atta. Māntāssu, Atta.*"

Simon smiled. "Okay."

"Will you carry me on your back like when I was little?"

"No. You're not little anymore."

She stood up on her knees and held out her arms. "*Māntāssu, Atta.*"

"Oh, all right." Simon stood and turned away from her. Bucky scrambled to her feet on the bed and climbed on his back.

Two hours later, when Simon turned back the covers on his side of the bed and switched off his bedside lamp and crawled in, he was surprised to find Bucky still awake. "If you don't go to sleep, you'll be dragging your feet around the park tomorrow morning."

"Every time I close my eyes, they spring back open like a Jack-in-the-box. Too many things to think about."

"I know."

"Maybe if you hold my hand." She felt under the covers for Simon's hand and then turned on her side to face him. With her left hand she reached up and ran her fingers through his hair.

"What are you doing?"

"I like your curls."

"If they're long enough for you to wrap them around your fingers, it's definitely time for a haircut."

"No," she said, drawing out the word. "Ian got his curls from you?"

"Probably."

"I wish I had curls. Madison Koeller has beautiful long curly hair. And it's red. You told me I had little red curls when I was born. I wish the Anarianu had not changed it to ugly old straight brown hair."

Simon squeezed her hand. "Your hair's not ugly. And you told me that whatever the Anarianu did to change you saved your life. I would much prefer to have a little girl with straight brown hair than...than the alternative."

"Is Mom's hair curly?"

"No. But she used to fluff it up a little with a blow dryer and a curling iron. Maybe she can teach you how to style yours."

Bucky didn't say anything for a while and Simon thought she had fallen asleep at last. He was still holding her right hand and her left hand was still touching his head. The moon was almost full and it bathed the room in a soft light. Simon tried to close his eyes but every time he opened them, he imagined he could see Meredyth in the shadows. He opened his hand that held Bucky's but she clasped it tightly again.

"Dad? Are you still awake?"

"Yes, but you shouldn't be."

"When Mom comes, I guess I can't sleep with you anymore, can I?"

"It would make it a little crowded."

"But what if I get scared in the night?"

"One of us will come to your room and make sure everything's all right."

"You come. Not her. Dad?"

"Yes?"

"How do we know all this isn't another dream? Maybe Mom's not coming."

"She's coming."

The next thing Simon knew was when he awoke to the sound of Bucky screaming. And kicking. One of her feet connected with his left leg, just below the knee. He sat up and gently grasped her upper arms to restrain her. "Lamb. Lamb, wake up. You're having a nightmare."

Bucky's eyes opened wide. In the moonlight Simon could see the wild look in them. "Dad! I-70! I-70!"

"What? Bucky, you were dreaming. It was just a—" Simon let go of her arms. The red, white and blue emblem interstate shield flashed in front of him, the white numeral 70 emblazoned on it. "I-70," he said aloud.

"We came here on I-70. Remember, Dad? You had me watch for the signs whenever we went through a city. Something's wrong. We have to warn Mom."

Simon tried to remember his own dream that was interrupted when Bucky screamed. *I-70.* The interstate highway crossed several states. He tried to recall the shield, to zoom in on the name of the state. "Ohio!" he said aloud.

"We have to warn Mom! Something bad's going to happen to her on I-70 in Ohio." Bucky was sitting up now with her legs crossed. The silver stars on her gown shimmered in the moonlight. "Call her. You said Matt gave her a phone."

"We can't… I can't call her. We aren't supposed to know she's on her way." Simon was out of bed and pacing across the room.

"What if there's a wreck, Dad? What if she dies? What if she dies like Ian's parents?"

"It was a… It was a shared dream. It must be from the Anarianu. But from which ones?" Simon put his hands on either side of his face and continued pacing. "Maybe it wasn't necessarily a warning for her not to take that particular route. If we tell her not to take it, perhaps the danger lies on whatever alternate she chooses."

"Call her, Dad. Please."

"I can't call her, Imala!"

Bucky stood up in the bed and screamed. "I'm not Imala!"

Simon stopped and closed his eyes. When he opened them, he spoke slowly and calmly. "Stay here, Bucky. Matt gave me her number. It's on my desk downstairs."

18

FIRST SATURDAY PRAYER WALK

Simon looked up from his desk to see a tangled-hair Bucky in a blue nightgown with silver stars standing in the doorway. "Good morning, sleepy head."

Bucky, bare-footed, joined him at the large, polished wooden desk where he spent much of his day. "I woke up in your bed. For a moment, I didn't know where I was."

Simon put his arm around her. "I was about to come up and wake you. We don't have too much time before we need to leave for the walk, but I thought I'd let you sleep as long as possible."

Bucky rubbed the back of one fist across her eyes. "I remember having a dream. Oh! I-70! Did you call Mom? What did she say? Was she all right?"

"She didn't answer. I had to leave a message."

"What did she sound like when she told you to leave a message?"

"It was a generic recording. It wasn't her voice."

"What do we do now?"

"There's not much we can do, Lamb. I've called several times. It's always the same. Either she has her phone turned off or she sees it's me on the caller ID and chooses not to answer."

"Maybe we should call the police."

"And do what? We don't know where she is, even what state she's in. Could be Pennsylvania or Ohio. Even Indiana if she were really pushing it. Matt didn't even tell me what kind of car she's driving. I don't think they'd shut down the whole Interstate because you and I had a dream something bad was going to happen."

"They might. Tell them you're a famous writer."

"Oh, yeah, they'd really listen then. We're just going to have to wait. And hope she gets the message and doesn't think her old husband is totally off his rocker." Simon picked at some of the knots in Bucky's hair and tried to smooth it out. "Why don't I fix you some breakfast while you clean up and get ready for the walk. It's supposed to be warmer today but it's still cool this morning. So put on some long pants and a long-sleeved shirt. Socks and shoes. You probably can get by with one of your zip-up sweatshirts with a hood. That way if you get too hot, it will be easy to take off and tie around your waist. You want me to work on these tangles or do you want to try?"

Bucky clasped her hands to her head. "I'll do it. It hurts when you brush them out."

"Okay. Off with you then. Don't dawdle. We don't want to be late. Come on down to the kitchen when you're dressed so you can at least eat a bowl of cereal before we leave."

Forty-five minutes later, Simon pushed the button on the remote control on his visor, and the iron gate at the end of the driveway swung shut behind them. Reaching into the back seat, he touched Bucky's knee. "You were awfully quiet at breakfast. You sure you want to go today?"

Bucky's eyes widened and her head jerked back. "We have to be there."

Simon put his hand back on the wheel and pulled onto the gravel road. "I know, but if you're too upset about…about things"

"I'm all right."

"You know I don't want you telling anybody about your mother coming. Is that understood?"

"Won't they know when she gets here?"

"I suspect Penny Crosson will see her driving through town and turning off on the road to come up here and it will be all over the county within an hour."

When they drove past the Fletcher's house, Bucky craned her neck to look out the window. She knew Ian wouldn't be outside, but she was hoping she might glimpse him through the living room window. She couldn't see in. "It's too bad Maggie and Ian can't go today. It'll be a whole month before the next one."

"I'll miss seeing Maggie walking with you," said Simon. "She always presents such a strong presence, especially if there's a confrontation with you know who."

"I wish Reverend Bergmann would leave us alone. But, Dad, you said you think the Anarianu have two sides, and he's on one side and we're on the other. He is a preacher, after all. How do we know we're on the right side?"

"That's easy. We're on the side of love and tolerance and respect. We don't get in people's faces and threaten them or tell them they're evil."

"But Jesus did. He cast out demons. That's what it says in the Bible. Maybe the Anarianu told Reverend Bergmann we have demons in us and he thinks he should cast them out."

"I thought we went all through that last summer, Lamb. You don't have any demons in you. You're not evil."

"Maybe it's demons that are making you upset and causing you to see things that aren't there."

"The demons I have inside me are of my own making. They are not from Satan, and I'm afraid it would take something or someone a whole lot more powerful than Reverend Bergmann to cast them out."

"You mean like Chip Crosson?"

Simon laughed. "Well, he's a start."

"Why didn't we ride to town in your new toy?"

"It's an off-road vehicle. Yes, I have driven it on this gravel road over to Maggie's or when we went looking for the cave yesterday morning, but I'm not really supposed to. I might get in trouble driving it into town." Simon glanced at the clock on the dashboard. "We're a little later than I'd like to be. I hope we can still park behind the hardware store."

"Dad, you don't seem happy about Mom coming. I mean I don't want her to come because she's going to kill me, but—"

"Bucky," Simon interrupted, "will you please stop saying that. Your mother is not coming here to kill you."

"But why were you crying yesterday and you're still… I don't know how to describe it. You're still upset."

"I am ecstatic she's coming, but at the same time…" He shook his head. "I don't know. It's been nine years. She will have changed. I've changed. We're going to have to get to know each other all over again. Assuming she wants to stay after she finds out…"

"Finds out what?"

Simon pulled into an empty space in the area they usually parked. He shut off the engine and undid his seatbelt, but he continued looking forward toward the brick wall that was the back of Crosson's Hardware Store. "Finds out that I'm crazy with all these people inside my head, people who are me, but not me."

Bucky unclasped her seatbelt and leaned forward. She put a hand on Simon's shoulder. "You're not crazy if it's true."

"And how about Ian? She left when she found out about him. What will happen when she learns he's living right next door?" Simon reached up and put his hand on Bucky's but still stared straight ahead. "I'll tell you what she'll do. She'll turn around and get in Matt's car and drive straight back to New York."

"Good."

Simon turned his head toward his daughter. "No, it's not good. And you don't mean that. And look at you. You're so adamant she's going to harm you because of a dream and yet you insisted we warn her about possible danger on her route here, danger you saw also in a dream. Well?"

Bucky withdrew her hand from her father's shoulder and sat back in the seat but didn't answer.

"Well?" Simon repeated.

"What does *adamant* mean?"

"Insistent, unyielding, unshakable."

"I don't want her to die. I just don't want her here. Because I don't want to die, either. It's complicated, isn't it?"

Simon opened the car door. "Let's go. It's almost time to start." He opened the back door for Bucky and she climbed out and took his hand.

As soon as they had driven into the outer edge of Turn Back, Simon had noticed there was an increase in the number of people who were walking the entire labyrinth which included all the streets of the town itself. He had had to stop three times to allow groups of walkers to clear the roadway. But that did not prepare him for the sight that greeted them when he and Bucky turned the corner from the alley where they had parked and walked down toward the center of town.

The street that circled the park was a mass of people, stretching all the way around the square and even spilling into the side streets and partially onto the lawn of the park. Simon counted eight tour buses parked at the edge of the road leading into town. Cars also lined both sides of the roadway.

Simon gripped Bucky's hand tighter as the two stepped up to the crowded sidewalk that ran in front of the storefronts on the south side of the square. "There must be ten thousand people here."

Music could be heard above the din of the crowd. "It sounds like the paleontology students from last summer," said Bucky, standing on her tiptoes, but it was useless for her to try to see over the heads of those in front of her. "Maybe they came down with Dr. Smallin this morning."

"Perhaps they're here because it's Saturday," suggested Simon, leaning down and speaking directly in Bucky's ear so she could hear him. "I see your ladies. Let's go."

They wound their way through the people standing on the sidewalk until they came to the front of the hardware store. There they stepped down into the street and finally made it to where the Lukefahr Ladies and others from the Methodist church were standing in their usual spot. The Methodists typically held the position at the head of the line, but today's crowd was such that it would be hard to define where the starting point was.

Several of the women immediately latched onto Bucky when she reached them. Simon reluctantly released her hand when they surrounded her.

"We missed you last Sunday," said Ruby Lower, "but I guess you had good cause. How are you finding Ian now that he's home?"

The women leaned in closer to hear Bucky's report. "He's getting better every day. I suspect he'll be good as new in no time."

"I'll bet Maggie is dog-tired," said Maxine Ross. "I offered to spell her when I took them a bite to eat, but she wouldn't hear of it."

"Oh, Maxine," said Bucky, "Maggie let my Dad and me have some of your roast beef and other stuff. It was really, really good." Bucky smacked her lips.

Maxine brushed Bucky's hair on her left side behind her ear. "How kind of you to say so."

"And I had some of your cookies, Ruby," said Bucky. "They were yummy dunked in milk. Oh, there's Sissy. I need to tell her something." Bucky squirmed away from the cluster of women around her and slipped beside Sissy Casteel who was talking with Ruth Mercer. Bucky waited politely until there was a break in the conversation and Sissy noticed her.

Sissy put an arm around Bucky's shoulder. "I'm so glad you made it. I was getting worried."

Bucky had been planning what she should say for over a week and now blurted it out quickly. "Sissy, I want to apologize for my behavior last Friday when you came to my house to see the new piano."

Sissy leaned down a little so she could hear her better.

Bucky continued. "I was supposed to tell you last Sunday but we went to the hospital to see Ian instead of to church. Anyway, I'm sorry I was rude to you. And... And I really do want to take piano lessons, but maybe not just yet."

"Why, honey, you don't have to apologize, but I accept it. Sometimes I come on a little strong to people. I don't mean to, but I scare them."

"No, it's not that. It's nothing you did. And someday I want to be able to play as pretty as you do."

"Why, thank you, Bucky."

From the corner of her eye, Bucky saw a tall, lanky figure. "Oh, there's Chip Crosson! Excuse me, Sissy, I need to talk to him before the walk begins."

Chip was leaning sideways a little to hear what his mother next to him was saying, but he straightened and smiled broadly when he saw Bucky wriggling between a couple of the elderly ladies to reach him. Penny Crosson turned away to speak to another woman from church, and when Bucky came close enough, Chip winked and said, "How's my favorite amphibian today?"

Bucky playfully slapped the tall doctor's arm. "My dad says I'm not an amphibian."

Chip laughed. "I'm just teasing you, Newt. You know that."

"What are you doing here?" asked Bucky. "I thought you said you didn't want to walk." She turned her head both ways. "Where's Dale?"

"Dale's minding the store although I doubt if anyone's shopping this morning. He doesn't really like crowds and this..." Chip swept his hand around. "I never imagined anything like this."

"There are an awful lot of people today. And it's strange with the sun over there." Bucky pointed toward the east. "Except for the first couple of weeks when we started last summer, the sun's always been over there going down behind the cliff." She pointed toward the massive rock wall that soared above the St. Francis River. "But you said you didn't want to risk having the dreams?"

"I guess my curiosity got the better of me. And after my mother told me what happened last week with Reverend Bergmann, I thought it was time I tried it. I want to study it objectively."

"Scientifically?"

Chip nodded. "And how have you been? Any more tear-induced…experiences?"

Bucky looked down at the pavement and scuffed her foot. "One. A couple of weeks ago. And some close calls."

"I thought I saw your father a few minutes ago."

"He's around here somewhere." Bucky raised her head and looked around but her short stature and the press of the bodies made it difficult to see. "He's not going to let me out of his sight. But where's your wife? Isn't she walking with you?"

"Lane's back at my parent's house. She wasn't feeling well this morning."

"Something's not wrong with the baby, is it?" Bucky slapped both hands over her mouth. She hadn't said it loud enough for anyone else to hear, she thought.

Chip almost bent over double to lean down in her face. "How did you know about the baby? No one knows. We only found out ourselves the day before Ian's accident. But you already knew that next night when I saw you at the hospital, didn't you?"

"Dale told me when you came to our house."

"That was the week before! How did *he* know?"

Bucky shrugged. "My dad told me to keep it secret so I haven't told anyone."

Chip straightened and put his hands on his hips. "We're going to announce it soon, anyway. And no, there's nothing wrong. It's morning sickness. But I'd be a little hesitant about her doing one of these prayer walks. Who knows what effect it might have on the baby? Although I'm sure there are pregnant women out here."

Simon suddenly appeared at Bucky's side and greeted Chip. "I think Pastor Bradley is about to announce that we're ready to begin. It's strange we haven't heard anything from Bergmann yet. After what he claims he experienced last week, I was sure he'd be here."

As if on cue, Reverend Bergmann's voice boomed over several loudspeakers placed in trees throughout the park.

Simon turned a complete circle. "Where is he?"

"There!" Bucky pointed up at the roof of the three-story brick building, the tallest structure in town. "He's on the roof of our museum."

"He's not going to be for long," said Simon as Bergmann began his tirade against the walkers. "That's private property. *My* private property. Chip, would you hold Bucky's hand if I'm not back before the walk begins?

Fortunately, there are more than two sheriff's deputies here this morning. Maybe I can get some official help ousting him."

Bucky took Chip's hand and soaked in the familiar feeling that spread through her. "Be careful, Dad."

Simon smiled to allay her fears. "As long as he doesn't have a sledge hammer, I'll be all right."

Stephen Bradley, the Methodist pastor, was in the bandstand at one end of the park, next to the Singing Spring and the mysterious Park Stone which had appeared the night of July fourth. He had already started twice to announce the start of the walk, but was having a difficult time being heard over the loudspeakers Bergmann's group had attached to the trees. One of the young men in the gazebo with Pastor Bradley worked to adjust the sound equipment the band had brought with them.

"I get the feeling you're not very happy today," said Chip, still holding Bucky's hand while they waited. They both were looking toward the roof of the tall brick building. "I thought these walks were supposed to put everyone in a good mood. Don't worry about your dad. He's not going to face Bergmann's group alone. He'll have officers with him."

"Chip, can I ask you something?"

"Sure."

"If something happens and I have to leave home, can I stay with you and Lane? The courts won't let me live with Maggie because she's too old and poor."

SONGS OF THREE

"What?" Chip stopped looking at the building and focused his attention on Bucky. "What's wrong? Is there something going on with your dad? You know you can tell me anything and I'll keep it confidential."

"No, it's a secret."

"Bucky, I want you to listen to me. There are good secrets and there are bad secrets. If there's something going on at home that's making you uncomfortable, you need to tell someone."

"You didn't call me *Newt*."

"That's because I'm not kidding now. Won't you trust me enough to tell me?"

"I can't. I promised Dad. But something big is coming and I'm afraid."

"But if you tell me, maybe I can help." Chip glanced back to the rooftop to see if there were any developments. The battle of the amplifiers continued around them.

Bucky's clutch tightened in his grasp. It took a moment for Chip to realize she was not responding. When he looked down at her, her eyes were squeezed shut and her right hand was curled into a fist, the arm straight at her side. The left hand he held was gripping his hand so hard now it was a little painful.

"Oh, no, no, no, no." Chip dropped to his knees in front of her. "Not here. Not now." He clasped her upper right arm, his left hand still holding hers. "I didn't mean to upset you."

"What's wrong with her?" Penny Crosson had been standing nearby the whole time but had been involved in her own conversations and had not been paying

321

attention. She put her hand on her son's shoulder. A few of the other women crowded around.

"Uh, you know, Mom, I think it's uh…" stammered Chip. "You know that condition Simon told Dad about last summer. I think she's having one of those."

"Well, do something, Son. You're a doctor."

Chip shook his head. "I don't think there's anything I can do."

"Is it epilepsy?" asked Lillian Thomas, leaning over her walker. "I heard you're to keep them from swallowing their tongue."

"It's not that," said Chip. "She'll be all right. Just give her a minute. There."

Bucky's eyes opened and she looked around at the faces staring down at her. "Uh oh." She loosened her hold on Chip's hand.

Chip, still on his knees, put his hands alongside her face, and took a couple of breaths. "Oh, Newt, you scared me to death. Are you all right?"

Bucky nodded.

"I'm so sorry. I didn't mean to upset you."

"Please don't tell, Dad," Bucky whispered in his ear.

"I can't promise that." Chip stood and gripped Bucky's hand again.

The crowd hushed as Pastor Bradley was finally able to be heard above the competing rants of Reverend Bergmann who was still broadcasting from the roof of the building. After welcoming everyone, the Methodist minister briefly stated the purpose and intent of the walk, that it was to be a solemn, slow walk of prayer and meditation. The Bible verse for the morning was the first part of James 4:8: *Draw near to God and He will draw near to you.*" Pastor Bradley tried to turn everyone's attention to the group of women who had started the walk and were the official leaders, but with the enormous number of people filling the town on this first Saturday in October, it was obvious today's walk would be different.

As the Lukefahr Ladies took their places, spreading out on both sides of Chip and Bucky and behind them, Chip leaned down to speak quietly to Bucky. "Do you feel like walking? I can always take you to the house to stay with Lane. It's just up the hill behind the store."

"I'm all right. And Dad wouldn't know where to find me."

He squeezed her hand. "Okay." He looked around at the elderly women on either side of them, all of them staring at him and Bucky. "Are they waiting for us?"

"I'm the leader," said Bucky. "Well, Maggie and I usually lead. I guess you're Maggie today."

Chip laughed. "I don't know if I can fill her shoes, but I'll try. Off we go then."

19

A VOICE ON THE PHONE

The sound of ten thousand pairs of shoes shuffling over the asphalt streets of Turn Back, mixed with the whispered prayers of many of the participants, filled the air during any lulls whenever Reverend Bergmann or one of his associates was not chastising the walkers and condemning them to Hell for participating in this demonic ritual. Bergmann spoke at length about his experience at the last walk when, according to him, he had been caught up in the Third Heaven and had received instructions from the angels about his role as God's messenger. He followed that with a full ten minutes of denigrations and insinuations against the moral character of Simon Carter and his daughter Bucky. This week, as on the last evening prayer walk, he also verbally attacked Simon's missing wife. He or someone in his group must have researched news articles from nearly a decade ago to uncover the events surrounding the mysterious disappearance of the spouse of the noted author.

During that particular minutes-long tirade, Bucky walked with her head down. She had pulled up the hood of her sweatshirt, not because she was cold, but because she didn't want anyone looking at her. She repeated the Bible verse over and over, but it was impossible to block out the preacher's amplified voice. Chip squeezed her hand every few seconds. She was glad the tall doctor was at her side, but she missed Maggie and wished she were here, too. She also wished her dad would either shut up Bergmann or come back to her side. But none of her wishes were fulfilled immediately.

When they reached the far end of the square where the bandstand stood, Chip leaned down and whispered, "How far do we go around?"

Bucky used her free hand to pull the hood back a little ways from her face. "Usually we turn into the park on over there a little bit in front of the museum, but there's too many people today. Maybe we should wait until we get back to where we started. There's a path there which goes toward the gazebo."

"Good idea," said Chip, straightening again.

It was when they reached the area in front of the future mastodon museum, from the roof of which Bergmann continued his verbal assaults and condemnations, that Simon at last slipped into the front line of walkers and took Bucky's other hand. Bucky felt agitation coming from her father, but it was tempered with the peace that came from knowing he was safe. The fact that Bergmann could still be heard, though, meant his mission to silence him and evict him from the roof had failed.

When she looked up at Simon, he could detect the questions in her face, shrouded as it was under her sweatshirt hood. "I'll tell you later," he whispered. "Some police protection we have," he muttered.

With the longer walk, a few of the elderly women from church with the most mobility issues remained at the edge of the park when the lead walkers turned onto the spiral pathway and wound their way to the far end to the bandstand. However, ninety-four-year-old Lillian Thomas, who had walked all the way on Bucky's right until Simon rejoined the group, kept pace and didn't stop until they stood in front of the bandstand. The musicians had broken away earlier from the mass of walkers and were already playing "I Have Decided to Follow Jesus." With the sun higher in the sky now but still in the east, there was no way the words would ever show up on the projection screen which had been in place on the previous walks. The screen itself was even too small to accommodate the growing crowds of the past. And the town could not afford a jumbotron, a giant LED screen. Besides, the addition of such a monster screen would block the natural beauty of the area and detract from the walk itself.

Many of those present knew the words, however, and the phrases repeated enough so that others easily could join in. When the band moved on to the even more familiar "Amazing Grace," the volume increased dramatically from the thousands of voices and overpowered Bergmann's attempts to shout them down.

After three more hymns, the park was shoulder-to-shoulder people with even more souls, unable to squeeze onto the grass, packing the street which encircled the square.

When Simon glanced around at the sea of people, he said, "Oh, Bucky, what have you done?"

Bucky had pushed back her hood when the singing began and she looked up at her father. "It's too crowded, Dad. We're not going to be able to lead people out like we usually do. There's nowhere to go."

She saw Simon gesture to Pastor Bradley behind them and whisper something in his ear. Bradley nodded.

After one more hymn, the Methodist pastor stepped up onto the gazebo with the college-student musicians and spoke into a microphone. "Those of us who host these walks are somewhat overwhelmed by the enormous numbers of people who have gathered to walk and pray with us today. If this is your first visit to Turn Back, it is a little difficult to see with so many people, but the streets of the entire town form a labyrinth. This morning we have just circled around the innermost part and because there are so many of you, some did not even get to walk that to any extent. You're welcome to come back any time and walk our labyrinth. We have a beautiful little town and it's set amidst the glorious wonders of God's creation, but it was never intended to hold this many people. As you leave this morning, note there are numerous food wagons set up around the perimeter of our square, but I'm sure those vendors, too, were not expecting this sort of turnout, so please be patient. As we disperse now and you make your way out of the park, I ask of you to walk slowly, to speak graciously, and to act kindly. And may the peace of God be with you this day and always. Amen."

A chorus of "Amens" reverberated through the crowd.

"And every last one of you is going to burn in the hellfires of damnation." Bergmann had been silent during Pastor Bradley's closing words, but his condemnation boomed out across the square.

The band quickly began playing "Just As I Am," and those in the crowd began to shuffle and slowly inch their way to the outside edges of the park.

Bucky still kept a tight hold to her father with her right hand and to Chip Crosson with her left. They eventually made it to the sidewalk which ran around the outside of the park. From there it was another couple of minutes to cross the street and step up onto the sidewalk in front of the future museum. Bergmann and his group had gone quiet and Simon wanted to be inside before they vacated the building. While Simon was trying to get help earlier from the sheriff's deputies he had discovered the glass had been broken on the back door to the building. The only way Bergmann could have reached the roof was through the inside since the fire escape stopped at the third floor. That meant they were not only guilty of trespassing, but of breaking and entering. Simon was hoping to find Dr. Michael Smallin in the crowd to discover what time he and his students had arrived and if they had been inside the building this morning, but there was no sign yet of the paleontology professor.

Lillian Thomas, with her walker, had managed to move through the press of bodies alongside Simon all the way. "I have no idea where my sister is," she said when they stopped in front of one of the two large plate glass windows. Newsprint covered the windows to keep the curious from peering inside. "I really needed to head home in the opposite direction but the tide was pulling me this way. Think I'll rest a spell here and maybe she'll find me." She took off her flowered-print headscarf. Her white hair, glowing in the harsh autumn sun, contrasted with her dark skin.

Chip took Bucky's left hand and transferred it to the front of Lillian's walker. "Miss Lillian, would you clamp your hand on top of Bucky's here and not let go. I need to speak with Mr. Carter and I wouldn't want her to get lost in this mess. Come on." He indicated for Simon to release his hold on Bucky, and then grabbed Simon by the arm and pulled him a few feet farther down the sidewalk.

Bucky, wide-eyed, watched them until Lillian drew her attention. The elderly woman realized that whatever Chip wanted to tell Simon, it was not meant for Bucky's ears. She engaged the girl with questions about Ian and Sadie Jane's French lessons and whatever else the ninety-four-year-old could think of to entertain Bucky for a few minutes.

People still pressed around them, but when Chip thought he was far enough away for Bucky not to overhear, he turned on Simon. "I'd like to come out to your place today. I think we need to talk."

"I don't really have the time," said Simon. "I'm...uh...meeting with the mastodon paleontologist this afternoon."

"I'm afraid this can't wait," said Chip.

"Why? What's so urgent? What's wrong?"

"Something's wrong with Bucky. I could tell today that she's not herself."

"She… She's just having a bad day. She'll be all right."

"I'm concerned about her. Concerned enough that…"

"That what?"

"It's the way she's acting. And what she said or, rather, wouldn't say. Is there something going on at home? As a doctor, I am mandated to report whenever I suspect—"

"Just what do you suspect? Are you talking about abuse?" Simon drew himself up to his full height which was still about five inches shorter than Chip. "I thought we hashed out all that before."

"She's scared. She's upset about something."

"Oh, I don't know why she'd be upset," said Simon sarcastically, but keeping his voice down. "She's having recurring nightmares about a woman she thinks is her mother who is trying to drown her. Her best friend was almost killed. She found out that best friend is also her brother. She discovered her perfect father is not so perfect after all. She is forced to listen to a deranged man shout from the rooftops that she's the devil's spawn. And because of her condition, she can't even cry like the rest of us to express her hurt and anger and frustration. And whenever she does cry, her back splits open in excruciating pain. And to top it all off we learned yesterday the mother who abandoned her, the mother she thinks is trying to kill her, is on her way here. She's just a child. How is she supposed to handle all that? You're darn right she's upset. She's terrified. Frankly, I don't know how she could even come out here today and walk. I don't know how she has the resilience to get out of bed every morning." Simon looked down at the small pits in the concrete sidewalk. "I'm sorry, Chip. This isn't like me. I'm tired. I'm just..."

Chip stood there, his head tilted almost like his brother Dale's, and listened to Simon's tirade before responding. "And how do you find the courage to face each day?"

"The knowledge that I have a little girl who needs me. That's the only thing that's kept me alive for nine years."

"But you told me you've had no contact for those years with your wife, that you didn't even know where she was. Now she's coming here? When?"

Simon shook his head. "Any day."

"Bucky told me something big was coming, but she wouldn't tell me what it was. Simon, the fact remains, she is scared. She asked if she could live with me."

Simon looked away and closed his eyes for a moment. He turned back to Chip. "Safety and security are among our most basic needs. And she doesn't feel safe right now. It started... I guess it started last summer with Bergmann's taunts. And then a few weeks ago, the nightmares began. And I don't know what else I can do to reassure her. I try to talk to her and she's all right for a while. Well, you saw how she was today. Before the walk she was talking with the ladies and I saw her speaking with you as if nothing's wrong, but then suddenly her whole attitude will shift and she'll fall into a dark place, and I have to struggle to bring her back to the light."

"She almost had one of her crying experiences after you left."

"Oh, God." Simon bowed his head. He looked at Bucky several feet away, talking to Lillian.

"Fortunately," continued Chip, "it went no further than her trance, but several people witnessed it. I think they were all people from church."

Simon rubbed his hands down the sides of his face. "Chip, I know being a neurosurgeon must be stressful, but you have no idea of what stress is until you become a parent."

"I guess I'm getting ready to find out."

Simon managed a wry smile and held out his hand to shake. "Congratulations."

Chip took the proffered hand. "We'd given up. The only reason Lane went to the doctor last week was because she hadn't been feeling well. I thought she was anemic. And here I am a doctor. We just never expected it to ever happen."

Bucky tells me it's a boy."

"Pfft," Chip scoffed. "It's a little early to determine the sex, but if Bucky says so... Does she scare you sometimes?"

"Astonish might be a better verb."

"I'd still like to come over, Simon. Maybe this evening? Perhaps we could do another session."

"Oh, I don't know. With all that's been going on and…"

"It might do you good. I've listened to the recording of our first session, oh, I don't know, four or five times, trying to understand it, trying to understand you."

"You're not planning to write me up in some journal, are you?"

Chip laughed. "I believe that would cost me whatever credibility I have as a neurosurgeon. I could probably sell your story to some check-out-stand tabloid, though."

"I'm sure it's too far-fetched for even that market." Simon caught sight of a uniformed deputy not far away. "Oh, there's an officer. They told me earlier they were too concerned with crowd control to take on Bergmann, and I could press charges later. I think they're too intimidated by him. Chip, I know you're anxious to get home, but would you watch Bucky for a couple more minutes while I talk to them and find out what I need to do?"

Simon let Bucky out at the front steps of the Mansion while he parked the car in the tiny garage. "We need to grab a quick bite," he said, unlocking the front door and letting Bucky go first into the foyer. "I never could find Dr. Smallin in that awful mess of people, but he said he'd be here at one o'clock to go see the cave. It's almost twelve-thirty. Let me check and see if he might have left a message on the phone."

Bucky trailed her father into his study. "Do I need to change clothes to go see Ian?"

Simon turned and looked at her. "I don't think so, unless you want to. We certainly didn't work up a sweat this morning. I think that was the slowest we've ever walked the labyrinth."

"Why were so many people there this morning? Where'd they all come from?"

"I don't know. Probably the news reports about You-Know-Who's experience last time. But I'm afraid it's getting out of hand. The town can't accommodate that many people. They're going to be backed up to the highway if it keeps going like this. Ah, look, we do have a message." The red light on the base of the phone on Simon's desk was blinking.

Simon sat while Bucky stood next to him, her elbows on the top of his desk, her chin cupped in her hands. Simon pushed *play*. The phone's recording announced "You have one new message. First message:"

Simon, this is Meredyth.

Bucky dropped her hands flat on the desk.

I got your message. I don't know if you heard the news but when I stopped for lunch, they said there had been a twenty-nine-car pileup in the fog on I-70, west of Morristown, Ohio. That's where I would have been this morning, Sie. I was in New Stanton, Pennsylvania last night. I had the same dream but I would have ignored it had you not called. I don't know how... The voice broke and then recovered. *I don't know how you knew to call or how to reach me. I guess Matt told you. I told him not to. But if you hadn't... Sie, I can't drive far at a time in my condition, but I should reach you probably Monday. I'm still a little fuzzy, but please promise me... I don't know what Matt's told you, but please promise me you'll hear my story before you tell me to leave. And please, Simon, tell my darling Bucky I love her.* There was a pause, and then, *I love you, Simon.* The mechanical voice added "End of messages. Remaining recording time is thirteen minutes, thirty-eight seconds.

Bucky whispered, "Was that really..."

Simon nodded and pushed *repeat.* Meredyth's message replayed.

"She called me her *darling Bucky.*"

"I never thought I would hear that voice again."

"Play it again, Dad."

Simon obliged and the two listened for a third time to the message left by Meredyth Carter who had disappeared over nine years earlier.

"She called you *Sie.* That's what she called you in the dream."

"It's short for Simon. Remember last summer, Nick Moyer, who's helping me translate the Hollow Stone, sometimes called me that."

"What did she mean in her *condition*? Is she sick? Did Matt Healey say something was wrong with her? Maybe she's dying."

Simon put an arm around Bucky's waist. "Shh. You're letting your imagination run away with you again."

"What does she mean she's *fuzzy*?"

Simon shook his head. "I don't know, Lamb."

"But, Dad, she's worried that you won't let her stay. But you told me you're worried she won't want to stay. Play it again."

"That's enough for now. We need to... Dr. Smallin will be here soon."

"Please. Once more."

Simon hit *repeat* and the two listened again to the voice Simon had not heard for almost a decade and Bucky had no memory of at all.

"She sounds pretty," said Bucky.

"You can't *sound* pretty," corrected Simon. "You *look* pretty. You should say she has a pleasant voice."

"Of course you can sound pretty," Bucky said defensively. "Take Miss Lillian. She's old and wrinkled and not very pretty to look at and her voice is kind of raspy and not pleasant at all. But when she talks you just know she's pretty inside. Mom sounds pretty inside."

Simon stood. "Then where has she been for nine years?"

❧

Chip left the Mansion that night about eight-thirty, and Simon went up to Bucky's room. He hoped she was as tired as he was and would be in bed early. He found her in her study room, sitting at the table with her Sunday school book and Bible opened in front of her.

"Studying your lesson for tomorrow?"

"It's about Joseph in Egypt. Dreams play an important part in the story."

Simon lowered himself into the chair opposite her. "I'd forgotten about that."

"Haven't you studied your lesson? It's about Joseph, too, isn't it? Don't you still use the same book we do?"

"I'll read it in the morning. I'm afraid I don't put as much effort in it as you because we mostly sit there and listen to Frank drone on and on."

"You should have Sadie Jane Woods for a teacher. She makes it interesting. Joseph lived back in the olden times, didn't he? Do you think he lived at the same time as the Hittites?"

"The Hittites were definitely around then. They and the Egyptians both struggled for supremacy in the region and clashed occasionally. I'm not sure where Joseph fits into the timeline, though."

"Maybe Etakkama knew Joseph."

"I don't think so. I was nev— Etakkama was never in Egypt."

"Did you and Chip talk about Etakkama tonight?"

"Among other things. I'm sorry he didn't bring Lane or Dale with him and you had to spend all evening up here by yourself."

Bucky shrugged. "I didn't mind."

"We talked about the cave so much when I picked you up at Maggie's this afternoon, I didn't get a chance to ask you how your visit with Ian went?"

"It was okay." Bucky closed her lesson book and traced the picture on the cover with her index finger.

Simon could tell in only the past twenty seconds she was starting to shut down again. Usually in the evening before bedtime was when she was the most talkative or, at least, was the most willing to share her thoughts with him. "Did you work on his assignments or just visit?"

Bucky didn't answer right away. She continued to move the tip of her finger across the slick cover. But Simon noticed now she was no longer tracing the outlines of the photo. She was inscribing a spiral.

"Bucky?"

She didn't respond.

"You need to talk to me, Lamb." Simon clasped Bucky's right hand in his.

"Do you think she's really coming or is this another one of those dreams?" Bucky kept her eyes fixed on the cover of the Sunday school lesson quarterly.

"I believe she's really coming."

"Why couldn't you stop Reverend Bergmann from saying all those awful things this morning?"

"I tried. I couldn't get help from the officers. Dr. Smallin was inside the building when they came in. He had left the back door unlocked and he couldn't stop them, he said. The window in the door broke when one of their microphone stands hit it. So they probably can't be charged with breaking and entering. But the sheriff's deputy said I could come to the station on Monday and press charges of trespassing and property damage. Maybe I can get the restraining order then."

"You can't go Monday if Mom's coming."

"I'll go another day then." Bucky's neck was still bowed and all Simon could see was the top of her head. "So what did you and Ian do this afternoon?"

Simon waited for a response but there was none. "Bucky?"

"We wrote a story." She raised her head finally and looked at Simon. "Maggie thought Ian should get some fresh air, so we sat on the front porch. She put up this little square folding table—"

"A card table?" interrupted Simon.

"Yeah." Bucky nodded. "That's what she called it. Ian was supposed to write an original story for school but he was supposed to write it with a partner. Madyson Koeller called him last night and said she would come over and help him write it, and he told her I was going to write it with him. Madyson got mad and said she was going to tell Mrs. Lannigan because that wasn't fair because I didn't go to school there. So Maggie called Mrs. Lannigan and asked her if it was okay if I worked with him on the story."

"And his teacher said it was all right?"

"Sure. So we wrote a lot of it today. We can probably finish it tomorrow."

"Are you going to let me read it?"

"Maybe, but after he turns it in. You know how you are. You'll be all picky and find all kinds of things wrong with it and make us do it over."

Simon put his palm on his chest. "I wouldn't do that, would I?"

"Yes, you would," Bucky said and smiled.

Simon sighed in relief. She seemed to smile so rarely these past few days. "Can you tell me what it's about?"

Bucky put her fist under her chin. "It's just a story about a boy and girl who spend a lot of time imagining themselves in different historical scenes and being heroes."

"Similar to what you and Ian do?"

"Yeah, but one day, something happens."

"What?"

"I'm not going to tell you, Dad. That would spoil the story for when you read it."

Simon laughed. "That sounds like a good story. But Bucky, you be sure you and Ian are working as partners. Don't you be doing all the work."

"Oh, we both think up ideas and what comes next and who says what."

"I think it's time you were in bed. Did you finish your lesson for Sunday school tomorrow?"

Bucky put her head down again. "There's something else I want to ask you."

Simon hesitated. "Okay."

"After church some of the Lukefahr Ladies are going over to Maggie's to eat. Maggie invited us, too, but I didn't think you'd want to."

"You're right about that."

"But…"

"But will I let you go without me?" Simon shook his head. "Not going to happen."

Bucky raised her head. "But you've let me go over there without you for the last two days."

"That was just with Ian and Maggie there. Chip tells me you almost had one of your episodes before the walk began this morning."

"But I didn't. I controlled it."

"But you worried and upset those around you. I would not want those sweet old ladies to witness what happens when you can't control it. I'm not going to risk it."

"But don't you risk it every Sunday when I go to church and every time we do the walk with all those thousands of people and every time I'm somewhere around anybody else?"

Simon put his fingers on his temples. "You see this gray hair? Most of that has come in since May when you started this nonsense. Up until then I was doing a pretty good job of keeping you apart from everyone, and my life was a whole lot less stressful."

Bucky lowered her gaze again. "I don't think it's nonsense."

Simon reached across the table and took both of her hands in his. "No, it's not. That was a poor choice of words. I'm sorry."

Bucky pulled her hands out his grasp. "This morning Miss Lillian told me she has very close veins but she's glad she doesn't have old-timers disease. I hope I don't have either of those."

Simon was never prepared for Bucky's abrupt change of subject. It usually took a few heartbeats for him to understand what she was talking about. "First of all, I think Miss Lillian was probably referring to varicose veins."

"She said *very close*."

"Sometimes when people have never seen a term in print and have only heard it, they try to interpret it with words which are familiar to them. It's varicose, and, no, you don't have them. And I believe the other condition she mentioned is Alzheimer's. And for the same reason, people tend to mispronounce that also. It's a form of dementia some people get when they're old, so, no, you don't have that either. But it's not your place to correct her pronunciation."

"Then how will she know she's saying it wrong?"

"Someone closer to her own age might correct her or she might discover it on her own when she reads an article or hears it on television. But children shouldn't correct adults. It's not polite."

"She's pretty old. I don't know if there is anyone else in Turn Back close to her age."

"It's getting late, Bucky. Why don't you go put on your pajamas and get in bed and we'll listen to your mother's message one more time. I put it on my cell phone so I can play it for you up here. Oh, let's see. It's Saturday night. Which pajamas are you going to wear? Don't tell me. The striped ones, right?"

Bucky got up and walked around the table and stood behind Simon. She put her palms on either side of his face. "Do you really believe Mom's coming here?"

Simon laid his hands on top of hers. "Yes, Lamb, I really believe she is coming."

20

A TURN BACK SUNDAY

Bucky hoped her father would relent and allow her to have lunch at Maggie's with the other Lukefahr Ladies after church. If the women stayed there and visited for a few hours, and Bucky did not go, then she would also miss her time with Ian. They had planned to finish their story on Sunday and she didn't want to postpone working on it. She didn't want to leave the Mansion on Monday for fear she would not be there when her mother arrived.

So Bucky waited before church for word Simon had changed his mind but none was forthcoming. She knew better than to press the issue, but she did drop a hint when they passed Maggie's house on the way to Turn Back. Simon appeared to be preoccupied, however, and did not respond to her subtle reminder of the invitation.

When she entered the classroom the women were discussing the dinner gathering and what each had prepared for it. Bucky slumped in her seat and listened to the talk of fried chicken and ham, potato salad, pickled beets, three-bean salad, corn casserole, green beans, chocolate cake and coconut cream pie. Her ears perked up at the mention of her favorite pie.

Lillian Thomas had come in behind her and had crossed over to sit in her usual spot but stopped and pushed her walker to the seat next to Bucky. "I've been sitting in that other chair for many years. Since Maggie's not here this morning, I think I'll try a change of scenery, if you don't mind, Miss Bucky. Might put a whole different perspective on things." The elderly woman lowered herself onto the stuffed theater seat.

"I don't mind," said Bucky. "Are you going to Maggie's for lunch?"

"Leona's not feeling well this morning. Maxine stopped and picked me up, but I think I should go on home after church and be with my sister. When you're as old as we are, you have to be extra careful about these little bugs that go around."

Bucky sat up straight. "Bugs?" Was Lillian referring to the Anarianu who took the form of lightning bugs?

"Viruses. The flu, that sort of thing," explained Lillian. "You're going, of course, aren't you?"

Bucky shook her head. "My dad. You know."

Lillian scoffed. "Sister and me—and we had a brother, Teddy—we just sort of ran wild when we was little. I don't even remember wearing shoes until I was six years old and started school. From what I hear on the news, people today have to be a lot more careful with their children, but your father does seem to be a tad over-cautious. Maybe he has a right after seeing whatever that thing that came over you yesterday before the walk."

Bucky did not want to get into a discussion about the narrowly-averted episode she experienced. "Did you go to the school here in Turn Back?"

"We wasn't allowed to go to that one. But there was other colored folks living here back then and we attended the colored school. It was just a little frame building up past the Baptist church, but the building's gone now."

"I never heard of a colored school."

"That was back in the days of Jim Crow. Segregation," she added when she saw Bucky's quizzical expression. "Coloreds and whites didn't mix much in those days. Here in little old Turn Back, things weren't quite as strict, but we knew our place, and we had our own school and our own church until it burned. But as the health resorts started closing—that's where most of our people worked—the colored families moved away to find jobs elsewhere. And now Leona and I are the only ones left."

"Did you ever work at the Mansion where I live now?"

"My grandma Euphemia did when she was young. Both of her parents—they would be my great-grandparents—were born slaves and then after the war, they stayed here and pretty much did what they had done before they were free. When Grandma left the Mansion she worked at the Halcyon. That was one of the other resorts. It was up on that ridge behind the school. And that's where my mama worked until she was married. And that's where Sister and me worked until they closed it."

"You should write all that down so people in the future will know about it."

"That was just life. Ain't worth writing about."

"Didn't you find it interesting in our lesson today that those people back in Egypt were having those strange dreams and Joseph could interpret them?" asked Bucky, changing the subject.

"Dreams have always fascinated me," said Lillian, "although the ones we've had all summer are certainly different. What you said Sunday before last about that woman in the cave dream being your mama, that's haunted me ever since. You still think that?"

Bucky nodded then leaned in close to Lillian's ear. "I'm not supposed to say anything, but if you promise not to tell anyone, I'll tell you a secret." She looked around but the other women were still talking among themselves and paying no attention to the oldest and the youngest members of the class.

Lillian inclined her head slightly toward Bucky who whispered, "She's coming back. Maybe tomorrow."

Lillian sat up straight, but whispered back, "From the grave?"

"She's not dead," whispered Bucky louder. "Just missing."

"Oh," said Lillian, "that must be what you said a couple of weeks ago. You had your head down then and were speaking so low, I couldn't understand you. Well, if she's coming here, you must be pretty excited."

Bucky shook her head and, still whispering, said, "I'm scared."

Lillian patted Bucky's hand on the polished wooden armrest of the old theater seat. "She might be scared, too.

I'd give anything to see my mama again. Course, I reckon it won't be too long before I do just that."

"But you told me your mama was dead. How can you see her?"

"I suspect I'll be passing on one of these days. I hope to see her in Heaven."

"You mean die? Like Clara?" Bucky clasped Lillian's forearm with both of her hands. "Oh, please, Miss Lillian, don't do that. There's been too many upsetting things in my life recently. I don't think I could take another one."

Lillian smiled and laid her other hand over both of Bucky's. "I'll try to stick around a while longer just for you. You know, I never had any children or grandchildren to tell all my stories to. Now that I think about it, maybe I should pass them on to you and you could write them down for me. I've lived a long time and parts of my life might be worth remembering for the future."

Bucky smiled and relished the warm feeling which flooded through her from being in physical contact with the old woman. "I'd like to know how we're related."

Lillian crinkled her nose. "That story might have to wait until you're older."

"That's what Maggie said, too. That's what my Dad says about his books." Both Bucky and Lillian had stopped whispering.

Lillian leaned close again and lowered her voice. "Having read a couple of your father's books this summer, I can understand why he'd say that. He's an excellent writer, but what he writes is definitely not for the eyes of a little girl."

Bucky smiled again. "He's going to let me read them when I'm your age."

Lillian shook her head. "I don't know. You might be better off waiting even a few more years than that."

They both giggled just as Sadie Jane Woods called the class to order.

⁓

As Simon backed the car out of the parking spot in the church lot after the worship service that morning, Bucky brought up part of the conversation she had had with Lillian Thomas before Sunday School.

"Did you know there was a colored school once in Turn Back and a colored church but it burned? Miss Lillian said there were lots more colored folks in town then but they all left when the resorts closed."

"No, I did not know that." Simon pulled out onto the street. "But the term *colored* is not really acceptable now, so you shouldn't use it."

"But that's what she said."

"Lillian is speaking from an historical perspective. The term was acceptable at one time in our society."

"What's acceptable now?"

"I suppose African-American or person of color."

"What's the difference between saying *colored* and saying a *person of color?*"

"It has to do with connotation and association and interpretation. The accepted use of certain words changes over time. You don't want to offend people with your language."

"I wasn't offended when she said it."

"That's because you're not African-American. But if you were to say it back to her, she might be offended, even if she uses the term herself. Understand?"

"No."

"Then I guess for now it's just one of those things you'll have to take my word on."

Bucky sighed. "There sure are lots of rules."

As Simon circled around the square, he slowed as he neared the Singing Spring so Bucky could hear it. She was sitting behind him and she rolled down the window. He pulled off the street to the side closest to the spring and switched off the engine. The day was sunny, although a little cool, and there were about two hundred people walking the various spiral pathways which wound through the park. Bucky unfastened her seatbelt and leaned her head out the window. As she focused on the ethereal sounds emanating from the fountain of water, Simon turned his attention from the park to the people he could see walking on the streets of the small town. Some of the license plates of the many cars parked around the square this morning were from out of state. He wondered if they had come for the big walk yesterday, but had been overwhelmed by the huge numbers and had taken Pastor Bradley's suggestion to walk when it was less crowded.

A car passed them on the right and tooted its horn. Both Simon and Bucky turned to look as the car full of women drove by.

"That's Ruby," said Bucky. "I guess they're headed to Maggie's for lunch."

"About that," said Simon. "If you still want to go, I'll drop you off there. You can call when you're ready to come home."

Bucky leaned across the seat to hug Simon around the neck. "You're the best dad in the whole world."

"You don't have a dish to take, but I'm sure there will be plenty to eat. But since you aren't providing any of the food, you help serve and do whatever else Maggie needs help with. Okay?"

"Thank you, thank you, thank you!" Bucky sat back down and fastened her seat belt. "And after lunch Ian and I can finish writing our story. But what will you do all afternoon at home alone?"

Simon started the car again and pulled back onto the roadway. "I have some writing of my own to work on."

Simon stopped on the gravel road in front of Maggie's house since her driveway already had three cars in it. He got out and opened the car door for Bucky.

"Don't worry," she said, hugging him. "Everything will be all right. I love you."

Simon wrapped his arms tightly around her. "I love you, too, Ima—Lamb." He squeezed his eyes shut against the tears welling up in them.

Bucky stepped back as he released her. "It's all right, Dad. If you were Etakkama, maybe I was Imala. You said she was headstrong like me."

Simon tried to smile as he smoothed down her hair. "Be good."

During the luncheon, Bucky divided her time between being in the company of the Sunday school ladies and visiting upstairs with Ian who was back in his bedroom for the day. Maggie had suggested he stay in her downstairs bedroom, but he much preferred to be out of the way of the women.

Bucky carried a tray piled high with food up to him. Maggie had filled a dinner plate for him, and Bucky had slipped an extra piece of chocolate cake onto the dessert plate. She carefully set the tray on the bed beside Ian who was sitting up with a pillow across his abdomen.

"Don't move," ordered Bucky. "I made it all the way up the stairs without spilling any of your iced tea. Let me set it here on your table." She used the back of her hand to brush aside some plastic dinosaurs and picked up the glass and set it on the small table beside Ian's bed. "Okay. Now if you wiggle, you won't have tea spilled all over your bed."

"Where's your tray?"

"Your gram fixed your plate first before they really had everything set out and organized. So it will be a few minutes yet before the others start eating. She said I can stay up here for a while." She reached for a bit of the ham Maggie had already cut into bite-sized pieces for him. "And nibble off yours."

"Just so you don't nibble off my chicken leg."

Bucky sat cross-legged on the bed next to the tray and lowered her voice so it wouldn't carry downstairs. "Ian, you know how we promised not to have any secrets from each other? Well, I have a big one I just found out yesterday."

"About the cave?"

"Bigger than that. But I'll tell you what Dad and Dr. Smallin plan to do about the cave first. In two weeks, Dr. Smallin's coming back and he's bringing Dr. Mason with him and Danny and Greg who were with him at the mastodon site last summer. He thinks by using some levers and muscle power they'll be able to move some of those rocks enough to get in there. They're going to treat it as an archaeological site, so they're going to go slow and record everything. Dad's going to try and see if the Moyers will come that weekend, also, in case there are more inscriptions inside."

"So I won't get to be the first one in there to see what's in the chest even though I discovered it."

"Dad says you should be well enough by then to go, too. You probably shouldn't go shoving those big boulders around, but he says both of us can tag along if we stay out of the way."

Ian used his fingers to fish one bean out of the small scoop of three-bean salad on his plate and popped it in his mouth. "I guess that's better than nothing."

"Well, we are just kids."

"So what's your big secret?" asked Ian.

Bucky picked at her lower lip with her thumb and index finger. "I should have told you yesterday when I first found out, but Dad made me promise not to tell anyone. But you're my best friend and my brother so you should know." Bucky took a big breath and let it out. "My mother's coming back. She left a message on our phone yesterday. She might be here tomorrow."

Ian's jaw dropped and he let his fork fall and clatter on his plate. "The woman from the dreams? She scares me."

"She scares me, too. She's tried to kill me. And now she's going to be here. In the same house as me."

"What are you going to do?"

Bucky shook her head. "I don't know. I'm worried that the dream will come true, and Dad won't be able to protect me."

"Maybe you could do to her whatever you did to Reverend Bergmann in the park a couple of months ago when you gave him that heart attack."

"Dad says that wasn't me."

"Everyone thinks it was you. I've heard some people say they're scared of you."

"That's another thing I've been thinking about."

"What?" said Ian as he resumed eating.

"Last Sunday when Reverend Bergmann came into your hospital room and threatened us, he said he now knew it was you, too."

"I don't remember the word he used," said Ian. "It wasn't devil. It was bom—something."

"Abomination," said Bucky. "Reverend Bergmann is always saying Dad is the Devil and I'm the Devil's spawn. He was at it again yesterday during the walk. Over and over. It was awful. But, Ian, if you're Dad's son, then you're the Devil's spawn, too. But how does Bergmann know that? Nobody knows but just a few of us. And why just pick on me? Why didn't he say those terrible things about you at the walk yesterday?"

Ian had speared a piece of potato from the potato salad with his fork and waved it around in a small circle. "Maybe he was listening at the door in the hospital room when I told you about the dream I had. He said they explained it to him when he was caught up to Heaven, but he could have been lying about that."

"And maybe he's really a coward and he didn't say those awful things about you at the walk because everyone around here knows you got injured and could have died. They won't stand up for Dad and me because we're newcomers, but you're part of this town and they might have ganged up on him if he went after you."

"Or," suggested Ian, "maybe he's saving up for next month when I'll be there in person." He put the potato chunk in his mouth and chewed thoughtfully. "Maybe you should just kill him. For good this time. Or since I'm the son of the Devil, maybe I can do it."

"Ian, Dad's not the Devil and I'm not killing anyone and neither are you. You've been watching too many movies. We're supposed to be Christians. Love is our weapon."

"But what are we supposed to do if he comes after us again?"

"I don't know," said Bucky. "I don't know what we can do to protect ourselves against either one of them. I think Mom tried to kill you at the cave and I think Bergmann might have tried to kill both of us in the hospital. And now when Mom comes tomorrow in person, I'm afraid she *will* kill me. Love just doesn't seem so powerful right now."

"Yeah, if love was something you could see, like a shield around you or a beam of light like you could shoot out of a ray gun, then you could tell if it was working."

"*Love your enemies and pray for those who persecute you*," said Bucky, quoting Matthew 5:44. "Those are easy words to say but a whole lot harder to do."

"Bucky!" called Maggie from the base of the stairs. "You need to come down and eat something before it gets cold."

Bucky carefully uncrossed her legs and scooted off the bed so as not to upset Ian's food tray or jiggle the bed and cause him discomfort. "I'll be back up later. We need to finish writing our story."

"Can't you bring your food up here?"

"I need to visit with the other women for a while. Do you need anything before I leave?"

"I guess not," said Ian sullenly.

Bucky stopped by the bedroom door and picked up a turtle shell from a shelf. "I never told you about the shell I found last week in the woods. It still has the bottom plate attached. Dad said I should give it to you but I'm keeping it to start my own collection." She waved her arms around Ian's bedroom, cluttered with his rocks and artifacts and fossils. "But it will be years before I have this much stuff." She replaced the turtle shell. "See you later, alligator."

"After 'while, crocodile."

When Simon glanced at the clock in the corner of his computer screen, he was shocked to see it was after four o'clock. He had been writing all afternoon. It had kept him distracted from thinking about what the next day might bring should Meredyth actually appear. And if she did show up, he was afraid he would have little time to write for the next few days. But he had not intended to leave Bucky at Maggie's all afternoon. He should have known better than to tell her to call him when she was ready to come home.

Simon wiped his hands down his face and then saved and closed the document. He had not been outside since returning home from church, but based on what he could see through the bay window in his study, it was a sunny, pleasant day. He considered walking over to Maggie's to retrieve Bucky but opted for the side-by-side instead. He enjoyed driving his new toy.

Maggie came out onto the porch with Bucky when he drove into the now-deserted driveway and tooted the horn of the UTV. The older woman had a plastic bag and some foil-covered dishes, all of which she shifted to one arm as she held the railing with her other hand and descended the steps. Simon jumped out and relieved her of the leftovers.

"It's some ham and salad and a few other things I thought you'd like for supper," explained Maggie as she handed then to him.

"I'm sorry I'm so late picking her up," said Simon. "The time got away from me, and..." he paused and looked down at Bucky who looked up at him. "I thought you were going to call."

Bucky shrugged. "Time got away from me, too. But we finished our story."

Simon thanked Maggie and told her goodbye and again looked at Bucky and tilted his head toward the older woman.

"Oh," said Bucky, picking up on his cue, "thank you, Maggie, for including me in your luncheon party today. I had a very nice time."

"Thank you for coming," replied Maggie, "and for helping Ian with his homework. He looks forward to your visits every day."

"Dad, don't you want to go inside and say hello to Ian? He's upstairs in his own room today because he didn't want to be down with all us old women."

Maggie playfully nudged Bucky with her elbow. "Who are you calling old?"

"No, it's late," replied Simon.

"Tomorrow I have to take him back up to Green River for a check-up at eleven," said Maggie. "So, Bucky, you won't be able to come over until the afternoon."

Bucky chewed on her lower lip and looked up at Simon who said, "We're expecting someone tomorrow. I'm not sure if...if...uh...Bucky will be able to come at all." He didn't have a free hand to take Bucky's hand but he nodded his head toward the vehicle, indicating for her to get in. "We'll let you know. Thank you, again, for the leftovers. We both appreciate them."

Simon heard the grandfather clock in the foyer strike seven o'clock. He laid aside the book he was reading and leaned his head against the back of the sofa and closed his eyes. After supper he had retreated to his study while Bucky had gone upstairs. He had considered resuming his writing which had been interrupted when he had gone to pick up his daughter, but instead opted to read. The events of the last few weeks had left him drained and exhausted. As he had told Chip, if it were not for Bucky, he didn't know how he would have survived the past nine years. He was not strong for himself, but he had to be strong for her. The phone message from Matt on Friday had almost sent him over the edge. And then to hear Meredyth's voice after all this time... All day yesterday and today he had waited for another call from her but none came.

"Dad!" Bucky's screams and her thunderous descent down the stairs broke Simon's reverie.

Running at full speed, she burst through the doorway and didn't stop until she was at the large bay window. "There's a fire! Maggie's house is on fire!"

Simon jumped up from the couch and joined her at the window. The way the Mansion sat downhill from the road, Maggie's house would have been visible to the left or north had not trees obscured the view. It was nearly dark out but no flames lit the evening sky.

"There's nothing there, Lamb. Were you dreaming?"

"Dad!" Bucky screamed near his ear. "Call 911! It's on fire!" She ran from the room.

"Bucky, get back here."

Simon rushed after her and chased her into the kitchen. She slammed into the French doors with both hands and rebounded when they didn't open. She fumbled with the lock and the doorknob as Simon reached her and attempted to stop her from opening them.

"Let me go! I've got to help them." She thrashed about like a wild animal, trying to get away from Simon and, at the same time, unlock and open the door.

The kitchen phone rang, and when Simon turned toward it, Bucky slipped through his grasp and was out the door and down the back steps before he could stop her. Simon grabbed the receiver off the wall. There was no one there. He slammed the receiver back on its cradle and turned to follow Bucky, but instead picked up the phone again and called 911. If there were no fire, it would be wasted call for the Turn Back Volunteer Fire Department. But if Bucky was right—and she had been right about Ian's fall—maybe they were needed.

After hurriedly giving the 911 operator the information, he grabbed his jacket off the hook and a flashlight from the shelf and hurtled down the steps, across the garden and through one of the doorways in the wall in the direction his daughter had fled.

21

FIRE

Bucky took the shortcut through the woods Ian used to get from his house to the Mansion. The boy had worn a path with his daily trips all summer and even in the dark, and despite the fact she had never gone that way, Bucky had no difficulty picking out the trail. The track took her to the back yard between Maggie's barn and the house. As she broke through the trees, she could see white smoke outlining the edges of the kitchen door and windows and eaves and then billowing upwards. Orange flames licked at the curtains at one window.

Bucky bounded up the steps to the back porch and pushed open the door. The sudden influx of oxygen caused the smoke and flames to vent through the open doorway, the smoke overcoming her for a moment.

"Maggie!" she tried to scream, but ended up coughing. She lifted the bottom of her T-shirt over her mouth and stepped into the kitchen.

Maggie was attacking the flames on one wall with a quilt.

"Maggie!" Bucky found her voice. "Where's Ian?"

"What is heaven's name are you doing here, child?" Maggie yelled, trying to smother the flames.

Bucky bolted through the dining room and into the living room. Opening the back door had drawn some of the smoke from these rooms, but there were no lights on. She had discovered years ago her night vision far surpassed her dad's, but here in the darkened room she could see only the black shapes of the furniture. A pile of covers and pillows were on the couch. Maggie must have been making Ian's bed again when the fire broke out which meant Ian was probably still upstairs. Bucky stood at the bottom of the narrow hallway which enclosed the stairs and called out to Ian, but there was no response. She flipped the wall switch at the base of the stairs, but the fire must have cut off the electricity. As she ascended the stairs in the dark, she repeatedly called his name. Why was he not answering?

There were three rooms upstairs and Ian's was the first one on the right. His door was closed, and he was sitting up in his bed, watching a video on his battery-powered laptop.

Bucky threw open the door and yanked the headphones off of him. "What are you doing, you idiot? Your house is on fire. You have to get out of here."

The glow from the screen illuminated Ian's surprised face. "Where's Gram?"

"She's trying to put the fire out in the kitchen. Come on!" Bucky pulled one of Ian's arms."

"Be careful." Ian doubled over in pain as Bucky tried to drag him out of the bed. "Let me do it." He shook her off and stood, hunched over. "Where are my shoes?"

"You don't need shoes," screamed Bucky. "We need to get downstairs."

Now that the door was open smoke began to fill the room.

"Here they are." Bucky bent down and picked up Ian's sneakers with one hand and put her other arm around Ian to support him. Her eyes were stinging.

"We're supposed to crawl," said Ian. "Less smoke near the floor." He moaned as he dropped first on one knee and then the other and pulled Bucky down alongside him.

Together they headed for the stairs just as Bucky heard her father's voice from the kitchen. "Maggie, you have to get out of here! Help is on the way. Where's Bucky and Ian?"

"Dad," yelled Bucky. "We're upstairs. We're coming down. Ian has to go slow."

The black shape of Simon appeared in the white smoke at the bottom of the stairs. "Bucky, get down here!"

"I have to help Ian!"

"Get down here!" ordered Simon, raising his voice. "I'll help him."

Bucky squeezed Ian's arm and crawled down the stairs on all fours.

"Go out the front door." Simon handed her his flashlight and pivoted back toward the kitchen. "Maggie, it's too big. There's nothing you can do. You have to get out now." Simon turned back to Bucky who was still beside him on the floor. "I told you to go!"

Headlights appeared in the driveway as the first of the volunteer firefighters arrived in pickups and cars.

Maggie came into the smoke-filled living room and grabbed some blankets from the pile on the couch. She wrapped one around Bucky who got to her feet and hurried with Maggie to the front door and out onto the porch.

Simon charged up the stairs in the darkness and tripped over Ian who was crouched near the top of them.

"Here," said Simon, "Put your arms around my neck. I'll carry you down."

Through the picture window Simon saw the firetruck arriving as he and Ian reached the bottom of the stairs. Two men had come in through the front door and shone their lights so Simon could see to exit the house.

The front yard was a flurry of activity. Simon carried Ian over near the driveway where Maggie and Bucky stood. Both of them were wrapped in quilts. Maggie took hers off and put it around Ian's shoulders after Simon had set the boy down on the grass.

"Maggie," called one of the men. Bucky recognized the voice as belonging to Jim Runnel from church. "Are your keys in the truck? We need to get it out of the garage in case the flames jump to there. You don't want to lose it, too."

The next hour was surreal, and, more than once, Bucky asked Simon if this was a dream or was it really happening. Maggie, who usually presented a strong front, looked worn out as she sat on an overturned five-gallon plastic bucket. Bucky sat in the gravel next to her and held her hand. The firefighters were able to contain the flames to the back of the house, mainly to the kitchen. A utility room and bathroom, additions to the original structure, also suffered damage. Smoke hung in the air even after the flames were out.

"Do you know how it started?" asked Simon.

"That old fuse box," said Maggie. "The whole thing was wired back in the forties when rural electric first came to the area. It should have been upgraded years ago. I had washed a load of towels and tablecloths from this afternoon and put them in the dryer. I didn't realize the oven had been left on all day. I guess it was too much and the box started sparking, and the next thing I knew there were flames going up the wall. I thought I could put it out."

Bucky patted Maggie's hand. "It's all right. You can stay with us until it's fixed."

"Bucky," Simon hissed, "are you forgetting who's coming?"

"But we have plenty of room."

"Who's coming?" asked Maggie.

Simon opened his mouth twice to speak, but could not answer her.

"You and Ian can stay at our house, of course." Penny Crosson had appeared behind them. Cars and trucks had been driving by and stopping for the past hour as news of the fire spread through the community.

"Dad?" Bucky pleaded in a soft voice.

"Can I stay in the Ian Michael Fletcher room?" asked Ian. He was sitting cross-legged next to Bucky, both of them huddled under blankets against the chill of the cold October evening.

"It doesn't have any furniture in it," said Bucky. "You'd have to sleep on the floor."

"I don't mind," said Ian.

"But we have those two guest rooms," said Bucky. "They have beds and everything. You can have one room and your gram can have the other one."

"But if you have a guest coming…" said Maggie.

"Oh, she'll sleep with Dad."

"What?" Maggie and Penny asked at the same time.

Simon cleared his throat. "Maggie, since Bucky seems to have the sleeping arrangements all figured out, you and Ian are more than welcome to stay at the Mansion as long as you need to. As soon as they say it's all right to go back inside here, you can get some clothes and whatever else you might need. Everything is going to smell of smoke, but we can do a load of laundry tonight so you have something to wear to Ian's doctor's appointment tomorrow."

"And we can tell Mrs. Lannigan all my school stuff burned up in the fire."

"No, we can't," said Simon.

"I hope our story's all right," said Bucky. "They might have gotten water all over it and ruined it."

"It appears most of the water damage was confined to the downstairs," said Simon, "but we won't know for sure until morning."

Maggie put her head in her hands. "I can't even think right now."

Penny, standing behind her, put her hands on Maggie's shoulders. "You're safe and Ian's safe. That's what's important. The two of you can stay the night at our house and then tomorrow we'll figure out what to do."

Bucky again took one of Maggie's hands from her face and squeezed it. Maggie raised her head and looked at Bucky. In the harsh glare of the spotlights illuminating the house and yard, Maggie could see the gold flecks sparkling in the young girl's eyes. And beyond her, in the dark tree line, flitted little green pinpoints of light. It was too late in the year for fireflies.

Maggie laid her free hand on one of Penny's which rested on her shoulder. "Thank you, Penny, but I think we'll stay at the Mansion tonight."

"If you think that's best," said Penny. "And don't worry about the milking tomorrow. Now that Dale has a taste for it, I think he'd be up here morning and night milking your poor Willow."

It was almost three hours later when Simon finally got everyone settled into the Mansion. He had a difficult time separating Bucky and Ian into their respective rooms, but managed it at last. When he walked by Maggie's room, her door was open and she was sitting on the stuffed chair, staring at nothing. He was unsure whether he should intrude on her, but decided to stick his head in and ask if there was anything else she needed.

Her hair was still wet from her shower and she was wearing one of Simon's robes.

"I'm just sitting here thinking of the million things I have to do tomorrow."

"We'll prioritize them. First thing we'll do is call your insurance agent. You do have insurance, don't you?"

Maggie nodded. "I have a high deductible, though."

"Don't worry about that."

"Simon, I *have* to worry about that. I have to worry about a lot of things that you don't."

Simon pulled out the desk chair and sat in it. "But money isn't one of them. We're going to—"

Maggie held up her hands to stop him.

"No, listen to me," Simon continued. "We're going to rewire that whole place. I'll not sit idly by and have you and Ian living in unsafe conditions. From what I could see tonight, the back wall is mostly gone and will have to be rebuilt, anyway. So, why don't we extend it out a few feet, enlarge the kitchen—you'll have more room to cook and can. We can enlarge and update that bathroom, too, and the utility room, so you can at least turn around in them. Heck, while everything is in disarray, we might as well replace the heating and cooling systems, also. How old's your roof?"

"Simon, I told you before. I don't want your money."

Simon reached over and took one of Maggie's hands. "For what you've done for my daughter in the past few months, I owe you more than I could ever hope to repay. Let me do this for you. And for Ian."

"Who's coming tomorrow?"

Simon, taken aback at the unexpected change in conversation, released her hand and sat back in the chair. He turned his head away from the woman's gaze.

"Is it that pretty young archaeologist that was here last summer?"

The question took Simon by surprise. "What? Who? Jennifer Brockman? No, why would you think that?"

Maggie smiled. It was the first time all evening she had smiled. "From what Bucky said about the sleeping arrangements."

Simon shook his head. "No. God, no. It's not her. It's uh… It's… It's Meredyth. It's my wife. We don't know for sure if it's tomorrow. Could be the next day or the next."

"Your wife?" Maggie whispered.

"She left a cryptic message on the phone yesterday. She hasn't called since."

"Then we really should not be here. Why didn't you say something?"

"It's a big house. And I think Bucky needs you here. She's scared to death of her. She's been having dreams—waking dreams and…and shared dreams with me—in which Meredyth is trying to kill her. I think she's torn between her fascination with seeing the mother she's never known but terrified of being near her." Simon told her what he had learned from Matt Healey about Meredyth. "So, that's where we stand. I guess we'll find out more when she gets here."

"You said Bucky's scared. How are you holding up emotionally?"

369

Simon turned away. "I don't know. I... I honestly don't know. It's been more than nine years."

"I think tomorrow I should take Penny up on her offer and we'll move to the Crossons'."

He turned his attention back to Maggie. "Please don't. I... I know you and Penny are close, but I really want you to be here. For Bucky. I really need you to be here."

"What happened to that writer's solitude you crave?"

"I think that went out the window some months ago. I still crave it, but it's not going to happen."

"I must admit having my own private bathroom right here is tempting."

"I'm sorry, Maggie. I know you must be exhausted. Do you need to leave by ten in the morning to get to the doctor's appointment?"

"I'm thinking I should call tomorrow and cancel that with all that's happened."

"No, you should keep it. I'm...a little concerned Ian is still in so much pain. I know it's only been a week since the surgery, but I think he should be a little better by now than he is. I wonder..."

"What?"

"I wonder if he's faking it."

"You mean for attention?" asked Maggie. "That doesn't sound like Ian. He's never been like that."

"He has been through a lot this past week. The surgery and then finding out...well...you know."

"You think he's looking for a little sympathy?"

Simon shook his head. "I just think you should keep the appointment tomorrow. There could be something physically wrong."

Simon said goodnight to Maggie and then went down the hall to Bucky's room. It was long past her bedtime but he found her sitting up in her bed.

"You should be asleep." Simon grasped her by her upper arms and tried to get her to lie down, but she resisted.

"I can't. That was scary tonight. What if this place catches on fire while I'm asleep?"

"You see that little round box with the green light up there on the ceiling?" Simon pointed to it. "That's a smoke detector just like in our apartment back in New York. It will make an awful noise if it detects smoke which will alert us to get out. Maggie didn't have those in her house and she should have. And she will have when her house is repaired. But, Bucky, you scared me terribly tonight. You are never, never to run into a burning building. Do you understand? That whole place could have gone up in an instant and I would have lost you."

"But I had to save Ian."

"I don't care. I could have lost you *and* Ian *and* Maggie."

"Dad?"

"What?"

"I don't think you can order me not to save someone's life. John 15:13 says *No one has greater love than this, to lay down one's life for one's friends.* So if I died, I would have died trying to save Ian."

"I'm not going to argue with the Bible. I'm just telling you to never run into a burning building. But, Bucky, Maggie's house wasn't on fire when you came downstairs to tell me and when you ran out alone into the night. I don't want you doing that again either. But it couldn't have been on fire. It would have been completely gone if it were already burning at the time you first said it was. How did you know?"

Bucky shrugged. "I just knew." She pointed to her head. "I could see it. Is that bad?"

"No, of course it's not bad."

Bucky sniffed the air. "Even though I took a bath, I still smell smoke."

"So do I. I think it's in the air outside. And our dirty clothes are downstairs and they smell of smoke." I'll put another load in before I go to bed."

"Dad, will you go talk to Ian tonight like you do to me? Except don't yell at him like you yelled at me."

"I didn't yell at you. I… I admonished you. I suspect he's already asleep."

"No, he's not. He's scared."

"Okay. I'll check on him. Now I think you need to lie down and close your eyes and try to go to sleep." On his way out, Simon bent over and removed something from one of the electrical sockets on the wall and slipped it into his pocket. He then turned off her bedside lamp with the switch by the door. "Good night, Lamb."

Ian's door was closed but light seeped out from beneath it. Simon knocked softly, but there was no response. He opened the door, expecting to find the boy asleep, but he, too, was sitting up in bed.

"May I come in?"

Ian nodded.

Simon pulled out the desk chair and sat down near the head of the bed. "Having trouble going to sleep?"

"Where's Gram? Is she all right?"

"She's in the room right next to this one. Remember? Her light was out when I passed by just now, so I think she's finally going to try to get some sleep. You should, too."

"I've only been in this place during the daytime. It's a lot scarier at night."

"As old as it is," said Simon, "you'd think everything would have settled by now, but it still creaks and groans like some old person. But it's only wood and stone, shifting a little. And if the temperature drops enough tonight, the heating system will kick on and that will be another sound added to the mix."

"I always heard it was haunted."

Simon shook his head. "No."

"What about the woman Bucky and I saw in the window downstairs last summer? She tried to dive-bomb us."

"If, indeed, you saw her, I don't believe she meant you any harm. I think it was the Anarianu, drawing your attention to the birth stone, Seraphina's song stone."

"Bucky says the woman in front of the cave in our dreams is her mom. She said she pushed me off the bluff and that's why I fell."

"Did someone push you?"

Ian squinted. "I don't think so. I think I stepped on a loose rock and it gave way. There sure wasn't no woman in no green dress up there with me."

Simon bit his lower lip to keep himself from correcting Ian's grammar. "Did Bucky tell you we're going to try to enlarge the opening of the cave so we can get inside? Dr. Smallin sent a little camera in there. I'll show you the video of what we saw sometime in the next couple of days."

"Did you see the pirate— I mean the chest?"

"Yes. Dr. Smallin and some of his crew are coming back, along with Dr. Mason and also the Moyers, the two experts in ancient languages you met last summer. They're all coming here in less than two weeks. You'll need to be mended so you can be there with us."

"I'll be all right by then, but…" Ian turned his head away, but not before Simon saw the young boy's eyes fill with tears.

Ian covered his eyes with his fists.

"It's okay to cry, Ian. You've had an upsetting evening."

"But my house is gone. And all my stuff." Ian spoke the words between sobs.

"No, it's not." Simon leaned forward and grasped one of Ian's shoulders. "I know it was hard to tell in the dark, but didn't you hear us talking? Only the back of the house is damaged. I'm sure most of your collections survived. You'll see tomorrow when you return from the doctor."

Simon fished the object he had taken from Bucky's room out of his pocket. "Here. I brought you a nightlight." He walked over by the door to the bathroom and plugged it in to the electrical outlet near the floor. "I'll put it here in case you have to get up during the night. It will provide enough light that you won't need these lamps on and maybe you'll sleep better."

"It's pink."

"Yeah." Simon chuckled. "I'm afraid it's a princess nightlight."

"I wish I could sleep in Bucky's room."

"The two of you would talk all night and not get any rest and neither would your gram nor I." Simon stood by the hallway door with his hand on the light switch. "Now, your gram is next door and I'm across the hall and down a little ways. I don't have a bell for you to ring, but if you need anything, just yell and we'll hear you."

"Mr. Carter?"

"Yes?"

"Are you the Devil?"

Simon shook his head and suppressed a smile. "No."

"Rats."

"Why would you want me to be the Devil?"

"Because Bucky says she's the Devil's spawn. And since you're my father, too, then that would also make me the Devil's spawn and I'd have powers like Bucky."

Simon's brow creased. "Bucky doesn't have any powers."

"Of course she does."

Simon hesitated a moment, surprised at the course of Ian's reasoning. The boy's last words reminded Simon of the response of the Anarianu when he questioned them in the Spring Room. "I'm afraid both you and Bucky will have to settle for just being the offspring of plain old Simon Carter. Good night, Ian." He flipped the switch and the room went dark except for the glow of the pink princess nightlight.

"Mr. Carter?"

"Yes?"

"I did what you told me."

"What was that?"

"About being nice to Gram and telling her thank you."

"Yes, I know you have and I appreciate it. Thank you. Good night."

"Mr. Carter?"

"Yes?"

"Bucky's really scared about her mother coming tomorrow. You should talk to her." In the darkness Ian was a silhouette still sitting up in the bed.

"I've tried. Nothing I say seems to alleviate her fears. I believe your presence here will comfort her more than my words. Good night, Ian."

When Maggie left in her pickup with Ian the next morning to drive the forty-five miles to Green River for her great-grandson's doctor's appointment, she considered turning right out of the Mansion's lane and taking the long road around the mountain. She was afraid if she drove by her house the tears which had pooled in her eyes ever since last evening would spill over. She didn't want Ian to see her cry, but she needed to view in the daylight what was left of the structure that had been built by her great-great-grandfather Arley Bolin in the 1870s. She turned left.

There were half a dozen cars and pickups sprawled in her driveway and parked on the side of the gravel road in front of her house. Ron Crosson's was not the only truck she recognized. She could name the owners of each of the others. She stopped her own truck in the middle of the road and left the motor running as she climbed out. Jim Runnel came out the front door and called to her.

"Maggie! Some of us thought we'd come over this morning and get some tarps over what's left of the wall and the roof in the back and clean up some of the mess we left behind last night. Hope you don't mind."

Maggie clasped her hands to her chest and turned back toward the pickup. "Stay here," she told Ian. "I'll just be a minute. She walked over and met Jim in the yard. "I tried to call you this morning, but Vera said you were out. I thought, as my insurance agent, you'd better come look at it in the light before I did anything."

"I already filed the claim to start the whole process," said Jim. "We'll get an adjuster in here probably tomorrow, but you should get an initial check in the mail tomorrow or the next day."

"Oh, Jim, thank you for everything. I'm just overwhelmed by it all."

He took one of Maggie's hands in his. "Try not to worry, Maggie. You've got a whole passel of friends and relatives who are going to do everything we can to get this old house fixed up good as new and get you back inside."

Ron Crosson came out onto the porch. "Maggie, good to see you. Penny said you had to be in Green River this morning."

"We're on our way there now. Thank you so much for all your help."

"We took the milk home with us this morning. Dale and I fed the chickens and we'll get the eggs for you today, too, when we come back this evening. Should we bring it all up to the Mansion?"

"You keep whatever you can use and give the rest to anyone who wants it. Oh, and I just thought of something. With no electricity, everything in my freezer is gone. And it's full of meat and peaches and blackberries and—"

"We've taken care of that, too," said Ron. "I've got a freezer in the back of the store that's almost empty. We transferred everything there already."

"Oh, Ron, how can I ever thank all of you?"

"I don't know about the others, but one of your peach cobblers this winter will be thanks enough for me and Dale."

"Oh, thank you again, Ron, and tell Dale thanks. I need to be on my way. Tell Penny I'll call her this afternoon when we get back."

"Dad!"

Simon looked up from his computer in the study to see Bucky standing at the door.

"She's here! She's coming down the lane."

Twisting in his chair, Simon looked out the bay window behind him. He glanced at his watch. It was eleven o'clock. Maggie had left at ten. He had told her to leave the gate open. "I don't see anyone."

"Wait." Bucky held up her index finger and cocked her head like she was listening.

"Oh, my God," whispered Simon. "Here she is."

A red Jeep Wrangler approached the front of the Mansion.

"What do we do, Dad?"

Simon stood and combed the fingers of his right hand through his hair. "We meet her at the front door, of course."

He crossed the room to where Bucky still stood by the door. She held out her hand and he took it out of habit. He could feel a slight tremor in her hand, but he was unsure which of them was trembling.

They walked out into the hall and to the spacious entryway with its marble floor. From their post they could hear the car engine outside and then it stopped, and the only sound was the short, rapid breaths of the two who waited in the foyer and the ticking of the grandfather clock behind them.

"What's taking her so long?"

"She has to park the car and get out and walk up the steps," said Simon.

"Maybe we should go out on the porch. She might think nobody's home or she might get scared and drive away."

"She's kept us waiting nine years. We can wait here a few more seconds."

They both jerked when the doorbell rang.

"Dad?" Bucky whispered.

Simon tried to let go of Bucky's hand to reach for the doorknob, but she clung tightly to him. He used his other hand, first taking a breath and then turning the knob of the right hand door and opening it.

"Hello, you handsome devil. I hope you don't mind I dropped in unannounced."

Both Simon and Bucky took a step back, their mouths opened.

Bucky was the first to recover. "Dr. Brockman?"

"Jennifer," whispered Simon.

22

EXPLANATIONS ARE IN ORDER

"Don't look so shocked." Jennifer stepped through the doorway. She was wearing khaki slacks and a pale yellow sweater with a scarf tied loosely around her neck. Her shoulder-length blonde hair was pulled back at the nape of her neck. "You did send me those photos of what you *say* are the remains of a smelter. Of course, there's no way they are millennia old. More likely they date from the time of the French in this area—1700s, possibly early nineteenth century." Jennifer wrinkled her nose. "What's wrong with the two of you?"

"Jennifer." Simon cleared his throat. "This is not a good time."

"I'm off through Wednesday," Jennifer said. "Thought I would pop in and have a look."

Bucky, still holding Simon's hand, yanked it. "But, Dad."

"Bucky," said Simon, "go up to your room. I need to visit with Dr. Brockman."

Bucky glared at the woman and released Simon's hand. She stepped away from them and then contorted her face as she twisted her right arm around to scratch her back. "Dad, that chigger bite I got from sitting on Maggie's lawn last night is itching something fierce. Would you put some more of that gel on it?"

"What are you talking about?" asked Simon. "We already had a hard freeze. There aren't any chiggers."

"Whatever it is, it itches. There's some of that ointment in the bathroom by the kitchen."

Simon, confused, creased his brow. "Then you put it on."

"I can't reach the itch. It's right about here." Bucky doubled over and switched to her left hand as she clawed at her back.

"Excuse me, Jennifer. Would you wait in my study while I tend to her?" Simon waved a hand in the direction of his study. He grabbed Bucky by the wrist and escorted her down the west hallway toward the kitchen and into the bathroom. He closed the door behind them. "Let me see your back," he said, keeping his voice low.

Bucky took a few steps away from him. "I don't have a chigger bite. I just wanted to talk to you. What is *she* doing here?"

"She told us. She's here to see the smelter ruins. I didn't invite her."

"But Mom's coming."

"I thought you said your mom was driving down the lane. I've come to trust your intuition, but you missed this one, didn't you?" Simon put his hands on his hips and turned his back to Bucky. "I'm sorry. I shouldn't have said that. But when you burst in and said she was coming, I thought you must have had...one of your...one of your feelings." He turned back around.

"No." Bucky shrugged. "Now that some of the leaves are gone, I can see the front gate from a window in one of the empty rooms upstairs near the end of the hallway. I've been keeping watch, and when I saw the car, I thought it was Mom. I didn't know we were expecting anyone else today."

"We weren't expecting anyone else."

"Can't you get rid of her?"

"She's come all the way from Philadelphia. I just can't turn her away. Besides, she's one of the leading experts in her field. I really want her to take a look at those stones."

Bucky took one of Simon's hands in hers. "Dad, I know you like her, but don't you still love Mom a little bit, too?"

"Of course I love your mother. It's not... I... I... Okay, here's what we'll do. I can show Jennifer on a map how to get to the clearing and she can take the UTV. That path's too rough even for that Jeep she's driving. I don't have to go with her."

"She won't like that." As soon as she spoke, Bucky's face went blank.

"What's wrong?" Simon leaned over and put his hands on her shoulders.

"Listen."

Simon straightened and cocked his head. "I don't hear anything."

The doorbell rang. They were some distance away from the foyer and behind a door but there was no mistaking the sound.

"Oh, God, no. Not now."

Simon took Bucky's hand and they left the bathroom and hurried to the entryway. The doorbell rang again. Simon took a breath and opened the door.

"Hi," said Ron Crosson. He was holding a large cardboard box. "Dale and I brought some of Maggie's belongings over here for her. Her computer and Ian's school stuff that we could find. A few other things."

Simon and Bucky stepped aside to let Ron and Dale enter.

"Bucky, why don't you show them upstairs to Maggie's room? They can put everything in there and she can sort through it when she returns."

Ron jerked his head toward Dr. Brockman's vehicle which was parked in front of his pickup. "Looks like you have company. Penny said you were expecting someone today."

"It's…uh…just an acquaintance."

Dale, carrying a computer tower, trailed his father.

"Believe it or not, Dale's the IT man in the family," said Ron. "He can get that thing hooked up for Maggie. We can get everything else out of the truck in a couple more trips. We don't want to take you away from your guest."

With a parting anxious look directed at Simon, Bucky led the way up the broad staircase with Ron and Dale following her. Ron made three more trips back to his pickup while Dale busied himself in Maggie's room, hooking up cables for the computer keyboard and monitor and getting everything in working order. Bucky stayed with Dale, sitting cross-legged on the floor beside him and watching him work. After Ron's last trip, carrying Maggie's possessions from the truck, he sat down in the recliner and waited for Dale to finish.

"Do…you…know…the…Wi-…Fi…pass…word?" Dale asked.

"I'll have to get it from my dad. It's probably in his desk."

Bucky ran down the stairs and came to a halt in front of the closed door to the study. She hesitated a moment before knocking. When she heard her father say, "Come in," she cracked open the door only wide enough to slip inside. Simon and Jennifer were standing at Simon's desk with a map spread out on it. Dr. Brockman's back was to Bucky.

"I'm sorry to interrupt, Dad, but Dale needs the Wi-Fi password." She tried to sound polite, but she hoped Simon could see from her expression she did not want Dr. Brockman here in their house. She knew she had conveyed her feelings when she saw Simon frown at her.

"Just a minute. It's here in the drawer." Simon pulled out a spiral notebook, thumbed through it, and wrote the code on a notepad. He tore off the paper and walked across the room to hand it to Bucky but stopped halfway.

Bucky's face had gone blank again.

"Bucky?"

Jennifer turned around.

Bucky started to pant, her eye wide.

Simon grasped her upper arms. "What's wrong, Lamb?"

"She's here, Dad. She's really here. I can… I can feel her."

Simon twisted around to look out the window, but there was no movement outside. Simon slapped the piece of paper into one of Bucky's hands. "Take this to Dale. Stay upstairs with them."

"No. Please, Dad."

"Do as I say. Now," he added when Bucky refused to budge. He forcibly turned her around and headed her out the door and closed it behind her.

"What was that all about?" asked Jennifer.

"Jennifer, you… You really have to leave." Simon crossed back to the desk and opened a drawer. "Here's the key to the UTV. It's charged, ready to go. Just follow the map."

Jennifer laid a hand on Simon's forearm. "Simon, I'd like you to go with me. I brought along a GPS-enabled drone to do both photogrammetry and LIDAR mapping. It's—"

"I can't. Not now. Someone's coming and I… I have to be here. And you…cannot be here. Please, Jennifer." Simon quickly folded the map and tried to steer Jennifer to the door of the study when he heard a motor outside. "Oh, God," he uttered and opened the study door.

"Dad!" Bucky hurled herself down the stairs.

Simon rushed over to her, leaving Jennifer standing in the doorway to his study. "I told you to wait with the Crossons."

Bucky took Simon's hand. "I can't."

"Let's go," said Simon. He pulled Bucky alongside of him to the double front doors and went out onto the porch.

A black sedan was now parked behind Ron Crosson's green pickup which was parked behind Jennifer Brockman's red Jeep.

"God, it looks like Grand Central Station out here," said Simon. "Now all we need is Maggie to come home." He looked down at Bucky who had gone quiet. She was chewing on her lower lip. He could feel her hand tremble. And this time he knew the tremor was hers. This was not the homecoming for Meredyth he had hoped for.

It was difficult to see the person behind the steering wheel through the tinted windows. The driver's side door finally opened. Simon felt Bucky take a sharp breath. It was a reminder to him to let out his own breath he was holding. The woman stood up out of the car and put a hand to her forehead. She took hold of the open car door for support. Simon released Bucky's hand and rushed down the steps, leaving Bucky on the porch.

He went around the car where the woman stood partially bent over.

"Are you all right?" He stopped about five feet away from her.

She straightened.

The woman standing before him was the same woman who had walked out the door nine years ago, never to return. Her hair, her skin, her hands, her eyes—it was the same Meredyth he had lost almost a decade earlier. She had not aged a day. Except this Meredyth was pregnant.

"Meredyth," Simon whispered.

"Sie, I think I'm going to be sick. The roads getting here were terr…"

Simon closed the gap between them and caught her as she crumpled. "I've got you, Mer."

Her eyelids fluttered. "I just need to lie down."

Simon lifted her and she put her arms around his neck.

"Not exactly the way I wanted to say hello," she said weakly.

Simon carried her up the steps to the broad porch as the front door opened to reveal Ron and Dale Crosson.

"Good Lord, what's happened? Here, let me help you." Ron Crosson was a larger man than Simon, and he held out his arms to relieve Simon of his burden.

Simon shook his head. "Just get the door, please. Bucky, run inside and make sure the library door is open. We'll put her on the couch."

"Should I call for an ambulance?" asked Ron, following Simon into the library. Dale came behind him.

"No, she's just… You know how these roads are for someone who's not used to them." Simon laid her on the couch and adjusted the pillows.

Jennifer had also followed them into the library. "What can I do to help?"

Simon shook his head. "Nothing. I… I need all of you to leave. Please. Please leave."

"Who is she, Simon?" asked Ron.

Simon sat on the low table in front of the couch and held Meredyth's hand. He looked up at the small group staring at him. "She's… She's my wife." He twisted to face Bucky who was standing behind him. "Go get a wash cloth from the bathroom. Run some cold water on it and bring it here."

Bucky stood frozen in place, her mouth half-open, her eyes fixed on the woman Simon said was her mother.

"Bucky, please," Simon whispered.

"Maybe I should stay here," said Jennifer, moving toward the couch. "If those ruins have been there all these years, they can last a few more hours."

"Jennifer, please go. Take the side-by-side." Simon turned back to Bucky, snapped his fingers and pointed toward the hallway door.

Bucky broke her gaze and looked at Simon who jerked his head toward the door. She fled from the room.

Simon released Meredyth's hand. He stood and held wide his arms as he ushered Ron and Dale and Jennifer through the doorway and into the foyer. "Please understand. I need to be alone right now."

All three seemed reluctant to leave, but they all walked out the front door. Simon closed it behind them as Bucky came back down the hallway with a dripping washcloth.

"Thank you, Lamb." Simon took the cloth from her. "You could have wrung it out first." A fake potted plant sat next to the grandfather clock, and Simon squeezed out the excess water into it. "Now, would you run upstairs and get a blanket?" He headed back to the library.

Bucky stopped him. "Dad, what's wrong with her? I can feel—" Bucky intertwined her arms. "It's all twisted like there are two of her. And she looks like she swallowed a basketball."

"She's… Bucky, she's pregnant."

Bucky's eyes widened. "What?"

Simon shook his head. "Please. Just go get a blanket. It's cool in there."

"But, Dad. She wasn't pregnant in the dreams."

"I told you it wasn't her in the dreams. They were only dreams."

Bucky backed away from him and then turned and ran up the stairs. Simon went back into the library.

As he placed the folded washcloth on her forehead, Meredyth opened her eyes. "I heard people talking. Who's Jennifer?"

"No one." Simon lowered himself to the table once again. "Well, she's not no one. She's a leading lithics expert from the University of Pennsylvania. She's here to check out some old ruins."

"We never allowed people to come over after Bucky was born."

"Times change. People change." Simon's eyes filled with tears. "Oh, Mer, where have you been? I searched for you. I waited for you. But you never... You never..."

Meredyth tried to sit up but a wave of nausea forced her back down. She put one hand over her lips and straightened the washcloth with the other.

Simon jumped up and grabbed a waste basket from the end of the couch. "You might need this."

Bucky appeared at the doorway with a blanket draped over her arms. Simon walked over and took it and sent her off once again to bring a glass of water. He spread the blanket over Meredyth and resumed his seat on the table.

"I want to see Bucky before you send me away, Simon. I think I caught a glimpse of her on the porch when I drove up. But I'd like to see her, to tell her I'm sorry, before I leave."

"Leave? Meredyth, you're not going anywhere. You're not well."

"I'm well enough to know you're not going to believe a word of my story. Oh." Meredyth lurched over on her side and vomited into the wastebasket. She lay back, her head on the pillow.

Simon took the damp cloth from her head and wiped her mouth.

Bucky, holding a glass and another washcloth, came to the doorway. "I wrung this one out," she whispered.

"Come over here." Simon beckoned her.

Bucky shook her head. From her position in the doorway she could only see the back of the couch and the library table behind it.

Simon walked over to where Bucky stood. "She wants to see you."

Bucky handed Simon the water glass and the damp cloth. "Please, don't make me."

"I'm not going to force you. Go on back up to your room, then."

"Uh, oh," said Bucky. "There's another car coming. I don't think it's Maggie and Ian."

Simon turned around to look out the window on the other side of the library but the angle was wrong for him to see the lane. "My God, we never get anyone here and now people are coming and going every few minutes. I need to be with your mother. Answer the door and send them away. But be polite about it." Simon stepped back into the library and closed the door.

Bucky's eyebrows arched a mile high as she stared at the closed door. He had never allowed her to answer the front door alone even when he knew who it was. Even on days when Sadie Jane Woods arrived for her French lesson, Simon always answered the door. On the day he had come home from the hospital, Bucky had opened the door for Dale Crosson without Simon's permission but he was asleep at the time. The doorbell rang and Bucky ran to the entryway. Skidding to a stop, she smoothed down her top and ran her fingers through her hair. She opened the right-hand door.

"Maxine!" Bucky exclaimed. "And Ruby!" she added when she saw the second woman behind the first. "What are you doing here?"

Maxine had bulging plastic bags hanging from her hands. More sacks filled the basket on the front of Ruby's walker. "We brought over some food," said Maxine, stepping through the doorway. "With Maggie and Ian staying here that's two extra mouths and…"

"We've heard your father doesn't do much in the way of cooking," said Ruby, completing Maxine's sentence. "And we certainly don't want Maggie to have to worry about cooking for all of you. Not with all that's happened to her."

Both of the Lukefahr Ladies were inside and Bucky closed the door behind them. She forgot all about Simon's instructions to turn away the person at the door.

"If I remember correctly the kitchen was down this hallway here unless the remodel changed things around," said Ruby.

"Follow me," said Bucky. "I'll show you."

When they reached the kitchen, the women set the bags on the counter and began to pull out of them plastic containers and baggies, each labeled with its contents.

"I think I can get the rest from the car," said Maxine.

"There's more?" asked Bucky.

"We wouldn't want you to starve," said Ruby. She pointed to a stack of containers. "Now all of these can go in the refrigerator."

Bucky helped her carry the items to the refrigerator, and Ruby shook her head and clicked her tongue a few times at how sparse it was. Aside from a half-empty gallon of milk, a bottle of orange juice and a carton of eggs, there was not much else in it besides some assorted condiments.

"Just what do you and your father eat, child?"

"There are frozen dinners in the freezer, and we eat sandwiches a lot. And soup."

Maxine came in with a cake pan balanced on two more bags.

"My gosh," said Bucky, "this will last us for a week."

"Oh, no," said Maxine, "this is just to tide you over for the next couple of days. Now all this isn't only from Ruby and me. Some of the others contributed. We'll get a schedule organized and keep you supplied until Maggie gets back in her home. We were already bringing her over a few things while she was having to care for Ian. We'll just have to double it."

"But now there's even one more," said Bucky. She turned and looked back down the hallway. "If she stays."

"Who else is here?" Maxine asked while Ruby stowed the rest of the food in the refrigerator, shifting things around until everything fit. "I was wondering about those two other cars out front."

"Now this pie and cake don't need refrigerating," said Ruby. "They can stay here on the counter." She rinsed her hands at the sink and then turned around. "So who else did you say is here?"

Bucky chewed on her lower lip, considering how she should answer the women's question. Her dad had told her it was a secret when they had first heard Meredyth was coming, but now Ron and Dale Crosson knew she was here, and Ron would tell his wife, and Penny would tell everyone. Maggie would find out as soon as she got home today, and she would probably tell anyone Penny missed. So it would not be a secret much longer. "One of the cars belongs to a visiting archaeologist, but she's not staying here. The other one, though." She swallowed. "My mom came home."

Both women visibly straightened.

"She's here now?" asked Maxine. "Where?"

Bucky tucked her chin. "In the library with my dad." She raised her head. "She's going to have a baby. The way she looks, she could have it any minute."

The two ladies, neither of them known for ever being at a loss for words, looked at each other without speaking. The only sound in the room was the faucet dripping from where Ruby had turned it off after washing her hands.

"My word," breathed Ruby, at last. "That is unexpected news. I guess it was unexpected, wasn't it?"

"We found out Friday she was coming," said Bucky.

"But a couple of weeks ago in Sunday school," said Maxine, "you told us the woman in the cave dreams is your mother. She's not in the family way in any of my dreams."

"If by that," said Bucky, "you mean she's not pregnant, she's not that way in my dreams either. And that's confusing to me."

"But Maggie told us she's been gone a long time— for years," said Ruby. "And now to show up like this, expecting a baby."

Maxine touched Ruby on the wrist and shook her head. "Bucky, we need to be on our way. You be sure and give Maggie our love when she gets back. It was generous of your father to take her and little Ian in like this. I know the two of them must be upset by the fire. And we all had such a nice time there yesterday. It just doesn't seem fair."

Bucky took Maxine by the hand and walked between her and Ruby back to the front door. "Thank you for all that food. All of you are such good cooks. I know it will be scrumptious."

When the two ladies had gone, Bucky went back to the closed door of the library. She slid down to the floor and sat cross-legged and listened. She could hear the deeper tones of her father clearly, but she had to strain to hear her mother's softer voice.

"Are you feeling better?"

Meredyth had vomited again into the wastebasket and Simon had wiped her face with the second washcloth. She nodded. "I need to try and sit up."

Simon grabbed another pillow from one of the other chairs and propped it behind her as she struggled to a sitting position.

"God, I'm as big as an elephant," she said. She focused on Simon's face after she got situated. "Guess you're wondering about that?"

"I'm wondering about a lot of things."

"Let me tell you. You're not going to believe it and there's a lot I don't know, but, please, just listen. The day I walked out of our apartment, the day I found that letter and the picture of the baby the woman claimed was yours, I now know that day was nine years ago. But to me it was last summer. It was July 5. Remember? We had watched the fireworks on TV the night before and had turned the sound down low so as not to wake Bucky."

"Of course, I remember. Every minute of that day is etched in my brain."

"I was hurt and upset, and I needed to get away from you for a while and think things through. I only intended to go to the park. Honest, Simon. I was just going for a walk to clear my thoughts. I was headed along my favorite part—"

"The Loch."

"Yes. And I was almost at Montayne's Fonteyn, the spring where it begins, when…"

"What?" Simon whispered the word.

"There was this thing—I don't know how to describe it. It was a swirling mass of colors. I was tired and hot and thirsty and I thought I was hallucinating and then it… It enveloped me."

Simon closed his eyes and leaned back, his palms flat on the low table where he was sitting.

"And the next thing I know I wake up and it's… It was almost dark and I could hear voices. One of them said, 'There's someone down there.' And I remember some people around me, but I couldn't tell them who I was or where I lived. And then I must have blacked out because I awoke next in a hospital, but I still had no memory. I learned later it was June 29 when I was admitted to the hospital. After a few days there I was sent to a residential care facility. I was declared a ward of the state. It was almost three months before even little bits of my memory returned and it's still not all there. But when it did start to surface, I realized nine years had passed since I walked out of our apartment. Nine years, Simon! I've lost nine years and I can't remember them. I don't know where... Just snippets and fragments. And then when I did remember who I was, I couldn't find you. But I found Matt. And he told me where you were."

Simon stood and paced back and forth a few steps but did not speak. He resumed his seat. "Why didn't you want Matt to tell me you were back?"

"For the same reason I walked out that afternoon. Simon, I messed up. I messed up really, really bad. I didn't know how to tell you that day and I don't know how to tell you now."

Simon took one of Meredyth's hands. "What are you talking about? I was the one who messed up. I got some girl pregnant I didn't even know while I was married to the most beautiful, most loving woman I could ever hope to have in my life *and* the mother of my child."

Meredyth turned her face toward the back of the couch for a moment before once again looking at Simon. "That's just it." She squeezed shut her eyes. "Matt and I had an affair. Simon, there's a chance Rose was not your child."

Simon released her hand. "You...and Matt?"

"When I found out I was pregnant with Rose, I told Matt. At first he wanted me to terminate the pregnancy. Of course, I refused, and then he said he would fix it. He would take care of things so you could never accuse me of infidelity since you would be as guilty as I was. I didn't know what he was talking about, but he told me later about Chicago, about how he fixed you up with some girl there. And he told me if ever you found out about him and me I could throw that in your face."

Meredyth was the one who now reached out and took Simon by the hand. "Simon, I swear to you my affair with Matt ended before Chicago. We never saw each other again without you present. And then after Rose was born and... And after... After Bucky came, well, he was never even over at the apartment any more, you know that."

Simon put his other hand over Meredyth's. "Let me get this straight. You and Matt Healey, my wife and my best friend, had an affair which you were afraid resulted in a pregnancy. So Matt gets me drunk and pushes me into the arms of a girl at a writers convention, hoping I will sleep with her. My wife disappears, and for the past nine years, Matt has continued to be not only my publisher but has remained my best friend."

Simon walked over to the bay window and looked out, his back to Meredyth. With his fists clenched and his jaw tight, he stood there, staring through the ripples in the old glass at the trees that lined the drive. Two minutes passed before he spoke. "So Matt Healey is to blame for all this…this misery I have experienced for all these years, this guilt you have borne, this... God, I feel like I've been kicked in the stomach."

"Simon, Matt was involved, yes, but he's not the one to blame for our sins. Deep down, you know that. We each made the decision to cheat on the other. We are the guilty ones."

Simon turned and paced from one side of the library to the other.

"It was a difficult period for both of us, Sie. But we came out on the other side okay. We had Rose to mourn and Bucky to focus on, and we rekindled the passion for each other we once had. We did, didn't we?"

Simon sniffed and fought back the tears pooling in his eyes. He stopped in front of the couch and nodded toward Meredyth's swollen abdomen. "Is that Matt's?"

"No, Simon. It's yours."

Simon sat down heavily on the table. "That's… That's impossible."

"Don't you remember I was sick every day there for a while? I did a home pregnancy test. In fact, I did it twice. I was planning to tell you that evening. I had a nice dinner planned, candlelight, the whole works. Simon, I was two months pregnant when I left the apartment that day for the park. The doctor at the hospital estimated I was four months pregnant when they found me last summer. Nine years later."

"But you said you can't remember those nine years. How do… How can you be so sure it's mine?"

"I just know."

Simon exhaled. "When are you due?"

Meredyth shook her head. "Maybe the end of November. I'm definitely in my last trimester." When Simon did not respond, Meredyth continued. "Simon, all of this makes no sense to me, but you're taking it awfully well. I mean you've always been reserved, but I expected—I don't know what I expected. Fireworks, maybe. Condemnation certainly."

Simon nodded. "I do have some things to say, but I wanted to hear your story first. To begin, Bucky *is* our Rose. There was no baby switch that awful night. Rose was dying and I believe she was taken to the same place by the same beings who took you. I don't know where that is— another dimension maybe—and I don't know who they are. But they cured her and returned her to us, somewhat changed, a few months older, but still our Rosebud."

"But her back. The blood whenever she cried."

"Part of her healing required her to be submerged in water. Her scars are from where her gills were removed when they returned her." Simon's head jerked when he saw Meredyth's face go blank. Twice today, and many times before, he had seen that same expressionless look on Bucky whenever she was sensing something. "What's wrong?"

"Gills. The 'Laya Song.' I remember something. Where I was it was all light and sounds and music, so much music. There was a song called the 'Laya Song' they sang to dry their tears."

"Yes," said Simon, "they told me, but I don't know it. They think I do. Evidently my subconscious knows it, but I can't remember the words. Can you sing it?"

"The words are there." She frowned. "If I could only remember. But Simon, she looked so different. Are you sure she's our Rose?"

"Positive. Which is another thing you needn't be concerned about. She's all mine. We had a DNA test. She's definitely my daughter. And, oh, Meredyth, wait until you get to know her. She's bright and funny and creative and...she has an imagination out of this world. And she's resilient and...and intuitive. I think that's her most important trait. I don't even know how to describe it. She's been raised in virtual isolation and yet, when she's around people, she just glows. She instinctively knows how to relate to them. She has this whole town wrapped around her little finger. Up until this month, every week we had what we called prayer walks. Thousands of people would show up and follow her around the park in the center of town."

"Is that why there were a gazillion portable toilets there when I drove through town this morning?"

Simon laughed. It was the first time he had even smiled since Meredyth arrived. "With that many people you have to provide for them. She even gets fan mail. I don't let her see it. I'm saving them, though, for when she's older."

"My God, Simon. This is just... This is all so unbelievable. It's something out of a fairy tale, and here we are talking about it as if it's ordinary. Our baby had gills, I was in some unknown place for nine years, I've been pregnant for those nine years, you say thousands of people follow our child like she's some Pied Piper…"

Simon smiled and shook his head. "Oh, it gets even better. Wait until you hear what's all been going on this past summer. And wait until I tell you about me."

"What about you?"

Simon looked away for a few moments. "I don't even know where to start." He sighed. "Remember when we were in Boğazkale in Turkey in that graduate class? And we went into that little shop and I picked up that stone with the spirals and the unknown inscription on it?"

"Of course I remember. It sat on your desk in the apartment. And then the night Rose was taken—that Bucky—that Rose became Bucky—we found a similar one in her bassinet." Meredyth's eyes widened and she caught her breath. "Oh, my God, Sie. They're song stones." She tried to get up off the couch. "I remember. They're the words to the 'Laya Song.' Where are they?"

Simon helped her stand, and he supported her with one arm around her shoulders. "You said you can't remember where you were for the past nine years, but in the past few minutes you seem to be remembering an awful lot."

"I told you the memories have come in bits and flashes for the past few weeks, but I swear, ever since I drove into Turn Back, I've had such a feeling of déjà vu. Except for the portable toilets. I don't remember them. But it's been almost overwhelming. And when I stepped through the doors of this place—well, I guess I didn't step. You carried me. I know I've never been here, and yet I feel I have been here. And the place—wherever it was where I've been— I feel I can almost reach out and touch it. It's here. It's all around here." She put a hand to her face and sobbed.

Simon could feel her shaking. "It's all right, Mer. I know… I know exactly what you're feeling. Let's…uh… Let's go into the kitchen. I'll… I'll fix you some tea and whatever else you think you can eat. We have… We have a whole lifetime ahead of us to catch up on the past few years. Come on."

"I really need to use the facilities first. I should have stopped at one of those toilets."

"There's a bathroom near the kitchen."

Bucky, still outside the library with her ear to the door, scrambled to her feet. There was an alcove down the hallway across from her father's study and she darted for it and flattened herself against the wall, hoping they would not see her when they emerged from the library. Fortunately, their attention was focused on each other, and they turned left and then right as they headed toward the kitchen. Bucky sprinted up the stairs and down a hallway. Creeping down the back stairs which came out in the kitchen, she planted herself on the landing where she would be out of sight and yet able to hear.

23

THESE THINGS TAKE TIME

Simon was standing at the French doors in the kitchen when Meredyth joined him a few minutes later. She put an arm around his waist and a hand on his shoulder. He had always assumed the feelings which flooded over him at her touch were the result of being in love with the perfect mate. But although these were more intense, he now recognized them as the same sense of familiarity he felt whenever he touched certain people here in Turn Back. And as Bucky had pointed out, he could also feel the presence of the baby growing within Meredyth, the life force of the unborn child entwined with Meredyth's own. Although why he was experiencing these sensations with Meredyth was something he was curious about, he decided any explanation could wait until later. For now he would simply enjoy her touch.

"It's so beautiful here," she said, her gaze on the walled back garden. "What's that boat?"

Simon smiled. "Oh, that's Bucky and Ian's craft they use for their adventures. Sometimes it's a pirate ship or the *Mayflower* or a canoe or a flatboat. It all depends on what story they're acting out."

"Who's Ian?"

Simon cleared his throat. "That's another thing I have to tell you. Ian is…the child…" He stopped and traced his index finger down the casing of the door. "He's the child of the woman in Chicago. He lives next door."

Meredyth withdrew her hands from Simon and stepped away. "Your love child and his mother live next door? Is that why you left New York to move here to the middle of nowhere? To be with her?"

"No. No. No." Simon tried to touch her but Meredyth shrugged him off. "What I told you that day in the apartment when you discovered that…that letter and the baby picture in it was true. I was only with her the one night. I never saw her again. I never had any other contact with her. And that letter was the last I received from her. What I didn't find out until I moved here was the reason I never heard from her again. She and her husband were killed in an accident when Ian was still a baby. He was brought here to live with his great-grandmother. But I swear, Meredyth, I didn't know any of that. I didn't even know for sure he was my son until a few weeks ago."

Meredyth put a hand to her face. "Simon, I want to believe you. I want us to try to work through all of these lies and deceptions on both of our parts, but I don't know if I can get past this. It's too much of a coincidence. The child you had with that woman in Chicago just happened to be living next door when you moved here and he's—"

"And he's Bucky's best friend. They both know the truth. Bucky seems to have accepted it. Not sure yet about Ian's feelings."

"And if I stay, how am I supposed to treat him? I mean every time I'd see him, it would be a reminder of what you did."

Simon cleared his throat again. "That's another thing. Their house suffered some fire damage last night. He and Maggie, his grandmother, are... They're staying here for the time being. He had a doctor's appointment in Green River this morning, but they should be back anytime."

"What's wrong with him?"

Simon briefly told her about Ian's fall and subsequent surgery.

Meredyth didn't speak but moved closer to the door and looked outside for a few moments. "What happened to my gardens, Southy?"

"What?"

"I mean..." Meredyth turned and looked at Simon. "I mean Simon. I don't know where I got Southy from. I just meant it's awfully bare in this walled section." Meredyth looked out toward the garden once more. "There's only that dry fountain and that little boat and a couple of bushes. I think you should build them a tree house."

"A tree house?"

"You said they acted out stories with the boat. Imagine all the wonderful adventures they could have with a tree house. I always wanted one. A boy down the street had one when I was young. I always envied him that tree house."

"There aren't any trees in the garden."

"Oh, silly." Meredyth put a hand on Simon's arm. "You don't need trees. It would be nice but you could build a free-standing one with two or three different levels with ladders connecting them and maybe a slide and swings. If her imagination is as big as you say—and being your daughter I don't doubt it—a tree house would lend itself to all sorts of adventures."

Simon turned away, still disturbed by her previous comment when she called him *Southy*. "I promised you some tea and something to eat." For the first time he noticed the desserts on the counter. Frowning, he opened the refrigerator. "Where did all this food come from?"

Bucky, hiding on the landing, yelled, "It's from the Lukefahr Ladies."

Meredyth, startled, turned toward the stairs and the sound of Bucky's voice.

"Why?" shouted Simon.

"Because they know you don't cook and they didn't want Maggie to have to work while she was here."

"But how did it get here?"

"Maxine and Ruby brought it," yelled Bucky, still out of sight.

"Bucky, if we're going to engage in conversation, you need to come down here so we can speak in a civilized manner. And if you will not, then you need to go to your room which is what I told you to do some time ago."

The only response Simon received was the sound of footsteps retreating up the stairs.

"It's past one o'clock," said Meredyth. "She's probably hungry."

"I'll take something up to her. It appears we have plenty to choose from." Simon took one of the plastic containers out of the refrigerator, read the label, and returned it to its place. "Why don't you search through here and see if there's anything you think you can eat. Or I can fix you some soup if you think it would be easier on your stomach." He opened a cabinet door. "I have a variety of tea. What sounds good?"

"Ginger, maybe." Meredyth rummaged through the refrigerator. "Oh, here's fried chicken. Cold fried chicken is one of my favorites." She patted her swollen abdomen. "I hope I can convince this little fellow to let me keep it down." She bowed her head and spoke to her midsection. "I'm eating this for you, you know." She looked at Simon. "It's just like with Rose. Remember? I was so sick and everyone kept telling me it would only last a few months…but they were wrong."

Simon put the tea kettle on the burner. "It's a boy, then?"

"I'm sorry. I thought I told you that. There's so much for us to catch up on."

It was late that night before Bucky, curled up on the cushions in her castle, heard Simon's footsteps. Except for a couple of hours that afternoon and again for a while after supper that she had spent with Ian in her study room, the castle had been her sanctuary from the maelstrom of emotions swirling inside the Mansion. She had refused to leave it when her father had brought her lunch, and then later when he had brought a tray for her supper. He had tried to coax her out both times, but, finally, had set the food on the table in her playroom and left her alone.

From within the castle, she cocked her head and listened for other, lighter footsteps that would mean he was not alone, but there were none.

"It's late, Lamb. You should have been in bed an hour ago."

Bucky unwound herself from the pillows and stood and stretched as much as she could within the confines of the structure. Ducking her head slightly, she walked out. "I thought you wouldn't come tonight."

He took her by the hand. "And how many times in your life have I neglected to come in and tell you good night?"

Bucky shrugged. She was already wearing her Monday night pajamas—light blue ones with puppies in various poses. "Did you tell Ian good night?"

"Yes, some time ago. We talked about some things. Did he tell you the doctor wanted him to go to physical therapy?" Simon turned back the covers on Bucky's bed and she crawled in, but twisted around and sat cross-legged.

"He wasn't happy about that," Bucky said.

"Neither am I. That's ninety miles round trip every day and that's too much for Maggie. So I'm setting up a regimen here for him. It will be a few weeks before they can get back into their house. I talked to the doctor about exactly what he needs and he's going to arrange for a physical therapist to come here twice a week, and in between visits, Ian can work out under Maggie's or my supervision to regain his strength. The initial injury and the subsequent surgery severely weakened his abdominal muscles. Walking is probably the best exercise for him, so he and you need to walk all over this place—indoors for the next few days—up and down the stairs and through all the corridors. Okay? Will you do that with him?"

"Sure."

"But just walk for now, not any faster, and let him set the pace at what he's comfortable with." Simon clicked his tongue. "Now, I suppose you have a whole lot of things you want to talk about."

"First of all, can I—may I—have a tree house?"

Simon smiled and shook his head. That was not at all what he was expecting her to say. He remembered Meredyth talking about it in the kitchen, though, while Bucky was eavesdropping from the back stairs.

"Ian has the perfect tree for one in his back yard, but Maggie's too old to help him build it. But we don't have to have any trees," continued Bucky. "I looked them up on the Internet today. They come already made. Well, you have to assemble them. They have all kinds. I found two I really liked."

"Don't you think you're getting a little old for a tree house?"

Bucky's jaw dropped. "I don't think I'd ever be too old for a tree house."

"First of all, we're going to concentrate on rebuilding Maggie's kitchen and other parts of her house which were damaged. And after that, well, we'll see. They can be dangerous. I'll have to think about it."

Bucky crossed her arms. "I know what that means. No."

"No, it doesn't. It means I don't want to rush into it. I don't want some plastic prefab piece of junk which will only last a year and not stand up to the elements. I'd want something substantial. Stone and wood. It would need to last a long time because after you've outgrown it—and there will come a time when you outgrow it—then your brother can also enjoy it."

Bucky squinted. "Oh, yeah, I forgot about him."

"I'm not talking about Ian."

"I know." Bucky pulled the covers up over her legs and lay back against the pillow. "The baby. When he's as old as I am now, I'll be—" She scrunched up her face, doing the math. "I'll be twenty! I won't even be here, will I? I'll be in college."

"Probably."

"He should just be...uhm...two years younger than me? We could have been having fun, playing together, all this time. That's not fair."

"There's little about any of this that's fair."

Bucky reached out a hand and grasped Simon's wrist. "Are you happy Mom came back?"

Simon laid his other hand on top of hers and smiled and nodded. "Yes. Yes, I am."

"Are you sure she's Mom?"

"Positive."

"Do you believe all the things she said?"

"Do *you* believe all the things she said? At least the part you heard when you were outside the library and on the stairs."

Bucky jerked her head. "How'd you know I was listening at the library?"

"I knew. But you missed a lot this afternoon and evening when you were holed up in here."

"I shouldn't have listened, should I?"

"No, you shouldn't have. Most of what we discussed was not meant for a child's ears."

"Do you think the Anarianu had her all these years?"

"I do."

"But I don't understand. They took me when I was four days old and returned me that same night, but I was several months older. That's what you told me I said that night you found me in the pool."

Simon nodded.

"And they took Reverend Bergmann and spit him back out just a couple of minutes later but he looked like he'd been gone for a week."

"Yes."

"But they took Mom for nine years and she looks like she does in her pictures. You said she'd be older when she came back."

Simon used the hand Bucky wasn't holding to reach over and pick up the framed picture of Meredyth and him from the bedside table. He studied it a moment. "I know."

"And I couldn't always hear through the library door what she said because sometimes she would speak real soft, but it sounded like she said she was two months pregnant when they took her and the doctors told her she was four months pregnant when they returned her. So that means they had her for nine years but she only grew two months older. That doesn't make any sense."

Simon snorted and returned the picture to its place. "Lamb, none of it makes sense. Listen, tomorrow Dr. Brockman and I and your mother are going to visit the furnace stones and also the Hollow Stone. I'd like for you to come along. We can call Sadie Jane and cancel your French lesson."

"I'll have to think about it."

Simon smiled. "Does that mean no?" He didn't wait for a reply. "But here's the thing. You were rude to ignore our guests by not coming down to eat with us and—"

"If she's staying, she's not a guest."

"I'm not talking about your mother. Dr. Brockman is here. Did you even know that? The bed and breakfast in town was booked, so she's sleeping in the library tonight. And Maggie and Ian are certainly our guests.

And after your church ladies went to all that trouble making that food for us, the least you could have done was sit at the table and eat it. So, you're not getting any more room service. Tomorrow you either come down and eat with the rest of us or you go hungry. Understand?"

"How's all those people fit around that little kitchen table?"

Simon shook his head at her comment. "We took the covers off of our old dining room table which has been in that huge dining room all these months, and that's where we ate tonight. It was...uh...interesting. If you listened closely and half-closed your eyes, you could almost hear the clinking of dinnerware and the hushed conversations of all those hundreds of people who must have dined there over the years."

Bucky wrinkled her nose. "Are you teasing me?"

"Maybe." He stood and adjusted her covers. "Now, it's time you went to sleep."

"Dr. Brockman could have slept in my bed tonight and I could have slept with Ian or Maggie."

Simon cleared his throat. "Uh...no, for various reasons. The main one is you kick in your sleep. Really hard. Poor old Maggie would be black and blue in the morning. Jennifer is fine on the couch."

"And Mom's in your room?"

Simon nodded and bent over and kissed Bucky's forehead.

"Be sure she stays there."

"Good night, Bucky."

A half hour later, Bucky was still awake. She reached over and turned on the lamp on her bedside table and picked up the picture of her dad and mom. It was a head and shoulders shot. Her mom was standing behind Simon and had her arms around his shoulders. Bucky traced her index finger over Simon's dark curls and down his nose. He was right. He did look older today than he was when this photograph was taken. But the smiling woman with the light brown wavy hair with him looked the same. She put her palm over Meredyth's face, blocking her out of the shot.

Bucky felt the sting of tears in her eyes, but she turned the picture over and suppressed them. She returned the framed photo to its place on her nightstand, threw off her covers, got out of bed, and tiptoed over to the closed door. Opening it a crack, she peered out into the empty, dimly-lit hallway. The great house was quiet. A sliver of light escaped under the door to Maggie's room. Maybe not everyone was asleep. Opening her door a little wider she looked both ways and then scurried over to Maggie's door and knocked softly. She heard a slight rustle inside the room. The door opened to reveal the older woman dressed in a gray robe and wearing house slippers.

"Bucky," Maggie whispered. "What are you doing up?"

"I couldn't sleep. May I come in?"

"Of course." Maggie stepped aside to allow Bucky to come in and then quietly closed the door behind her.

The older woman crossed over to the desk where her computer monitor and keyboard sat amidst a clutter of papers. She clicked on something with her mouse and the screen changed to her home page. She turned around and sat in one of the stuffed chairs. "I was working on genealogy and sometimes I get so engrossed in it, I forget what time it is. I'm so glad Ron brought my computer over here."

"But Dale was the one who hooked up all the cables and got the Wi-Fi working." Bucky stood by the arm of the chair.

"I didn't know that. Penny just mentioned Ron and Dale brought some of my things over. I figured Ron was the one who hooked it up."

"People sometimes forget about Dale, don't they? They think he can't do things."

"I suppose you're right." Maggie patted Bucky's hand which rested on the arm of the chair. "I guess this has been a strange day for you, hasn't it?"

Bucky bit her lower lip and brushed her hair behind her ears. "Am I too big to sit on your lap?"

"Oh, I don't think so. Let's try it and see. I'll let you know if you're about to crush me." Maggie opened her arms and then wrapped them around Bucky when the young girl had found a comfortable position. "We missed you at supper tonight."

"How long can a person go without food? In the Bible it says Jesus fasted forty days. That's an awfully long time."

"Are you planning on fasting?"

"Dad says I have to go downstairs and eat with everybody else from now on." She shook her head slowly. "I don't know if I can do that." She tilted her head back so she could look at Maggie's face. "Do you suppose you could slip me something when he isn't looking?"

"I don't think I should go against your father's wishes."

"But he doesn't understand."

"I think he does, Lamb. But he also knows it's important you connect with your mother. I've visited with her twice today—once when we came home and then I had a nice conversation with her at supper." Maggie smoothed Bucky's hair. "She wants to meet you so bad she almost cries whenever she talks about you. I know these things take time. But the longer you put it off, the harder it will be."

"It's complicated, though, Maggie. All my life I've wanted her to come back, but at the same time I've always been mad at her for going off and leaving Dad and me. And then when I started having those dreams where she was trying to kill me... Why would I dream those things if they weren't true?"

"Because they were just that—dreams."

"But the mastodon dreams came true and the ship dreams. And now Ian has found the cave, so that one's true. Why shouldn't this one be true? I don't think she's really my mom. Dad said the woman in the dreams wasn't Mom. And now I think he's right. I think this woman was sent here by the Anarianu, pretending to be my mom, so she could kill me."

"She's not an imposter, Bucky. She's family. Your father told me you felt her...and the baby."

"That doesn't mean anything."

"Sure it does. It means she's related to us."

"Even if she is my mom, she wouldn't be related to you."

"Then how should I explain the feeling I got when I first shook hands with her, and again at supper when I brushed up against her when we were putting the food on the table. She's family. I know it."

Bucky had been leaning against Maggie but she sat up. "Seraphina's family? How?"

"That's what I've been working on all evening. And I think I've finally made a breakthrough. Last summer you told me you were named for your two grandmothers and that your father's mother's name was Bucilla. That's the information I've been working from off and on for the past few months and getting nowhere. Tonight at supper I learned Bucilla was your *maternal* grandmother's name. Rose was your father's mother's name."

Bucky snuggled back down and twirled one end of her hair around her index finger. "Oh, I always get them mixed up. They both died before I was born so I didn't ever know them."

"Once I had the correct name, things just sort of fell into place tonight. I'm not certain yet, but I think I can trace your mother back to Seraphina through Seraphina's daughter Saphrona who disappeared."

"Disappeared?"

"She left without a trace, leaving her newborn daughter to be raised by Seraphina."

"How about Saphrona's husband?"

"She didn't have one."

"Maggie, do you suppose she was taken by the Anarianu the same as my mom was and Reverend Bergmann, although they didn't keep him long?"

"Your dad told me your mother's story this afternoon while she was taking a nap. I don't know, Lamb. From reading Seraphina's diary and from the stories my mother and grandmother told, I'd always assumed Saphrona just ran off, maybe to the city."

"But they might have taken her and left her someplace else after a few years."

"More likely she was just a young girl who was tired of living back here in the hills and wanted to see the world."

"But to leave her baby behind. What kind of mother does that?"

"Bucky, from what your father told me, your mother did not abandon you. It sounds like she was kidnapped by these Guardian beings, whoever or whatever they are, and held prisoner for nine years."

"That's her story, anyway."

"At any rate, I think tomorrow you'd better swallow some of that pride of yours and face some of your fears and come downstairs and have breakfast with the rest of us. And afterwards, your dad said he and your mom and that archaeologist are going off somewhere. I have to stay here with Ian, of course, but I think you should go with them. It will give you a chance to get to know your mother a little."

Bucky examined one of her fingernails and did not reply.

"And now I think it's time you were in bed."

"But, Maggie, she's right next door to me."

"Would you like to sleep in here in my room tonight?"

Bucky tucked her chin. "Dad said I couldn't because I kick in my sleep."

"If you can stand an old woman's moans and groans in her sleep, I think I can take a few kicks."

Bucky raised her head and smiled. "Really? I can sleep here with you?"

"Get on in there. You take the far side over there. I've got some business to take care of in the bathroom and then I'll join you."

Bucky reached up and hugged her neck. "Thank you, Maggie. You won't hear a peep out of me, and I'll be as still as…as still as…a rock."

24

ANCIENT WORDS

An hour later Simon awoke. He slid his left hand across the sheet and touched Meredyth. She was still here. Today had not been a dream. She was back in his life and back in his bed after nine years. He released a long breath he felt he had been holding all day and stared at the ceiling, hidden in the shadows. The waning gibbous moon was still large enough to bathe the room with a soft light. His fingers lingered on Meredyth's wrist and he let the warmth of that touch fill him. He could feel that other life, too. He tried to separate them, but they insisted on rejoining and entwining. Had it been that way when she was pregnant with Bucky? He tried to remember. Bucky!

Simon sat up and listened. Had she woken him? Had he heard her cry out? The room was quiet except for the soft breathing of Meredyth. He put his bare feet on the floor and stood.

"Simon?" Meredyth reached for him and then saw his silhouette standing by the bed. "What's wrong?"

"I thought I heard Bucky. Maybe I should check on her."

"I'll come, too."

"No. Stay here. I'll just be a minute."

"No. I want to." Meredyth got up and pulled on her robe which was lying across the end of the bed.

Simon switched on the lamp and Meredyth joined him, hooking one hand through the crook of his elbow. He led the way to Bucky's room and opened the door. The room was dark except for the moonlight and he could not tell from the doorway if the lump of covers in her bed was actually her. With Meredyth in tow, he crossed the room and laid his hand on the pile of blankets and then ran his palm over the bed.

"She's not here." Simon switched on the lamp to reveal the empty bed. "My God."

"Calm down, Simon. Maybe she's in the bathroom."

"You don't understand." Simon shrugged off her clasp of his arm and rushed to the bathroom door. He could see by the light from the bedside lamp there was no one in there. He hit the switch beside the door of her study room and hurried through it to the playroom. He turned on the lights and bent down to look in the castle. That was where he was hoping to find her, but it, too, was empty. "Oh, God." He turned around to see Meredyth, her mouth open, standing in the doorway to the playroom.

"This is her room?"

"Mer, stay here. I have to go the Spring Room." He threw open the door in the playroom which led to the hallway and ran toward the stairs.

Meredyth followed him as quickly as she could. "Simon, wait!"

Maggie's bedroom door opened and she stepped out into the hall, closing the door behind her. "What's wrong?"

"Bucky's not in her room," said Meredyth.

"She's in here," Maggie said. "I think she's having a nightmare."

Meredyth went to the top of the stairs and called for Simon but he was already down the stairs and racing toward the lower hallway.

"Stay here," ordered Maggie. "I'll get him."

Left alone in the hallway, Meredyth hesitated for a moment and then pushed open the door to Maggie's room. It was dark and the dim lights from the hall did little to illuminate it. She heard moans coming from within, though, and as her eyes adjusted to the moon-lit room, she picked out the bed where Bucky lay, thrashing wildly. She crossed to it and fumbled with the bedside lamp, trying to find the switch. In the soft light of the low-watt lamp she saw her daughter, Bucky, bathed in sweat, flailing her arms and legs.

Meredyth had barely caught a glimpse of Bucky earlier that day and this was the first time she had seen her up close. She wanted to touch her, to hold her and banish whatever terrors she was facing in her dream, but Simon had explained Bucky's fears and the reason she was reluctant to meet the mother she had never known. Meredyth was afraid of what Bucky's reaction would be if she woke her now. And so she stood there, staring at the little girl who looked nothing like the baby she had left behind when she walked out of the apartment last

July. No, not last July, a July nine years ago. Bucky was not even fifteen months old on that fateful day. How could this little girl in the bed be her daughter?

"Meredyth, what are you doing?" Simon spoke slowly and deliberately from the doorway.

"Just looking. She's having a terrible nightmare, but after what you told me, I certainly didn't want her to wake up and see me looming over her."

Simon sat on the bed next to Bucky. He was breathing heavily from his quick run down and back up the stairs. He tried to pin Bucky's arms, but she fought him. "Bucky, Lamb, you're having a bad dream. You need to wake up."

"Does she have these often?" asked Meredyth.

"More so in the past few weeks. I guess that's what woke me a few minutes ago."

Maggie came into the room. She had returned from going after Simon and had first gone to check on Ian before coming back to her room. "Ian's still asleep," she whispered. "When Bucky cried out, it woke me. I'm sorry, Simon. I didn't think you'd mind if she slept in here tonight."

Simon shook his head. "I panicked when she wasn't in her room. I was afraid she... I thought she might be in the Spring Room again."

Despite Simon's attempts to hold her still, Bucky sprang upright, shouting, "No, you can't take her. Get away! You can't have her!" Her eyes opened wide and she gaped at Simon. "Dad! Help her! Please." The last word was a drawn-out wail and then tears started to flow and she screamed.

"Oh, God, no." Simon hugged her to his chest.

Bucky cried out in agony as the scars on her back opened and began to bleed.

"The song stone you got in Boğazkale. Where is it? " asked Meredyth, putting her hands on Bucky's back as blood began to seep through her pajama top. "It has the words to the 'Laya Song' on it."

"What good is it? We can't read it."

"I... I think I can. I can almost hear it in my head. Maybe if I see the words again."

"Bucky's is on the table in her study room. It's closer."

Meredyth collided into Jennifer Brockman as she rushed from the room.

"What's all the commotion?" asked Jennifer, watching Meredyth hurrying across the hall to Bucky's room. "What's going on?" The archaeologist turned back around and saw Simon holding the screaming and bleeding Bucky. "Oh, my god. Do you want me to call 911? Is there even 911 service out here?"

"No, don't call," said Simon in between the soothing words he was saying to Bucky. "It's a... It's a condition she has." He fell back on the explanation he had invented should anyone ever witness one of her episodes. "She'll be all right."

Bucky's screams grew louder and more piercing.

"My Lord," said Maggie, "this is what Ian witnessed that night in the woods, isn't it?"

Meredyth returned with the inscribed rock in her hands. She sat down on the bed with Simon and Bucky and tilted the stone so the dim light fell across the symbols. "I think it's—" She stopped.

"What's the matter?" asked Simon, hugging Bucky as tightly as he could without crushing her. "Sing it."

Meredyth squeezed her eyes shut for a moment and two tears rolled down her cheeks.

Ah te o ki u ma
Sa pa ah ku me
Le pa ti ah su me tu
Ki ah as ah ku me
La ya

Meredyth softly intoned the syllables, singing them almost as lullaby. When she reached the end and started again, Simon joined her, his tenor voice harmonizing with her higher pitch.

Bucky's cries quieted to a gurgling sound and then she fell silent. Simon felt her relax in his grip. He gently laid her back down, her head on her pillow.

"Simon?" Maggie whispered, "is she all right?'

Simon turned his head to where Maggie and Jennifer were standing at the foot of the bed. "She will be. I'm sorry. I know it's a frightening thing to witness."

"What causes it?" Jennifer kept her voice low.

Simon shook his head. "Early childhood trauma." He recalled how Chip had once commented how he could lie so glibly. But maybe, he thought, it wasn't much of a lie. After all, being taken in the night, having your DNA altered to become a water breather for a few months, and then having your gills removed before being replaced in your own crib had to have been traumatic. "Maggie, I'll put her back in her own bed and…uh…find you some clean sheets."

"You just see to her. Tell me where they are and I can change the bedding."

"I'll help," said Jennifer.

A few minutes later, Meredyth emerged from Bucky's bathroom where she had rinsed the blood-stained blue pajamas with the puppies on them and had draped them across the bathtub. She sat down on the edge of the bed near Simon who was sitting in the chair. Together they had washed the blood from Bucky's back and pulled a nightgown over her head without waking her. She lay on her back, the covers drawn up to her chin.

"She always slept for a long time afterwards and then was lethargic for a day or two," said Meredyth, speaking softly so as not to wake her. She adjusted the blankets at Bucky's neck.

"That's still the pattern," Simon said. "Although the last time, when I sang the song, she wasn't quite as bad the next day. She seemed to recover a little faster. Hopefully, it will be the same this time."

"You said you didn't know the words."

"If I had to say them now or write them, I don't think I could. But when I heard you sing, I don't know… They are there somewhere in my brain. Can you really read the inscription?" Simon picked up the song stone from where Meredyth had set it on the bedside table and turned it over in his hands.

"Yes, but I don't know how. I must have learned when I was with them."

"If so, then perhaps you can read the writing on the Hollow Stone when we go there tomorrow. Or I have lots of pictures of it. They'd probably be easier for you to look at since the inscription is at the bottom of the stone and you'd have to bend over. We have it behind plexiglass now to protect it. That makes it a little more difficult to pick out some of the fainter symbols."

"Simon, earlier when you came back into Maggie's room and saw me standing over Bucky, there was an accusatory tone to your words when you asked what I was doing. Do you not trust me with her?"

Simon tightened the corners of his mouth and turned away from her for a moment before replying. "I'm sorry. I'm just... I've been so protective of her for all these years. It's only been since we moved here I've even let her out of my sight when we're out somewhere and even then only under guarded conditions."

"But I'm her mother."

"But I've had some of the same dreams she's had—the ones I told you about, and... I know it's not you in the dreams, but they've... They've planted that same doubt in me, too. I'm so sorry, Meredyth. There's a reason for those dreams. They've put those terrible thoughts in our brains for some nefarious purpose. I'm certain of it."

429

"Perhaps I'll remember more about my life there and I'll— Oh!" Meredyth jerked up right and put a hand on her abdomen.

"What is it? What's wrong?"

Meredyth smiled. "The little darling just kicked unexpectedly. He's been pretty quiet since I arrived."

"Why don't you go on back to bed," Simon suggested. "I'm going to sit here for a while."

"How many times have you sat beside her bed after one of her attacks?"

Simon shook his head. "There's little else I can do. They're not as frequent as they were when she was younger. She's better at controlling them, but…" Simon's voice caught in his throat. "But my heart breaks every time."

Meredyth leaned over and brushed one hand along the side of Bucky's face and then laid the same hand along Simon's jaw. "I'm sorry you've had to deal with this all alone. I should have been here beside you. That's where I want to be tonight."

Simon took her hand and kissed it.

The next morning Bucky appeared at the bottom of the back stairs. Her hair was a rat's nest and she was wearing a long-sleeved yellow nightgown that reached almost to her bare feet. Simon, Meredyth, Maggie and Ian were seated at the small kitchen table, eating a breakfast of scrambled eggs and bacon. Jennifer was nowhere in sight, but Bucky could hear water running in the bathroom just down the hallway from the kitchen.

"Where am I supposed to sit?" asked Bucky, walking over to the table to stand by Maggie who put an arm around her.

Maggie said, "We didn't think you'd be joining us."

"Dad said I had to if I wanted to eat."

"I would have made an exception after last night," said Simon.

Bucky looked at each adult in turn and then focused her attention on Meredyth. "Why? What happened last night?"

Simon stood and walked over to stand by her. He put a hand on her shoulder. "You had... You had one of your episodes during the night. You don't remember?"

Bucky ran her palms down either side of her face. "Oh, that's why I feel like I was rode hard and put away wet."

"Where on earth did you learn that expression?" asked Simon.

"Probably from me," said Maggie, smiling. "It's a fairly common saying in these parts."

"Do you feel like eating something?" Simon bent over slightly so he could see Bucky's face. "Do you want some eggs?"

Bucky nodded, still watching Meredyth who laid her napkin on the table and stood.

"I'll fix you some," Meredyth said.

"No," Bucky answered quickly. "I want Dad to."

Simon and Meredyth exchanged glances. Meredyth resumed her seat.

Bucky looked down at her gown. "This isn't the right. It should be my puppy pajamas."

Simon walked over to the stove, to reheat the skillet. "The nightgown is one of your new ones. Remember? You just haven't worn it."

Ian, on the other side of Maggie, pointed his fork at her. "Your hair looks like it got caught in Gram's mixer."

Bucky reached across Maggie's plate and tried to grab his fork but he snatched it away. "Well, your hair looks like a bunch of curly fries."

Simon, a whisk in one hand, turned around and raised his voice. "No fighting at the table."

Bucky cocked her head and looked at him. "When can we fight?"

"Ian," Maggie said, intervening. "You scooch over a little so Bucky can share your chair." She pushed Ian's plate and glass of milk further over, and Bucky went around her and slid into the seat with Ian.

Simon poured a glass of milk for her and brought it and some silverware over to the table. "There are two pieces of bacon there for you already cooked." He indicated a plate in the middle of the table. "Your eggs will be ready in a minute. Oh, I need to fix some toast."

"I was going to eat those," said Ian, reaching for the bacon.

Maggie swatted his hand. "You've had enough."

Ian and Bucky continued to tease each other until Simon brought Bucky's plate of scrambled eggs and toast over to her and resumed his seat at the table and his plate of now-cold eggs.

"Bucky, I told you last night I wanted you to accompany us to the Hollow Stone and the smelter rocks this morning, but I think you'd better stay home and rest."

"I don't feel that bad." She had felt out of sorts when she woke up this morning and came downstairs, but the lethargy she usually experienced as an aftermath of one of her episodes was dissipating already. She had perked up considerably in the past few minutes.

"I wish I could go," said Ian, sitting back and crossing his arms.

"I think you're feeling better this morning, too," said Maggie to Ian, "but jostling over that uneven terrain is something you're not ready for."

Jennifer Brockman, wearing a long-sleeve thermal knit Henley shirt and khaki pants, came into the kitchen, towel-drying her wet hair. She draped the towel around her shoulders. "It smells like a country breakfast in here."

"I'll fix you some eggs." Simon started to stand, but Jennifer put a hand on his shoulder.

"I can scramble my own eggs. Just point me in the direction of a coffee cup."

Bucky eyed the two pieces of bacon she had transferred to her plate alongside the fluffy yellow mound of eggs. "Dr. Brockman, there are only two pieces of bacon left." She held up one with her fingers. "But you can have one."

Meredyth, noting the small gesture, smiled at Bucky, but Bucky did not return the smile.

"Thanks, sweetheart," replied Jennifer, "but I'll pass. I'm not a bacon eater."

Forty-five minutes later, Simon, Meredyth, Jennifer and Bucky were in the utility vehicle, headed to The Hollow. They took the gravel road that wound around the mountain before intersecting with the old logging road which led to the natural amphitheater. There the mysterious stone had appeared last summer, entwined in the roots of an fallen ancient oak. The large monolith was inscribed with Hittite cuneiform and Minoan Linear A and an unknown script which contained some symbols that matched those on the song stones. Spirals and ship motifs also covered the Hollow Stone.

Soon after its discovery, Simon had invited Nick and Jan Moyer to examine it. He had known them since their graduate course of study together at Brown University. While Simon and Nick had worked the last few months on translating the Hittite inscription on the stone, Nick's wife Jan had focused her attention on the Minoan writing. Linear A was a language which frustrated scholars in their attempts to decipher it. Jan was one of those scholars. She had been so excited over the discovery of the stone, hoping the Hittite inscription would lead to the translation of the Minoan Linear A inscription, and that she would be the one to finally crack

434

Linear A. But so far her efforts at linking the two inscriptions were fruitless.

Upon arriving at The Hollow, Bucky hung back as the adults examined the ten-foot-high chain link fence, topped with barbed wire, that Simon had ordered to be erected around the monolith. It would keep out anyone who happened upon the site by accident, but a serious intruder could still breach it, although it would be difficult. There were three motion sensor security cameras positioned in the trees, and Simon and Bucky had already enjoyed watching the videos of the wildlife, including a black bear, captured by the cameras.

Simon unlocked the gate and stepped aside as Jennifer and Meredyth entered the enclosure dominated by the huge sandstone block encased in plexiglass. Jennifer had not been there since the security measures were installed, and she walked around the stone, inspecting the acrylic covering. Simon heard a sharp intake of breath from Meredyth as she laid a palm flat against the surface.

"Oh, Simon," said Meredyth, "this is remarkable. How old is it estimated to be?"

Jennifer replied from the other side of the stone. "My tests indicated it was buried anywhere from a thousand to two thousand years ago. How long it stood before that I have no idea."

"It quite possibly dates back thirty-five hundred years," said Simon.

"You said you had translated the Hittite. What does it say?" Meredyth ran her palm over the cuneiform letters behind the glass. There had not been time this morning before they left for Simon to show her the detailed photos he had taken of the inscriptions.

"Oh, I hadn't heard that you and Nick had finished the translation," said Jennifer, coming around to the front of the monument.

"We aren't totally in agreement on a couple of the words or some of the syntax, but basically it goes something like this. Simon traced the Hittite cuneiform with his index finger as he read them in English.

Sing and rejoice
Etakkama from the land of the Hatti be praised
The sacred spring gives life
And Etakkama gives back life to our water breather baby
The song of the lamb is heard again
The name of Etakkama will be remembered forever
The Anarianu bless his children to the thousandth generation
The Anarianu bind his family to us forever.
Rejoice and sing the songs of life.

"Wait," said Jennifer, "isn't the name *Etakkama* also on that stone in the park? Sounds like whoever wrote this thought pretty highly of this Etakkama fellow, whoever he was."

Meredyth, her hand still touching the plexiglass, turned partly toward her husband and wavered slightly. "Sie."

Simon reached out a hand to steady her. "Are you all right?"

Meredyth leaned in close to one ear and whispered to him, "I've been here before." Louder, she said, "I... I think I need to sit down."

Bucky stayed outside the fence, standing in a ring of sunlight that penetrated the dense foliage, while the adults examined the huge stone. She loved to visit The Hollow. The leaves of the massive oaks were turning brown but most still clung to the branches. The spring that had been dry when she first visited this sacred place with Ian now bubbled up continuously as it had done ever since the night of the earthquake that had also started the flow of the Singing Spring in the town square. She wondered if there were any Anarianu present here today. If her mother had indeed been with them for nine years, surely they would recognize her. When she heard Meredyth ask what the Hittite inscription said, she stepped closer. It was the first time she had heard her father recite the entire translation and now she knew why. He was Etakkama and the verse was about him. It was a song in praise of him.

Bucky hooked her fingers through the wires of the chain link fence.

Simon put an arm around Meredyth. "We can go back."

Jennifer interrupted. "If she's not well, I understand, but I'd really like you to look at this one corner back here. I think it's settling."

"Bucky," Simon said, "would you see your mother to the UTV. We'll be along in a minute."

Bucky's mouth dropped open. He didn't phrase it as a question. It was an order. She looked at him and he gave her one of his looks that said there would be no back talk. Bucky let go of the fence and held out a hand through the open gate. She didn't take Meredyth's hand though. She held on to the fabric of Meredyth's jacket sleeve and walked beside her to the vehicle.

On the way to The Hollow, Meredyth had sat in the front with Simon who drove, and Bucky and Jennifer had sat in the back. But now Meredyth climbed into the back seat. Bucky crawled in beside her but still avoided touching her and scrunched up as far away from her as she could get in the small space.

"Oh," Meredyth said, a hand covering her mouth, "I experienced a wave of vertigo when I heard your father recite the inscription. I think I'm all right now. How are you feeling this morning?"

"I'm okay, I guess." Bucky crossed her arms. "Just a little out of sorts. Not nearly as bad as usual."

"Maybe the song helped," said Meredyth. "If we could have sung it when the tears first started you might have avoided it all together."

Bucky frowned and looked at her sideways.

"Don't you remember us singing?"

Bucky nodded slowly. "I do now. You know the song?"

"Not by heart, but I was able to read it off of your song stone. But I'll learn it and I'll teach it to your father and we'll teach it to you. Maybe those terrible experiences you suffer will be a thing of the past."

Bucky nodded toward the Hollow Stone where Simon and Jennifer were. "It's probably not a good idea to leave them alone like that."

"Why?"

"Dr. Brockman was all over him last summer when she was here."

Meredyth raised her eyebrows. "What do you mean?"

"She was after him. Making goo-goo eyes and holding his hand and rubbing up against him and touching his face. I think she's still after him. Didn't you see her this morning at breakfast? She came in and put her hands on his shoulders just like you weren't sitting right there. I don't like her."

"But you offered to share your bacon with her."

"My dad told me I have to learn to act nice even when I don't like someone. He said it's how people get along in the world. Besides, I remembered from when she was here before she didn't eat bacon."

Meredyth smiled. "And what about me?"

Bucky had been watching the two at the monolith, but now she stared at the floorboard. "It's not that I don't like you. I... I'm..."

"Scared?" Meredyth reached across to touch her but Bucky hugged the far side of the vehicle even closer, so Meredyth withdrew the gesture.

"I'm not going to hurt you, Lamb."

Bucky's head jerked. "The inscription Dad read. There was a line with the word 'lamb' in it. That's what he always calls me. And Gram—I mean Maggie—she calls Ian that sometimes."

"So?"

"Don't you think that's strange?"

"I think it's just a term of endearment, like sweetheart or honey. It's something he and I always called you."

"Did he tell you about Etakkama? That inscription was all about him, wasn't it?"

"He told me a little yesterday afternoon. This—all this—is so much to take in all at once." Meredyth shifted position. "Now that I'm here, maybe I can help take some of the pressure off him, help with some of his workload. And I'd like to be a mother to you, or at least a friend. Maybe I can help you with some things that he can't."

"He does everything just fine for me." Bucky returned her gaze toward Simon and Jennifer at the Hollow Stone, but continued to speak. "Except hair. He can't do hair. He tries. I show him pictures of how I want it done. He just can't do it. Especially braids. He can't braid."

"That might be something I can help with."

"I hate my hair. I wish I had long red curly hair like Madyson Koeller. She's a girl in Ian's class. She's in love with Ian but he doesn't like her. I don't like her, either. But I love her hair."

Meredyth reached out again and lifted a few strands of Bucky's brown hair. Bucky flinched but didn't pull away. "Everyone's hair is different. But I could try working with it if you'd want me to. Or is there a beauty shop in town? We could go together and get our hair done."

Bucky's face brightened for the first time since she escorted Meredyth back to the UTV. She turned to look at her. "By the grocery store. It's where Dad gets his hair cut and most of the women in my Sunday school class go there, although a few of them go to Garton, and there's one or two I think do their own hair."

"Then we'll check that out in few days when things calm down."

"But talking about hair makes me sound like that's all I care about," said Bucky. "I'm interested in lots more things. I want to know how the Romans managed to build Hadrian's Wall clear across England. And how Lewis and Clark made it all the way to the Pacific Ocean and right back where they started without any maps or GPS, or how Magellan made it clear around the world. Well, I guess he didn't make it because he got killed, but his expedition sailed all the way around. And I want to know how people first learned to write and I want to be able to translate Hittite like my dad. Did you know Hittite is the oldest known Indo-European language?"

"Yes, I did know that. But it sounds as if you really like history."

"I do."

"I do, too. In fact, it's your dad's and my love of history which brought us together in the first place."

"In graduate school. Dad says you used to work in a museum."

"I loved my job there. I worked in interpretation."

"Like translating one language into another?"

"No. In the context of a museum, interpretation means the way we set up a particular exhibit so people can understand it. How do we want them to move through it? What do we want them to take away from their experience? What emotions do we want them to feel? Some people will stand for hours and read every description and label. And others will only pause and look at the headlines and maybe look in detail at a few of the artifacts or photos. And others will breeze through and stop only if something really grabs their attention. But we need to design the exhibit to speak to each of those types of people."

"Did Dad tell you about our museum in Turn Back?"

"Just briefly. I think we're going to go see it soon, but maybe not today."

"There's not much to see yet. Dr. Smallin is going to be in charge until Ian gets old enough and smart enough. Maybe you could work with Dr. Smallin in setting it up. Why did you quit your job at the museum if you liked working there?"

"I worked up until the time you were born. And I was planning to return after my maternity leave, but then…"

Bucky made a face. "But then you had this problem child to take care of."

Meredyth touched Bucky's cheek. "I never saw you as a problem child. You were an extraordinary child and I wanted to spend every moment with you, protecting you and...and comforting you."

"But you never saw me as your child, did you? You didn't know I was Rose."

"No, I didn't know you were Rose. I'm still having trouble digesting that. But I loved you. I'm sorry I haven't been here for you. I've missed so much of your life. You were barely walking and talking when I left. I didn't get to share in any of your childhood joys and accomplishments. I didn't get to sit beside you when you were sick. I didn't get to hold you whenever those awful scars opened and bled and you were in such agony. And now you've grown into this beautiful young lady I don't even know."

"I've never been sick."

"Never?"

Bucky turned her head away.

"Bucky, do you feel that...that sensation when we touch?"

Bucky nodded. "Didn't you feel it when you shook hands with Maggie?"

There was a sharp intake of breath by Meredyth. "I did."

"You probably felt it when I was baby, didn't you?"

Meredyth's brow creased. "Maybe. But not like this."

"Maggie says folks around here don't notice it so much anymore. That's probably how it was when I was little. You were used to it so you didn't notice."

"What causes it?"

"It means we're family. It means we're all descended from Seraphina. Dad, me, you, Maggie, Ian, and half the county."

"Seraphina." Meredyth breathed the name but not as a question.

"Does it hurt to have a baby inside you?"

Meredyth blinked. It was a sudden change of subject. "No, not hurt exactly. It's uncomfortable sometimes. Most of the time. All the time. But knowing you have this life growing inside of you. That's so incredible and it makes up for all the pains and little twinges and the bloating and the all the other stuff that goes along with being pregnant."

"Was I inside of you?"

Meredyth smiled. "Yes."

"Does it hurt coming out?"

"That part does hurt. Yes. Oh, it looks like they're done."

Bucky turned to watch Simon and Jennifer shut and lock the gate and head in their direction.

"We've been so busy talking," said Meredyth, "I forgot to watch out for what you warned me about." She lowered her voice to a whisper. "But I'll keep an eye on her."

"So will I," said Bucky.

25

TWISTED TREES AND TANGLED TALES

"Simon, I know you don't want to be bothered, but I think you ought to see this."

Simon looked up from his desk to see Maggie standing at the door to his study. "It's all right. Come in." He stood and gestured for her to enter.

"No, sit back down. I have a bunch of papers to spread out."

Simon cleared off an area on the right side of his desk, shuffling some papers and books to the other side of his computer monitor and keyboard.

"I've made a major breakthrough in the family," said Maggie, "and it's... Well, it's mind-blowing, but it explains a lot."

It had been five days since Meredyth had arrived at what had once been the Mansion Mineral Springs Resort to be reunited with the husband and daughter she had not seen for nine years. It was nine years from their perspective. For Meredyth just over four months had passed from when she had walked out of their New York apartment, although she could not deny her toddler was now ten years old, and her husband, who should have been a boyish-looking thirty-two was now a mature forty-one, although still handsome. All week Bucky had maintained an emotional and a physical distance from her, except where the situation forced them to be close such as mealtimes and in the car. Meredyth thought their talk on Tuesday during the visit to the Hollow Stone and later to the smelter chimney had broken the ice and would lead to further mother-daughter discussions, but Bucky conducted herself in a reserved manner whenever the two were near each other. Furthermore, Bucky insisted the two of them never be alone in the same room.

On this Saturday afternoon, Bucky and Ian were on one of their walkabouts (as Bucky termed their twice-daily excursions throughout the Mansion, up and down stairs, down and around hallways, checking the many vacant rooms). Today they were also circumnavigating the back garden. Ian had improved sufficiently and was going to be able to return to school on Monday. Bucky was not looking forward to that. It had been a fun week with Ian living under the same roof. She had even enjoyed his physical therapy sessions, doing the exercises along with him. And she had used him as a buffer between herself and Meredyth. She could not yet bring herself to call Meredyth "Mom" to her face. She wasn't sure what to call her.

Dr. Jennifer Brockman had gone home on Wednesday. She did not make any flagrant advances toward Simon during her stay, but there were subtle gestures both Bucky and Meredyth picked up on. Simon appeared oblivious to them. His attention this week was focused on Meredyth.

"Meredyth should probably see this, too," continued Maggie, standing over Simon as he resumed his seat at his desk, "because it concerns her, but I thought you might want to look at it first."

"She's upstairs resting."

"Let's start here." Using the eraser end of a pencil, Maggie pointed to the family tree chart she had brought with her into Simon's study. "Here's Southy and Drucilla MacAdoo who built this place and founded the town. They had the one daughter Seraphina, who, I am absolutely certain now, suffered the same experience as Bucky as a baby and was taken by the Guardians and returned somewhat changed. Seraphina had three children, and you've heard me mention that one of her daughters disappeared, and I've never been able to find out any more about her. That is until this week. I had tried last summer to research Bucky's family tree when she told me she didn't know anything other than her grandmothers' names, Bucilla and Rose. I didn't get anywhere because she had the names mixed up. She said Rose was Meredyth's mother's name."

"No, my mother's name was Rose," said Simon.

"But I didn't find that out until Monday night at supper when Meredyth said Bucilla was her mother's name. Everything suddenly fell into place. All sorts of records popped up in my searches. You aren't going to believe this, Simon."

"What could possibly be stranger than all that's happened here in the past few months? I think I'm ready to believe anything now."

"Look at this." Maggie pointed to the chart again. "Here is Seraphina and here is her daughter Saphrona who left one day, never to be heard from again. Saphrona had a baby out of wedlock before she disappeared, and Seraphina ended up raising that baby, whose name was Vera. Vera had two daughters. One of them was Sadie Jane Woods' mother. The other daughter was Carl Bergmann's grandmother."

Simon raised one eyebrow. "Indeed."

"But I already knew that," continued Maggie. "This is the exciting part. I discovered this week that when Saphrona left, she evidently went to Chicago, got married and had two more children, both of them daughters, Leola and Delphia. Leola later had a daughter, Talitha. See here?" Maggie drew his attention to the diagram.

Simon nodded.

"And I find Talitha later living in western New York. And there Talitha had a daughter named…Bucilla Sarah Collins who married Lowry Joel Durragh."

Simon pushed back his desk chair and stood. "Meredyth's parents. How sure are you of all this?"

"Oh, Simon, that's not even half of what I've found."

"What more could there possibly be?" Simon ran his hands through his hair. "Maggie, I confessed to you a few weeks ago I think I am…or…rather…I was…Southy MacAdoo. And now you tell me Meredyth is one of my descendants."

"Simon." Maggie straightened and put a hand on Simon's shoulder. "You're going to want to be sitting down for this next part."

Simon dropped heavily onto the chair and put his hands over his face. "What?"

"Look."

Simon removed his hands and looked at Maggie's chart.

"I told you Saphrona had two daughters in Chicago, Leola and Delphia. Leola is Meredyth's great-grandmother. Delphia married and had a daughter, Camilla. Camilla, evidently, never married but she had a daughter, Lovina. Lovina married a Charles Ganaway and they had one daughter." Maggie had been hunched over the desk as she pointed out the names, but now she raised her head and looked at Simon. "Their daughter was Kara Ganaway and she married my grandson Seth."

Simon stood and leaned over the chart, running his index finger down the lines, pausing at the names Maggie had indicated.

Maggie stepped back out of the way and let him study the genealogy diagram for a couple of minutes, but she kept talking although Simon appeared to no longer be listening. "I guess Camilla being an unwed mother was why I could never find the records for who Lovina's parents were. Kara's mother, Lovina, died the year before Kara and Seth were married. And her father died when Ian was just four and his memory had been affected by his heart attacks, I guess, because he was no help at all with names. So that's why I could never get further back than Ian's maternal grandparents, so I had no idea Kara's line went back to Seraphina. But when I traced Meredyth's line back to Saphrona and found the records for Saphrona's other daughter and came down that line, well, that's how I figured it out."

Simon straightened. He shoved his hands in his pockets, turned and looked out the window.

"Simon, say something." Maggie touched his shoulder and he flinched.

He pressed both palms flat against the window pane. "What do you want me to say? I married my own granddaughter and had an affair with another one and…" His voice broke. "Had a child by both? Oh, God, help me." He turned and spun his chair around and collapsed into it. Leaning over, he buried his face in his hands.

The desk chair Bucky sat in sometimes was on the other side of the desk. Maggie dragged it around and sat next to him. "Simon, whose name did you not see anywhere on this chart except next to Meredyth's? Yours! Simon, you're not on this except for marrying your wife. You're not a descendant of Southy MacAdoo. Not one I can find, anyway, and I think now I have tracked down all of them. And you're certainly not Southy MacAdoo. He died in 1909."

Simon cleared his throat. "So…if you attempted to trace Bucky's family tree last summer, did you try to look for my side?"

"I told you, because she gave me the wrong grandmothers' names I didn't get anywhere, but, yes, I have tried looking up yours this week, also."

"And? You think I'm family." He waved a hand over Maggie's papers. "I must fit in here somewhere."

"Your parents emigrated here from England."

"I already know that."

"That's as far back as I can go."

Simon creased his brow. "Why?"

"Because I can only look up U.S. records. To research the international ones, I'd have to upgrade to a premium membership. That's...uhm...that's expensive."

"Maggie, I will pay the increased fees if you will do the work. I... I need to know how I fit in to all this. And I know the names of my grandparents in England and even where they lived. That ought to be enough to get you started."

Maggie glanced back toward the papers lying on the desk. "At least all this research this week has told me how I'm related to Ian. He may not be my great-grandson, but he is my third cousin, twice removed. I guess that's something. I just... I always thought there was a part of me that was passed on down to him."

Seeing the tears pooling in her eyes, Simon took her hand. "Maggie, you are a part of him. The fine young man he's becoming is because of you. It's all because of you. You live in him."

Maggie sniffed and forced a smile. "Course he would have fit right into our twisted family tree if he was Seth's son. Seth and Kara are fourth cousins, once removed."

The five people now living in the Mansion ate dinner that evening in the kitchen. On Thursday, Ron Crosson had dropped by with milk and eggs and had helped Simon move the large dining room table into the kitchen so they wouldn't have so far to carry the food and dishes back and forth for each meal. There was ample room in the kitchen for it and the smaller square table Simon and Bucky had always used. The Lukefahr Ladies had continued to bring food all week. Tonight's meal was ham, sweet potato casserole, broccoli salad, and a few other side dishes and leftovers from the previous meals.

After everyone had filled their plates and had begun eating, Simon announced, "While we're all together, I want to call a family meeting."

"We've never had one of those," Bucky said.

"That's because you and I were the only ones living here. Whenever we talked it was a family meeting. But now there are more of us and we are rarely all together and we need to be a little better about communications."

Bucky frowned and slunk down in her chair. She knew Simon did not approve of the way she had been avoiding Meredyth and she was certain he was going to chastise her in front of everyone.

Simon, sitting at the head of the table to her right, reprimanded her for her posture with just a look and she straightened. "We're all going to church tomorrow," Simon began. "I realize the number one pastime in this town is rumor mongering and tales are already running rampant about Meredyth." He nodded at her on his right. "Especially since we've been seen together in town when I showed her the park and the future mastodon museum. And that's by people besides the ladies and Ron who have dropped in here this week. So, we need to get our stories straight."

Bucky set down the glass of milk she had been holding. "You mean you want to make sure we're all telling the same lie."

Simon exhaled a long breath and tried to contain his exasperation with his daughter. Her behavior all week had been so unlike her. He realized it was only a ten-year-old's reaction to the events that had shaken her world, but he longed for the return of the Bucky he had always known. "If you want to phrase it that way. I prefer to think of it as a viable explanation should anyone ask. And since the locals are extremely forthright in expressing themselves, I have no doubt there will be questions." He took a sip of coffee. "All right. Here's the official version. Meredyth and I separated nine years ago but we reconciled briefly last...uh...February?" He glanced at Meredyth who nodded. "At that time she wasn't sure if she wanted to make the move here, but now she has decided to join us. Does everyone understand? It's simple. If anyone wants more details, they can ask me."

Ian raised his hand. "Mr. Carter? What does *reconcile* mean?"

Bucky, sitting next to him, pulled his hand down. "Honestly, sometimes I think you have cotton stuffed between your ears instead of a brain. Reconcile means they got together and made a baby."

Meredyth put a hand over her mouth to hide her smile.

Maggie chuckled out loud.

"That's not exactly the definition of reconcile," said Simon. "It means to restore friendly relations, to settle differences. In this case, yes, our reconciliation resulted in a baby. But don't word it like that. You don't even have to use the word reconcile. You can say we got back together."

"What class is she going to?" asked Bucky.

"What?" The question caught Simon off guard. "Oh, what Sunday school class? I hadn't thought about it."

"There's the Faith Class," suggested Maggie. "That's mostly couples."

"I really don't know those people as well," said Simon.

"But you go to the Men's Class," said Bucky, "and she can't go to it. And she's too young for the Lukefahr Ladies."

"Aren't you a Lukefahr Lady?" asked Meredyth.

Bucky cocked her head. "They made an exception for me."

Maggie spoke up. "There's not an age restriction and some of the Lukefahr Ladies have husbands in the Men's Class. Betty and Penny. You'd have to split up, but, Meredyth, you can come to class with Bucky and me, and that way Simon can stay in the Men's Class."

Meredyth reached over and took Simon's hand. "Or we could just stay home."

Simon shook his head. "No, we need to show them that…" He trailed off, unable to complete the sentence.

"You know we're Methodists now," said Bucky. "Not Presbyterian."

Meredyth looked at Simon. "So I hear."

"Okay," said Simon. "So, now, does everyone have the story straight?"

Everyone nodded except Bucky. Simon ignored her for the moment and they continued the meal in silence for the next few minutes.

Maggie finally spoke up. "Ron Crosson has found someone to buy half of my chickens. The flock has grown so large it was difficult to sell as many eggs as they were producing."

"You aren't selling the one that lays the blue eggs, are you?" asked Bucky.

"Oh, no. I told Ron specifically not to get rid of her."

"Simon," said Meredyth, "we used to have a little brown hen that laid blue eggs. Remember? Her name was Willow."

Simon and Bucky looked at each other with identical shocked expressions, remembering the dream they had shared two weeks earlier in which Bucky had made the comment, "Willow lays blue eggs."

Simon shook his head and looked at Meredyth. "We never… We never had chickens."

"Willow's the name of our cow," said Ian with a laugh. "We don't name our chickens."

"That's another thing," said Maggie. "You children enjoy that milk. There's just enough left for tomorrow and then we'll have to start drinking store-bought milk again."

"Why?" asked Ian, with a mouth full of sweet potatoes. "Has Willow gone dry?'

"No," said Maggie. "I sold her and Jack to Russ Woodson over by Garton. "Well, Ron made all the arrangements."

"Sold them!" Ian exclaimed. "Why?"

"Because winter's coming on and I'm getting too old to get up at the crack of dawn to milk her and do it all over again in the evening. And you're too young yet to do the milking. This way I don't have to worry about feed and vet bills and a host of other things."

"But Jack was mine."

"No, Ian, he was mine. And it was for the best. And when Mr. Woodson butchers him next year, he's going to split the meat with us."

Bucky dropped her fork on her plate at the word *butcher*.

"I don't want any old meat. I want Jack back." Ian jumped up from the table so abruptly he knocked his chair over backwards. Holding one arm against his stomach he fled up the stairs.

Bucky slid from her chair and started after him, but a word from Simon stopped her.

"Bucky, what do you say?"

She turned around to look at her father. "Ian didn't say it."

Simon shot her a disapproving glance.

"May I be excused?"

"You don't want dessert?" asked Simon. "Someone brought over a coconut crème pie, I think because they knew it was your favorite."

Bucky turned her head and looked toward the stairs then back at Simon. "May I have some later?"

"There's no guarantee there'll be any left," Meredyth said. "If it tastes as good as it looks, we might eat the whole thing."

Bucky mentally counted the people at the table and cocked her head. "I'll take my chances."

"You may be excused," said Simon. "Go make sure Ian didn't hurt himself."

"You never came down for your pie." Simon entered Bucky's room and sat down in the chair next to her bed.

Bucky closed her Sunday school book and set it on the bedside table. "Ian was in my castle, crying. He was inconsolable. Is it inconsolable or unconsolable?"

Simon laid a folded paper on top of her quarterly. "They're both correct. Maggie probably could have broken the news to him a little differently."

"I think he understood the part about Maggie getting older and it's too hard on her to do the milking, but there have just been so many things happening recently. Him getting hurt so bad, and then finding out you're his father, and then the fire and moving in here and now Maggie up and sold his cow without telling him. So many upsetting things. I think I handle all that much better."

"Oh, you do, do you?"

"Yes. He's a lot more sensitive than I am. And he cries every time something happens."

"Maybe you've learned to brace yourself against those things which upset other people. But I think Maggie could have left out the part about Jack being butchered."

"That part did upset me. I don't think I could eat Jack after watching him being born and all, but I don't think it bothered Ian. It's happened before with their cows. But Maggie should have talked to him ahead of time and told him what she was going to do."

"I guess parents don't always think about how their decisions will affect their children."

"We talk about things, don't we?"

Simon nodded. "That's what I want to speak to you about tonight. You've been acting out all week and that's not like you. I'm afraid it's partly my fault because I haven't paid as much attention to you."

"You haven't even been in to tell me 'good night' for the last two nights."

"What? Two nights? Oh, God, Bucky, how could I have missed two nights and not even realized it? I'm so sorry. I will try to do better. I promise. But this week has been... God, it's been unbelievable."

"I know, Dad. It's all right. You have other people than just me to worry about now."

"That's no excuse for ignoring you. Especially because I realize having these extra people in the house affects your... Your what? Your emotions? Your senses?"

"It's kind of like a buzzing in my head. It makes me jittery. But I like having Maggie and Ian here. I wish Ian didn't have to go back to school Monday."

"You like Maggie and Ian being here, but you haven't accepted your mother yet, have you?"

Bucky put her head down and chewed on her lower lip.

"She wants so much to be your mother. You know now, don't you, it wasn't her fault that she's been gone all this time?"

Bucky raised her head and looked at Simon. "I don't trust her."

"What can she do to gain your trust? She was so excited on Tuesday about the conversation you had with her. She got a glimpse of what an extraordinary little girl you are and then... And then you clammed up and have avoided her ever since. She doesn't know what she did or what she said to turn you away from her."

Bucky's chin was tucked again and she plucked at the front of her teal-and-gray-striped pajamas.

"I think she just wants to hear you call her *Mom*. Can't you do that?"

"Dad, I know you think she is who she says she is, but how do you explain what happened at dinner when she said you and she had a chicken named Willow that laid blue eggs? That was in our dream. How could she know that if she wasn't in it also? If she wasn't one of the Anarianu who are causing the dreams?"

"That was not the first unusual comment she made this week," said Simon. "This evening, after dinner, we had a long discussion about it in light of something Maggie had told me this afternoon, which I will share with you in a minute." Simon paused and took a deep breath. "Remember how ever since I got hit on the head I keep having these flashbacks and memories about being other people in other times?"

"Etakkama?"

"He's the main one, but there are numerous others. Even Southy MacAdoo who built this place."

"Seraphina's father."

"Yeah, well, we often hear about Mr. MacAdoo but, of course, he had a wife, Drucilla."

"I know. Her name is on one of the doors down near the Spring Room. Ian thought it said *Dracula*." Bucky giggled and Simon smiled in response.

"Well," Simon continued, "I might not be the only one in this house who has lived other lives. Meredyth... Your mother...has been having similar memory episodes this week. Especially this week, but she says they began a couple of months ago, but she…" Simon turned away from Bucky as his eyes filled with tears. "She thought she was mentally ill. That's what the psychiatrist told her when the people at the group home sent her to him."

"Dad?" Bucky reached out a hand to touch him and he closed both of his hands around hers.

"I first noticed it the day she came. On Monday. We were talking and she called me *Southy*. And I swear, Lamb, for a moment, just for a moment, I saw her standing there in a long navy blue skirt and she was wearing a white blouse with…uh…poofy sleeves and her hair was all done up on top of her head. For an instant, she was Drucilla. It was only a flash, but she…she was Drucilla. And that's not all. "

Simon, keeping a firm grip on Bucky's hand, brought it down to rest on his knee. "The next day when we went to The Hollow and, remember, she got a little sick and went back with you to the UTV?"

Bucky nodded.

"She told me it was when I read the inscription about Etakkama, that for a moment, she saw me as Etakkama and she knew me because…" Simon cleared his throat. "Because she was Aiyana"

"Who?"

"Imala, Etakkama's daughter that was taken and healed by the Anarianu just as you were, her mother was Aiyana. Aiyana was my wife. She was a Native American. And she… She died giving birth to Imala. I took her from her home and…she died." Simon's eyes filled with tears again and he brought Bucky's hand to his mouth and bowed his head. "She was so beautiful."

This close to him, and with him holding her hand in both of his, Simon's emotions cascaded over and through Bucky. "Dad," said Bucky softly, "Meredyth was more than just Aiyana and Drucilla, wasn't she? You and she have been together many times."

Simon raised his head. "Many times. We don't know how many. We're both starting to remember but the memories just come in bits and pieces. And they don't always coincide. We've been talking for the past couple of hours, trying to match them up. Maybe we'll never know for sure."

Bucky slipped her hand out of her father's grasp.

Simon reached for the papers he had laid on her night stand. "I want to show you something." He unfolded the copy of the family tree Maggie had explained to him that afternoon. "Look here." He pointed to Southy's and Drucilla MacAdoo's names. "Here's where we'll start." He proceeded to show her how she and Meredyth were descended from Southy and Drucilla through Saphrona, their daughter who had left, presumably, for life in the big city. He did not show her how Ian, through his mother Kara, was also descended from Saphrona, leaving that for Maggie to explain to her great-grandson. He had folded back the paper so Bucky wouldn't see that section.

"They all had funny names, didn't they?" said Bucky.

"The women certainly did, although for the time period when some of them were born, some of those names were common. Given names are similar to clothing fashions. Just as clothing styles change over time, certain names go in and out of fashion. Maybe Maggie will show you the whole chart she has. It's fascinating but also a little confusing, especially when you had some descendants marrying other descendants."

"Like Ron Crosson and Penny."

"I didn't actually see them on there. I didn't take a lot of time studying it."

Bucky peered at the chart. "Here they are." She pointed at their names. "See? They're both related to us. Can't you tell when you shake hands? Maggie told me they were distant cousins, so it's all right they married."

"They certainly weren't the only ones. Oh, and your French tutor, Sadie Jane Woods, is also descended from Saphrona like you are, through her daughter Vera. When Saphrona disappeared, she left Vera behind." Simon pointed to Sadie Jane's name. "I always get a little confused, describing the relationships, but I think you and Sadie Jane are second cousins, twice removed."

"What does that mean?"

It's a way of describing how far down the line you are from a common ancestor, in this case, Saphrona. If you were both, for example, her great-granddaughters, then you would be second cousins. And Sadie Jane is her great-granddaughter. But you are her great-great-great-granddaughter, so you are two more generations removed from Sadie Jane. See?" Simon pointed again to the chart.

Bucky gasped and pointed to a name. "There's Carl Bergmann."

"I know. He's also descended from Saphrona through her first child Vera."

"I knew we were related but I had never seen how. What kind of cousins are we?"

"Let me figure it out." Simon mentally counted back up the generations on the diagram. "I think you're third cousins, once removed."

"I see your name here where it says Meredyth Lowry Durragh m Simon Leander Carter. The *m* I guess means married?"

"Yes."

"But where are your parents? You're descended from Seraphina, also."

"Maggie doesn't think so."

Bucky latched onto Simon's wrist. "But I can *feel* you. Maggie can, too. She told me."

"I don't know, Lamb. She's doing more research. And knowing Maggie, she's not going to rest until she figures it out."

Bucky was quiet for a moment, her eyes on the genealogy chart. "So are you and...and Meredyth any of these other people on here, besides Southy and Drucilla?"

Simon held his tongue when he heard Bucky again refer to her mother by name. He shook his head. "I don't think so. I haven't had any images or memories of anyone else. I think we skipped from them to present day."

Bucky shrugged. "I wonder where you were in the meantime."

Simon chuckled. "I don't know."

"So you and Drucilla had a chicken named Willow that laid blue eggs?"

"No, that's what's...crazy. It was further back. Somewhere, sometime in England. Maybe sixteenth century."

"I wonder if every time you had a little girl, it was actually me. Perhaps I am Imala and...and Seraphina. What were the names of some of your other children?"

Simon shook his head. "Don't know."

"Maybe if I get hit on the head, I'll remember my past lives."

"I wouldn't want you to experience either of those things. I certainly wouldn't want you to sustain a head injury, and remembering this jumbled collection of earlier lives is...disconcerting, to say the least."

Bucky lay back against her pillow and put her hands under her head. "Things were sure simpler back before we left New York, weren't they?"

Simon looked away. "We were secluded up in that apartment, high above the city streets, shut away from everything. We were in our own little world. No labyrinths, no little green lightning bugs, no crazy, ranting preacher, no old ladies. Just you and me."

Bucky sat up and touched Simon's cheek. "Shouldn't that be 'just you and I'?"

Simon smiled and covered her hand with his. "Yes, it should."

"Dad, things were simpler back then, but it was kind of boring. I didn't know it was boring until we came here. I don't think I could ever go back to that life."

Simon kissed her hand, released it and stood. "It's time you were asleep."

"Two things first. She said she would learn the 'Laya Song' and teach it to you and then you would teach it to me to dry my tears."

"Oh." Simon put his hands on his hips. "God, I'm sorry. I've been so busy this week, I forgot. But your mother has been working on it and the translation of the Hollow Stone. After church tomorrow, we'll see about it. I am so sorry, Bucky. I feel like this whole week I've practically ignored you with everything else that's been going on. I'll make it up to you."

"Second thing, you need to see Ian before he goes to sleep."

"He's probably already asleep."

"No, he's not."

Simon shook his head and frowned. "How do you know?"

Bucky shrugged. "He's still upset about Willow and Jack and he thinks you don't like him."

"Why would he think that?"

"Because you never do anything with him. You haven't even been doing his exercises with him. Maggie's been doing that."

"I told him I would leave it up to him what kind of relationship we would have. I'm not going to push myself on him if that's not what he wants."

"Dad, he's just a kid, remember?"

"Okay. I'll stop by his room. Now, lights out." Simon switched the lamp off and headed toward the door.

"No, one more thing. What's the Hittite word for mother?"

Simon turned around. With her closed door shutting out the light from the hallway, he could barely distinguish the lump in the bed that was his daughter. "*Anna.*"

Light slipped from under the door to Ian's room. Simon rapped twice softly and spoke barely above a whisper, "Ian, may I come in?"

Simon heard a "Sure," and he stepped inside and closed the door behind him.

Ian was sitting up in bed, propped against two large pillows. He closed a large book and set it to the side.

"What are you reading?" asked Simon, sitting on the edge of the bed.

"It's about how they built castles a long time ago. I got it out of your library downstairs. Bucky said you wouldn't mind."

"I don't mind. I used it for a little research for one of my books."

Ian tucked his chin. "Have you come to yell at me?"

"I wasn't planning on it. Why?"

"For knocking the chair over at supper and running out like that. Gram says we're guests here and I'm supposed to be on my best behavior. She's already yelled at me for it, so you don't have to."

"She must have yelled quietly because I didn't hear her. I guess you're pretty upset with her for selling Willow and Jack."

Ian nodded.

Simon could see tears glistening in the boy's eyes. He fought the urge to wrap his arms around him as he so often had done to Bucky at the first sign of her tears. He reminded himself Ian was not Bucky. He could cry normally without his back opening up and bathing him in blood.

"She could have told me before they were gone." Ian's words were followed by a sniff. "I didn't even get to tell Jack goodbye. The next time I see him he'll be hamburger." The tears spilled over and trickled down his cheeks.

Simon did reach one hand out then and grasped his shoulder. "I know something about how you feel. The same thing happened to me when I was only a little older than you. We had a dog named Shep that I grew up with. My parents had him before I was even born, so by the time I was in seventh grade, he was pretty old. He got really bad and my dad had him put to sleep without telling me. In fact, they didn't tell me for a couple of days. They acted like he must have run off, and finally my mother told me what had happened. I cried for a week."

"You did?"

Simon nodded. "I still tear up just thinking about him. He was a good dog." They both were silent for a moment before Simon spoke again. "Do you think it would help if we drove over to the Woodson's farm, and you could see Willow and Jack, make sure they're all right and being cared for? It would give you a chance to say goodbye."

"I don't think Gram would do that."

"I can find out where he lives and take you."

Ian's face brightened.

"But not this week. I have too much to do with the Moyers coming next weekend. But probably the week after. And the repairs on your house might be close to being done by then. They're moving incredibly fast on it."

"I like living here, but I kind of miss my old room and all my stuff."

"I know Bucky likes having you here. I'm really glad the two of you are such good friends. And I know she hates that you're returning to school Monday."

"I don't have to go back, do I? Couldn't you teach me like you do Bucky?"

"If Bucky were the same as other children, she would be in school."

Ian screwed his face. "You mean if she weren't as smart as she is?"

"No, I mean her...her condition, what happens when she cries."

"Oh, yeah. I guess if she went and did that at school it would kind of freak everybody out."

"Your grandmother told me when you saw the doctor last week he said you could go back to school this

Monday if you felt well enough to do so, but you have another appointment on Wednesday. I don't see any reason why you should go Monday and Tuesday and then have to miss Wednesday. We could wait and make sure the doctor says everything's okay on Wednesday."

"You mean I might not have to go back until Thursday?"

"It's up to your grandmother, of course, but I'll talk to her about it tomorrow."

"Mr. Carter, I've been thinking. Next summer, I'll be eleven. Gram says I can start mowing our yard then. Could I mow yours, too? I mean for money?"

"Oh, I don't know about that."

"But you paid someone to mow it last summer. And I won't charge much."

"It's not the money. Mowing can be dangerous. And eleven is not very old."

"But Gram's going to let me."

"Maybe we should wait until spring and have this discussion then."

"I just thought it would be a way for me to earn some money. If Gram's not going to have so many eggs to sell and she's going to have to start buying milk, well, money's going to be tight. If I had my own, then I could buy the things I want and not have to pester her."

"Do you get an allowance?"

Ian shook his head.

"As I said, we'll revisit this topic of mowing in the spring. But, maybe with her permission, I could give you an allowance in return for chores around the house when you move back in. There will probably be more work to be done next spring and summer when you can help in the garden and mowing the yard, but even now you could help with the chickens or the housework."

"You'd pay me to help Gram?"

"She might not agree to it."

"Will you ask her?"

"I will suggest it to her. And now, if we're all going to have to get up and go to church tomorrow, then we'd better get to bed. Oh, and about tomorrow. You realize there were an awful lot of people worried about you after your accident and then concerned about you and your grandmother after the fire. So when they see you tomorrow, they're going to want to make over you."

"You mean like kiss me?"

"No, but they'll probably rub those curls." Simon touched the top of Ian's head. "And they'll want to hug you. Although don't let them hug too tightly and hurt you. But what I'm saying is I want you to grin and bear it. Don't pout and don't run off and hide. Just let them do their thing and tell you how happy they are that you're okay. Do you think you can do that? I know Maggie will be tickled and so proud of you."

"It sounds awful."

"It will only be for a few minutes before Sunday school. And then you can disappear downstairs until the worship service begins."

"Bucky will be jealous because she's usually the one who gets all the attention."

"She will just have to get over it."

"Okay, Mr. Carter." Ian shuddered. "I'll try. I won't like it, but I'll try."

"Thank you. Lights out. No more reading tonight." He took the book from Ian's bed and laid it on the night stand. "Good night, Ian."

26

A LESSON ON RECONCILIATION

Hoping to avoid being greeted by many people, Simon wanted to arrive at church earlier than usual the next morning, but it didn't work out as he had planned. Getting the other four occupants of the household fed, dressed and out of the Mansion and into the car took longer than expected. Instead of a smattering of cars on the parking lot, the lot was even fuller than usual. Simon had told Ian what the boy could expect this morning, but Simon was unsure what the reaction would be to his pregnant wife suddenly showing up after a nine-year absence. Anticipating the gauntlet which awaited them in the entryway, Simon squeezed Bucky's hand a little tighter than usual as they crossed the parking lot. Meredyth walked on the opposite side of him and she tightly clasped his other hand. It was the first time since Meredyth's arrival the three of them held hands and walked together. Simon could feel their energy coursing up both his arms. He could also detect the tendrils of his unborn son, wrapped around the pulses emanating from Meredyth. The feeling excited him and emboldened him. By the time they reached the front doors, he was braced and ready to face the onslaught of questions and possible slurs.

Maggie and Ian walked up the steps ahead of the others and Ian started to open the door, but Ron Crosson was on the inside and held it open for them.

Maggie and Ian stepped through into the crowd waiting for them. The reception was much like Simon had described to Ian, even the hair tousling. The exuberant hugs and well wishes from her friends and relatives quickly brought Maggie to tears. Ian allowed himself to be petted and hugged without complaint. He shook hands with the men, most of them clasping his shoulder or upper arm. He even managed a smile for some of them.

The reception Meredyth received was much more subdued, but courteous. It was not at all what Simon had expected. People shook her hand and welcomed her to church. Some engaged in small talk, questioning how she liked the town so far or was the weather like what she was used to.

Simon stayed by Meredyth's side as they made their way through the church members, but Bucky, no longer holding her father's hand, hung back a little and listened to the whispered remarks made after the couple had passed. She observed that while most everyone smiled as they spoke to her mother, some of the comments afterwards were not so polite. She didn't even understand some of the references, but the remarks often resulted in snickers between the speakers, and she had a feeling whatever was spoken was not nice.

She skirted around the large cluster of people and saw Lillian Thomas standing with her walker in the hallway leading to the classroom. "Where's your sister?" asked Bucky. "She's not still sick, is she?"

"Oh, no. We were both in the room already when I heard all this hubbub and came out to see what was going on."

"Maggie and Ian are back today," explained Bucky.

"Is Ian better, then? I heard Maggie was worried about him."

"He's getting better," replied Bucky. "Although getting hugged by all these people is sure not like him. I expected him to bolt like a scared rabbit at the first sign of affection and he's just standing there, taking it and grinning like a possum eating a sweet potato."

"Lands, child, you're sounding like a native. Are you sure you weren't born and raised here?"

Bucky and Lillian shared a laugh. With Lillian being short and hunched over her walker, she and Bucky were at eye level.

"And is that pretty young thing with your papa the one I've heard tell of all week—your mother come back after all these years?"

Bucky nodded. "I guess she came back briefly last February and no one told me."

"So now you're going to be a big sister?"

Bucky sighed. "Looks that way."

"Well," said Lillian, patting Bucky's hand which rested on her walker, "I've been a big sister since I was four years old. It's not so bad. Puts a little more pressure on you cause now you'll be the oldest. But it takes some pressure off cause now you won't be the onliest. So it evens out pretty good."

Ian was finally through the well-wishers and came up to Bucky and whispered in her ear. "You don't have to stay in class since your mom will be there. You can come downstairs with me."

Bucky bit her bottom lip and considered Ian's suggestion. She shook her head. "No. She wouldn't try anything with all the other women present. I'll be all right."

"Suit yourself. Gram says I can ride the stair lift down." Ian was no longer whispering but the adults were talking among themselves and not paying any attention to the conversation of the children.

"She's babying you. You know you can walk up and down those stairs just fine. If you're well enough to go to school tomorrow, you're well enough to—"

Ian interrupted her. "Your dad told me last night I don't have to go back to school till Thursday."

"He did?"

"I asked him if I could stay home all the time and be home-schooled like you, but he didn't go for that."

"Maybe he'll change his mind. He does sometimes. But at least we get three more days."

Ian started for the stairs as the clusters of people in the entryway began breaking up and the members headed to their classes. Lillian had already walked back down the hallway while Bucky and Ian were talking. Bucky flattened herself against a wall and waited while

Simon and Meredyth, followed by Maggie and several of the other Lukefahr Ladies, passed by. She followed them down the hall.

Outside the door of the women's classroom, Simon and Meredyth stepped aside and allowed the ladies to enter. "That wasn't so bad," Simon said, keeping his voice low. "I'll just be in that room we passed back there. You'll be all right?"

"I'll be fine," Meredyth reassured him. "Maggie will be there…and Bucky. Where is Bucky?"

They both turned and looked back down the hallway. Bucky was standing in the middle of the now-deserted corridor.

"Come here," Simon whispered, motioning to her with his hand. "Take your mother inside and find her a place to sit. Most of the women met her just now, but I don't know if all of them did." He tried to place Bucky's hand in Meredyth's but Bucky snatched hers away.

"Come on," said Bucky. "You can sit in Clara's old seat. She died."

Simon and Meredyth exchanged parting glances and Simon left her there.

Bucky was hoping the only empty seat would be on the opposite side of the semi-circle of chairs from her, but the women had left two open spots on Maggie's right. Bucky heaved a heavy sigh and led Meredyth to them. Bucky sat next to Maggie, and Meredyth, none too gracefully, lowered herself into the seat on Bucky's right.

"These look like old theater seats," said Meredyth, "except they're nicely padded."

"They're from the Mansion," said Bucky. "They used to be in that big room with the stage, didn't they, Maggie?"

"That they did," confirmed Maggie. "Ladies, some of you have met Meredyth Carter either a few minutes ago or when you brought those mountains of food to us this past week. Before I forget, I want to thank all of you for being so generous. The food has been delicious. However, I do not thank you for the ten pounds I've gained."

The women all laughed good-naturedly at Maggie's comment.

"But if you haven't met her yet, this is Meredyth— and I believe she spells her name with a *y* instead of an *i*. She's Simon's wife and Bucky's mother and with a little one on the way."

Meredyth put a hand on her swollen abdomen. "Not so little, I'm afraid."

Some of the ladies tittered.

Maggie continued. "Bucky told her she was too young for our class, but I disagreed and told her we would welcome her."

There were nods all around.

"Oh," said Sadie Jane at the teacher's desk. "Clara's daughter was going through some of her things this past week and she brought over Clara's quarterly. Bucky, would you come get this and give it to your mother so she'll have a book?"

Bucky avoided eye contact with Meredyth when she handed her the Sunday school lesson book.

"And, Sadie Jane," said Maggie, "I don't want to take up any more of your class time, but I also want to tell everyone how much I appreciate all of your calls and prayers and offers of help and…" Maggie teared up and had to pause for a moment. She dabbed at her eyes with one hand and Bucky reached across the arms of their two seats and took her other hand. "And just everything. I don't know what people do when something terrible happens if they don't have a church family."

"We're all so thankful you and Ian weren't hurt," said Maxine.

"That's right," said Ruby. "Things can be replaced but not people."

"And Ron says the repairs are coming along nicely," added Penny. "You'll be back home before long."

Maggie nodded, too choked up to speak. She squeezed Bucky's hand.

"All right, then," said Sadie Jane, getting everyone's attention. "Let's continue our lesson on Joseph in Genesis that we began last week. Sissy, would you read the scripture for us?"

As the class continued, Bucky tried to relax, but it was difficult with Meredyth just inches away from her. In the mix of fragrances in the room—some of the ladies tended to overdose on the application of their perfume—Bucky could smell her mother's. The scent was the same as in the bottle Simon kept in the second drawer of his dresser. Over the years, he had sometimes removed the cap, allowing Bucky to inhale the delicate aroma. He would take a whiff, as well. On the rare occasion, Simon let

Bucky dab a drop behind each of her ears. Bucky squeezed her eyes shut for a moment. She must not let pleasant memories cause her to let down her guard. She reminded herself the woman beside her had tried to kill her in her dreams.

She tried to imagine how Joseph must have felt, seeing for the first time his brothers who had tried to kill him, now standing before him, asking to buy food. But Joseph pulled a dirty trick on them before he told them who he was. And his father was stunned at first and then overjoyed to learn his son was alive. That's how Simon feels about Meredyth coming home, Bucky thought. Whereas Bucky cast herself in the role of the brothers who were probably scared Joseph would retaliate and kill them now that he was in a position of power. And yet Joseph forgave his brothers and they were reconciled. There was that word her dad had used at supper the night before.

Throughout the Sunday school hour, Bucky continued to mull over her relationship to the woman sitting on her right, sitting so close Bucky could feel her and the baby without even being in physical contact. She wondered whether any of the ladies who shook hands with her a few minutes ago felt the family connection her dad had showed her last night on Maggie's genealogy chart. Should she trust her as Joseph's brothers trusted him enough to go home and get their families and flocks and bring them back to settle in Egypt? Should she be reconciled to her? She and Simon obviously had reconciled this past week, if not last February in the lie

Simon had told them to tell. Her dad had forgiven his wife after hearing her story and had accepted her back into his life. Bucky felt like she could forgive her now for leaving, but how could she know for certain the Anarianu were not using her mother to bring harm and even death to her. She wondered how her father could know for sure.

Bucky was so lost in thought she didn't hear Sadie Jane ask her to read a paragraph in the quarterly. Maggie nudged her to get her attention and Sadie Jane repeated the request. Bucky quickly flipped to the right page and found the spot and read it. The words *reconciliation* and *forgiveness* were both in the sentences Bucky read. It was as if Sadie Jane knew what had been swirling around in her brain, Bucky thought, and perceived the youngest member in the class was trying to come to grips with her dilemma.

The bell rang just as Bucky finished reading. The class closed by saying in unison the prayer printed at the end of the lesson. The word *reconcile* appeared in the prayer, also. Bucky felt as if the entire lesson was sending her a message.

As everyone was gathering their belongings and visiting for a few moments before going into the sanctuary, several of the women gathered around Meredyth who had used the arms of the old seat to maneuver herself into an upright position. Bucky slipped around everyone and plopped into the chair vacated by Leona, Lillian's sister. Sadie Jane Woods put her books into a bag and came over and sat in the seat next to her.

"My star French pupil seemed a little distracted in class today. *Est ce que ça va ?*" At Bucky's quizzical expression, Sadie Jane translated for her. "Are you okay?"

Bucky shrugged.

Sadie Jane kept her voice low. "From the way you acted on Thursday during our French session and from watching you today, I don't think you have warmed up to your mother yet, have you?"

Bucky shook her head and lowered her gaze. She turned up the corner of her class quarterly on her lap.

"She seems congenial from my brief conversation with her before Sunday school. Are you jealous there will be a new baby in the house?"

Bucky shook her head and looked around. Most of the women were heading into the hallway.

"Come on, Bucky," Meredyth said. "You need to show me where the sanctuary is."

"Maggie will take you, *Anna*, won't you, Maggie?"

Both Maggie and Meredyth raised their eyebrows when they heard Bucky refer to Meredyth as *Anna*, but Sadie Jane said, "We're going to have a little talk. Go on and I'll see that Miss Bucky gets there."

Maggie took Meredyth's elbow and escorted her from the now-deserted room.

"Why did you call her *Anna* just now?" asked Sadie Jane.

"That's the Hittite word for mother."

"So why not call her Mother or Mom?"

Bucky shrugged again.

"Is it because you don't want to be close to her yet? Saying *Mother* in a foreign language—and a dead language at that—puts a little distance between you, doesn't it?"

"I've had too many dreams where she's tried to hurt me," said Bucky. "And then this week, some nights I dream she is being pulled into one of those colored spinning cloud things like Reverend Bergmann got taken in. And I try to stop her but can't, and Reverend Bergmann is standing there laughing. Last night, I told him I was glad she was gone."

"I'm afraid those dreams which have plagued us for months are having an effect on all of us. I don't know what I can say to make you feel better." Sadie Jane laid her hand on Bucky's head and smoothed down her hair. "I can tell you this, though. I would be overjoyed to see my mother again if only for a day, or an hour, or even a minute. Maggie has told me you have no memories of your mother, but this is a chance for you to get to know her. You can't do that if you shut her out."

"So you think I should reconcile with her?"

A smile cracked Sadie Jane's bony features. "That was today's lesson, wasn't it? Come on. I think we'd better go or your father will be calling out a search party for you."

"That is one interesting thing about her coming back. He pays a lot of attention to her and sometimes I think he forgets I'm even around." Bucky stood with the elderly woman and took her hand. "Sadie Jane, when you shook hands with her, did you feel something like what you feel when you hold my hand?"

"Yes. Yes, I did, but I don't know why. I usually only feel that with relatives."

"She is a relative. Maggie figured out how she's descended from Southy and Drucilla MacAdoo. They're the ones who founded Turn Back and built the Mansion where I live."

"The MacAdoos are my third great-grandparents on my mother's side," said Sadie Jane. "But that means you're descended from them, too, so that makes us cousins, doesn't it?"

"According to Maggie's chart, my dad says you and I are second cousins, twice removed."

Sadie Jane raised Bucky's hand in the air as they walked down the hall. "Well, cousin, I knew there was something special about you all this time, but I had no idea we were family."

All through the worship service and on the ride home and throughout lunch, Bucky considered since it had been a week since her mother's return, and Meredyth had not tried to harm her during that time, maybe she should relax her guard a little. Maybe she should try talking to her, try getting to know her better. She admitted to herself she had enjoyed their brief conversation in The Hollow on Tuesday. And from listening to her talk at mealtimes, she seemed to be every bit as intelligent and knowledgeable as Simon, and Bucky considered Simon to be the smartest person in the whole world. But how could she be sure it was not an act, an elaborate scheme to lull her into thinking this woman was a sweet, caring mother when she was really the Wicked Witch of the West?

When the noon meal was almost over, Simon announced, "Bucky, before you and Ian go off to do whatever you have planned for this afternoon, you need to come into the music room."

Bucky stiffened. "But, Dad, that's where— You know, the dream."

"Bucky," said Meredyth, "I think it will be easier to learn the 'Laya Song' if you hear the words along with the notes played on the piano."

Bucky looked at her father and pleaded, "Can't you teach them to me?"

"I'm trying to memorize them, also," said Simon. "I'm going to be there, too."

"Can I come learn the song?" asked Ian. "You never know. Something might happen like that night in the woods and I'd be the only one around to help."

"What happened in the woods?" asked Meredyth.

Ian shuddered. "It was awful."

"Bucky...uh...had one of her episodes and Ian witnessed it," explained Simon. "He probably saved her life that night."

"What were you doing in the woods at night?" Meredyth looked at Bucky who had slouched down in her chair.

"I'll tell you about it later," said Simon.

Bucky spoke up. "There's an awful man who lives around here named Reverend Bergmann who's always trying to interrupt our prayer walks. He says things like how Dad is the Devil and I'm the Devil's spawn."

"And he's a preacher?" Meredyth leaned forward toward Bucky who was seated across the table from her.

"One night, after one of the prayer walks, he scared me really bad. He knocked Maggie down and I thought he was going to hurt me so I took off running and ended up lost in the woods."

"Oh, my gosh," said Meredyth. "You must have been terrified." She turned to Simon. "Where were you during all this?"

"I...uh... I wasn't there."

"You let her go to these prayer walks alone, knowing this maniac is there? You're supposed to protect her."

"I have been protecting her all these years." Simon raised his voice and his face reddened. "It was one time."

Bucky's mouth dropped open as she watched and listened to this verbal exchange between her parents.

Maggie stepped into the conversation. "Meredyth, it was my fault. I convinced him to let her go with me that evening. I thought she'd be safe with me and the other women from church. I never expected the confrontation with Carl Bergmann to turn violent. It all happened so fast."

"So, where is this nut now? In jail, I hope."

Simon gave a slight shake of his head. "I wish."

"But," said Ian, holding up a bite of pie on the end of his fork, "it all had a happy ending. Because that's how we found the Hollow Stone. If Bucky hadn't led us there, it could have been months or maybe years, before anyone discovered it."

"That's little solace," said Meredyth, bringing her napkin to her mouth.

Bucky thought she, too, should defend her father's decision that fateful night. "It was a good thing Dad stayed home from the prayer walk that evening, because he made a really good deal that brought in lots of money, didn't you, Dad?"

Simon narrowed his eyes at her and said softly, "That's not necessary."

"What profit a man to gain the whole world and lose his daughter?" Meredyth said scornfully.

"That's not how that verse goes," said Bucky, frowning. "Shouldn't it be *lose his soul*? In fact, in the New Revised Standard Version, it says *forfeit his life*."

Simon laid his hand on top of Bucky's on the table. "Believe me, Lamb, if I had lost you that night, I would have forfeited my life *and* my soul." He smiled at her but she did not return it. "Okay, it's Meredyth's and my turn to clear the table. While we clean up in here, why don't you two go on into the music room and wait for us. Maggie, you can join us there and learn the song, too, if you wish."

"I need to go to my room first and change into more comfortable shoes," Maggie said. " I'll be there in a few minutes."

❧

"I don't think your mother likes me," said Ian. He and Bucky were alone in the music room and sitting on the bench at the grand piano.

"Of course, she doesn't," said Bucky matter-of-factly as she raised the fallboard and exposed the keys. The ivory keys had yellowed over the years.

"Why not?"

"Because of who you are, silly."

"Who am I?"

"Really, Ian." Bucky threw up her hands. "Do I have to explain everything to you? My dad is your dad, but my mother is not your mother. Get it?"

"No. What difference does that make?"

Bucky exhaled in exasperation. "Think about it, Ian. We're just a couple of months apart in age. My dad was married to my mom when he made a baby—you—with your mom. I thought he explained all that to you."

"I think he tried, but you know how he is. He takes a long time to explain things sometimes, and I get a little lost."

"It's not that she doesn't like you, exactly, but you remind her of the awful thing my dad did and how he cheated on her."

"But that's not my fault. I couldn't help being born."

Bucky slung an arm around Ian's shoulder. "Course not. Maybe she'll grow to like you."

"Are you two ready to sing?" Meredyth, followed by Simon, entered the room and came over to the piano. Meredyth held some papers in her hand.

Bucky removed her arm from Ian's shoulder and slid off the bench to stand by Simon as Meredyth took her place.

Meredyth put the papers on the music rack. "I think there's room on here for you, too." She patted the bench next to her. Ian had moved to the edge on the other side of her.

Bucky shook her head, remembering the dream in which the woman—her mother?—yanked down the fallboard, almost crushing her fingers. Talking about reconciliation in the comfort of a Sunday school room was easier than putting it into practice with someone she thought had tried to drown her in her sleep.

Simon put his hands on Bucky's shoulders and physically guided her onto the bench. "Sit down there so you can see the words. I'll be right here behind you."

Meredyth had translated the Anarianu symbols from Bucky's song stone into English syllables. The symbols on the stone also indicated the notes which accompanied each symbol. Since Meredyth could remember the tune from her time with the Guardians, she was able to translate those signs, as well. She had printed some blank staff paper off the Internet and created the score and words to the "Laya Song."

Maggie joined them and stood next to Simon, behind the children and Meredyth. The five of them spent the next forty-five minutes going over and over the words and music they hoped would counteract the effects of Bucky's tears. There was no way of knowing if it would work, of course, until the next time Bucky started to cry.

27

GONE

"**D**ad, you and *Anna* were yelling at each other at lunch today." Bucky was sitting up in bed. The sparkles on the front of her pink princess gown flickered in the light of her bedside lamp.

"We weren't yelling." Simon crossed the room and sat in the chair next to her bed. "We both raised our voices slightly but we were merely having a disagreement."

"It was about me."

"It was about my poor decision to allow you to go to that one walk last June without me."

"It sounds like she wants to keep me on an even shorter leash than you do."

"You have picked up some idioms since we've been living here and I'm unsure as to whether I like you using them. Do you mean your mother sounds as if she might be even more protective of you than I am?"

Bucky turned her head away and pretended to look out the window. It was dark. There was nothing to see.

"Everyone in this town is protective of you. It's something you're going to have to live with."

"Not everyone."

"No," said Simon. "Not everyone. I think that's the greatest blessing about having the prayer walks only once a month now. We don't have to put up with him every week."

Bucky turned back to look at her father. "I think *Anna* might call him out if he tries anything when she's around."

Simon exhaled loudly. "Why can't you say *mom?* That's how you used to refer to her."

Bucky shrugged. "Ian and I were talking about that this evening. He said he might start calling you *Atta.*"

"I didn't realize Ian spoke Hittite." Simon smiled and this time it was enough to coax a smile from Bucky.

Her smile was fleeting. "Where are the Moyers going to sleep when they come next weekend? Maggie and Ian have the guest rooms."

"I figured since it appears we're running a boarding house now, I should furnish a couple more rooms. I have some bedroom sets and a few other things coming this week. I thought maybe I would set up two of the rooms on the first floor, down from my study. In fact, Maggie might want to move down there. I'm sure going up and down these stairs all day is hard on her."

"How about a nursery?"

"Your mother and I have been discussing that. It would be nice if this room were available. We could cut a doorway—" At Bucky's horrified expression he quickly continued. "I didn't say we were taking your bedroom. I said it would be nice because we could cut a doorway to connect to our room. But we'll probably use the vacant room across the hall from us."

Bucky sighed in relief. "That's still pretty close. He'll probably wake me up crying all night."

"He probably will for a while."

"Have you picked out a name for him yet?"

"Since you are named for both of our mothers, we thought we'd name him after our fathers."

Bucky scrunched her nose, trying to remember her grandfathers' names. "Lowry and Brennan?"

"Brennan Lowry. We'll probably call him Brennan. Although you never know. After he's born, he might look like he should have an entirely different name." Simon yawned. "I think I'm ready for bed. I'm going to call it a day." He stood and helped Bucky get under the covers and started to switch off the lamp but stopped. "Our lesson in the Men's Class this morning was about Joseph and his brothers and reconciliation and forgiveness. I'm certain yours was, too. Did you understand any of that and consider maybe it is applicable to your current situation with your mother?"

Bucky stuck out her lower lip and crossed her arms on top of her blankets.

"After all," Simon continued, "Joseph didn't just dream his brothers tried to kill him. They almost did had not Reuben convinced them not to, and then Judah suggested they sell him as a slave. And yet he forgave them all and they were reconciled."

"But they didn't reconcile until years later," said Bucky. "I'll bet he was pissed enough when they threw him in the cistern that he could have killed the whole bunch."

Simon huffed in exasperation. "Bucky, *pissed* is not a word you are allowed to use and I don't want to ever hear you say it again."

"Miss Lillian says it's not a bad word."

"I don't care. I'm telling you not to use it. Now you are intelligent enough to think of a synonym for it. Give me a word you could use instead."

Bucky's lower lip protruded even further this time.

"Well?" demanded Simon.

"Angry?" Bucky spoke the word through clenched teeth.

"Yes. Any others?"

"He was…furious." She opened her mouth this time. That's a good one."

Bucky smiled impishly. "I'll bet Joseph was fit to be tied."

Simon shook his head at her use of another idiom. "Good night." He leaned over and kissed her forehead.

Simon awoke to someone pounding on his bedroom door

"Mr. Carter! Mr. Carter!"

Simon threw off his covers and bounded from the bed and across the room. He opened the door. "Ian, what's wrong?"

"It's Bucky! She's gone!"

"What? Where?" Simon tried to focus after coming up from a deep sleep.

"I woke up because I thought I heard her yelling. She's not in her bed and she's not in her castle."

Simon hit the light switch by the door and spun around. "Oh, God, no." His bed also was empty. Meredyth was gone.

Maggie opened her bedroom door and stepped into the hall. "What's wrong? What's happened?"

"Is Bucky with you again?" asked Simon.

Maggie shook her head "No."

All three of them turned their heads toward the distant sound of a scream piercing the darkness. It came from somewhere on the first floor.

"The Spring Room," announced Simon, but Ian was already sprinting toward the stairs, faster than he had moved since before his accident. "Ian! Don't go there. Stay up here." Simon flipped the switch to light the stairs and rushed after Ian but the boy outpaced him easily and was at the bottom of the stairs and fleeing down the hallway toward the lower level before Simon was halfway down the grand staircase. Ian ran in the dark, but Simon stopped along the way long enough to hit the switches to light the passageways. Both of them were led forward by Bucky's anguished cries for help.

Ian reached the Spring Room first. The door was open and he didn't hesitate to enter, but he halted in horror on the landing. A swirling multicolored cloud filled the room, but it was what he saw at the base of the cloud above the lower pool that made him stop and grip the railing for support.

The water in the pool was spinning into a massive whirlpool. Meredyth and Bucky were both standing in the air inches above the gaping hole in the water. The spiraling, twisting cloud almost completely engulfed Meredyth who was struggling against being drawn into it. Bucky was holding on to one of her arms. There were no lights on and the waning crescent moon had not yet risen, but an eerie green glow illuminated the room.

"No!" screamed Bucky. "You can't take her. She's my mother."

Recovering quickly from his initial shock at the sight, Ian descended the stairs. Bucky and her mother were too far from the edge of the pool for him to reach them. He was a good swimmer but his abdomen was hurting from the exertion of his race here. But he had no choice.

Simon arrived at the top of the stairs just as Ian plunged into the churning, cold water. Simon hit the light switch, but he, too, stopped on the landing, unable for a moment to comprehend the spectacle until Bucky's screams spurred him to rush down the steps.

Ian bobbed in the water and grabbed one of Bucky's ankles. Simon dove into the pool and surfaced next to Ian. He grasped Bucky's other leg but the way the cloud was sucking Meredyth into it, there was nothing of his wife Simon could reach. The whirlpool was dragging down both Simon and Ian into its gaping maw.

Without warning, the entire cloud collapsed and the pool became placid. Meredyth and Bucky disappeared, and Simon and Ian were left holding only air.

"No!" Simon's protest was a harsh, guttural sound. "You can't have them. Not this time."

"Ian!" screamed Maggie from the landing. She had followed them both through the corridors and had finally reached the Spring Room.

With the lower spring pool calm now, Simon's feet could reach the smooth rock bottom with the water only coming up to his neck, but it was over Ian's head. Terrified and in pain, Ian was having trouble staying afloat. Simon slipped an arm around the boy's chest and helped him to the edge and up onto the stone walkway. Simon climbed out and sat next to him.

"I tried to save her. I tried," sobbed Ian.

Simon, exhausted from his run and numb from shock and shivering with the cold, wet pajamas plastered to him, put an arm around his son. "I know." He looked around the room, but there were no Anarianu visible, no green lightning bugs nor red ones.

Maggie joined them and took off her bathrobe and wrapped it around her grandson. "Where?" was all she could say.

Simon shook his head. "I don't know. Oh, God." He put his head in his hands. "God, please help me."

"We need to get the two of you upstairs and into dry clothes," said Maggie. She had sat down next to Ian and he huddled against her, crying. "It's freezing down here."

"I can't," moaned Simon. "I can't leave them. I can't… Either of them."

"They're not here, Simon. There's no one here."

"But she's coming back, isn't she?" Ian raised his head away from Maggie's protective clutch. "Bucky's coming back. She has to come back."

"I don't know, Lamb." Maggie rubbed his upper arm through the robe.

"But the Guardians only took Reverend Bergmann for a few minutes," said Ian.

Simon, his hands still cradling his head, whispered hoarsely, "But they took Meredyth for nine years."

"Simon, you can't stay here. We need to go."

Simon shook his head. "My life is forfeit."

"Come on, Lamb." Maggie struggled to her feet and helped Ian stand. "Hold up the robe so you don't trip on it. Do you think you can make it up the steps?"

Ian, holding one arm across his stomach, nodded. He put the other hand on Simon's head. "She'll be back, *Atta*. They both will."

A disturbance in the upper pool, the one into which the spring water flowed continuously, caused all three to turn their heads in that direction. They watched as a water spout formed, reaching to the high ceiling. Within a few seconds, it sunk back into the pool, leaving behind a little girl in a pink princess gown, floating face down in the icy water.

"Oh, God!" Simon scrabbled on his hands and knees across the stone floor to the edge of the pool. This pool was smaller and he could reach one of Bucky's ankles to pull her toward him. He hauled her out of the water and wrapped his arms around her, willing her to be alive.

Maggie and Ian knelt beside the huddled pair.

"Simon, is she…"

"I don't know," Simon sobbed.

Bucky's eyes popped open and she gulped a deep breath. "Dad!"

Simon hugged her even more tightly to him. "Bucky. Oh, God, Bucky."

Bucky raised her head from Simon's hold on her. "Why are you wet? Why am I all wet?" She noticed Ian and Maggie. "Why are you in my room?" Her eyes widened. "Oh! Oh, Dad! I was there! I was there again."

Simon tried to bring her head again his chest once more. "God, Bucky, what happened to your mother? Where is she?"

"She'll be back. They're going to send her back. But, Dad, listen to me. I might forget again."

"She's freezing, Simon," said Maggie. "You all are. We need to get upstairs and into some dry clothes."

"We need to hear her out, Maggie," Simon said. "Last time she forgot almost immediately."

"It was all light and colors and music like you said I told you before." Bucky spoke rapidly. "I was there a while. And they told me… They explained things to me about what's going on." Bucky shifted in Simon's grasp to see his face better. "What you said you thought or what they told you about the Reds and the Greens being two different groups, it's kind of true. But they look alike there. When they show themselves in our world is when they appear red or green. The red ones, the Discordants, are tied more to the physical forces of the universe—the supernovas and…and…the solar flares…And I don't really know how to explain it. But here on earth it's like they feed off of earthquakes and volcanoes and storms and hurricanes. But it's not only the physical forces which feed the Discordants, but emotions like hate and anger and…and fear. And the green ones get their energy from…from peace and harmony and good will and order in the universe. Things like gravity and rotation. Oh, Dad, it made sense when they were telling me, but it doesn't make much sense now. But they don't hate each other. They're just different. They're opposites, but they go together."

"So is it the Reds who have your mother?"

"They both have her. They both remember Etakkama and what he did to save the baby and they almost— What's the word? It begins with an r."

"Respect?" suggested Simon.

"To us, it happened thousands of years ago, but they act like it was yesterday. Oh, the word is revere," said Bucky. "They don't worship him but he's really important to them. And I kept hearing them say over and over, *protect the three.*"

"That's what you told me the ones said who were with you when you ran to get help for Ian."

"Dad, on the Park Stone, remember where it says the *songs of three are powerful?* You thought it referred to the three birth stones or song stones we have—mine and Seraphina's and the one you got in Turkey. Because the line right above it says something about the return of the song stone. But that's not the three it's talking about. The three are me and Ian and Baby Brennan. We three are the children of Etakkama—you!"

"Who's Baby Brennan?" Ian spoke up for the first time while listening to Bucky's tale.

"Brennan is the name we've chosen for Meredyth's unborn baby," said Simon. "But, Bucky you still haven't told me where she is or why they took her."

Bucky frowned at Ian for interrupting. "We are the three, and the songs of three are powerful. I'm not sure what that means but that's why they have to protect us. That's why they took Mom. It's about time for the *Turning*, when our worlds will not be together, in…in…in sync. And if anything is wrong with the baby, they won't be able to help it like they did with me. So they want to make sure he's all right before the *Turning*. She's coming back, Dad. We just have to wait."

Simon exhaled heavily and shook his head. "So what was the purpose of the terrible dreams we've been having?"

Bucky wrinkled her nose. "It's complicated. When the last *Turning* ended—the one Mom was caught in accidently—and they sent her back, they weren't in agreement about that. They took her originally because they wanted to protect the baby. And then the *Turning* caught them by surprise. I guess it's not always predictable. The Reds wanted to keep her until she had the baby, but the Greens knew that because of the *Turning*, they couldn't return her to the time when she left. And the Harmonics, the Greens, thought we should be together, but the Discordants, the Reds, thought the best way to protect us was to keep us apart. They could have returned her here last summer but they…they compromised and returned her to the spot in New York where they took her from. The Reds were hoping we would never be reunited, at least until the baby was older and could protect himself. So when they became aware Mom was planning on coming here, that's when they started sending the terrible dreams. They thought if I hated her enough or if you didn't trust her, she would go back to New York."

"Simon," whispered Maggie, "are you following all of this?"

"A little," said Simon.

"Dad, when I was listening outside the library, I heard Mom say she reappeared in Central Park on June 29. What happened here on June 29, during the prayer walk?"

"The earthquake and the Singing Spring," whispered Simon.

"That wasn't a coincidence. The Greens were overjoyed we would all be together soon. Remember when the Park Stone suddenly appeared overnight? July 5, the anniversary of the day they took Mom nine years ago. Even though the Greens agreed to return her to Central Park, they knew she would find her way here to us and the stone was their way of celebrating. On the Park Stone, it says something about Etakkama's *scion*.

That's referring to Baby Brennan because he makes the *three*."

Simon raised his voice. "But where is your Mother?"

"I told you. They have her because they want to make sure the baby's all right. They're going to send her back."

"When? Are they going to send her back today? Tomorrow? Next year? In ten years? In fifty years?"

Bucky put her hands on Simon's face. "I don't know. We have to wait."

"I waited nine years already."

"So what about Carl Bergmann?" asked Maggie. "He was taken in a similar fashion as you and yet he came back spewing just as much hatred toward the two of you—and Ian now, too— as before."

Bucky scrunched up her face. "I think the Reds liked it at first because he ag…agi…"

"Agitated?" suggested Simon.

"Yeah, he agitated the crowd, but both the Reds and the Greens became concerned later because they saw him as a threat to me, so that's why they took him and tried to show him he was wrong, but he twisted everything they said." Bucky closed her eyes and began to shiver uncontrollably.

"Simon," ordered Maggie, "we have to get her into some warm, dry clothes."

Simon clasped Bucky's chin in one hand. "Is Meredyth safe there?"

Bucky nodded.

"What's this?" Simon pulled a leather-bound book from a fold in the front of Bucky's wet nightgown. He opened it and there scrawled on the title page, above the words *The Holy Bible*, was the name *Carl Bergmann*. A drop of water from Simon's hair dripped on the preacher's name and smudged it, but the rest of the pages were not even damp, despite having been in the pool with Bucky.

"I have to give it back to him," said Bucky through chattering teeth.

"Not tonight. Let's go upstairs." Simon handed the Bible to Maggie. He shifted Bucky so he could get to his feet.

She put her arms around his neck. "Please don't let me forget this time. I haven't told you everything."

Bucky opened her eyes and immediately closed them again against the morning light flooding her room. Two seconds later, she opened them again and sat up. This wasn't her room! She looked to her right at the man lying next to her. Simon lay on his back, his eyes staring blankly at the ceiling.

She shook his shoulder. "Dad, it's light out. Why are you still in bed?" It was only then she became fully aware of her surroundings. She was in her father's bedroom, but where was Meredyth. "Dad?" She shook him again.

"You go ahead and get up." Simon's voice was gravelly. "I'm staying here a while. Ask Maggie to fix you some breakfast."

"What's wrong? Where's *Anna*?"

Simon turned his head and looked at her. "You don't remember, do you?"

Bucky's eyebrows knitted in confusion as she tried to remember what he was talking about. "Did we have another dream? Was this whole last week a dream? Mom never came home, did she? There's no baby."

Simon clasped one of her wrists. "It was no dream. But last night—"

"What happened? Where is she? Why did you let me sleep in your bed?"

"Bucky, I... I don't want to talk about it right now. Ask Maggie. She and Ian were there. They'll tell you."

"But—"

"Don't argue. Just let me be for a while."

"Your coffee's ready." Bucky could see the green light on the small coffee maker on the table next to Simon's dresser and smell the pleasant aroma. "Want me to bring you a cup?"

Simon shook his head. "Go on. Get some clothes on and go downstairs for breakfast."

Bucky looked down at the front of her gown. It was Monday morning. She should be wearing the pink princess gown she wore every Sunday night. This one was the long-sleeved yellow nightgown, one of the new ones her dad had bought for her. Someone also had put it on her a week ago after she had one of her episodes. But she didn't feel bad this morning. She was not experiencing any of the aftereffects she normally had as a result of her tears. "Dad, did I cry last night? Did you sing the 'Laya Song'?"

Simon shook his head. "Please, Bucky, I need to be alone."

Bucky slipped off the bed and, with one last glance at her father lying there motionless, she left his room and went to her own. The first thing she saw when she went into her bathroom was her princess gown draped over the tub. She touched it and discovered it was wet but there were no blood stains. Had she again been in the pool in the Spring Room during the night? All this past week she had dreamed of hanging onto her mother, trying to save her from the swirling cloud that was sucking her in. She thought she could recall having the same dream last night or, maybe, it wasn't a dream.

Confused over what had transpired and concerned about her dad's uncharacteristic behavior and the absence of her mother, she changed into leggings and a long-sleeved top. She tried to brush out the worst of the tangles in her hair and noticed it, too, felt slightly damp. Simon had said Maggie could tell her what had happened, so she headed downstairs.

She heard the grandfather clock in the hallway at the bottom of the grand staircase chime eight o'clock as she walked slowly down the back stairs. Maggie usually had roused Ian out of bed by this time, but Bucky had not yet heard anything from him this morning. She hoped he was in the kitchen. Simon had said he was there, too, last night—wherever *there* was.

But Maggie was sitting alone at the small square kitchen table, not the larger dining room table they had moved in to accommodate the expanded household. She was staring into her coffee cup but looked up when she heard Bucky come in. "How are you feeling this morning?"

Bucky walked over to her and allowed Maggie to slip one arm around her waist. "I don't know. Dad's acting strange. He's just lying there in bed. And I woke up in his bed this morning and my mom wasn't there. Have you seen her?"

"He said you might not remember."

"What happened, Maggie? Was I in the Spring Pool last night? Did Mom try to drown me like in my dreams?"

Maggie shook her head. "No, Lamb. You were in the pool but you were trying to save your mother. Your father and Ian also tried to save her and you, but they…" Maggie's voice broke. "They took both of you. You returned a few minutes later in some kind of water tornado. But not your mother. She hasn't come back."

Bucky broke free of Maggie's grasp and plunked down in the chair to Maggie's left. "Is Ian okay?"

Maggie smiled through the tears that had gathered in her eyes. "He's fine. He's upset, as we all are, so I'm letting him sleep in this morning."

Bucky tried to digest what Maggie had told her. "I can't… I can't remember. It was just another dream. I don't remember Ian and Dad being there, nor you."

"But it wasn't a dream, I'm afraid. And your father is devastated. To lose her again just days after getting her back, I can't even imagine what he's going through. But you said they would return her."

"I did? What else did I say?"

Maggie tried to relate to Bucky her account of where she had been when the cloud took her and her mother. But Maggie herself was still trying to understand Bucky's confused tale of what the Anarianu told her. Maggie had been sitting here all morning trying to sort the Reds from the Greens and what both sides wanted. "I'm sorry. Maybe your father can explain it to you better. I'm worried most about your phrase *protect the three*. Protect you from what or who?"

"Whom," muttered Bucky, looking down at the table.

"I'm sorry, Lamb. You must be hungry. Do you want some cereal or I can fix you some eggs, or pancakes or French toast."

"The ladies don't want you to have to work while you're here. I can get my own cereal." Bucky started to get up, but Maggie put a hand on her wrist.

"Pfft. You stay right there. Pouring a bowl of cereal ain't work. Work is pulling weeds in the garden or milking a cow when it's ten degrees below zero."

28

AND THEN THERE WERE THREE

For the next two days, Simon refused to leave his room. No amount of cajoling from Maggie or Bucky or Ian could drag him from his bed or from the stuffed chair he occasionally sat in next to it. Maggie would open the heavy drapes, but the next time she passed by they would be closed again. The furniture he had ordered for the two guest rooms arrived on Tuesday, and the delivery men set up the pieces in the downstairs rooms where Bucky directed them. Linens for the beds and baths came with the delivery, so Maggie busied herself cleaning the two rooms and getting them ready for the Moyers and anyone else who might need them this weekend.

Bucky repeatedly reminded Simon that Nick and Jan Moyers, the ancient language professors from Chicago, were coming in only a few days, but Simon expressed as little interest in that as he did in everything she told him. Dr. Michael Smallin, the paleontologist in charge of the future mastodon museum, and Dr. Daniel Mason, the archaeologist who had assisted Smallin on the mastodon dig last summer, were scheduled to be here, too, along with some graduate students, to examine Ian's cave.

Only a few days ago, Simon had been excited about their arrival, but now he didn't seem to care about anything.

On Tuesday evening, Maggie had spoken sharply to Simon. She had told him he had a right to grieve, but he also had a responsibility to his daughter. She finally received a response when he turned his head toward her and said, "You take care of her."

"I have been taking care of her," said Maggie. "She needs her father."

Simon faced away from her and said, "I can't go through this again. I told you when Meredyth disappeared nine years ago, I was investigated, humiliated in the press, accused of… It was probably only a blip in the news here, if even that much, but it was a big story in New York." He shook his head. "And now for her to return and be gone again in just a week, it's going to happen all over again. What defense do I have? Little red and green bugs took her?"

"The first time," said Maggie calmly, "you obviously filed a missing person's report. No one has filed a report this week. No one except us even knows she's gone. I was there, Simon. I can't explain what I saw, but I did see it. And Bucky said she's coming back."

Simon clenched one fist and pounded the arm of the chair. "Bucky says, Bucky says, Bucky says. I need to know when."

"If she doesn't return soon," said Maggie, "we can make up another story. The reconciliation didn't work out. She went back to New York. People around here would accept that. They know you by now. They know you for a rather stern and detached and…difficult person who doesn't quite fit in. They wouldn't doubt for a minute she walked out on you."

Simon huffed. "Is that really what people think of me?"

Maggie patted his hand. "You're behaving exactly the way Bucky did last summer when she retreated into her castle for several days. It's obvious where she gets her disposition from. You need to get up, shave, shower, change out of those pajamas and rejoin the world of the living. You haven't even eaten anything since Sunday. Sitting here brooding is not going to bring Meredyth back any faster."

"I will sit here and brood as long as I like."

Maggie held her tongue at his last remark, but finally said, "I have to leave tomorrow at noon for Ian's doctor's visit. I'll take Bucky with me."

On Wednesday morning, Bucky went in to check on Simon before going downstairs for breakfast. She had smelled coffee and was hoping it meant he was back to himself, but he was sitting slumped over in the bedside chair. Maggie must have prepared the coffee on his dresser in his room the night before and set the timer, hoping the aroma the following morning might revive him a little.

Bucky sat on the arm of the stuffed chair. "How are you feeling this morning, Dad?" She ran the palm of her hand down the side of his bristly face. She never liked to feel his beard stubble on those rare days when he did not shave. "I've missed you coming in the past two nights to tell me good night. I guess you've been busy, sitting in here thinking. Do you want me to pour you a cup of coffee? It sure smells good."

Simon shook his head.

At least she had received a small reaction from him.

"Sadie Jane came yesterday for my French lesson and I pretended that nothing was wrong. I learned the names of colors in French. Do you want to hear them?"

"No."

Bucky sighed and continued talking. "I've been keeping up with my regular lessons, but I didn't understand something in science. Ian couldn't explain it, either. I really needed your help. I took one of the self-tests in math but I only made an eighty-two percent. I'll study some more and try for a hundred. I want you to be proud of me."

Simon took one of her hands in his. "Lamb, I am proud of you."

Bucky twisted the hem of her shirt in her hands. She was afraid the tears were ready to start. "She's coming back, Dad."

"Did Maggie tell you that's what you said?"

"Yes, but I remember them telling me. *Before the Turning*, they said."

"You're remembering?"

"Not much, but I feel like I don't have to hate Mom anymore. I don't have to be scared of her. Maggie tried to tell me why, but she didn't make a whole lot of sense."

Simon scoffed. "Nothing about any of it makes sense. I wish our lives had never crossed paths with the

Anarianu. If I could go back thirty-five hundred years as Etakkama, I don't think I would save their baby."

"Dad! Of course you would because you are good and kind and loving and the best dad in the whole world. You couldn't have let that baby die in the cold. Besides the Anarianu saved Imala's life and Seraphina's and who knows how many others. And if it hadn't been for them I would have died, too, as a baby…and Ian."

"When Ian fell off the cliff?"

"No, when he was a baby in the accident which killed his parents. He told me he was thrown clear of the car, clean out of his car seat, but that's not what happened. They took him. His skull was cracked and they repaired it. They knitted it back together with their music. They didn't change his DNA like they did mine, I think, because he was too old and because the bone was easier to fix.

"But the scar on his forehead?"

"When they left him on the ground away from the wreckage, he got up and fell over and cut his head. He was as clumsy as a baby as he is now."

"They told you this when you were there Sunday night?"

Bucky shrugged. "I guess so. Maggie said I told you the line on the Park Stone about *the songs of three are powerful* refers to me and Ian and Baby Brennan. And that's why they have to protect the three. What do you think that means?"

Simon squeezed her hand. "I don't know. I know you want me to have all the answers, Lamb, but I don't. And right now, I have such a fog in my brain, I can't even think about it. All I can think of is… I don't think I can do this anymore."

"No, Dad!" A jagged black and red image formed in her head, a feeling so horrible, so terrible and terrifying, she had no words to describe it. She jerked her hand away from him and took his head in both of her hands. "I love you more than anything. Please, please, Dad, don't leave me."

"Bucky, I… I've changed my will. I wrote it on my laptop up here, but it should have printed a copy in my study. It won't stand up in court without a fight because it wasn't witnessed, but if anything should happen to me, I want you to live with Maggie. I won't have you living with Matt Healey, not after what he did. You fight for it, okay?"

"Dad, please don't talk like that. Nothing's going to happen to you. Mom's coming back. You have to be here for her and for the baby. You have to raise him like you raised me."

"It's rear," corrected Simon without emotion. "You raise cattle and corn. You rear children."

"That doesn't sound right. Are you sure?"

"Pretty sure."

Bucky slid off the arm of the chair. "Think of all the exciting things you have to live for. The museum and…and the cave. We have to find out what's in the cave. You have to finish your book and the new book you started about Etakkama."

"I'm far behind on the book for Matt, although I don't really care since it's the last one he'll ever publish for me. If it wouldn't cost me a fortune, I'd break the contract in a minute."

Simon closed his eyes for a moment. When he opened them, Bucky wrapped her fingers around one of his wrists. She detected his old spark from deep within him. "Drink some coffee, Dad. It always makes you feel better in the mornings."

"All right. Bring me a cup."

"I can bring you up some toast."

"I don't think I could eat it."

"Sure you could. I'll put a smidgen of strawberry jam on it."

"Smidgen," Simon repeated and a half smile cracked his lips. "Is that another word you've picked up from Maggie?"

"Is it a bad word?"

"No. I just never heard you use it before."

When Bucky reached up on Simon's dresser to pour him a cup of coffee, she saw a leather-bound book lying next to the coffeemaker. She reached for it.

"Don't touch that!"

Simon's harsh tone startled her and she drew back her hand.

"It's Bergmann's Bible. You brought it back from...from...wherever you were."

Bucky turned to face her father. "Shouldn't we give—"

"No," interrupted Simon before she could finish the question. "Not until…" He sighed. "I can't think right now. Just leave it be. I'm sure he has other Bibles. We'll see to it later."

❧

"Bucky, are you sure you'll be all right here alone?" Maggie and Ian were standing in the entryway, ready to leave for the doctor's appointment. Bucky had pleaded with Maggie to allow her to remain at the Mansion instead of accompanying them.

"I'm not alone. Dad's here."

"But he's not himself. Listen, you stay in your room or, better yet, take a book and sit in his room and read while we're gone. Don't answer the door for anyone. You lock it after we leave. And don't answer the phone. I'm going to lock the front gate on my way out. Here's the number of the doctor's office if you have to get ahold of me." Maggie handed her a slip of paper. "And Penny's number is on there, too."

"I'll be okay, Maggie. I'm not four."

Maggie gave her a quick hug, and she and Ian left.

Bucky and Ian had worked on lessons all morning so Bucky had not had a chance to investigate her father's will he said he had sent to the printer in his study. She did that now before she went back upstairs. But there were so many pages to it, the printer had run out of paper and the "load paper" light was flashing. She put a stack of paper in it and pushed "OK" and the device began spitting out even more pages. She tried reading the first two pages in the document, but it had so many legal terms in it, she was unsure what it meant. She sighed. It was another one of those things she was too young for.

She trudged upstairs and retrieved a book from the bookshelf in her study room and took it into her father's bedroom. He seemed not to have left the chair where he was earlier this morning. She plopped on the edge of the bed. "Do you want me to read to you?"

"No."

"It's *Laddie* by Gene Stratton-Porter. It's one of my favorites."

"Then you read it to yourself, preferably in your own room."

"Maggie said I should sit with you while she's gone."

"I don't need a nursemaid."

Bucky eyed the piece of toast she had brought him earlier. It sat on the table next to his half-empty cup of coffee. It appeared he had nibbled only a bit at one corner of the toasted bread with a little red smear of strawberry jam. "Dad, I'm worried about you. We all are."

"I'll be all right. I just need time. Go on back to your room and— Wait!" He straightened a little. "Maggie and Ian are gone? She said she was taking you with her."

"Somebody needed to stay here with you. Dad, this is Wednesday. You haven't shaved since Sunday morning. You're looking awfully scruffy."

"Bucky, please leave. I don't feel like talking—or listening."

Bucky sighed and hopped off the bed. She kissed Simon on his prickly cheek. "I love you."

"I love you, too, Lamb."

Bucky walked back into her room and tossed the book on her bed. Her father didn't want her in his room and she saw no reason to stay in her room as Maggie had ordered her, so she went back out into the hallway. She had wanted to slide down the smooth, curved, dark bannister of the staircase ever since they moved in last April. With Simon unlikely to emerge from his room and catch her, she might not get a better opportunity. She hesitantly approached the stairs. There were handrails on both sides but one side of the stairs butted up against the curving wall and the railing was attached to the wall at intervals. The other side was open. She peered over the edge. If she fell it would be a long way down, but if she held on tight, she wouldn't fall.

She mounted the bannister, facing backwards, and tightly gripped the rail. If she kept a firm grasp, she would have a controlled descent. An idea popped into her brain, and she slipped down to the landing. After tip-toeing past her father's room, she went into her playroom. Retrieving a red cape from her supply of costumes, she fastened it around her shoulders and returned to the stairs. She realized it would look better if she faced downward and allowed the cape to billow out behind her, but she felt safer going down backwards. Once again, she climbed up on the bannister, grasped it securely, took a deep breath, loosened her hold and slid down. She tightened her grip in the last few feet so she wouldn't crash into the newel post and arrived safely at the bottom.

It had been an exhilarating experience and she couldn't wait to share it with Ian. But what to do now? Based on Maggie's story of what Bucky had said after being sucked into the cloud on Sunday night and the flashes of memory she had been experiencing, Bucky had come to accept she no longer needed to fear her mother when Meredyth returned. That meant there was no reason to fear the piano in the music room. She had closely observed Meredyth's hands on the keyboard as she taught the "Laya Song." Bucky wondered if she could duplicate the tune.

She headed to the music room and closed the double doors behind her. Seating herself on the bench, she lifted the fallboard. Meredyth had left a copy of the sheet music on the piano and, with one finger, Bucky plunked out the notes.

A pounding noise woke Simon, who had been dozing in his chair. It was faint but seemed to be coming from downstairs. He sat upright with a start, remembering Bucky was home alone. He pushed himself up from the chair and experienced a momentary wave of vertigo. He waited until it had passed and then slipped his arms into the robe that lay draped across the end of the bed. He headed out into the hall. The noise was definitely coming from downstairs. It sounded as if Bucky was pounding on the grand piano in the music room, banging the fallboard up and down.

"Bucky!" Simon threw open the double doors to the music room. "Will you please stop that infernal racket."

Bucky, sitting on the bench, looked up in surprise as Simon, in pajamas and bathrobe, strode into the room. She stopped playing and cocked her head and listened. "That's not me."

Simon stopped and listened. The loud knocking continued. It wasn't coming from this room, but from the lower level.

"Dad, it's the dream! It's the shared dream when Mom returned."

"This is no dream. Stay here." Simon sprinted down the hall to his study and yanked open one of the bottom desk drawers. He fished around in it and came up with a set of keys.

The pounding grew louder as Simon descended the short flight of stairs to the lower level, the original rooms of the Mansion. Someone or something was knocking on the locked door from inside the Spring Room. Simon unlocked the box above the right side of the door and hit the switch to disconnect the motion sensor. His heart was pounding.

"Who's there?" He thought he could hear a low keening sound in response, but the wooden door was several inches thick. Even the sound of the spring pouring into the pool could not be heard from this side.

He scanned the hallway for something he could use as a club, a cudgel for protection. There was nothing.

The intervals between the knocks were growing longer, the raps themselves fainter. Perhaps, whoever or whatever was making the noise was weakening. He fumbled with the key as he tried to insert it into the lock and the entire ring clattered to the floor. He picked them up, found the correct key and tried again and heard the click. Grasping the ornate metal handle, he pulled, opening the door only a couple of inches.

The love of his life slumped against the door frame, her right hand raised to knock once more. Her wet hair fell over her shoulders onto a long green dress which clung to her as if she had just stepped from the pool. It was the same dress as in the dream. In her left arm she cradled a baby wrapped in a wet blanket.

"Meredyth. Oh, my God. Meredyth."

The woman collapsed into Simon's arms and he sunk to the floor beneath her weight.

"My God. Meredyth." He stroked her hair and face. There were tiny droplets of water—or tears—on her cheeks which were tinged with a slight blush. Her lips parted slightly as she tried to speak. Only a quiet moan escaped.

"Dad?"

Simon looked up to see Bucky standing at the turn of the hall.

"I told you she was coming back."

"I know." Simon's voice broke as he tried to force back tears. "Come here and take the baby. I'll try to carry her to my study."

Bucky had never held a real baby, only dolls. She reached for it, but before Meredyth transferred the child to her, Bucky grabbed her head and cried out in a long, drawn-out wail. She fell to her knees and then crumpled to the floor.

"Bucky, what's wrong?" With one arm supporting Meredyth and the baby, Simon reached for his daughter."

"They're gone," moaned Bucky. "All of them."

"It's the *Turning*," said Meredyth, weakly. "Our worlds are no longer in sync. She feels it, as do I."

"Bucky, Lamb," said Simon. "Can you get up? I can't carry both of you—all three of you,"

Bucky struggled to her hands and knees. "It's like someone cut a cord and yanked it out of my head."

"I think I can walk, Sie, if you'll support me." As Meredyth shifted position, the baby began to cry. "Just help me to my feet."

A few minutes later, Simon had pulled up a chair to the couch in his study where Meredyth now lay, the baby nestled in the crook of her arm. "We have to get you out of those wet clothes."

"Let me rest here a few minutes."

Bucky stood behind the couch. Whatever she experienced at the *Turning* had passed and she suffered no further ill effects.

"Lamb," said Simon, "would you get a bath towel from the linen closet so we can wrap the baby in it. And then go upstairs and get a blanket off my bed."

"There are some new blankets just down the hall," said Bucky, rushing out.

When she returned, Simon took his new son and wrapped him in the soft, white towel. He held him in his arms. "My God, Meredyth. How…"

"They wanted me to stay long enough to give birth and to make sure there were no defects like…with Rose. Look at him, Simon. He has the same little red wisps of curls as Rose did." She looked up at Bucky. "I'm sorry, Bucky. As *you* did. And his dimples. Wait till he smiles at you."

"I don't guess they ever considered I would have liked to have been there to see my son come into this world—or whatever world."

"I wish you could have been there, darling. We could learn a few things from them. It was in water and absolutely painless. The vibrations from their music do something—I don't know—but it was a wonderful experience. And, of course, they were so excited because he was your son. I don't remember much of what all transpired there, but I remember that."

"But how are we ever going to explain…"

"He obviously arrived earlier than we anticipated," said Meredyth matter-of-factly.

"He's a mighty big baby for a preemie. But, Mer, we need to get you to a hospital."

"I'm fine, Simon. People have had babies at home for thousands of years."

"But you didn't exactly have him at home. Are you sure you're all right?"

Meredyth nodded. "Absolutely. He's not a newborn. It's been at least two months, maybe more since the delivery. But, Sie, what's wrong with you? You look terrible."

Simon smiled through eyes that were filling with tears. "I'm all right."

"Dad," said Bucky, meekly, "can—may I hold him?"

"Of course. Pull up that chair over there by the desk." Simon carefully placed the baby in Bucky's arms and showed her how to support him.

Both Bucky and the baby opened their mouths in surprise as an invisible spark passed between them. "I can feel him," whispered Bucky. She adjusted the towel under his chin. "Hi, little Brennan. I'm your big sister."

"But we don't have anything here in the house for a baby," said Simon. "We're going to need diapers and a crib and bottles and lotions and there's probably some paperwork we have to file with the county or state for a home birth."

"Calm down, Sie. I'm nursing for the moment, and we can always use towels or sheets or some of your T-shirts for diapers until we can get to the store. Where's Maggie? Is she back in her house? How long have I've been away this time?"

"Three days." Simon's voice broke. "A lifetime. Let's get you upstairs and into some dry clothes. Maggie took Ian to the doctor for a check-up. She ought to be back—" He swiveled and looked at the clock on the wall. "In an hour or two."

Meredyth lay propped up on the bed. She wore a nursing gown she had brought from New York with her. They had arranged some rolled-up towels in a rectangle and the baby had been nestling contently inside them, but now began to fuss.

"I'm going to shower and get cleaned up," said Simon. "You'll be all right?"

Meredyth looked at Bucky, sitting cross-legged on the bed, and smiled. "We'll be fine. I think he's hungry."

"Can I watch?" asked Bucky.

"Absolutely not," said Simon.

"Of course, you can," said Meredyth, picking up the baby.

Simon rolled his eyes and shook his head and retreated to the bathroom.

Bucky waited until she heard the water running so Simon wouldn't be able to hear them, and then she lifted her top up to her chin. "I'm getting them, too. But they're not much, yet. I see some of the other girls at the walk or the ones in Ian's class, like Madyson Koeller, and I think I'm behind."

"People mature at different rates. Don't rush it. You have the rest of your life to be all grown up. But I'm glad I'm here to help guide you through it. Your father is brilliant, but you're entering into a stage in your life that is unknown territory for him. I think he'd have a hard time navigating it alone."

Bucky watched in fascination as Brennan fed. "I thought Dad was going to die when you were gone this time. He just sat here in his room like a zombie. If you had been gone much longer, I don't know what would have happened to him."

"All I could think of was getting back here to him…and to you."

"I'm sorry for the way I treated you last week," said Bucky. "I don't remember much from when I was there Sunday night, but Maggie told me what I said when I came back. It sounds like they were trying to protect us by keeping us apart."

"They're hard to understand," Meredyth said. "But both groups certainly think highly of your father, or, rather, Etakkama in his present reincarnation as your father."

"I think pretty highly of him, too," said Bucky.

"I can tell you do. He has done such a marvelous job rearing you. I am so lucky to have found him."

"From what Dad told me, the two of you have found each other several times in the past."

"So maybe it's not luck. Maybe it's fate. Oh, Bucky, I hope someday you meet someone as kind and generous and loving and forgiving as he is."

Bucky bit her lower lip. "Speaking of forgiving, I know Ian reminds you of the terrible thing Dad did, but it wasn't Ian's fault. He's my best friend…and my brother. Don't you think you could like him a little?"

Meredyth shifted the baby. "It's difficult, Bucky, but I'll work on it. I promise. He is a cute little boy and he says the funniest things."

"Did you nurse me when I was a baby?"

"For the first few days until…"

"Until the fourth night and you thought I wasn't yours. You thought I was a changeling."

"It was still my milk for a while. You just drank it from a bottle instead of directly." Meredyth's eyes filled with tears. "I'm so sorry. If only we'd been able to read the song stone back then."

"It's all right, Mom."

Meredyth smiled. It was the first time Bucky had called her "Mom" directly. "I should have gotten a hand towel from the bathroom before your father went in there. I'll need one for a burp cloth in a few minutes."

"I'll get you one out of my bathroom." Bucky uncrossed her legs and scooted carefully off the bed.

"I think you're going to make a wonderful big sister."

29

INSIDE THE CAVE

"Oh, my," said Maggie. "Oh, good Lord." She sat down heavily on the bench next to the grandfather clock near the foyer. Bucky had met her and Ian at the door when they returned and told them about Meredyth and the baby.

"Okay, let me get this straight," said Ian, standing next to the bench. "He's my little brother, right?"

"Yeah," confirmed Bucky, "but by the time he's big enough to play baseball with you, you'll be in high school."

"And how's your father?" asked Maggie.

"He's just fine, now."

"But they haven't bought anything yet for the baby," said Maggie, "and I don't have any of Ian's baby things left."

"Mom's not too concerned. She says there's plenty of time to go shopping. But Dad's worried about what people will think."

"People will think what they will."

"Maggie, I didn't hear you come in." Simon, looking like his old self, appeared on the stairs above them. He had shaved and was wearing khaki slacks and a long-sleeved henley shirt. His dark curls were still damp from his shower. When he reached the bottom step, he said, "I suppose Bucky has already filled you in."

Maggie stood. "Oh, Simon, it takes this old woman's breath away. How's Meredyth? Are she and the baby okay?"

"As far as I can tell, they're both perfect."

"Can I see him?" asked Ian.

Simon laid a hand on Ian's head. "The two of them are napping at the moment. And how was your checkup? All cleared to return to school tomorrow?"

"Yeah, but I can't take P.E. for at least another two weeks."

Simon nodded. "That's understandable. I'm famished. I'm going to go rummage in the refrigerator and see if I can find something to eat."

"I'll fix you something," offered Maggie.

"You've done enough the past few days while I was… Well, you know. Thank you, Maggie, for taking care of things and watching after Bucky."

Bucky punched Ian in the arm. "Let's go upstairs and play."

"Keep the noise down," admonished Simon.

By the time the Moyers arrived on Friday afternoon, Maggie had made two trips to Garton to purchase baby supplies. Simon was reluctant to leave Meredyth and his new son, so he gave Maggie his credit card with instructions to buy whatever she felt was needed. During that time, word spread that Meredyth had delivered her baby unexpectedly at home with only Simon's and Maggie's help. Maggie wasn't sure how the story expanded to include her, but she accepted the role of midwife. In most people's minds, her experience with livestock over the years made her aptly qualified for the task, and her no-nonsense attitude toward most things added plausibility to the tale.

"We'll be fine," said Meredyth for what felt like the hundredth time. She, Simon, Bucky, and Nick and Jan Moyers were in Simon's study. "If you don't leave soon, there won't be enough light left to see the cave."

"I'm really torn," said Jan. She was sitting on the couch next to Meredyth and holding the baby. "I want to see the cave and the smelter remains, but I could also just sit here and hold this little guy for the rest of the weekend."

Bucky was looking out the bay window. "Maggie and Ian are here," she announced. Maggie had picked up Ian at school instead of having him ride the bus. Even though they wouldn't try entering the cave until the next day when Smallin and Mason and a few of their students arrived to help move boulders, Simon knew Ian would be disappointed if they made the trip there this afternoon without him.

Jan handed Brennan back to his mother. "Professional duties call."

Simon leaned over and touched the baby's chin and his hand then brushed Meredyth's cheek. "We'll lock the gate on the way out."

The four of them intercepted Maggie and Ian on the front porch. Ian handed his backpack to his grandmother and joined the others as they climbed into Simon's UTV. Nick took the front passenger seat and Jan sat in the back along with Bucky and Ian.

When the rough trail through the woods ended, they got out and walked the rest of the way to the clearing and stopped at the tumbled stones of what Simon claimed were the ruins of a Minoan smelter.

"You said Jennifer Brockman was here last week and took samples for conducting luminescence tests on these rocks," said Nick, circling around the rubble. "Have you heard back from her?"

"You aren't going to like it," said Simon. "As with the Hollow Stone, what she discovered flies in the face of current North American theoretical scholarship and archaeological evidence."

Nick stopped and put his hands on his hips. "How old?"

"Those stone blocks on the bottom last saw the light of day more than three thousand years ago." Simon knelt next to two large stones, one resting on top of the other. "And she got in between these two and took scrapings. Same result."

Nick made a *pfft* sound.

"So not some settler's chimney," said Jan. "Native American?"

"Unlikely," said Simon. "But Jennifer's been the only professional to look at it so far besides Michael Smallin and he's a paleontologist. Dan Mason—you met him last summer, also—will be here tomorrow and his background is in Native American archaeology."

Jan was running a hand lightly over some of the stones. "I wish there were some writing on them."

"That'd make it too easy," said Simon.

"So, why do you think it's Minoan?" asked Nick. "That stone in The Hollow has Minoan and Hittite glyphs. We almost agree on what the Hittite says. The inscription doesn't make much sense, but we agree. What is it about these rocks that says Minoan to you and not Hittite?"

Simon shrugged. How could he tell these friends, colleagues from his university days, professional epigraphers, that he was here on this spot and helped work this smelter over three thousand five hundred years ago?

"Dad." Bucky pulled at Simon's sleeve. "Shouldn't we go look at the cave? It'll be dark on our way back home if we don't hurry."

Simon did not know if Bucky interrupted on purpose so he wouldn't have to answer Nick's question, but he was thankful for her interjection. "Bucky's right. The path down the bluff face is just over there."

The group carefully picked their way down the bluff, scrambling over and around the massive boulders, until they reached the trail which ran alongside the stream. It was only a few yards until Simon stopped and pointed about halfway up the cliff.

"You two kids stay down here," ordered Simon.

"But—" started Ian.

"We're not going inside. We're just going to look," explained Simon. "We can't get in until we get some help tomorrow enlarging the entrance. Stay here."

He led the way up to the ledge in front of the mouth of the cave, where large stones still blocked the entrance. "Jennifer also took scrapings from some of these boulders."

"Let me guess," said Nick. "They tumbled down here over three millennia ago."

Simon laughed. "More recently, I'm afraid. They most likely were the result of the New Madrid earthquakes, 1811-1812."

"So the cave was open up until two hundred years ago," said Jan. She was watching her husband who was down on his knees with a flashlight, peering into the slit Ian had discovered and which Dr. Smallin and Simon had slightly enlarged two weeks earlier. "Anything exciting?"

Nick backed out and stood up, relinquishing his place to Jan. "I can understand how seeing whatever that shape is could fuel a young boy's imagination that it's a pirate's chest. It's enough to fire up mine. Is the image from the camera any clearer?"

"I'll show it to you this evening. It's definitely a chest."

"Which must date to prior to the New Madrid earthquakes," said Nick, "unless, of course, there's another way in."

"I've considered that," said Simon. "Now that we're losing a lot of the vegetation, another opening might be easier to spot. I haven't had time to investigate further."

"That's understandable," said Nick. He shook his head. "I can't believe Meredyth's back in your life. And with a son. I just can't imagine. And seeing the two of you together this afternoon, I mean, it's like old times. And yet, this past summer when we were here…"

Jan stood up and brushed off her jeans. "Are you saying if I left you for a decade and then showed back up, you wouldn't take me back?"

"I don't know," said Nick. "I'd have to think about it."

"Don't think too hard. I wouldn't want you to strain that little brain of yours." Jan turned and playfully slapped Simon's upper arm. "But you could have told us about the baby when we talked to you last week!"

"Too much going on," said Simon. "If you've seen enough for today, we probably should be heading back."

"Let me get a couple more pictures," said Jan.

"All right, Ian, keep your head down and crawl forward in a straight line. Try not to touch anything except the floor of the cave. That includes the chest when you reach it. If you see anything else unusual, stop and don't go any further." Simon knelt beside Ian at the opening which was now large enough to admit people on their hands and knees.

The ledge in front of the cave was crowded with Nick and Jan Moyer, Michael Smallin and two of his graduate students, and Daniel Mason and one of his students. Bucky sat off to the side and toyed with the headlamp Dr. Mason had given her to wear. She was glad her father was allowing Ian to be the first one inside. After all, he had been the one to discover its location. It was only right he should be first. She could tell from the expressions of the three students they did not agree with that decision.

"Off you go, then," said Simon. "Dr. Mason will be right behind you and I will be behind him."

Ian adjusted the headlamp on the band around his head, stuck the slender flashlight between his teeth, and took off on his hands and knees. It was a short crawl, only about eight feet, before he was past the rock rubble and into the cave. The chamber was taller than a man and about twenty feet wide. The light on his forehead didn't reach to the back wall, so he could not tell how far back the cavern extended. He wrinkled his nose at the musty, earthy smell.

Directly in front of him rested the chest he had glimpsed when he had originally found the cave! He circled to the left of it and halted.

Despite Simon having said that any wood would have long ago disintegrated, the chest appeared to be made of wood. A layer of dust enshrouded the roughly two feet by one foot case which stood just over a foot high with a camel-back lid. The dust obscured the metal bands encircling the chest and the two rectangular copper inlays decorating the top. Those features would not be fully revealed until the artifact was safely in a laboratory.

"Oh, my," whispered Dr. Daniel Mason, coming to a stop behind Ian.

Simon, entering the room behind Mason, sat back onto the dry packed dirt of the cavern floor.

With their combined lights illuminating the wooden coffer, Dr. Mason approached it and examined it for any markings but found none. "It's in a highly fragile state," he announced. "I'm afraid any attempt to move it will cause the whole thing to crumble."

"Can we open it?" asked Ian.

"Not without compromising its integrity. I brought an endoscope camera with me, hoping we could insert it into a tiny opening to peer inside, but I'm hesitant to do that now, seeing its condition." While he talked, Daniel Mason moved around the chest, taking pictures from various angles. "If they're not handled correctly, artifacts can disintegrate when exposed to air or moisture. Just our presence here, our breaths and the lint from our clothes and the light and air we've let in, are all probably already causing irreparable damage."

Ian and Simon stayed still and watched as the archaeologist made his initial examination.

"Oh, wait," Dr. Mason exclaimed. "With your lights shining from this angle, it appears there are some faint letters etched into the lid. The dust has settled into the engraving."

"What's it say?" asked Ian.

"We'll have to call in the language experts," said Mason.

As if on cue, Nick Moyer, followed by Jan, crawled in through the opening. Even though the room was large enough to stand up in, everyone except Ian remained kneeling. Nick made his way to the chest and Dr. Mason held his flashlight so as to reveal the letters, careful not to disturb the dust.

"It looks like Latin," said Nick. "Definitely missing a few letters—probably an abbreviation. Best guess is *Christus Rex,* Christ is King."

"I think we should jacket the chest and block the bottom if we intend to move it," said Mason.

"What does that mean?" asked Ian.

"Similar to what we did with some of the mastodon bones last summer when we put them in a plaster cast in order to remove them from the site. We can encase this the same way. We need to make a sturdy support system for it by wrapping it first with gauze and then cotton batting soaked in plaster. But we also need to get underneath it, to include a pedestal of soil in the jacket. If we lifted it without doing that, the bottom would probably fall out. From what Simon told me when he called, I thought that might be a possibility so we brought the materials with us."

Ian sat down again on the dirt floor. "It'll take forever before we find out what's in it."

Simon, sitting beside him, put a hand on his shoulder. "One of the first lessons you have to learn in archaeology is patience. If you go too fast, you might end up destroying important evidence."

"Simon, Nick, I think you'd better take a look at this." While the attention of the others was focused on the chest, Jan had crawled to the wall on the left side of the room. She stood up and shone her light at an angle, splaying it across the uneven limestone surface. Faint symbols covered one section of the wall, but many of them had been marked out, obliterated by lines scratched across them.

Getting to their feet, Nick and Simon left the chest and carefully walked across the dark chamber to where Jan stood.

Nick let out a low whistle.

"Minoan," whispered Simon.

"The underlying marks are definitely Minoan," said Jan. "Linear A. See, here and here." She pointed out a few which had escaped the brunt of the slashes. "But who would have tried to destroy them?"

"Here's your answer, maybe." Nick pointed to some Latin letters at about eye level. He squinted at the etched lines in the dim light. "*Sancta Maria, Mater Dei.* Holy Mary, Mother of God."

"Here's some more," said Jan, moving slightly to her right. "*Retribuet Deus.* God will repay. And what looks like *fidelibus coronam vitae dabo.*"

"I'm afraid most of my Latin has fallen by the wayside," said Simon.

"To the faithful I will give the crown of life," Jan translated.

"Oh," said Nick, "Here's an unusual one. *Quom fideles constellationes*. When the faithful are constellations. Not sure I've heard that one."

"*Dominus mihi adjutor*," said Jan. "The Lord is on my side or the Lord is my helper."

"We obviously had some religious people in here who spoke Latin," said Simon. "But when? Can you tell by the shape of the letters or the phrasing?"

"Here's an example," said Nick. "*Solus deus me iudicet*. God alone may judge me. *Iudicet* can be written with a J today, but an I was more common in Medieval Latin, since Romans had no letter J. I believe what we are looking at here is Ecclesiastical or Liturgical Latin, and I'm going to be bold and say before 1600."

"So…" started Jan.

"You're going to dispute me, aren't you, darling?"

"Not at all," replied Jan. "I concur. So do you think whoever was in this cave in maybe the sixteenth century was offended by obviously pagan writing—the Minoan—on the walls and they tried to mark it out and leave behind more Christian sentiments?"

Daniel Mason had finished photographing the chest and had joined the Moyers and Simon at the wall. "Wait. What is this talk of Minoans? Minoans were never in North America and they certainly were never here in southeast Missouri."

"Who knows, Dan?" said Simon. "If you agree to carry out the excavation in this cave, you might be the one to prove they were here. What a paper that will be."

"I'd be the laughing stock of the archaeological community."

"Not if you have irrefutable evidence." Simon looked around. It was only now he noticed his daughter was missing. "Where's Bucky? I thought she followed me in."

"She was still outside when we came in just now," said Jan, laying a hand on Simon's wrist. "I'm sure she's all right."

Simon could feel his heart racing. He made his way to the opening, dropped to his knees and crawled out. The brightness of the fall day almost blinded him for a moment. He shielded his eyes with one hand. The three students and Dr. Smallin were making a cursory survey of the ledge and the bluff face. And there was Bucky sitting off to the side.

He carefully picked his way across the narrow, uneven ledge and sat beside her. "I thought you were right behind me when I went in. What are you doing out here? Don't you want to see inside?"

"I thought I did. But when it actually came time for me to crawl in after you, I guess I got scared. Are you mad at me?"

"Of course I'm not angry with you. But there's nothing to be frightened of. It's just a big, empty room."

"They were here, though, weren't they? See where that spring comes out down there?" Bucky pointed down the bluff face to where a trickle of water emerged from some rocks about five feet above the base of the cliff. The rivulet flowed down and on into the stream. "That's one of their springs. Maybe they don't want us in there."

"But they're gone now. Remember? They're in the *Turning*. You can't feel them, can you?"

Bucky flipped the switch on the head lamp she held in her lap. "Are there bats in there?"

"Maybe. But it's daytime, so they're probably asleep."

"Snakes?"

"I didn't see any."

Bears?"

The opening was too small for them to get in. Don't you want to see Ian's chest?"

Bucky nodded. "How come you can't open it? Is it locked?"

"No, but it's quite fragile. But we found some writing on the wall. Minoan and Latin."

Bucky raised her head. "I heard Jan Moyer last night say she can't read the Minoan Linear A yet on the Hollow Stone."

"No, and this writing is mostly marked out. But she and Nick can read the Latin."

"I don't know Latin."

Simon laughed. "I don't know it well, either—just the rudiments. But you can learn when you're older."

"Any Hittite?"

"No, but we've only had time to look at a small portion. Who knows what discoveries await us?"

"Dad," Bucky whispered, cupping her hand to Simon's ear, so the others could not hear. "Did it look familiar to you in there? Was that where you stayed when you were here before? When you were Etakkama?"

"It…uh… It took my breath away. I don't think the others noticed. They were focused on the chest and the inscriptions. It's where… It's where Imala was born and where… It's where Aiyana died."

"It made you sad."

"Yes, it did."

"There's probably not any Hittite writing in there. I don't think you were the kind of person to go around writing on walls."

Simon smiled. "Etakkama was a scribe, remember. He might have."

"If I go in there, will you hold my hand and not let go?"

"Of course, but I'm not forcing you to go in there. I thought you were as excited as the rest of us to look inside."

"I want to see it." She stood.

Simon got to his feet and adjusted her light around her head. "We have to crawl single file for a few feet, but as soon as it's clear we can stand up and I'll take your hand."

That night Bucky and Ian were playing cards on the floor in Bucky's bedroom. Baby Brennan, alert and making cooing sounds, was propped up in a baby carrier on the floor with them. They would deal him a hand each round and take turns playing his cards for him. Sometimes he would reward them with a smile. Maggie was in her room. Simon and Meredyth and the Moyers were downstairs in Simon's study. Dr. Smallin was staying at the future museum in Turn Back and Dr. Mason and the three students were camping at the cave site.

Bucky stood up on her knees and dug in her pocket. "Look what I found today." She opened her hand to reveal a red bead, about a quarter inch in diameter.

"Let me see." Ian took it from her and held it up to the light. "Where'd you find it?"

"In the cave. Toward the mouth next to where Dr. Mason thought there was a hearth but that most of it was under the rocks that had fallen."

"Bucky!" hissed Ian. "That's an artifact. You weren't supposed to touch anything in there, and you sure weren't supposed to pick up anything."

"It's just a bead."

"But it could be thousands of years old. I'm telling *Atta*."

"No, you're not." Bucky snatched the bead out of his hand and stuffed it back in her pocket.

"Then you're telling him."

"He doesn't need to know. And don't you tell or I'll pound you."

"Hey!" Simon appeared in the doorway and crossed over to where the children sat on the floor. "Don't talk that way in front of the baby. He'll pick up your bad habits." He knelt down and unhooked the restraining strap around Brennan and lifted him out of the carrier. Holding Brennan against his shoulder, he indicated the playing cards in front of the carrier. "What's this? Are you teaching this innocent little thing to play poker?"

"Yeah," said Ian sullenly, "but he cheats like his big sister."

Bucky threw down her cards. "I don't cheat. You cheat."

"It sounds to me like it's time for the two of you to be off to bed. You had a long day today." Simon sat down with the baby in the chair next to Bucky's bed.

Ian gathered up the cards and straightened them. "Mr. Carter, what do you think is in the chest?"

"I don't know. We can't even tell how heavy it is until tomorrow when we lift it. The jacketing material they put on it this afternoon is supposed to harden overnight so we'll be able to transport it tomorrow. They're going to transfer it to a wooden crate to get it out of the cave and down the bluff and back up the bluff to the vehicles. Even with the plaster jacket and all the padding inside the crate, that's going to be tricky. And they're worried about the vibrations of the UTV over the rough terrain. Dr. Mason or one of the students will probably hold it on his lap."

"Are they taking it to St. Louis?" asked Bucky.

"No. Dr. Smallin has one room in the museum that's temperature-controlled and humidity-controlled. They're putting it in there for now."

"I think it's full of gold," said Ian, "and jewels."

"And pearls," added Bucky. "I heard those guys talking about the clam shells they found where Dr.

Mason thinks is a hearth. That's where pearls come from."

"They come from clams in the ocean," said Ian. "Not clams from the St. Francis river."

"There are such a thing as fresh-water pearls, aren't there, Dad?"

"I think so," said Simon. "And I remember seeing quite a few clam shells on that gravel bar when we were fishing a few weeks ago. Maybe that's something you should research this week."

"I can't wait until we open it," said Ian. "I think there's a wonderful treasure inside."

"And it's on our property, so it'll be ours, won't it, Dad?" said Bucky.

Simon smiled and rubbed Brennan's back. "My greatest treasure are the two of you and this little one here."

Bucky leaned against the arm of the chair and took Brennan's hand. He made some babbling sounds and closed his tiny fingers around her finger.

"Now," said Simon, "I want to talk about tomorrow. It's going to be another long day. Remember last summer when the two of you helped Dr. Brockman do the survey of the area around the Hollow Stone, looking for ancient artifacts or even gum wrappers? We're going to do a detailed surface survey of the floor of the cave and the walls tomorrow and there's going to be enough of us that there really won't be anything for the two of you to do, so…you're going to stay here."

Both children uttered a chorus of protests.

Simon held up one hand to silence them. "Maggie's not going to church tomorrow. She's staying here with Meredyth and the baby and you're staying home, too."

"Gram's not going to church?" asked Ian. "But they always recognize the people at church on their birthday and tomorrow is Gram's."

"What?" said Simon. "Why am I just hearing about this? I didn't know it was her birthday."

Ian shrugged.

"Well, then, I know what the two of you are going to do tomorrow morning. You're going to bake her a cake."

"A cake? I've never made a cake before," said Bucky.

"I'm sure we have everything you'll need," said Simon. "I have some cookbooks somewhere in the library and I'll find a recipe for you. You're both smart enough. Just follow the directions. And tomorrow afternoon, when we come back from the cave, we'll have cake and ice cream. Nick and Jan don't have to leave until Monday morning. Now, how about you get ready for bed?"

Ian caught Bucky's eye and frowned. Bucky glowered at him.

"I have the distinct impression one of you has something to tell me," said Simon.

Bucky lowered her gaze and chewed on her bottom lip.

"And I'm pretty sure it's you," said Simon, looking at Bucky.

Bucky sighed and fished the red bead out of her pocket. "I found it in the cave. You were talking to Dr.

Mason and it was lying right there at my feet. I didn't
think anyone would mind. It's just an old bead."

Simon took the bead in his hand that was not
supporting Brennan and examined it under the light of
the bedside lamp. "You're right. It is an old bead. I can't
tell whether it's glass or ceramic, but either way, it's not
Native American, although they could have possessed it
as a trade good."

"What does that mean?" asked Ian.

"The European explorers would often carry trade
goods as gifts for the Native Americans or to trade for
items. Beads and metal objects were popular."

"Guns?" asked Ian.

"I think guns as trade goods entered the picture
later," said Simon. "But, Bucky, this isn't just an old
bead. It's an artifact."

"That's what I told her," Ian said, smugly.

"In an archaeological site," explained Simon, "every
little bit of information is a piece of the puzzle the
archaeologists put together to tell the story of the people
who once lived there. Dr. Mason and his students are
going to be studying that cave for a long time. They'll
take soil samples and run a pollen analysis to determine
what kinds of plants grew in the area. They'll collect
charcoal from the hearth for radiocarbon tests to see how
old it is. You saw this afternoon, before they wrapped it,
how Dr. Mason took a sample of wood from the chest to
send off for a carbon-14 test. And they'll try to locate the
midden. That's where whoever lived there dumped their
garbage. Think of all the things that could tell us about

what they ate and what kinds of animals lived there. You know how frustrating it is when you're putting together a jigsaw puzzle and discover a piece is missing? This little bead could turn out to be an important piece of the puzzle of how the cave was used and who lived there over the years. Its location needed to be marked and it needs to be bagged and labeled. Do you understand?"

Bucky nodded. "I'm sorry I took it."

Simon transferred the bead to his hand that was on Brennan's back and put his other hand alongside her face. "I know you are. We all make mistakes. The important thing is to learn from them." He stood. "I told your mother I'd just be a minute, so I'd better get back to our guests. I think she wants to feed the baby before she puts him down for the night. You two need to hit the sack and I'll see you at breakfast in the morning before we take off."

30

SIDEWAYS RAIN

"**O**kay. Next it says *three eggs*," said Bucky, reading from the cookbook Simon had left on the table for them.

"My suggestion," said Meredyth, sitting at the larger table in the kitchen, "is to crack the eggs into a small bowl first. That way you can make sure none of the shell gets into the cake mix."

Ian reached up into one of the cabinets and retrieved a cereal bowl. He handed it to Bucky who set it on the small square table next to the mixing bowl. "Let's each crack one," he said, "and then whoever does the best job cracking gets to crack the third one."

"Tap it gently on the side of the bowl." Meredyth reached over to take one of Brennan's hands. The baby was in the carrier on top of the table.

"How's it coming?" Maggie came down the back stairs into the kitchen. "I don't smell any cake baking yet."

"You're not supposed to be in here," said Bucky, shooing her away from the table.

"I just came down to get a cup of coffee and to rest my eyes for a minute. I've been staring at that computer screen ever since breakfast and the words are starting to run together." Maggie got a cup from the cabinet and poured some coffee into it. "It's supposed to rain this morning. I hope the humidity doesn't affect your cake. I'm looking forward to eating it with a big scoop of vanilla ice cream."

"What are you working on?" asked Meredyth.

"Simon asked me to try to trace his family tree in England."

"Any luck?"

Maggie shook her head. "Oh, I don't know. Sometimes I think I'm just going in circles."

"He showed me a copy of your tree," said Meredyth. "Of our tree," she corrected. "It's a wonder we don't all have two heads as twisted as it is with all the intermarrying." She patted one of Brennan's socked feet. "I hope this one is as perfect as he looks when we take him for his first checkup this week."

"He seems so happy and contented all the time," said Maggie. "I think second cousins are the closest of any of our intermarriages. It just looks worse on paper."

A crash startled both women. Maggie turned around toward the children as Meredyth jumped to her feet. Ian was on his knees trying to salvage the vegetable oil running out of the jar Bucky had dropped. Bucky, holding a measuring cup, was backing up, her eyes wide, her mouth open.

"Oh, what a mess," said Maggie, looking at the oil pooling on the stone floor.

"Bucky, what's wrong?" asked Meredyth. The baby started fussing, but she ignored him for the moment and went to where Bucky had stopped, her back against the French doors. "What's wrong?" Meredyth repeated.

"S-s-something," stammered Bucky. "S-something's coming. Someone."

Brennan, in his carrier on top of the table, began thrashing and crying.

"Has something happened to your father?" Meredyth put a hand on Bucky's shoulder. Bucky flinched.

"Here." Maggie got a towel off the counter beside the sink and covered the oil on the floor with it. "Ian, put the lid back on the jar and set it on the table. Get some paper towels and wipe off your hands." Maggie then turned her attention to Bucky who had slipped down to her knees.

"Has something happened at the cave?" asked Maggie. "Has someone been injured?"

Maggie and Meredyth both turned in the direction Bucky was staring, which was toward the wide kitchen doorway that opened into the hall leading to the front section of the house.

"Who's coming?" asked Meredyth.

Bucky blinked and shook her head. "Reverend Bergmann," she whispered.

"Oh, good Lord," said Maggie.

"He can't get in," said Meredyth. "Simon told me again this morning when he left he'd lock the front gate."

"There are other ways in," said Maggie. "Maybe not with a car, but on foot."

"Why would he come here?" asked Meredyth. "What does he want?"

"He's threatened these children. He's an evil, demented man who thinks he's doing God's will."

Ian threw the paper towel from his hands in the trash. He knelt beside Bucky and put an arm around her. "He can't hurt us, Bucky. Gram and your mom are here to protect us. And I'm here."

The baby had progressed to screaming. Meredyth unhooked the strap and picked him up. Maggie reached behind Bucky and Ian to check the lock on the door.

"Ian," ordered Maggie, "run to the front door and make sure it's locked."

Inside the cave, Simon and the Moyers examined the walls, looking for any marks, and recording and photographing whatever they found. Michael Smallin, Daniel Mason, and the three students had laid out a string grid on the floor of the cavern so they could systematically survey for any artifact or ecofact which appeared on the surface in each square. The ceiling sloped toward the back of the cave, but the back wall was still about five feet high. There at the back, another small opening at the bedding plane where the ceiling met the wall, hinted more cave lay beyond this room. But for this first weekend, everyone restrained themselves from crawling into it to see where it led. The students, who were all experienced cavers, had already called dibs on who would be first when they returned.

As Simon inched his way along one section of the wall, flames shot from the limestone, engulfing him and forcing him to jump back and trip over one of the grid lines. He sprawled on the cave floor. Nick Moyer was immediately at his side.

"Simon," said Nick, "are you all right? What happened?"

"Seraphina," whispered Simon. "I have to get out of here." He struggled to his feet and lurched toward the entrance and then dropped to his knees once more to crawl out.

Nick followed him. Jan crawled out behind her husband. When they were all outside and standing, Nick grasped one of Simon's arms to help support him. The blood had drained from Simon's face and he was breathing rapidly.

"What's wrong?" asked Jan.

"I… I have to get home. Something… Something's wrong."

Michael Smallin emerged from the cave. "Take my four-wheeler. It's faster than that little toy truck of yours. The key's in it." The paleontologist kept an ATV at the future museum so he could use it for his trips to the mastodon site every weekend when he came down from St. Louis. He had ridden it to the cave yesterday and today.

"Do you want one of us to come with you?" asked Nick.

"No, everything's probably fine. It was just… It was nothing." How could he tell him about the vision he had experienced in the cave? He had seen the Mansion in flames and his little daughter Seraphina at an upstairs window. Simon squeezed shut his eyes. No, he told himself. His daughter's name is Bucky. He shook off Nick's hold on his arm. "I just have to go home to tell myself everything's okay. I'll be back." He looked at Smallin. "Tell Dan I'm sorry I messed up the grid. Hope I didn't hurt anything."

Jan stepped in front of Simon as he started off down the bluff. "Are you sure you're all right? I can ride with you on Michael's four-wheeler."

"I'm fine. Really. Sorry I frightened you."

Thunder rumbled in the distance.

"Hope you don't get caught in the rain," said Jan.

Simon descended the path they had worn between the boulders and then raced along the trail next to the stream to where he could climb up the bluff to the open area where the smelter ruins lay.

The students had worked yesterday afternoon on clearing a track so they could ride their sports vehicles all the way to the clearing and across it to the edge of the cliff. Dr. Mason had hauled one four-wheeler and one side-by-side, similar to Simon's UTV, from St. Louis for the weekend. They needed the side-by-sides to carry supplies.

On the ride back to the Mansion, Simon could not shake the feeling of dread. He knew it had been only a vision he had seen in the cave, but he could not remember an incident where there had been a fire. His past life as Southy MacAdoo remained a memory that was difficult to access. Occasional flashes or even auditory hallucinations were all he experienced from that time period. Even though he had never before seen Seraphina, Southy's daughter, in any of his visions, he knew the young girl at the window, trying to escape the blaze, was the same Seraphina whose song stone was set into the fireplace surround in the lower level room which bore her name.

The ATV skidded as Simon pulled out onto the gravel road. Slow down, he told himself. You won't do anyone any good if you wreck this thing.

As he came down off of the hill and neared the front gates of the drive leading to the Mansion, he saw several vehicles parked along both sides of the road. He pulled alongside them. He didn't recognize any of them and they were all empty. Backing up a little, Simon pulled his cell phone out of his pocket, and took pictures of the cars and trucks and their license plates. He then punched in the code which would open the gates and drove through.

"Who's that?" asked Meredyth. She was dividing her attention between Bucky, sitting in a heap on the kitchen floor, and Brennan, crying in her arms, but a movement in the back yard caught her eye.

"Oh, Lord," said Maggie, looking out the back door.

Two men, one carrying a gasoline can, were in the walled enclosure where Bucky and Ian had played since their first meeting last May.

Bucky struggled to her feet as Ian came running back into the kitchen. "There's some men out in front of the house," Ian announced. "Reverend Bergmann is one of them and I recognized a couple of the others from the walks."

"I'll deal with him," said Maggie, marching out of the kitchen. "You children stay inside."

"Wait," said Meredyth, handing the baby to Bucky. "I'll come with you."

When Maggie reached the front door, she paused. "He probably thinks we're all at church this morning." She inhaled deeply to brace herself and then opened the right-hand door and stepped out onto the porch. Meredyth followed closely behind her.

Two of the men were on the porch with gasoline cans and they jumped off and joined five others who were standing with the preacher. They all looked surprised as the two women emerged from the house.

Maggie caught her breath against the pungent smell of gasoline. The walls of the Mansion and the floor of the porch were stone, but there were wooden pillars and railings and the front door and woodwork around the door and windows. Bergmann's men had doused the whole area with gas. "Carl Bergmann, I want you and these men off this property right now. I don't know what the heck you think you're doing, but the fact is you are trespassing and committing arson."

From his expression, it was obvious the women had caught Bergmann off-guard, but he quickly found his voice. He had spewed his rhetoric so many times in the past four months it rolled off his tongue with ease. "Maggie Fletcher, you are siding with Satan. We've come as the hand of God to rid this town once and for all of the Devil and his spawn. See what a coward he is to send you out to do his bidding."

"I said, *get off this property!*" Maggie pointed up the lane.

"When the Judgment comes, we will be the ones around the throne of God and you will be cast into the fires of damnation along with those you serve."

"He's crazy," whispered Meredyth, standing beside Maggie. "We need to get back inside."

Maggie shook her head. "Go in and call 911. I'm going to keep him talking."

Meredyth started to back toward the front door when the sound of an engine on the lane caught everyone's attention. Simon, on the four-wheeler, came into view around the curve. The group of men split as he drove into their midst and jumped off the vehicle.

"What's going on here?" Simon demanded. "What's this all about?"

Meredyth rushed down the steps to stand by her husband. Maggie followed more slowly.

When Maggie and Meredyth hurried out of the kitchen, Bucky and Ian and the baby were left alone. Brennan had quieted a little in Bucky's arms, but he was still fussing.

"Call 911," ordered Bucky, starting for the hallway, carrying Brennan.

"They're not going to listen to me," said Ian. "I'm just a kid. They'll think it's a prank."

"Here." Bucky turned back and thrust the baby at Ian. "I'll call."

After Bucky hung up the kitchen receiver, she took Brennan back from Ian, and they hurried down the hall and into the library where they could watch from the large bay window.

Maggie and Meredyth were on the front porch, confronting the men who stood below them, but the children could not hear what was being said.

"Look!" Bucky held Brennan in her left arm and pointed up the lane with her other hand. "Here comes Dad."

"That looks like Dr. Smallin's four-wheeler," said Ian.

"I'm scared," said Bucky. "What if they start fighting? There are lots more of them."

"Gram says Reverend Bergmann is all talk."

"I don't think he's all talk after what he said to us when you were in the hospital. And that's gas, Ian. He was going to set fire to this place if your gram and Mom hadn't gone out there."

"I wish we could hear them. Maybe we should go out."

"No. Your gram told us to stay inside." She gently bounced the baby up and down like she had seen her parents do. "I wish the cops would hurry up and get here."

"They're trying to burn us out," said Maggie, reaching Simon and Meredyth. She raised her voice. "They're cowards, the whole lot of them. Calling themselves Christians. You all don't know the meaning of the word."

"The hand of God is upon me," shouted Bergmann. "He has ordained me to fight his battles. He showed me his truth when his angels took me up into Heaven."

"He showed you no such thing," said Maggie.

"They were trying to tell you the truth," said Meredyth, "but you twisted it into a lie."

"As Satan's unholy consort, of course you side with him."

"You've gone too far, this time, Bergmann," Simon said. "I have pictures of your vehicles. The law's going to take care of you."

The two men Maggie and Meredyth had seen earlier in the back yard came around the far corner of the Mansion. "We went ahead and lit it," said the one holding the gas can.

Everyone looked up as black smoke billowed up from behind the Mansion.

One of the men standing near Bergmann flicked a lighted match onto the front porch. It immediately ignited the gasoline that had been poured there and the whole porch erupted in fire. The flames raced up the pillars and railings and across the door and window frames.

"My God!" shouted Simon. "My children are in there." He broke from the group but couldn't even get up the steps before the flames drove him back.

Bergmann's men grabbed Simon and pinned his arms behind him. Two other men seized Maggie and Meredyth, who had also rushed toward the blazing porch.

Another man had a rock wrapped with a gasoline-soaked rag. The cloth had a tail on it. He lit it and hurled it through the library window.

Bucky and Ian watched the events unfold outside with increasing horror. When the fiery rock smashed through the window, it barely missed them and landed on the carpet which covered much of the hardwood floor in this room. Flames spread from the rock to the carpet and smoke began to fill the room. That triggered the smoke alarm which began its high-pitched beeps.

"Come on!" Ian started for the door. "We have to get out of here!"

"No!" Bucky lunged for Ian and grabbed him by the arm. "We have to stop the fire."

Ian halted. The electric jolt that passed through him was greater than anything he had ever felt whenever he and Bucky were in physical contact.

Bucky felt the power surge also. Brennan, in her arms, quieted and his mouth made an O shape.

"Hold my hand," ordered Bucky, taking Ian's left hand in her right one. "We can do it. We just have to sing the right song. *The songs of three are powerful.*"

"What song? What are you talking about?" The thickening smoke was making Ian's eyes water and the jarring sound of the alarm was hurting his ears.

Bucky bit her lower lip. "I don't know. Uhm... Let's try 'One Two, Buckle My Shoe.'"

"What?"

"Just sing it."

"Why? It's not even a song," protested Ian.

"It'll work," said Bucky. "Just chant it. Come on, Brennan, you sing, too."

Bucky squeezed shut her eyes as she sang the nursery rhyme Simon had taught her when she was a toddler. Ian joined in hesitantly. Brennan made cooing noises. While they sang, Bucky visualized rain pouring over the Mansion and dousing the flames.

> One, two, buckle my shoe
> Three, four, shut the door
> Five, six, pick up sticks
> Seven, eight, lay them straight
> Nine, ten, begin again

When they started the verse again, Bucky saw the rain needed to go sideways to get under the porch roof so that is what she pictured in her mind. She even imagined a spray of water hitting her face as the rain came in through the broken library window, putting out the carpet fire. They sang the verse for a third time and then again and again.

A clap of thunder startled them, and Bucky opened her eyes. Rain was pouring outside. It was such a heavy downpour it was impossible to even see the trees at the far edge of the lawn.

Ian let go of Bucky's hand and stomped his foot on the carpet, smothering the last of the flames that were being drenched by the rain coming in the window. All three children were dripping wet as the shower of water continued to wash over them.

"You did it, Bucky! You put out the fire."

"We did it," said Bucky weakly. "Oh, Ian, I don't feel so good."

She held out the baby to Ian who took him in one arm and tried to catch Bucky with his other arm as she sunk to the sodden carpet. He kept her head from hitting hard against the floor.

"Bucky!"

The microburst of rain caught everyone outside off guard. The wind whipped up so suddenly it was difficult to stand. The men dropped their holds on Simon and the two women. The driving rain blew horizontally toward the front of the Mansion and quickly extinguished the flames. Two sheriff's cars arrived on the scene seconds after the deluge began. Bergmann and his followers scattered toward the trees, but the wind and rain impeded their escape.

"I'm going to see to the children," shouted Simon over the storm. He and Maggie and Meredyth had taken refuge on the covered porch, but they were still being beaten by the stinging rain.

And then the rain stopped as quickly as it had begun.

31

SONGS OF THREE

Bucky opened her eyes and looked around. She was in her bedroom but it was light. She pulled down the cover a little bit and noted she was wearing the yellow nightgown again.

"Oh, you're awake. How do you feel?"

She turned her head to the sound of Meredyth's voice. Her mother was sitting beside her bed in the chair where Simon usually sat. "Where's Dad? Is he all right?" Bucky bolted upright.

"He's fine." Meredyth smiled and reached out a hand to smooth her hair. "He went back to the cave, but they should be returning soon. You've been asleep for most of the day."

"Most of—" Bucky craned her neck to look at the clock on the bedside table. Four thirty-five. "Where's Ian and the baby and…and Maggie? Are they all right?

"Everyone's fine, Lamb. Maggie is watching Brennan for me in her room. I think Ian is in your playroom.

"Are you sure they're all right? No one got hurt in the fire?"

"I'm sure. Everyone was concerned about you. You passed out in the library."

"How about Reverend Bergmann?"

"I don't think we're going to have to worry about him for a while. The sheriff arrested him and the other men with him this morning. They'll be charged on numerous counts, including attempted murder. Ian said you were the one who called 911. Fortunately, there were two deputies in town this morning because of numerous walkers, they said, so they were here in a matter of minutes. But I still tremble whenever I think about what might have happened."

There was a soft knock on the bedroom door and it opened a few inches to reveal Maggie. She had the baby with her. "Thank God, you're awake." Maggie crossed the room to Bucky's bed. "You gave us quite a scare. Again."

"I'm all right." Bucky stretched and yawned. "I don't know why I'm so tired, though."

"You've been through a lot," said Meredyth.

Maggie handed Brennan to Meredyth. "I just got off the phone with Penny for the third time today. You remember her, the wife of the hardware owner? You met her last week at church."

"I think she was one of the women who brought some food."

"Oh, that's right. Anyway, some of the Sunday school ladies want to treat me to supper tonight for my birthday at Joe's Café. He didn't even used to be open past two on Sundays, but I guess with all the increased traffic in town, it pays him to have longer hours. Anyway, they've already reserved the big table in the back for us."

"Oh, Maggie," wailed Bucky. "What happened to your cake? We didn't get to finish it."

"After all the hubbub calmed down, I helped Ian with it while your mother sat up here with you. He even piped some lettering on it. We can still have it with some ice cream tonight after I get back from the restaurant. But, Meredyth, what I wanted to suggest was that you and Simon and the Moyers come on down to Joe's, too. Lord knows we have enough food in the house, but with all that's happened today, it'll be nice to go out."

"I'll ask Simon when he comes," replied Meredyth.

"What about me?" asked Bucky. "If it's the Lukefahr Ladies, I should be there, too."

"Of course you should," said Maggie, "if you're feeling up to it. If your parents say 'yes,' you can go with me if they don't go, and, if they do go, you can come with them."

That night, Simon went to Ian's room first before his nightly chat with Bucky. Ian was sitting up in bed, reading, but he closed the book when Simon came in and sat on the bed.

"I'm still full of fried chicken and cake and ice cream," said Simon. "How about you?"

"I probably could eat another little piece of chocolate cake," said Ian, "and maybe two scoops of ice cream."

"I think you would wake up in the night with a stomach ache. I don't know how much of the supper conversation with the Moyers you followed, but we gated the cave to protect it." Simon and Meredyth and Ian, along with Nick and Jan Moyers, had eaten in one of the booths at Joe's Café in Turn Back while most of the Lukefahr Ladies had sat around the large table at the rear of the room. Bucky had divided her time between the two groups, carrying her plate back and forth. Simon had started to reprimand her, telling her she needed to stay at one table or the other, but Meredyth silenced him with a look and a hand on his wrist.

"Can we get in the cave if we want?"

"They left a key with me, but I think we'll leave it to the archaeologists. Dr. Mason is going to have students continue to work on it for a few weekends, and, if they find enough to make it worthwhile, he might make it and the smelter ruins a site for a field school next summer, similar to what Dr. Smallin did last summer with the mastodons."

"Do you think he'll find enough?"

Simon smiled. "From my own observation and what we collected from the surface survey yesterday and today, and the inscriptions on the walls, I think we're looking at an occupation there thirty-five hundred years ago and another one much more recent, maybe four hundred and fifty to five hundred years ago, both of them European."

"Not Indians?"

Simon shook his head. "No evidence yet. I think perhaps it was a sacred site to the Native Americans. They were in the area, but didn't live in the cave. Bucky thinks the spring below the cave is another one of the Anarianu springs. Maybe the Native Americans, who were more attuned to such things, picked up on that."

"So, who were the Europeans?"

"I would say the Minoans, who also built the smelter, and Spaniards."

"Spaniards? Like Hernando de Soto?"

"Possibly. Scholars don't think he made it this far north, but…" Simon shrugged. "Who's to say? It's probably another group of Spanish priests or explorers for which we have no record. But the biggest artifact they left behind, the chest, hopefully will tell us more when we open it. It is safely in the museum now. Dr. Mason is going to consult with some of his colleagues before attempting to look inside."

Ian frowned. "So we have to be patient a while longer."

"Afraid so."

Ian was quiet for a moment and then spoke timidly, "Mr. Carter, I know you don't think Bucky has any powers, but she's the one who made it rain this morning and put out the fire."

"And how could she possibly do that?"

"I don't know. She made us hold hands—she and me and the baby—and we sang a song. It wasn't really a song. It was a nursery rhyme. 'One Two, Buckle My Shoe.'"

Simon shook his head and exhaled. "Ian, does that make sense to you?"

Ian shrugged. "Did you ever see rain like that? And it was blowing sideways and coming right through the window."

"But we were expecting rain this morning."

"Not like that."

"At any rate, I am so thankful you children are safe. I hope… I hope this is the last we hear from Bergmann for a long time." Simon stood. "Good night, Ian. I need to stop in and see Bucky and then visit with the Moyers for a while yet. They're leaving in the morning for Chicago."

Simon left Ian's room and crossed the hall to Bucky's room. She, too, was sitting up in her bed, reading. After they found her unconscious on the library floor after the fire, Simon had carried her upstairs and Meredyth had removed her wet clothes and slipped the yellow nightgown on her. But now she was wearing her sparkling pink princess gown Simon recognized as her traditional Sunday night sleeping attire.

Simon took the book from her and put a bookmark in it and laid it on her table. "Exciting day, wasn't it?"

"I slept through most of it."

He took one of her hands in his and held it for a few seconds without speaking.

"Dad, why did you show up this morning when you did? Did you forget something?"

Simon shook his head. "I had a premonition, a vision, a warning something was wrong. I saw flames. Except it was Seraphina who was in danger."

"Seraphina?"

"Maggie told me this evening the Mansion had suffered a fire not long after Southy MacAdoo built it. It was deliberately set by some raiders during the Civil War. But it wasn't destroyed. Seraphina was a young girl at the time, about your age, and according to what she wrote years later in her diary, a freakish rain storm blew up and dumped water on it and..." Simon looked away.

"Dad, last summer when Reverend Bergmann hit you in the head and I told him I wished he was dead and he fell over dead, you told me it was just a coincidence, but that wasn't a coincidence, was it? I killed him. You told me that to make me feel better, didn't you?"

Simon looked back at his daughter and placed his other hand over the one which still held hers. He knew she could detect his feelings and he wanted to be honest with her. "I told you that because it was the truth. You don't have that kind of power. If you did, people would be scared of you. I would be scared of you."

Ian says people are scared of me because they think it's true."

"And so today you believe that by reciting a nursery rhyme you made it rain?"

"Not by myself. What I did to Reverend Bergmann I did alone, but today I had help. Ian and Brennan. *The songs of three are powerful.*"

"And why would 'One Two, Buckle My Shoe' accomplish that?"

"I don't think it's the words that are so important. It's the tone and the... I'm not sure what the word is. It's the way the words go up and down. I think it starts with a C."

"Cadence?"

"Yeah, that's it"

"But if Seraphina made it rain all those years ago, she did it alone."

"Last summer, Maggie told me Southy MacAdoo had twin sons who died when they were little, before Seraphina was born. Maybe their spirits were there that day, helping Seraphina. And, Dad, after I did that to Reverend Bergmann, I was tired, but not as tired as I was today. Do you think using that power sort of drains me?"

Simon's lips disappeared into a thin line as he considered an answer. "Bucky, you are a beautiful, brave— What was the other word I used to describe you?"

"Bodacious."

"You are a beautiful, brave, bodacious girl and I love you. And I will always love you." Simon paused. "That reminds me of a verse in the Bible. Do you know 1 Corinthians 13:13?"

"Sure. 'And now faith, hope, and love abide, these three; and the greatest of these is love.'"

"Love is a power that we can all share. So I want you to put all this talk of any other power out of your head and just concentrate on being a smart, creative, imaginative, loving young lady. Do you think you can do that for me?"

"Ian told me the fire in the backyard burned our boat."

"I'm afraid it's a charred mess," said Simon.

Bucky sighed. "That boat carried Marquette and Joliet up and down the Mississippi, and it took Lewis and Clark as far west as it could go on the Missouri River. It was at the Battle of Lake Erie with Admiral Perry and crossed the Atlantic with the Pilgrims. It even took Vasco da Gama to India and Captain Hook to Hawaii. I'm going to miss it."

"Maybe after the work on Maggie's house is finished, we can get you another boat to go along with a jungle gym and a tree house."

Bucky's face brightened and then clouded over again. "At supper tonight and again when we were back here having cake and ice cream, Jan Moyer was talking about the difficulty she was having with translating Minoan Linear A. She was hoping the Hollow Stone was the breakthrough she needed, but evidently yours and her husband's translation of the Hittite on it didn't help. So what I was wondering, if you are Etakkama and he could write Hittite but he lived and traveled with the Minoans, couldn't he write Minoan, too?"

"I've wondered about that same thing. You'd think since he was a scribe he would naturally be interested in other writing, especially since he made his home with the Minoans. But, remember, he dropped out of scribal school early, so maybe he just didn't care for writing. At any rate, so far, I haven't been able to recover any memories of being able to read and write Linear A. That would be a major benefit to Jan, though, wouldn't it?"

"Would you help her instead of taking the credit yourself?"

"Of course." Simon yawned. "I need to get back to the Moyers. Anything else?"

"Well, I was wondering one thing. I'm glad Reverend Bergmann finally got arrested—"

"But I'm worried he'll get out on bail," interrupted Simon. "I hope the judge doesn't allow that."

"But," continued Bucky, "despite all the terrible things he's said and done, I feel kind of bad that a preacher is in jail because of us. Aren't we supposed to forgive our enemies?"

"If you can find it in your heart to forgive him after everything he has put you through, then I applaud you. You have the makings of a true Christian. Perhaps someday, I can do the same. But for now, we're going to let the law and the courts handle it."

"Why?"

"Let me see if I can explain it to your understanding. When people believe a certain thing and they are willing to act on those beliefs, they also must be willing to accept the consequences. For example, we are Christians. We go to church on Sunday. We have Bibles we read here in our house. You have one here in your room. We pray. But there are some places in this world, some countries, where those things are illegal. And if we lived in one of those places and believed in our faith enough that we were willing to still do those things, then we'd also have to be willing to face the consequences and, perhaps, be arrested, be imprisoned, even be killed for our beliefs.

Lots of Christians, including preachers, have done just that. Look at Martin Luther King, Jr., for example. He was willing to go to jail because he believed certain laws in this country were wrong. He stood up for his beliefs and he accepted the consequences."

Bucky nodded.

"So," continued Simon, "when we consider Reverend Bergmann and his followers, they believe a certain thing—that you and I are evil. We know that to be false, but they believe it, and they are willing to act on that belief. In their case, their actions were against the law and now they must face the consequences. Understand?"

Bucky nodded. "It's like when I do something wrong even though I think it's right, but you've told me not to do it, and you make me do two pages of math questions, I have to be willing to accept the punishment in exchange for the wrong thing I did."

"Pretty much."

"I slid down the bannister."

"What? When?"

"The day Mom came back. I didn't get hurt. I made it all the way to the bottom."

"You could have been hurt. You could have broken your neck. That's a… That's an eighteen or twenty-foot drop. Please don't ever do that again. Promise me?"

"I won't. I promise."

"Good. And you tell Ian the same thing. Okay. I really need to get back downstairs. Good night, Lamb."

Simon started to help her scoot under the covers, but she stopped him.

"Are you going to give Reverend Bergmann's Bible back to him?"

"Someday. I'll have to think of a plausible story of how we acquired it. Or maybe I can leave it on their doorstep while he's in jail and let his wife find it."

"I'd like to get baptized. Ian told me he wasn't ever baptized and I've never been. Are you baptized?"

Simon sighed. "Yes, I was baptized when I was an infant."

"Oh, so Brennan could get baptized with me. I think I'd like to get baptized in the Singing Spring in the park."

"Let's put that off until things calm down a little, all right?"

"Dad, if I don't have to worry anymore about Reverend Bergmann and I don't have to worry about Mom and I don't have to worry how some of the Anarianu want to keep us all apart because they're gone in the *Turning* now, then all my big worries are taken care of, aren't they?"

"And that's how it should be when you're ten years old."

"Do you think the Anarianu will come back? If the people who come to Turn Back to walk the labyrinth don't have the dreams anymore, those people might stop coming."

"I think the Anarianu provided for this town in such a way people will continue to come. The labyrinth itself will always be there, providing a peaceful, worshipful experience for those who walk it. The museum will be open someday to attract people to see the mastodons and learn about the history of the area, including the jaw-dropping discovery that Minoans visited here thousands of years ago. Perhaps we'll have a Spanish treasure chest on display, too. And maybe we'll have walking trails so people can visit the Hollow Stone and the cave and the smelter ruins. Yes, I think the Anarianu will come back when our worlds are in sync once more, and there will be plenty of people here to provide them with the energy they need."

Bucky sighed and lay back against her pillow. "We are good people—you and I—aren't we?"

"I like to think so."

"And Ian and Brennan?"

"Brennan's a little young yet to be anything but good."

Bucky smiled.

"What?"

"*The songs of three.* I think our songs are going to be powerful but they're going to be good because you're good."

Simon bent over and kissed her forehead. "Good night, Lamb."

"What's the Hittite word for Lamb?"

"*Ākunas.*"

"*Ākunas,*" Bucky repeated.

Simon switched off the lamp. He crossed the room and paused at the door.

From the darkness Bucky quoted the line from the Hollow Stone, "*The song of the lamb is heard again.*"

THE END

EPILOGUE

I celebrated my seventy-eighth birthday eating cake and ice cream in the kitchen of the Mansion Mineral Springs Resort. If anyone had told me a year ago I would be sitting there in that restored stately residence in the company of a man who believed he was the reincarnation of old Southy MacAdoo, my third great-grandfather who had built the Mansion in the mid-nineteenth century, I would have thought them about a half bubble off plumb. And not just Grandpa Southy. Simon Carter believes he has lived many past lives, the earliest one back to the days of the Hittites in the Old Testament. Not that I believe in all that reincarnation talk, but it's what a person believes about himself that's important for it dictates his actions. Simon's reserved demeanor has made it difficult for him to fit into our little community, and he will never be one of the local good ol' boys, but he is generous, extremely generous, lavishly generous. He doesn't use his wealth to buy our friendship. His generosity is a part of him, a part of who he is. He lives generously.

Bucky was also at the birthday table that night. What can I say about Bucky? She's a mystery. She's quicksilver. She slips and slides in and out of moods so quickly it's hard to keep up. She sees and senses things the rest of us pass by unnoticed, and the cumulative effect is a burden no ten-year-old should have to bear. That fall when I turned seventy-eight was especially hard on her. She perhaps lost a little of her innocence. She learned her father and her mother could make mistakes. She learned sometimes others have your best interests at heart and still harm you. Most importantly she discovered a power buried deep within her and began bringing it to the surface. Her father denies the power, but he can't stop it. All in all, though, Bucky emerged on the other side of those experiences just fine.

Meredyth, Simon's wife and Bucky's mother who had been missing for nine years, ate cake and ice cream with us that night. Where does a person go for nine years and not grow any older? What did she learn in that place? She and Simon are two sides of the coin. For all his quiet manner, she is outgoing, talkative. She loves to laugh. She brought sunshine to that dark, foreboding Mansion. And she is family. We are cousins.

In fact, except for the Moyers, the visiting ancient language experts from Chicago, everyone at the table that night was related in some way. In my great-grandson Ian's case, however, the relationship is different than what I had always assumed. The revelation Ian was not the son of my grandson, Seth, haunted me for many days and cost me more tears than I'd cried in a long time. Even sometimes today when I think about it, I still tear up. But what's done is done. You can't change the past. And as Simon pointed out, even though I won't be passing anything of myself to future generations in the physical sense, maybe, through Ian, there is something of me that will live on.

And speaking of physical family, Simon asked me to trace his family tree. I was curious also as to how he fit in with the MacAdoo descendants. But the *how* still eludes me. I've not given up, though. Some record, some scrap of paper, still resides in a dusty book somewhere that's going to tie all this together.

Three weeks after my birthday, we were able to move back into my house. As in everything he did, Simon went overboard, but it was a wonderful remodeling job. The kitchen was larger with all new appliances. The utility room had a new washer and dryer. There was a walk-in pantry for my canned goods. Both bathrooms had been redone. And there was even a tree house for Ian. But my favorite part was the addition of a glass sunroom off of the kitchen. I can sit out there in all kinds of weather and look beyond the barn toward the river. Living in the Mansion was nice, but there's no place like home.

The next two months flew by. We had prayer walks on the first Saturdays of November and December. The numbers were down some but there were still several thousand, even though the cave dreams had ended. Maybe most were hoping a new dream would begin. They didn't know that the Anarianu, the Guardians responsible for those dreams, were gone.

Dr. Daniel Mason and some fellow archaeologists opened Ian's treasure chest the first week in December. It was empty. Ian was crushed. Simon tried to explain to him the chest itself was an important artifact because it was most certainly Spanish. But when you're ten years old, the box is no longer the best part of the present. When you have your heart set on gold and jewels, it's hard to find out there's nothing inside.

Simon and Meredyth and Bucky and Brennan joined Ian and me for Thanksgiving at my house. The week before Christmas, the Lukefahr Ladies had dinner and a party at the Mansion. The music room there had been transformed into a winter wonderland with a tree that was all of twelve feet tall. Bucky had started piano lessons with Sissy Casteel the week after my birthday in October. Sissy accompanied us when we sang carols at the party but she reserved "Silent Night" for Bucky to play for us. During her performance I glanced at Simon and Meredyth. Their love and their pride in their daughter was almost tangible. As Bucky played the notes perfectly, I looked around at all of the Sunday school ladies that evening. Each face glowed in the multitude of tiny lights in the room, but their faces weren't only reflecting the Christmas lights. They were reflecting the love of a little girl who had adopted them as her own.

Bucky had picked Sunday, January 22, as the date she would be baptized. We tried to discourage her and get her to change it either to an indoor baptism at the font in the sanctuary or wait until the weather warmed if she insisted on having it at the Singing Spring. There was no dissuading her. Ian joined forces with her and decided he, too, should be baptized. Bucky insisted that Brennan be baptized that day as well. She claimed the weather would be perfect for a January day.

Turn Back awoke that Sunday morning to a cold drizzle. The temperature was just above freezing so the roads weren't slick, but it was awful weather. All of the ladies showed up for Sunday school, though, to support her. All of us were sure she would opt to do it indoors.

But just as Sadie Jane led us in the closing prayer, the room lightened. Betty Fischer pulled back the heavy curtain. The rain had stopped and the sky was clearing. Bucky smiled at me and winked but didn't say anything. Meredyth had made her a white dress with pale blue lace trim at the collar and cuffs. She looked like a little angel in it. Brennan also had on a white outfit. According to the birth certificate we had filled out at the courthouse, he was three months old here at the end of January. He looked all of six months and maybe more. He had already started to crawl.

During the worship service, the stained glass windows on the east side continued to reveal the sunshine. At least it wouldn't be a miserable, soggy day for the baptism. When the service ended, Pastor Stephen Bradley invited everyone to the Singing Spring at the west end of the park and nearly the entire congregation attended. The temperature had climbed into the upper fifties. While not a heat wave, it was pleasant for a January day in Missouri.

There were a few walkers that morning and they, too, stopped to witness the ceremony. Simon and Meredyth had chosen Chip and Lane Crosson as godparents for Brennan, and the couple stood beside them. Lane's pregnancy was now clearly visible. I stood with Ian who was wearing a new suit. No one in town, except the Crossons, yet knew Simon was Ian's real father. There's no reason for them to know, but I was surprised the rumor hadn't started, especially since I had told Penny, who loves to gossip. Bucky had chosen me as a godparent as well as Chip and Lane, but she also insisted Dale

Crosson and ninety-four-year-old Lillian Thomas join her. She would have had the entire Lukefahr Ladies Bible Class stand with her had her parents allowed it.

It was a beautiful ceremony. Pastor Stephen spoke about the meaning of baptism and added a few words about the importance of water in the history of Turn Back. He baptized the baby first, Simon and Meredyth answering the questions for Brennan. The pastor held his hand in the spray of the spring that still shot up into the air with its ethereal sound, and then placed his hand on the baby's head and spoke the words, "I baptize you in the name of the Father and of the Son and of the Holy Spirit." As he made the sign of the cross on the baby's forehead, Brennan giggled, and quiet laughter rippled through the congregation. Next it was Bucky and Ian's turn. They were old enough to answer the questions for themselves. Pastor Stephen repeated the gesture on both of them. Bucky was all smiles. Ian, not so much. The pastor ended the service by asking all those present if they would endeavor so to live their lives that these children would grow in the knowledge and love of God through our Savior Jesus Christ and do all in their power to increase their faith, confirm their hope, and perfect them in love. More than one of our members was misty-eyed as they answered in the affirmative to that age-old question.

The ceremony itself was memorable on that sunny January day, but I have a special framed photograph from Penny Crosson to remind me of how remarkable these three children are. When we were posing for pictures afterwards in front of the Singing Spring, someone suggested that the children hold hands. Brennan was in Simon's arms with Meredyth at her husband's side. Bucky, in front of them, took the baby's right hand, and Ian, on the other side, took his left hand. As soon as the children touched, the same surge they had reported on the day of the fire swept through them, and in the picture all three have their mouths wide open in surprise. But that's not all. Just as Penny snapped the photo, Meredyth turned and whispered something in Simon's ear. His mouth, too, is open. It's an amusing family portrait of an amazing family, one I'm proud to be a part of.

Margaret "Maggie" Fletcher
Turn Back, Missouri

APPENDIX I

Index of Characters from Books 1 and 2

* Indicates that the person is a descendant of Seraphina

LUKEFAHR LADIES

*Margaret (Maggie) Fletcher (age 77) — widowed; Bucky's mentor; great-grandmother of Ian Fletcher; birthday is October 22.

*Maxine Ross — widowed

*Pernecia (Penny) Crosson — wife of Ron Crosson; mother of grown twins Chip and Dale

Ruby Lower (age 85) — widowed

Sissy Casteel — widowed; church organist; singer; artist; Bucky's piano teacher

*Lillian Thomas (age 94) — never married; African-American; sister to Leona

*Leona Thomas (age 90) — never married; African-American; sister to Lillian

*Sadie Jane Woods — never married; retired French professor; Bucky's French tutor

Ruth Mercier — widowed

Betty Fischer — wife of Frank Fischer

Clara Keller (age 83) — widowed

*Gladys Earlene Bauer — widowed

Bertha (Birdie) Weber —widowed

OTHER PEOPLE IN THE BOOKS

Aiyana — Native American who Etakkama took for a wife; she died giving birth to Imala

Anarianu — also called the Guardians; mystical beings, perhaps from another dimension; associated with certain springs.

Arley Bolin — Maggie's second great-grandfather; he built the house where Maggie and Ian live

*Brennan Lowry Carter — Simon and Meredyth's son;

*Bucilla (Bucky) Rose Carter (age 10) — daughter of Simon and Meredyth Carter

*Carl Bergmann — non-denominational, evangelical preacher who verbally harasses Simon and Bucky at the prayer walks which he also denounces

Caitlyn — paleontology student in Dr. Michael Smallin's class; worked at the Mastodon Site

Corrine LaMotte — owns the Bluff House Bed and Breakfast in Turn Back

*Dale Crosson — Ron and Penny's grown son; twin brother of Darrin (Chip) Crosson; suffered a brain injury at birth; worked to restore the park

Dana Lannigan — Ian Fletcher's fifth grade teacher at the Turn Back school

Daniel Mason, PhD — archaeologist; assisting at the Mastodon Site; lead archaeologist for the excavation of the cave and the smelter ruins

Danny — graduate paleontology student under Dr. Michael Smallin

*Darrin (Chip) Crosson, M.D. — Ron and Penny's grown son; twin brother of Dale Crosson; neurosurgeon at a St. Louis hospital

Drucilla MacAdoo — wife of Southy MacAdoo; mother of Seraphina

Etakkama —Hittite who travelled in a company of Minoans to present day US in approximately 1500B.C.

Euphemia — grandmother of Lillian and Leona Thomas; had a daughter, Zenobia, by Darius Whitener, son of Seraphina

*Frog Bryland — mailman

Greg — graduate paleontology student under Dr. Michael Smallin

Helen — one of the Baptist women

Hilda — one of the Baptist women

*Ian Michael Fletcher — (age 10) great-grandson of Maggie Fletcher; birthday in June 16

Imala — Etakkama's daughter

James Dumont — anchor man on the Morning Show on television station KDRS-TV in Cape Girardeau, Missouri

Jan Moyer, PhD — from the University of Chicago; expert in ancient languages, specializing in Minoan Linear A; friend of Simon Carter's; called in to investigate and assist in translating the Hollow Stone; married to Dr. Nicholas Moyer

Jennifer Brockman, PhD — from the University of Pennsylvania; expert in lithic (stone) artifacts; called in to examine and verify the age of the Hollow Stone

Jewel Bergmann — Carl Bergmann's wife

Jim Runnel — from the Faith Class at the Methodist church; runs the projector in the park

*Joe Freiland — owns the Turn Back Café

*Kara Fletcher — Ian's mother

Khalil Bukhari, M.D. — Muslin doctor from Pakistan; has a clinic in Garton; has a wife and grown daughter

Kendra — waitress in the Turn Back Café

Kena Lacey — music teacher at the Turn Back School

*Kevin and *Angela Albright – a couple who participate in the walks;

Kyle — paleontology student in Dr. Michael Smallin's class; worked at the Mastodon Site; runs the projection system in the park for the summer walks

Lane Crosson — wife of Dr. Chip Crosson

*Lydia Schell — one of the Baptist women

Madyson Koeller — classmate of Ian's

Masie — paleontology student in Dr. Michael Smallin's class; worked at the Mastodon Site; played guitar during the summer prayer walks

Matt Healey — Simon's publisher and friend

*Meredyth Lowry Durragh Carter — Simon's wife; Bucky's mother

Marty Neale — classmate of Ian's

Michael Smallin, PhD — paleontologist from St. Louis University; director of the excavation at the Mastodon Site; developing the Carter Fletcher Museum of Natural History in Turn Back

*Palmer Reagan — the mayor of Turn Back

Mrs. Koeller — Madyson Koeller's mother

Nicholas Moyer, PhD — from the University of Chicago; expert in ancient languages; friend of Simon Carter's; called in to investigate and assist in translating the Hollow Stone; married to Dr. Jan Moyer

Pearl — one of the Baptist women

*Ron Crosson — Penny's husband; owns the hardware store in Turn Back

Seraphina MacAdoo — daughter of Southy and Drucilla MacAdoo; married Myles Whitener

*Simon Leander Carter (age 41) — father of Bucky; husband to Meredyth; mystery writer; Hittite epigrapher

Sophie — classmate of Ian's

Southy MacAdoo — built the mansion; founded Turn Back; husband of Drucilla MacAdoo; father of Seraphina.

Tikatara — the Anarianu baby that Etakkama saved

Stephen Bradley — pastor of the Turn Back Methodist Church

*Teddy Thomas — brother to Lillian and Leona Thomas; deceased.

Vera Runnel — married to Jim Runnel

Willow — Maggie's cow; had a calf, Jack, on Ian's birthday

APPENDIX II

Bucky's Pajamas

Sunday — pink princess gown with sparkles

Monday — blue pajamas with puppies

Tuesday — blue pajamas with dolphins

Wednesday — pink unicorn gown with sparkles

Thursday — purple pajamas with kittens

Friday — navy blue gown with silver stars

Saturday — teal and gray striped pajamas

APPENDIX III

Hittite Words

Lamb: *ākunas* (Hittite scholar Olivier Lauffenburger invented this word for me. Since Hittite for *lamb* is always written with a logogram, scholars don't know how it was said. *Ākunas* would be cognate to Latin *agnus*, Old Greek *amnos*, English to yean.)

Father: *atta*

Mother: *anna*

Be strong: *dassus ēs*

Go to sleep: *it sēs*

Please: *māntāssu* (Hittite scholar Olivier Lauffenburger coined this word for me, also, since there is no Hittite word for *please* that he can find, except phrases such as "if it pleases the king.")

Ship: *nāhhus*

Fish: *parhus* (This word is always written as a logogram, but some scholars think this is the word it might be.)

APPENDIX IV:

Seraphina's Family Tree

(This is not the complete tree. In some of the later generations, there are siblings who are not shown. There are also more "entanglements" than those indicated here. The blank boxes can be filled in after Book 2 is read.)

Descendants of Seraphina MacAdoo Whitener,
the Daughter of Southy MacAdoo and Drucilla Wisdom

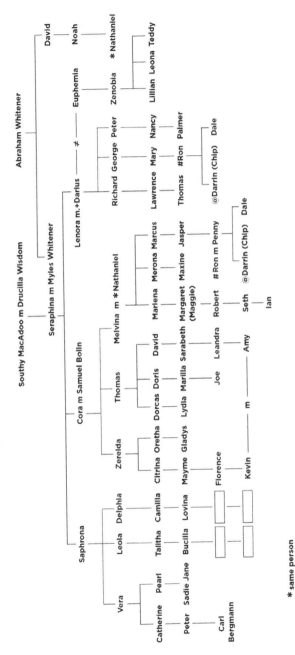

* same person
# same person
@ same person
+ Darius Whitener inherited te Mansion Mineral Springs Resort, and ownership passed down his line to Thomas who sold it to Simon Carter

APPENDIX V:

Map of Turn Back, Missouri

Annotated

1. The Hollow Stone
2. The Mansion
3. Mastodon Site
4. Maggie Fletcher's House
5. St. Francis River
6. Three-Story Brick Building
7. Hardware Store
8. Joe's Café
9. Park
10. Park Stone
11. Singing Spring
12. Gazebo
13. Methodist Church
14. School
15. Baptist Church
16. The cave is farther south

ACKNOWLEDGEMENTS

I would like to thank my beta readers for their corrections and suggestions and especially their encouraging words:

Michael Blacksher
Penny Bolin
Renee Branch
Nancy Carter
Michael Gilmore
Vera Huffman Hayman
Elizabeth Mardis
Bruce Miller
Cadence Probst
Gretchen Probst
Amrita Singh

Thank you to the following people for their invaluable contributions to the story:

Tauseef Ahmed, (username on Fiverr.com is Toxictax), illustration artist, for his drawing of the Mansion

Nurul Akmal, (username on Fiverr.com is nurakmal23), for organizing Seraphina's family tree in Adobe Illustrator.

Emily D. Aulicino, genetic genealogist, author of Genetic Genealogy: The Basics and Beyond, for her assistance with DNA interpretation.

Sandra Beale, for her assistance with a portion of racial/cultural dialogue.

Christelle Billard, for her help with a French translation.

Gabrielle Cox, for her help with a French translation.

Bobette Crump, fifth grade teacher at Marquand-Zion Elementary, for answering questions about her class routine.

Bobby Daniels, EMT-P, FP-C Flight Paramedic with Cox Air, for answering questions about medical helicopters.

Nathan Gilmore, IT superintendent for Dubuque County, Iowa, for his IT expertise.

Mark Henderson, Chupadero Archeological Resources, for suggesting how to treat the chest found in the cave.

Najla Kay (Najlakay on Fiverr.com), archtist, for the map of Turn Back and surrounding area.

Peggy Knott, for her gardening expertise.

Olivier Lauffenburger, author of Hittite Grammar, for translating several words into Hittite and for creating plausible Hittite words in cases where the Hittite word is unknown.

All songs used in this book are in public domain:

"Amazing Grace." Words by John Newton, 1779. Music: 19th century USA melody.

"Bringing in the Sheaves." Words: Knowles Shaw, 1874. Music: George Minor, 1880.

"I Have Decided to Follow Jesus." Words by Anonymous, but some sources attribute it to Sundat Singh (1889-1929). Music: Indian folk tune.

"In the Garden." Words and Music: Charles A. Miles, 1913.

"It is Well with My Soul." Words: Horatio G Spafford, 1873 Music: Phillip P. Bliss, 1876.

"Just a Closer Walk with Thee." Words: Anonymous. Music: American melody.

"Just as I Am." Words by Charlotte Elliot, 1835. Music: William B. Bradbury, 1849.

"My Hope Is Built on Nothing Less." Words: Edward Mote, 1834. Music: William B. Bradbuy, 1863.

"One Two, Buckle My Shoe." Nursery Rhyme.

ABOUT THE COVER

The colorful fractal swirl was downloaded from Pixabay.com, under a creative commons license and is free for commercial use. It was created by Coyotechnical.

The font used on the front cover is Sell Your Soul created by Christopher Hansen. (The Reverend Bergmann would most assuredly not approve.)

The font on the back is Calibri.

The Hittite cuneiform script running along the top and bottom are part of the inscription from the Hollow Stone.

The Minoan Linear A on the back cover is a TrueType font by that same name. It is there so you can see what Linear A looks like. Linear A has not yet been translated. Downloaded from:
http://ancientroadpublications.com/Fonts.html

The little green and red blobs are bits of photos of leaves in the author's woods.

ABOUT THE AUTHOR

Shirley Gilmore, the author of *Bucky and the Lukefahr Ladies: Songs of Three,* is a teacher. "No matter what job I have, I will always be a teacher," she says. "It's in my DNA. If I had lived in Paleolithic times, I would have been the storyteller of the clan, preserving our people's history and tales and passing them on to the next generation."

Shirley taught history and various social studies classes to students in grades 7-12 for twenty-five years and earth science for four years at the university level. She currently lives in the woods at a mystical place she calls Glendragon. She built her cottage there on the spot where she had been inexplicably drawn for many years. Whatever force resides there not only continues to attract her, but it also messes with a compass.